Sigrid Undset

The Axe

Sigrid Undset was born to Norwegian parents in Denmark in 1882. Between 1920 and 1922, she published her magnificent and widely acclaimed trilogy of fourteenth-century Norway, *Kristin Lavransdatter* (composed of *The Bridal Wreath*, *The Mistress of Husaby*, and *The Cross*). And between 1925 and 1927, she published the four volumes of *The Master of Hestviken* (composed of *The Axe*, *The Snake Pit*, *In the Wilderness*, and *The Son Avenger*). Ms. Undset, the author of numerous other novels, essays, short stories, and tales for young readers, was awarded the Nobel Prize for Literature in 1928. During the Second World War, she worked with the Norwegian underground before having to flee to Sweden and then to the United States. After the war, she returned to Norway, where she died in 1949.

THE AXE

THE AXE

THE MASTER OF HESTVIKEN, VOLUME I

SIGRID UNDSET

VINTAGE BOOKS

A DIVISION OF RANDOM HOUSE, INC.

NEW YORK

VINTAGE BOOKS EDITION

Copyright © 1928 by Alfred A. Knopf, Inc.
Renewal Copyright 1956 by Alfred A. Knopf, Inc.

Translated from the Norwegian by Arthur G. Chater.

Library of Congress Cataloging-in-Publication Data
Undset, Sigrid, 1982 – 1949.
[Olav Audunssøn i Hestviken. I. English]
The axe / Sigrid Undset.
p. cm. — (The master of Hestviken / Sigrid Undset ; v. 1)
Originally published in Norwegian as part 1 of Olav Audunssøn i
Hestviken (2 v.).
ISBN-10: 0-679-75273-0
ISBN-13: 978-0-679-75273-8

1. Norway—History—1030 –1397—Fiction.
2. Middle Ages—History—Fiction.
I. Title. II. Series: Undset, Sigrid, 1882 – 1949.
Master of Hestviken ; v. 1.
PT8950.U5061513 1994
839.8'2372—dc20   94-16662
CIP

146028962

PART ONE

Olav Audunsson

Takes a Wife

I

THE STEINFINNSSONS was the name folk gave to a kin that flourished in the country about Lake Mjösen at the time the sons of Harald Gille held sway in Norway. In those days men of that stock held manors in every parish that bordered the lake.

In the years of trouble which later came upon the land, the Steinfinnssons thought most of keeping their estates unshorn and their manors unburned, and for the most part they were strong enough to succeed in this, whether the Birchlegs or any of the opposing bands were to the fore in the Upplands. They seemed not to care greatly who in the end might be kings in Norway; but some men of this line had served King Magnus Erlingsson and later Sigurd Markusfostre faithfully and well, and none of them had aided Sverre and his kinsmen more than they could help. Old Tore Steinfinnsson of Hov and his sons joined the cause of King Skule, but when there was once more peace in the land they paid allegiance to King Haakon.[1]

[1] The period preceding that of this story (that is, the late twelfth and early thirteenth centuries) had been one of anarchy in Norway. Harald Gille (or Gilchrist; he came of Norse stock in Ireland) reigned 1130–6. His sons were Inge, Sigurd Mund, and Eystein, who at first reigned conjointly. Inge was the last to be killed (1161), and the crown then went to

Haakon II	1161
Magnus V, Erlingsson	1162
Sverre	1184
Haakon III	1202
Inge Baardsson	1204
Haakon IV, the Old	1217
Magnus VI	1263
Eirik	1280
Haakon V	1299

Sigurd Markusfostre was a son of Sigurd Mund; he was proclaimed King in 1162; in the end he was executed. Sverre was the famous adventurer

3

But from that time the family began to lose something of its repute. The country was now quieter and law and justice prevailed between man and man; their power was then greatest who held the King's authority or had served in the royal body-guard and won the King's trust. But the Steinfinnssons stayed at home upon their lands and were content to govern their own estates.

They were yet a wealthy kindred. The Steinfinnssons had been the last of the great Uppland lords to own thralls, and they still took the offspring of their freedmen into service or made them tenants on their land. Among the people round about, it was whispered that the Steinfinnssons were a race greedy of power, but they had the wit to choose such liegemen as should be easy to deal with. The men of the kin had no name for being of the wisest; but foolish they could not be called, since they had shown such good sense in the preserving of their estates. And they were not harsh lords toward those of less degree, so long as none offered to raise his voice against them.

Now, two years before King Haakon the Old died, young Tore Toresson of Hov sent his youngest son, Steinfinn, to the royal body-guard. His age was then eighteen; he was a handsome, well-grown man, but it was with him as with his kinsmen: folk knew them by their horses and their clothes, their arms and jewels. But if young Steinfinn had donned a coarse peasant's cloak, many a man would hardly have known him, of those who had called him friend and boon companion over the ale tankards the night before. The Steinfinnssons were goodly men for the most, but, as the saying was, they were lost in the crowd of church folks; and of this Steinfinn his fellows used to say that his wit was none too bad, but that it was as naught to his arrogance.

Now, Steinfinn was in Björgvin,[2] and there he met a maiden, Ingebjörg Jonsdatter, who had her place at the King's court with

whose followers were known as Birchlegs (*Birkebeinar*), from the shifts they were put to for foot-gear and clothing. He won his way to the crown in spite of the fierce opposition of the Church. Skule was the brother of Inge Baardsson, at whose death he claimed the throne. The Birchlegs however supported Sverre's grandson, Haakon Haakonsson, who was proclaimed king at the age of thirteen. Skule continually rebelled against Haakon, who finally defeated him at the Battle of Oslo; after this Skule was captured and slain by the Birchlegs 1240, and the civil wars came to an end.

[2] The modern Bergen.

Queen Ingebjörg. She and Steinfinn took a liking for each other, and he had his suit preferred with her father; but Jon answered that his daughter was already promised to Mattias Haraldsson, a dear friend of young King Magnus and one of his body-guard. But it seemed Steinfinn could not take his rejection in earnest: he came again many times, and had men of mark and at last Queen Ingebjörg herself to plead his cause. It availed nothing, for Jon Paalsson would not break his word to Mattias.

Steinfinn followed King Haakon in his last warfaring west oversea. In the fight at Largs he won fair renown for valour. While the King lay sick at Kirkevaag,[3] Steinfinn often had the night watch by his side, and at least he himself thought that King Haakon had shown him great favour.

The next summer Steinfinn was again in Björgvin. And one fine morning just after John's Mass,[4] as some of the Queen's maidens were coming from Nonneseter toward the King's house, they met Steinfinn and his body-servant riding through the street. They were leading a fine horse which Steinfinn said he had bought that morning, as they saw it, with bridle and woman's saddle. He greeted the damsels with courtesy and blithe jesting and would have them try this horse of his. They then went all together to a meadow and diverted themselves awhile. But when Ingebjörg Jonsdatter was in the saddle, Steinfinn said that she must have the loan of the horse to ride back to the King's court, and he would go with her.—The next that was heard of these two was that they had passed through Vors and taken to the hills. At last they reached Hov; Tore seemed at first ill pleased at his son's misdeed, but afterwards he gave him a homestead, Frettastein, which lay remote in the forest tracts. There he lived with Ingebjörg Jonsdatter as though they had been lawfully wedded, and he held a christening ale with the most lavish hospitality when she bore him a daughter next spring.

Nothing was done to him, either for the rape of the woman or for his flight from the body-guard. Folk said he could thank Queen Ingebjörg for that. And at last the Queen made a recon-

---

[3] After being defeated at Largs in Ayrshire by Alexander III of Scotland (in 1263) King Haakon retired to Kirkwall (Kirkevaag) in Orkney, where he died in the Bishop's palace, some remains of which are still to be seen close by the newly restored cathedral.

[4] June 21.

ciliation between the young couple and Jon Paalsson; he gave Steinfinn his daughter in marriage and held their wedding at the King's court in Oslo, where he was then a courtier.

At that time Ingebjörg was expecting her third child; but neither she nor Steinfinn showed becoming humility toward Jon or thanked him as they ought for his fatherly kindness. Steinfinn gave costly gifts to his wife's father and her kinsmen, but in other ways both he and his wife were very overweening and behaved as though all their life had been honourable, nor had they any need to humble themselves in order to retrieve their position. They brought their elder daughter, Ingunn, to the wedding, and Steinfinn danced with her on his arm and showed her to all who were there; she was three years old, and her parents were proud beyond measure of this fair child.

But their first son died, whom Ingebjörg bore close upon their marriage, and after that she had still-born twins, both boys. Then the two bowed the knee to Jon Paalsson and besought his pardon with contrite hearts. Thereafter Ingebjörg had two sons who lived. She grew fairer with every year that passed; she and Steinfinn lived together in affection, maintained a great house, and were merry and of good cheer.

One man there was of whom none seemed to take thought: Mattias Haraldsson, Ingebjörg's rightful bridegroom, whom she had played false. He went into foreign lands at the time Steinfinn's wedding was held and he stayed away for many years. Mattias was a little man and ill-favoured, but mettlesome, hardy, and of great wealth.

Steinfinn and Ingebjörg had been married seven years or thereabouts and their daughters, Ingunn and Tora, were ten and eight winters old, but the sons were quite small—when Mattias Haraldsson came one night with an armed band to Frettastein. It was at haymaking, and many of the house-folk were away on the outlying pastures; those who were at home were overpowered as they lay asleep. Steinfinn did not wake until he was pulled out of the bed, where he slept with his wife. The summer was warm that year, so folk lay naked; Steinfinn was bare as his mother bore him as he stood bound by his own board with three men holding him.

The lady Ingebjörg defended herself like a wild beast, with tooth and nail, while Mattias wrapped the coverlet about her, lifted her out of bed, and set her on his knees. Mattias said to Steinfinn:

"Now could I take such vengeance as ye two deserve—and you, Steinfinn, should stand there a bound man with no power to protect your wife, if I had a mind to take her who was promised to me and never to you. But I have more fear of breaking God's law and I take more heed of good morals than you. So now I shall chasten you, Steinfinn, by letting you take back your wife inviolate, by my favour—and you, my Ingebjörg, dwell with your man and peace be with you both! After this night I trow ye will remember to thank me each time ye shall embrace in joy and gladness," he said with a loud laugh.

He kissed the lady and laid her in the bed, calling to his men that now they should ride away.—Then he turned to Steinfinn.

Steinfinn had not uttered a word, and, as he saw he could not break loose, he stood still; but his face was a deep crimson and he did not take his eyes off Mattias. The other went close up to him.

"If you have not the grace, man, then maybe you have the wit to thank me for the mercy I have shown tonight?" asked Mattias with a laugh.

"Be sure I shall thank you," quoth Steinfinn. "If God grant me life."

Now, Mattias was dressed in a kirtle with open, hanging sleeves and tassels at their points. He took the flap of his sleeve in his hand and whisked the tassel across Steinfinn's face, laughing yet louder. And of a sudden he drove his fist into the face of the bound man, so that the blood flowed from Steinfinn's mouth and nose.

That done, he went out to his men. Olav Audunsson, Steinfinn's foster-son, a boy of eleven years, ran forward and cut Steinfinn's bonds. The lad, Steinfinn's children, and their foster-mothers had been dragged into the outer room and held there while Mattias was speaking to his faithless betrothed and her man within.

Steinfinn snatched a spear and, naked as he was, ran out after Mattias and his men as they rode down the steep slope, straight across the plough-land, laughing scornfully. Steinfinn flung the spear, but it fell short. Meanwhile the boy Olav ran to the men's room and the byre and let out the serving-men who had been barred in, while Steinfinn went back to the house, dressed himself, and took his arms.

But all thought of pursuing Mattias was vain, for there were but three horses left at Frettastein and they were loose in the paddock. Nevertheless Steinfinn rode off at once, to seek his father and brothers. As he dressed, he had spoken in private with his wife. She came out with him when he was ready to set out. And now Steinfinn declared to his house-folk that he would not sleep with his wife until he had repaired the shame, so that no man could say she was his by the favour of Mattias Haraldsson. Then he rode forth, but his lady went into an old outhouse that stood in the courtyard, and locked herself in.

The house-folk, men and women, streamed into the hall, eager to learn what had happened. They close-questioned Olav, who sat half-clad on the edge of the bed that Steinfinn's weeping daughters had crept into; they turned to ask the two little maids and the foster-mother of Steinfinn's youngest son. But none of these could tell them aught, and soon the servants grew tired of questioning and went out.

The boy sat in the dark hall listening to Ingunn's obstinate weeping. Then he climbed up into the bed and lay down by her side.

"Be sure your father will take vengeance. You may well believe he will do that. And I trow I shall be with him, to show that Steinfinn has a son-in-law, though his sons are yet too young to bear arms!"

It was the first time Olav had dared to speak straight out of the betrothal that had been made between him and Ingunn when they were children. In the first years he spent at Frettastein the servants had sometimes chanced to speak of it and tease the children with being betrothed, and it had always made Ingunn wild. Once she had run to her father and complained, and he had been angered and had forbidden his people to speak of such things— so wrathfully that more than one of them had guessed that maybe Steinfinn repented his bargain with Olav's father.

That night Ingunn took Olav's reminder of the plans that had been made for them in such wise that she crept up to the boy and wept upon his arm, till the sleeve of his shirt was drenched with her tears.

. . .

From that night a great change came over the life at Frettastein. Steinfinn's father and brothers counselled him to bring a suit against Mattias Haraldsson, but Steinfinn said that he himself would be the judge of what his honour was worth.

Now, Mattias had gone straight home to the manor in Borgesyssel where he dwelt. And the following spring he went on a pilgrimage in foreign lands. But when this was noised abroad and it was known that Steinfinn's wrath was such that he shunned folk and would not live with his wife any more, then there was much talk of the vengeance that Mattias had taken upon his faithless betrothed. Even though Mattias and his men told no different tale of the raid from what was heard at Frettastein, it turned out that the farther the rumour spread over the country, the more cheaply folk judged that Steinfinn had been held by Mattias. And a ballad was made of these doings as they were thought to have fallen out.

One evening—it was three years later—as Steinfinn sat drinking with his men, he asked if there were any who could sing the ballad that had been made upon him. At first all the house-carls made as though they knew naught of any ballad. But when Steinfinn promised a great gift to him who could sing his dance, it came out that the whole household knew it. Steinfinn heard it to the end; now and then he bared his teeth in a sort of smile. As soon as it was done, he went to bed together with his half-brother Kolbein Toresson, and the folk heard the two talking behind the bed-shutters till near midnight.

This Kolbein was a son of Tore of Hov by a concubine he had had before his marriage; and he had always cared more for his children by her than for those born in wedlock. For Kolbein he had made a good marriage and got him a great farm to the northward on Lake Mjösen. But there was little thrift in Kolbein; he was overbearing, unjust, and of a hasty temper and was ever in lawsuits both with lesser men and with his equals. So he was a man of few friends and there was little love between him and his true-born half-brothers, until, after his misfortune, Steinfinn took up with Kolbein. After that these two brothers were always together and Kolbein charged himself with Steinfinn and all his affairs. But he ordered them as he ordered his own and brought trouble with him even when he acted on his brother's behalf.

Assuredly it was not that Kolbein had a will to harm his

younger brother; he was fond of Steinfinn in his own way, after that the younger in his perplexity had put himself wholly into his half-brother's hands. Careless and lazy Steinfinn had been in his days of prosperity; he had thought more of lordly living than of taking care for his estate. After the night of the raid he shunned all men for a time. But afterwards, by Kolbein's advice, he took a whole band of house-carls into his service—young men well trained to arms, and by choice such as before had done lord's service elsewhere. Steinfinn and his men slept in the great hall, and they followed their master wherever he went, but they neither could nor would do much work on the estate, so that he had great cost and little gain of the whole band.

Nevertheless the farm work at Frettastein was seen to in a way, for the old bailiff, Grim, and Dalla, his sister, were children of one of Steinfinn's grandmother's thralls, and they had no thought beyond the welfare of their young master. But now, when Steinfinn had need of a return from his outlying farms, he cared neither to see nor to speak with his own tenants and bailiffs—and Kolbein, who took charge of all such matters in his stead, brought with him trouble without end.

Ingebjörg Jonsdatter had been a skilful housewife, and in former days this had made great amends for her husband's lavish and indolent ways. But now she hid herself in the little outhouse with her maids, and the rest of the household scarcely saw her. She spent her days in pondering and repining, never inquired of the condition of the house or estate, but rather seemed to be angered if any disturbed her thoughts. Even with her children, who lived with their mother in the outhouse, she was silent, caring little for how they fared or what they did. Yet before, in the good days, she had been a tender mother, and Steinfinn Toresson had been a happy and loving father, proud of their strong and handsome children.

So long as her sons, Hallvard and Jon, were still small, she often took them in her lap and sat rocking them, with her chin resting on their fair-haired crowns, while she moped, lost in sorrowful thought. But the boys were not very old before they grew weary of staying in the outhouse with their mournful mother and her women.

Tora, the younger daughter, was a good and pretty child. She saw full well that her father and mother had suffered a grievous wrong and were now full of cares and sorrow, and she strove to cheer them, kindly and lovingly. She became the favourite of both. Steinfinn's face would brighten somewhat when he looked at this daughter of his. Tora Steinfinnsdatter was delicate and shapely in body and limbs, she ripened early into womanhood. She had a long, full face, a fair skin, and blue eyes; thick plaits of smooth, corn-yellow hair hung over her shoulders. Her father stroked her cheek: "A good child you are, Tora mine— God bless you. Go to your mother, Tora; sit with her and comfort her."

Tora went, and sat down spinning or sewing beside her sorrowful mother. And she thought herself more than rewarded if Ingebjörg said at the last: "You are good, Tora mine—God preserve you from all evil, my child." Then Tora's tears began to fall— she thought upon her parents' heavy lot, and, full of righteous wrath, she looked at her sister, who had never enough constancy to sit still with their mother and could not come into the outhouse without making her impatient with her continual restlessness—till Ingebjörg bade her go out again. And Ingunn made for the door, carefree and unrepentant, and ran out to play and shout with the other children of the place—Olav and some boys belonging to the serving-folk at Frettastein.

Ingunn was the eldest of all Steinfinn's and Ingebjörg's children. When she was little, she had been marvellously fair; but now she was not half as pretty as her sister, people thought. And she had not so much sense, nor was she very quick-witted; she was neither better nor worse than are most children. But in a way she was as much liked by the people of the place as the quiet and beautiful younger sister. Steinfinn's men looked upon Tora with a sort of reverence, but they were better pleased to have Ingunn among them in the hall.

There were no maids of her own age either at Frettastein or any of the farms and homesteads round about. So it was that Ingunn was always with the boys. She took part in all their games and all their pursuits, practised such sports as they used—she threw the spear and the stone, shot with the bow, struck the ball, set snares in the wood, and fished in the tarn. But she was clumsy at all these things, neither handy nor bold, but weak, quick to give up and take to tears when their play grew rough or the game went against her. For all that, the boys let her go with them everywhere. For one thing, she was Steinfinn's daughter, and then Olav Audunsson would have it so. And it was always Olav who was the master of their games.

Olav Audunsson was well liked by all on the estate, both great and small, and yet none would have called him a winning child. It seemed that none could come at the heart of this boy, although he was never unfriendly toward any living soul—rather might it be said that he was good-natured and helpful in his taciturn and absent way.

Handsome he was, though he was fair of skin and hair as an albino almost, but he had not the albino's sidelong glance or bowed neck. Olav's blue-green eyes were pale in colour, but he looked the world straight in the face with them, and he carried his head erect upon his strong, milk-white neck. It was as though sun and wind had little power upon that skin of his—it seemed strangely tight and smooth and white—only in summer a few small freckles appeared over the root of the nose, which was low and broad. This healthy paleness gave Olav's face even in childhood something of a cold, impassive look. His features too were somewhat short and broad, but well formed. The eyes lay rather far apart, but they were large and frankly open; the eyebrows and lashes were so fair that they showed but as a golden shadow in the sunlight. His nose was broad and straight, but a little too short; his mouth was rather large, but the lips were so finely curved and firm that, had they not been so pale in the colourless face, they might have been called handsome. But his hair was of matchless beauty—so fair that it shone like silver rather than gold, thick and soft and lightly curled. He wore it trimmed so that it covered his broad, white forehead, but showed the hollow in his neck between the two powerful muscles.

Olav was never tall for his age, but he seemed bigger than he was; of perfect build, sturdy and muscular, with very small hands and feet, which seemed the stronger because the wrists and ankles were so round and powerful. And indeed he was very strong and supple; he excelled in all kinds of sport and in the use of arms— but there was none who had ever taught him to practise these exercises in the right way. As things stood at Frettastein in his growing up, Olav was left to his own devices. Steinfinn, who had promised to be a father to him when he took charge of the boy, did nothing to give him such training as was meet for a young man of good birth, heir to some fortune and destined to be the husband of Ingunn Steinfinnsdatter.

That Steinfinn Toresson was Olav's foster-father had come about in this way:

One summer, while Steinfinn was still in goodly case, it chanced that he had business at the Eidsiva Thing. He went thither with friends and kinsmen and took with him his wife and their daughter Ingunn, who was then six years old. The parents had such joy of the pretty child that they could not be without her.

Here at the Thing Steinfinn met a man, Audun Ingolfsson of Hestviken. Audun and Steinfinn had been bedfellows in the King's body-guard and good friends, though Audun was older than the other and the men were of very unlike humour; for at that time Steinfinn was merry and loved to talk of himself, but Audun was a silent man and never spoke of his own affairs.

In the spring of the same year that King Haakon was away warring in Scotland, Audun was married. He took a Danish wife, Cecilia Björnsdatter, Queen Ingebjörg's playmate, who had been with her at the convent of Rind. When the Bishop of Oslo took young King Magnus's bride by force and carried her to Norway, because the Dane King slighted the compact and refused to send his kinswoman thither, Cecilia went with her. At first the young Queen would fain have kept the damsel always with her; but a year later the Lady Ingebjörg seemed already to have changed her mind and she was eager to have Cecilia married. Some said it was because King Magnus himself liked to talk with the Danish maid more than his wife cared for; others declared that it was young Alf Erlingsson of Tornberg who had won her heart, but his father, Baron Erling Alfsson, would not let his son take a foreign wife who owned neither land nor powerful kinsfolk in Norway. Young Alf was a man of fiery nature and wont to have his will in all things, and he loved Cecilia madly. The Queen therefore took counsel to marry off the maid, lest some misfortune might befall her.

However these things might be, the maid herself was chaste and full of grace; and after Audun, who at first had seemed somewhat unwilling, had spoken two or three times with Cecilia, he himself was eager to take her. Their wedding was held at the

King's court in Björgvin; old King Haakon gave the bride a marriage portion. Audun carried his wife to Hestviken. There she was well secured, whether from King Magnus or from Alf Erlingsson.

In the course of the summer Audun with his ship joined the King in Herdluvaag and followed him westward oversea. And when the King died in the Orkneys before Yule—it was in the winter of 1263—Audun commanded the ship that brought the news to Norway. Then he journeyed on to the east, home to his manor. In the summer he came back to King Magnus's bodyguard. His wife had then died in giving birth to a son, who lived. Audun had grown even more silent than before, but now he uttered one thing and another of his affairs to Steinfinn. At Hestviken dwelt his grandfather; he was old and somewhat self-willed. He had been against his grandson's marriage with a foreign wife without kindred. Besides him there was in the house an old uncle of Audun; he was mad. Most of the time Cecilia had lived at Hestviken she had been left alone with these two old men: "It misgives me she had no happy life there in the east," said Audun. In the great-grandfather's honour Cecilia had named the child after him—it was the Danish custom—but Olav Olavsson was greatly angered thereat: "In Norway no child is called after a living man—save with the thought of putting him out of life," said he. It fell out that Audun was left sole heir to these two old men, but he let it be known that he would not go home to Hestviken for a while; he was minded to bide in Björgvin with King Magnus.

It was a short time after this that Steinfinn carried off Ingebjörg, and since then he had neither heard nor sought tidings of Audun Ingolfsson until he met the man at the Thing. Audun was leading a boy of seven years by the hand and was asking for certain men from Soleyar whom he was to meet there. He looked very sick. Audun was a tall man and had always been very spare and slim, with a narrow face, a thin and sharp hooked nose, and his skin and hair were fair to whiteness. Now he was bent in the back and gaunt as a skeleton, wan-faced and blue about the lips. But the boy was a strong and comely child, broad-shouldered and of good build; he was as fair of hue as his father, but in other ways he bore him no great likeness.

Steinfinn embraced his friend with riotous joy, but it filled him with grief to see that Audun was so sick. He would hear of naught else but that Audun must go with him to the house where Steinfinn and his following lived while the Thing lasted.

On the way thither Audun told him that these men he was to have met were the sons of his grandfather's nephew: "And nearer kinsmen have I none; it will fall to them to be the guardians of Olav here, when I am dead." The two old men at Hestviken were still living, but they were clean decrepit; and for himself he had an inward scathe in his stomach, so that he had no good of meat or drink; he could not live many weeks more. He had been with King Magnus all these years until lately, before Yule; then he went home to Hestviken, being very sick. He had not seen his own house more than once since his wife's death, so it was only this winter that he had come to know his son. But now the child's future lay heavily on his heart—and here these kinsmen from Sole-yar had failed to come, and he scarce had the strength to ride up to them, it gave him such pain to ride—and this was the last day but one of the Thing. "The Fathers of Hovedö [5] would gladly take him—but should the boy have a mind to stay there when he grows up and make himself a monk, then our kin would die out with him."

When Ingebjörg saw the fair child who would soon be both motherless and fatherless, she was fain to kiss the boy. But Olav wrested himself from her and fled to his father, while he stared at the lady with his great blue eyes, full of ill humour and surprise.

"Will you not kiss my wife, Olav?" asked Steinfinn with a mighty laugh.

"No," answered the lad. "For Aslaug kisses Koll—"

Audun smiled somewhat uneasily—these were two old folks who served at Hestviken, he said; and at that all the grown people laughed greatly, and Olav turned red and looked at the ground. Then his father chid him and bade him greet Ingebjörg courteously and properly. So he had to go forward and be kissed by the lady; and when little Ingunn came out and said that she too would kiss the boy, Olav dutifully went up and bent forward so that the little maid could reach his lips. But his face was red as fire, and his eyes were full of tears, so that the men laughed and

[5] The Cistercian monastery on Hovedö, the largest island in the fiord off the town of Oslo.

bantered Olav that he set so little store by the favour of fair women.

But as the evening wore on, when the folk had supped, and sat over their drink, Olav seemed to thaw a little. Ingunn ran about among the benches, and where she found an empty place, she climbed up and sat for a while swinging her legs; then slipped down again, ran to another place, and crept up there. This made the grown ones laugh; they called to her and caught at her, and the child grew more and more wanton and wild. Then it seemed that Olav had made a great resolution—he rose up from beside his father, straightened his new knife-belt, walked across the hall, and sat down by Ingunn's side. And when she slid down and ran to another seat, the boy followed her, holding back a little, and seated himself again beside her. Thus the children played hither and thither among the benches, with laughter and cries from Ingunn—while Olav followed, steady and serious; but now and again he glanced at his father, and a faltering smile came over the boy's mute and handsome face.

The children were nodding in a corner by the time Steinfinn and Audun came and led them out to the hearth in the midst of the hall. The guests formed a ring about them; they were far gone in drink. Steinfinn himself was unsteady on his legs as he took his daughter's hand and laid it in Olav's. Then Steinfinn and Audun clenched the bargain of their children's betrothal with a hand-clasp, and Audun gave Olav a gold ring and helped him to set it on Ingunn's little hand and hold up the child's fingers so that all might see the massive ring dangling there. Ingebjörg Jonsdatter and the women laughed and cried by turns, for no fairer sight than this little bridal pair had any of them seen.

Then she handed her daughter a horn and bade her drink to her betrothed, and the children drank and spilled the liquor over their clothes. Steinfinn stood holding his friend round the neck; with tears in his voice he swore solemnly that Audun had no need to grieve for the child he left behind him; he would foster Olav himself and stand in his father's stead till the boy was a man and could bring home his bride, said Steinfinn, and kissed Audun on both cheeks, while Ingebjörg took the children in her arms and promised to be a mother to Olav, for the sake of Cecilia Björnsdatter, whom she had loved as her own sister.

Then they told Olav he must kiss his betrothed. And now the

boy went forward right boldly, laid his arms about Ingunn's neck, and kissed her as warmly as he could, while the witnesses laughed and drank the health of the affianced pair.

But it seemed as though Olav had now learned to like the sport— all at once he sprang at his young bride, took her round the neck again, and gave her three or four smacking kisses. Then all the company roared with laughter and called to him to keep on with it.

Whether it was the laughter that made her ashamed or a whim of the little maid—Ingunn tried to struggle out of the boy's arms, and as he only clasped her the closer, she bit him in the cheek with all her might.

Olav stood staring for a moment, fairly amazed. Then he rubbed his cheek, where drops of blood were oozing out. He looked at his bloody fingers—and then made to fly at Ingunn and strike her. But his father lifted him in his arms and carried him away to the bed where they were to sleep. And then the affianced bride and bridegroom were undressed and put to bed, and soon they fell asleep and forgot the whole company.

Next day, when Steinfinn was sober, he would fain have been quit of his bargain. He dropped some hints that it was all done in jest—if they were to make any compact for their children's future, they must first take counsel about it. But Audun, who had been kept from drinking by his sickness, opposed him in this. He bade the other remember that he had given his promise to a dying man, and that God would assuredly avenge it if he broke his word to a forlorn and fatherless child.

Steinfinn pondered. Audun Ingolfsson came of a good and ancient kindred, though it was now short of men and had little power. But Olav was an only child, and even if he could not look for much heritage beyond his ancestral seat of Hestviken, this was nevertheless a great estate. He himself might yet have many children in his marriage—Olav might well be a fit match for Ingunn, with her daughter's portion after him. So Steinfinn sober took up the word he had spoken in his drink, promised to foster Olav and give him his daughter in marriage when the two children should come to years of discretion. And when he rode home from the Thing, he took Olav Audunsson north with him.

• • •

17

The same autumn there came tidings to Frettastein that Olav's father was dead, a short time after his grandfather and the mad uncle. The messengers brought with them a part of the child's heritage from his father and mother in chattels—clothing, arms, and a casket of jewels. His estate of Hestviken was left in the charge of an old kinsman of the boy—one they called Olav Half-priest.

Steinfinn took his foster-son's goods in keeping, and he so far bestirred himself that twice he sent messages with folks who had errands in Oslo, to appoint a meeting with Olav Half-priest. But nothing came of it at that time, and afterwards Steinfinn took no further step. It was the way with Steinfinn that he was no very active man even when his own affairs were at stake. Both he and Ingebjörg were kind to Olav, and he was treated as a child of theirs, till the trouble came upon them. And after that their foster-son was haply no more neglected than their own offspring.

In a way Olav had been quick to feel at home at Frettastein. He liked Steinfinn and Ingebjörg well enough, but he was a quiet-mannered, rather reticent child, so he was always something of a stranger to them. He never had any true feeling that he belonged to the house, though he was happier here than where he came from. As far as he could, he left off thinking of his first home, Hestviken; but now and then memories of that time came up in him. And it caught him with a clutch of despondency when he called to mind all the old folks there.—The serving-men were worn out with age, and his great-grandfather was ever plaguing his mad old son, whom folk called Foulbeard—he had to be fed like a child and kept away from fire and water and edged tools. Olav had mostly been left to fend for himself. But he had never known any other ways, and the filth and evil stench that followed Foulbeard had been part of the life of the place as far back as the boy could remember, and he had also grown so used to the mad-man's fits of howling and shrieking that they frightened him not so much. But he shrank from these memories.—Sometimes in his last years his great-grandfather had taken him to church with him, and there he had had a sight of strangers, women and children too; but he never had a thought that he might mix with them or talk with them; they seemed to be a part of the mass. And for many years after he had come to Frettastein it might chance that he would have a sudden feeling of loneliness—as though his life here with these people were unreal or not an everyday thing, like a church Sunday, and he were only waiting to go away, back to the life from which he had come. This was never more than a flash of memory that came and vanished again at once—but he never came to feel wholly rooted at Frettastein, though he had no longing for another home.

But at times memories of another kind arose, which stabbed his heart with a sharp longing. Like the return of an old dream he remembered a bare outcrop of rock in the midst of the yard at Hestviken; there were cracks in the warm rock and he had lain there picking out moss with a splinter of bone. Pictures floated before his eyes of places where he had once wandered alone, filling them with his own fancies, and these memories brought an aftertaste of unutterable sweetness. Behind the cowsheds in the yard, there was a lofty cliff of smooth, dark rock over which water trickled, and in the swampy hollow between the cliff and the outhouses it was always dark and shady, with a growth of tall green rushes.—And there was somewhere a stretch of beach where he trod on seaweed and rattling pebbles, and found snail-shells and bits of rotten wood, water-worn and green with slime. Outside, the water lay glittering into the far distance, and the old housecarl, Koll, used to open mussels and give them to him—Olav's mouth watered when he recalled the fine taste of sea-water and the rich yellow morsel that he sopped up from the open blue shell.

When such memories glimmered within him he grew silent and answered absently if Ingunn spoke to him. But it never came into his head to go away and leave her. He never had a thought of parting company with her, when she came and wanted to be with him, any more than he thought he could part from himself. Thus it was with Olav Audunsson: it seemed his very destiny that he should always be with Ingunn. It was the only sure thing in his life, that he and Ingunn were inseparably joined together. He seldom thought of that evening when they had been betrothed—and it was now many years since any had spoken of the children's affiancing. But amid all his thoughts and feelings it was as firm ground under his feet—that he should always live with Ingunn. The boy had no kinsmen to rely on; he knew that Hestviken was now his own, but with every year that went by, his images of the place grew fainter and fainter—it was but fragments of a dream he remembered. When he thought that one day he would go to live there, the fixed and real part of his thought was that he should take Ingunn with him—together they would face the uncertain future.

He never thought whether she was fair or not. Tora was fair, it seemed to him, perhaps because he had heard it said so often. Ingunn was only Ingunn, near at hand and everyday and always at his side; he never thought of how she might be, otherwise than as one thinks of the weather; that has to be taken as it comes. He grew angry and scolded her when she was contrary or trouble-some—he had beaten her too, when they were smaller. When she was kind and fair-spoken with him and the other boys, their play-mates, he felt happy as in fine weather. And mostly they were good friends, like brother and sister who get on well together—at whiles they might be angry and quarrel, but neither thought the other's nature could be changed from what it was.

And among the band of children at Frettastein, of whom none took any heed, these two, the eldest, kept together, because they knew that, whatever happened, one thing was certain—that they should be together. This was the only sure thing, and it was good to have something sure. The boy, growing up alone in the home of a stranger kin, struck root, without knowing it, in her who was promised to him; and his love for the only one he well knew of all that was to be his grew as he himself grew—without his mark-ing the growth. He cherished her as a habit, until his love took on a colour and brightness that showed him how wholly he was filled thereby.

Things went on this wise until the summer when Olav Auduns-son had ended his sixteenth year. Ingunn was now fifteen winters old.

2

OLAV had inherited from his father a great battle-axe—with pointed barbs, steel edge, and inlays of gold on the cheeks; the shaft had bands of gilt copper. It had a name and was called Kin-fetch.[6]

[6] Norse, *Ættarfylgja:* the fetch or "doubleganger" of his race.

It was a splendid weapon and the boy who owned this treasure thought its match was scarce to be found in Norway, as was like enough. But he had never said this to any but Ingunn, and she believed it and was as proud of the axe as he himself. Olav had always kept it hanging above his sleeping-place in the hall.

But one day this spring Olav saw that the edge was notched, and when he took it down, he found that the steel edge had parted from the iron blade and worked loose in the welding. Olav guessed that it would be vain to try to find out who had used his axe and spoiled it. So he said nothing to any but Ingunn. They took counsel what he should do and agreed that next time Steinfinn was from home Olav must ride to Hamar; there dwelt a famous armourer, and if he could not set it to rights, no man could. And one morning in the week before John's Mass Ingunn came and told Olav that today her father was going north to Kolbein; so it might be a timely occasion for them to go to the town next day.

Olav had not thought to take her with him. It was many years since either of the children had been in the town, and Olav did not rightly know how far it was thither; but he had thought he might be home again to supper if he rode down early in the morning. But Ingunn had no horse of her own, and there was none in the place that he could take for her. If they were to take turns at riding his horse, Elk, they could not reach home again till far on in the night—and then it would be so that she must ride and he walk the whole time; that he knew well from the many times they had gone together to mass in their parish church, in the village below. And they would surely be very angry, Steinfinn and Ingebjörg, if they heard that he had taken Ingunn with him to Hamar. But Olav only made answer that they would have to go down to the shore and row to the town—they must set out betimes in the morning.

It was a good while before sunrise when he stole out of the hall next morning, but it was daylight outside, calm and chilly. The air was cold with dew—good as a bath after the dense fumes of man and dog within. The boy sucked it in as he stood on the threshold looking at the weather.

The wild cherry was white with a foam of blossom between the cornfields—spring had come even here in the hills. Far below, the lake lay glistening, a dead grey with dark stripes where the current ran: it gave promise of showers. The sky had a wan look, and dark shreds of cloud drifted low down—there had been rainstorms in the night. When Olav stepped out on the grass of the yard his high boots of yellow undyed leather were darkened with moisture—little reddish splashes appeared on his boot-legs. He sat down on the doorstone and pulled off his boots, tied the laces together, and slung them over his shoulder to carry them with his folded cloak and the axe.

Barefoot he went across the wet courtyard to the house where Ingunn had slept that night with two of the serving-maids, that she might be able to slip away without being seen. For the journey to town Olav had dressed himself in his best clothes—a long kirtle of light-blue English cloth and hose of the same stuff. But the dress was somewhat outgrown—the kirtle was tight across the chest and short at the wrists and it scarce reached to the middle of his calf. The hose too were very tight, and Ingebjörg had cut off the feet the autumn before; now they ended at the ankle. But the kirtle was fastened at the neck with a fine ring-brooch of gold, and round his waist he wore a belt set with silver roses and Saint Olav's image on the buckle; his dagger bore gilt mounts on hilt and sheath.

Olav went up into the balcony and struck three light blows upon the door. Then he stood waiting.

A bird began trilling and piping—it burst forth like a fountain above the sleepy twittering from the thickets round about. Olav saw the bird as a dot against the sky—it sat on a fir twig against the yellowing northern heaven. He could see how it drew itself in and swelled itself out, like a little heart beating. The hosts of cloud high up began to flush, a flush spread over the hillside with a rosy reflection in the water.—Olav knocked at the door again, much harder—it rang out in the morning stillness so that the boy held his breath and listened for a movement in any of the houses.

Soon after, the door was opened ajar—the girl slipped out. Her hair hung about her, ruffled and lustreless; it was yellow-brown and very curly. She was in her bare smock; the neck, which was of white linen, was worked with green and blue flowers, but below, it was of coarse grey stuff, and it was too long for her and trailed about her narrow pink feet. She carried her clothes over her arm and had a wallet in her hand. This she gave to Olav, threw down her bundle of clothes, and shook her hair from her face, which was still flushed with sleep—one cheek redder than the other. She took a waist-band and girt up her smock with it.

She was tall and thin, with slight limbs, a long, slender throat, and a small head. Her face was a triangle, her forehead low and broad, but it was snow-white and finely arched at the temples under the thick folds of hair; the thin cheeks were too much drawn in, making the chin too long and pointed; the straight little nose was too low and short. But for all that her little face had a restless charm of its own: the eyes were very large and dark grey, but the whites were as blue as a little child's, and they lay in deep shadow beneath the straight black lines of her brows and her full, white eyelids; the mouth was narrow, but the lips were red as berries—and with her bright pink and white complexion Ingunn Steinfinnsdatter was fair now in her young girlhood.

"Make haste," said Olav, as she sat on the stair winding her linen hose tightly around her legs; and she took good time about it. "You were best carry hose and shoes till the grass be dry."

"I will not go barefoot on the wet ground in this cold—" the girl shivered a little.

"You will be warmer when once you have made an end of putting on your clothes—you must not be so long about it—'tis rosy morning already, cannot you see?"

Ingunn made no answer, but took off her hose-band and began again to wind it about her leg. Olav hung her clothes over the rail of the balcony.

"You must have a cloak with you—do you not see we shall have showers today?"

"My cloak is down with Mother—I forgot to take it with me last night. It looks now like fine weather—but if there comes a shower, we shall find some place to creep under."

"What if it rains while we are in the boat? You cannot walk in the town without a cloak either. But I see well enough you will borrow my cloak, as is your way."

Ingunn looked up at him over her shoulder. "Why are you so cross today, Olav?"—and she began to be busy with her footgear again.

Olav was ready with an answer; but as she bent down to her shoe, the smock slipped from her shoulders, baring her bosom and upper arm. And instantly a wave of new feelings swept over the boy—he stood still, bashful and confused, and could not take his eyes off this glimpse of her naked body. It was as though he had never seen it before; a new light was thrown on what he knew of old—as with a sudden landslip within him, his feelings for his foster-sister came to rest in a new order. With a burst of fervour he felt a tenderness that had in it both pity and a touch of pride; her shoulders sank so weakly in a slant to the faint rounding of the shoulder-joint; the thin, white upper arms looked soft, as though she had no muscles under the silky skin—the boy's senses were tricked with a vision of corn that is as yet but milky, before it has fully ripened. He had a mind to stoop down and pat her consolingly—such was his sudden sense of the difference between her feeble softness and his own wiry, muscular body. Oft had he looked at her before, in the bath-house, and at himself, his hard, tough, well-rounded chest, his muscles firmly braced over the stomach, and swelling into a knot as he bent his arm. With child-ish pride he had rejoiced that he was a boy.

Now this self-glorious sense of being strong and well made be-came strangely shot through with tenderness, because she was so weak—he would know how to protect her. He would gladly have put his arm around that slender back, clasped her little girlish breasts beneath his hand. He called to mind that day last spring when he himself had fallen on his chest over a log—it was where Gunleik's new house was building—he had torn both his clothes and his flesh. With a shudder in which were mingled horror and sweetness he thought that never more would he let Ingunn climb up on the roof with them at Gun-leik's farm.

He blushed as she looked at him.

"You are staring? Mother will never know I have borrowed her smock; she never wears it herself."

"Do you not feel the cold?" he asked; and Ingunn's surprise was yet greater, for he spoke as low and shyly as though she had really come to some hurt in their game.

"Oh, not enough to make my nails go blue," she said laughing.

"No, but can you not get your clothes on quickly?" he said anxiously. "You have goose-flesh on your arms."

"If I could but get my smock together—" The edges at the throat were stiff with sewing; she struggled, but could not get the stuff through the tiny ring of her brooch.

Olav laid down the whole load that he had just taken on his back. "I will lend you mine—it has a bigger ring." He took the gold brooch from his bosom and handed it to her. Ingunn looked at him, amazed. She had pestered him to lend her this trinket before now, but that he himself should offer to let her wear it was something new, for it was a costly jewel, of pure gold and fairly big. Along the outer edge were inscribed the Angel's Greeting and *Amor vincit omnia*. Her kinsman Arnvid Finnsson said that in the Norse tongue this meant "Love conquers all things," since the Lady Sancta Maria conquers all the malice of the fiend by her loving supplication.

Ingunn had put on her red holy-day garments and bound her silken girdle about her waist—she combed her tangled hair with her fingers.

"You must even lend me your comb, Olav!"

Although he had but just collected all his things again, he laid them down once more, searched out a comb from his pouch, and gave it to her without impatience.

But as they plodded along the road between the fences down in the village, Olav's dizzy exaltation forsook him little by little. The weather had cleared and the sun was broiling hot—and as time went on, it *was* a load: wallet, axe, cloak, and boots. True, Ingunn had once offered to carry some of it; but that was when they were passing through the forest and it was cool beneath the firs, with a grateful fresh scent of pine-needles and hair-moss and young leaves. The sun barely gilded the tree-tops, and the birds sang with full throat—and then the boy was still swayed by his new-born emotion. She bade him stop, she had to plait her hair anew, for she had forgotten her hair-band—ay, 'twas like her. But her tawny mane waved so finely over her forehead as she loosed the braids, making shady hollows at the temples, where the first short hairs lay close and curly, it softened his heart to look at it. So when she spoke of carrying, he only shook his head; and afterwards he heard no more of it.

Down here on the fiord it was full summer. The children climbed a fence and made straight across an enclosure; the meadow was a slope of flowers, pink clouds of caraway and golden globe-flowers. Where there was a thin patch of soil among the rocks, the violets grew thick as a carpet, and within the shade of the alder brake red catchflies blazed amid the luxuriant green. Ingunn stopped again and again to pluck flowers, and Olav grew more and more impatient; he longed to get down to the boat and be rid of his burden. He was hungry too—as yet neither of them had tasted food. But when she said that they could sit down and eat here in the shade by the brook, he replied shortly that it would be as he said. When they had got hold of a boat, they could make a meal before rowing away, but not till then.

"You will always have your way," said Ingunn querulously.

"Ay, if I let you have yours we might reach the town tomorrow morning. But if you will listen to me, we shall be back to Frettastein by that time."

Then she laughed, flung away her flowers, and ran after him.

All the way down, the children had followed the brook that ran north of the houses at Frettastein. On nearing the village it became a little river—on the flat, before it fell into the fiord, it spread out and ran broad and shallow over a bed of large smooth stones. The lake here formed a great round bay, with a beach strewed with sharp grey rocks that had fallen from the mountain-side. A line of old alder trees grew along the bank of the stream right out to the lake.

At high-water mark, where beach and greensward met, the path led by a cairn. The boy and girl stopped, hurried through a Paternoster and an Ave, and then each threw a stone upon the cairn as a sign that they had done their Christian duty by the dead. It was said to be one who had slain himself, but it was so long ago that Olav and Ingunn at any rate had never heard who the poor wretch might be.

They had to cross the stream in order to reach the point where Olav had thought he could borrow a boat. This was easy enough for him, who walked barefoot, but Ingunn had not gone many steps before she began to whimper—the round pebbles slipped under her feet and the water was so cold and she was spoiling her best shoes.

"Do but stand where you are and I will come and fetch you," said Olav, and waded back to her.

But when he had taken her up in his arms, he could not see where he put his feet, and in the middle of the river he fell with her.

26

The icy water took away his breath for a moment—the whole world seemed to slew over. As long as he lived, this picture remained burned into him—all that he saw as he lay in the stream with Ingunn in his arms: light and shade dropping in patches through the alder leaves upon the running water, the long, grey curve of the beach beyond, and the blue lake glittering in the sunshine.

Then he got to his feet, dripping wet and ashamed, strangely ashamed with his empty arms—and they waded ashore. Ingunn took it ill, as she swept the water from her sleeves and wrung out first her hair-plaits and then the edge of her dress.

"Oh, hold your mouth now," Olav begged in a low and cheerless voice. "Must you always be whining over great things and small?"

The sky was now blue and cloudless, and the fiord quite smooth, with small patches of glittering white sunshine. Its bright surface reflected the land on the other shore, with tufts of light-green foliage amid the dark pine forest and farms and fields mounting the hillside. It had become very warm—the sweet breath of the summer day was heavy about the two young people. In their wet clothes it felt cold merely to enter the airy shade of the birches on the point.

The fisher-widow's cot was no more than a turf hovel boarded at one end, in which was a door. There was no other house in the place but a byre of stones and turf, with an open shed outside to keep the stacks of hay and dried leaves from the worst of the winter weather. Outside the cabin lay heaps of fish refuse. It stank horribly and swarms of blue flies buzzed up as the children came near. These heaps of offal were alive and crawling with maggots—so as soon as Olav had made known his errand and the widow had answered that they might have the boat and welcome, he took the wallet and went off under the trees. It was an odd thing about Olav that ever since he was a little boy it had given him a quite absurd feeling of disgust to see maggots moving in anything.

But Ingunn had brought with her a piece of bacon for the widow, Aud. She came of the folk of Steinfinn's thralls and now she was eager for news of the manor, so Ingunn was delayed awhile.

The boy had found a dry and sunny spot down by the water; there they could sit and dry themselves as they ate. Soon Ingunn came, carrying in her hands a bowl of fresh milk. And with the prospect of food, and now that it was settled about the boat, Olav was suddenly glad at heart—it was grand after all to be out on his own errand and to be going to Hamar. At heart he was well pleased too that Ingunn was with him; he was used to her following him everywhere, and if at times she was a little troublesome, he was used to that too.

He grew rather sleepy after eating—Steinfinn's house-carls were not used to early rising. So he stretched himself on the ground with his head buried in his arms, letting the sun bake his wet back, and he made no more ado about the need of haste. All at once Ingunn asked if they should bathe in the fiord.

Olav woke and sat up. "The water is too cold—" and all at once he turned red in the face and blushed more and more. He turned his head aside and stared at the ground.

"I am freezing in my wet clothes," said Ingunn. "We shall be so fine and warm after it." She bound her plaits in a ring about her head, sprang up, and loosened her belt.

"I will not," muttered Olav in a hesitating voice. His cheeks and brows pricked with heat. Suddenly he jumped up and, without saying more to her, turned and walked up the point into the grove of firs.

Ingunn looked after him a moment. She was used to his being vexed when she would not do as he said. He would be cross for a while, till he grew kind again of himself. Calmly and caring nothing, she undressed and tottered out over the sharp grey stones, which cut her feet, till she reached a little bank of sand.

Olav walked quickly over the grey moss, which crunched under his feet. It was bone-dry already on these crags that jutted into the lake—the firs stifled it with their vapour. It was not much more than a bowshot to the other side of the point.

A great bare rock ran out into the water. Olav leaped onto it and lay down with his face in his hands.

Then the thought came to him—she could never drown? Perhaps he ought not to have left her. But he *could* not go back—

Down in the water it was as though a golden net quivered above stones and mud—the reflection of sunlight on the surface. He grew giddy from looking down—felt as if he were afloat. The rock he lay on seemed to be moving through the water.

And all the time he could not help thinking of Ingunn and being tormented by the thought. He felt plunged into guilt and shame, and it grieved him. They had been used to bathe from his canoe in the tarn above, swimming side by side in the brown water, into which a yellow dust was shed from the flowering spruces around. But now they could not be together as before—

It was just as when he lay in the stream and saw the familiar world turned upside-down in an instant. He felt as if he had had another fall; humbled and ashamed and terrified, he saw the things he had seen every day from another angle, as he lay on the ground.

It had been so simple and straightforward a thing that he should marry Ingunn when they were grown up. And he had always looked to Steinfinn to decide when it should be. The lad might feel a tingling when Steinfinn's house-carls told tales of their commerce with women. But to him it had been clear that they did these things because they were men without ties, while he, being born to an estate, must keep himself otherwise. It had never disturbed his rest to think that he and Ingunn would live together and have children to take the inheritance after them.

Now he felt he had been the victim of a betrayal—he was changed from what he had been, and Ingunn was changed in his eyes. They were wellnigh grown up, though none had told them this was coming; and these things that Steinfinn's serving men and their womenfolk had to do with—ah, they tempted him too, for all she was his betrothed and he had an estate and she a dowry in her coffer.

He saw her as she lay there face-down on the short, dry grass. She rested on one arm beneath her breast, so that her dress was drawn tight over the gentle rounding of her bosom; her tawny plaits wound snake-like in the heather. When she had said that about bathing, an ugly thought had come over him—together with a meaningless fear, strong as the fear of death; for it seemed to him that they were as two trees, torn up by the spring flood and adrift on a stream—and he was afraid the stream would part them asunder. At that fiery moment he seemed to have full knowledge of what it meant to possess her and what to lose her.

But what was the sense of thinking of such things, when all

who had power and authority over them had ordained that they should be joined together? There was no man and no thing to part them. None the less, with a tremor of anxiety he felt his childish security shrivel up and vanish, the certainty that all the future days of his life were threaded for him like beads upon a string. He could not banish the thought that *if* Ingunn were taken from him, he knew nothing of the future. Somewhere deep down within him murmured the voice of a tempter: he must secure her, as the rude and simple serving-men secured the coarse womenfolk they had a mind to—and if anyone stretched out a hand toward her that was his, he would be wild, like the he-wolf showing his teeth as he stands over his prey; like the stallion rearing and snorting with rage to receive the bear and fight to the death for his mares, while they stand in a ring about the scared and quivering foals.

The boy lay motionless, staring himself dizzy and hot at the play of light in the gliding water, while he strove with these new thoughts—both what he knew and what he dimly guessed. When Ingunn gave a call just behind him, he started up as though waked from sleep.

"You were foolish not to care for a swim," she said.

"Come now!" Olav jumped down to the beach and walked quickly before her. "We have stayed here far too long."

After rowing awhile he grew calmer. It felt good to swing his body in steady strokes. The beat of the oars in the rowlocks, the wash of the water under the boat, lulled his agitation.

It was broiling hot now and the light from the sky and lake dazzled and hurt the eyes—the shores were bathed in heat haze. And when Olav had rowed for wellnigh two hours, it began to tell on him severely. The boat was heavy, and he had not thought how unpractised he was at rowing. This was not the same as poling and splashing about the tarn at home. He had to keep far out, for the shore wound in bays and inlets; at times he was afraid he might be clean out of his course. The town might lie hidden behind one of these headlands, invisible from the boat—perhaps he had already passed it. Olav saw now that he was in strange country; he remembered nothing from his last journey in these parts.

The sun burned his back; the palms of his hands were sore; and his legs were asleep, so long had he sat with his feet against the stretcher. But the back of his neck ached worst of all. The lake gleamed far around the tiny boat—it was a long way to land on every side. Now and again he felt he was rowing against a current. And there was scarce a craft to be seen that day, whether far out or close under the shore. Olav toiled at the oars, glum and morose, fearing he would never reach the town.

Ingunn sat in the stern of the boat facing the sun, so that her red kirtle was ablaze; her face under the shade of her velvet hood was flushed with the reflection. She had thrown Olav's cloak about her, for the air on the water was chill to her, sitting still, she said; and then she had drawn the hood down to shade her eyes. It was a fine cloak of grey-green Flanders cloth with a cowl of black velvet—one of the things Olav had had from Hestviken. Ingunn had a well-dressed look in all the ample folds of her garments. She held one hand in the water—and Olav felt an envy of the senses; how good and cool it must be! The girl looked fresh and unweary; she sat and took her ease.

Then he pulled harder—all the harder for the pain he felt in hands and shoulders and in the small of his back; he clenched his teeth and rowed furiously a short space. It was a great deed he had undertaken for her sake, this rowing; and he knew, with pride and a melancholy sense of injury, that he would never have thanks for it: "there she sits playing with her hand over the side and never has a thought of *my* toiling." The sweat poured off him, and his outgrown kirtle chafed worse and worse at the arm-holes. He had forgotten that it was *his* business that brought them; once more he pursed his lips, swept his arm across his red and sweaty face, and took a few more mighty pulls.

"Now I see the towers over the woods," said Ingunn at last.

Olav turned and looked over his shoulder—it hurt his stiff neck past believing. Across the perfectly hopeless expanse of a fiord he saw the light stone towers of Christ Church above the trees on a point of land. Now he was so tired that he could have given up altogether.

He rounded the point, where the convent of preaching friars lay far out on raised foundations; it was a group of dark timber houses about a stave-church, with roofs of tarred shingles, one above another, dragon heads on the gables and gilt weathercocks above the ridge-turret, in which the mass bell hung.

Olav put in to the monks' pier. He washed the worst of the sweat from him before he climbed up, stiff and spent. Ingunn was already at the convent gate talking with the lay brother who had charge of some labourers; they were bearing bales of goods down to a little trading craft. Brother Vegard was at home, she told Olav as he came up—now they must ask leave to speak with him; he could best advise them in this business.

Olav thought they could ill trouble the monk with such a trifle. Brother Vegard was wont to come twice a year to Frettastein and he was the children's confessor. He was a wise and kindly man and always used the opportunity to give them such counsel and exhortation as the young people of that house lacked all too often. But Olav had never spoken a word to Brother Vegard unbidden, and to put him to the pains of coming to the parlour for their sake seemed to him far too bold. They could well inquire the way to the smith of the brother porter.

But Ingunn would not give in. As Olav himself had hinted, it was perhaps a hazardous thing to hand over such an heirloom to a smith of whom they knew nothing. But maybe Brother Vegard would send a man from the convent with them—ay, it was not impossible he might offer to go with them himself. That Olav did not believe. But he let Ingunn have her way.

She had a motive for it, which she kept to herself. Once, long ago, she had visited the convent with her father, and then they had been given wine, which the monks made from apples and berries in their garden. So good and sweet a drink she had never tasted before or since—and she secretly hoped that Brother Vegard might offer them a cup of it.

The parlour was but a closet in the guest-house; the convent was a poor one, but the children had never seen another and they thought it a brave and fine room, with the great crucifix over the door. In a little while Brother Vegard came in; he was a middle-aged man of great stature, weatherbeaten, with a wreath of grizzled hair.

He received the children's greeting in friendly fashion, but seemed pressed for time. With awkward concern Olav came out with his errand. Brother Vegard told them the way shortly and plainly: past Christ Church eastward through Green Street, past the Church of Holy Cross, and down to the left along the fence of Karl Kjette's garden, down to the field where was a pond; the smith's house was the biggest of the three that stood on the other side of the little mere. Then he took leave of the children and was going: "You will sleep in the guest-house tonight, I ween?"

Olav said they must set out for home after vespers.

"But milk you must have—and you will be here for vespers?"

They had to say yes to this. But Ingunn looked a little disappointed. She had expected to be offered other than milk and she had looked forward to hearing vespers in the minster; the boys of the school sang so sweetly. But now they durst not go elsewhere than to St. Olav's.

The monk was already at the door when he turned sharply, as something came into his mind: "So that is how it is—Steinfinn has sent for Jon smith today? Are you charged to bid the armourer come to Frettastein, Olav?" he asked, with a trace of anxiety.

"No, father. I am but come on my own errand." Olav told him what it was and showed the axe.

The monk took it and balanced it in both hands.

"A goodly weapon you have there, my Olav," he said, but more coolly than Olav had ever thought a man could speak of *his* axe. Brother Vegard looked at the gold inlay on the cheeks. "It is old, this—they do not make such things nowadays. This is an heirloom, I trow?"

"Yes, father. I had it of my father."

"I have heard of a horned axe like this which they say was at Dyfrin in old days—when the old barons' kin held the manor. That must be near a hundred years ago. There was much lore about that axe; it had a name and was called Wrathful Iron."

"Ay, my kindred came from thence—Olav and Torgils are yet family names with us. But this axe is called Kinfetch—and I know not how it came into my father's possession."

"It must be another, then—such horned axes were much used in old days," said the monk; he passed his hand along the finely curved blade. "And maybe that is lucky for you, my son—if I mind me rightly, bad luck followed that axe I spoke of."

He repeated his directions, took a kindly leave of the children, and went out.

. . .

Then they went off to find the smith. Ingunn strode in front; she looked like a grown maid in her long, trailing dress. Olav tramped behind, tired and downcast. He had looked forward so much to the journey to town—scarce knowing what he looked for in it. Whenever he had been here before, it was in the company of grown men, and it had been a fair-day in the town; to his serious and inquiring eyes all had been excitement and festivity: the bargaining of the men, the booths, the houses, the churches they had been in; they had been offered drink in the houses, and the street had been full of horses and folk. Now he was only a raw youth wandering about with a young girl, and there was no place where he could turn in; he knew no one, had no money; and they had not time to enter the churches. In an hour or two they must set out for home. And he had an unspeakable dread of the endless rowing and then the walk up through the fields—God alone knew what time of night they would reach home! And then they might look for a chiding for having run away!

They found the way to the smith. He looked at the axe well and long, turned it this way and that, and said it would be a hard matter to mend it. These horned axes had gone wellnigh out of use; 'twas not easy to fit an edge on them that would not spring loose with a heavy blow, on a helm, to wit, or even on a tough skull. This came from the shape of the blade, a great half-moon with barbs at either end. Ay, he would do his best, but he could not promise that the gold inlay should come to no harm by his welding and hammering. Olav considered a moment, but could see naught else to be done—he gave the axe to the smith and bargained with him as to the price of the work.

But when Olav told where he came from, the smith looked up and scanned his face: "Then you would have it back in all haste, I trow? So that is the way of it—are they making ready their axes at Frettastein these days?"

Olav said he knew naught of *that*.

"Nay, nay. Has Steinfinn any plan, he is not like to tell his boys of it—"

Olav looked at the smith as though he would say something, but checked himself. He took his leave and departed.

. . .

They had passed the pond, and Ingunn wished to turn into a road between fences which led up to Green Street. But Olav took her by the arm: "We can go here."

The houses in Green Street were built on a ridge of high ground. Below them ran a brook of dirty water at the edge of the fields behind the townsmen's outhouses and kale-yards. By the side of the brook was a trodden path.

Ashes, apple trees, and great rosebushes in the gardens shaded the path, so the air felt cool and moist. Blue flies darted like sparks in the green shadows, where nettles and all kinds of coarse weeds grew luxuriantly, for folk threw out their refuse on this side, making great muck-heaps behind the outhouses. The path was slippery with grease that sweated out of the rotting heaps, and the air was charged with smells—fumes of manure, stench of carrion, and the faint odour of angelica that bordered the stream with clouds of greenish-white flowers.

But beyond the brook the fields lay in full afternoon sunshine; the little groves of trees threw long shadows over the grass. The fields stretched right down to the small houses along Strand Street, and beyond them lay the lake, blue with a golden glitter, and the low shore of Holy Isle in the afternoon haze.

The children walked in silence; Olav was now a few paces in front. It was very still here in the shade behind the gardens—nothing but the buzzing of the flies. A cowbell tinkled above on the common. Once the cuckoo called—spectrally clear and far away on a wooded ridge.

Then a woman's scream rang out from one of the houses, followed by the laughter of a man and a woman. In the garden a man had caught a girl from behind; she dropped her pail, full of fishes' heads and offal, and it rolled down to the fence; the couple followed, stumbling and nearly falling. When they caught sight of the two children, the man let go the girl; they stopped laughing, whispered, and followed them with their eyes.

Instinctively Olav had halted for a moment, so that Ingunn came up beside him and he placed himself between her and the fence. A blush crept slowly over his fair features and he looked down at the path as he led Ingunn past. These houses in the town that Steinfinn's house-carls had talked so much about—for the first time it made him hot and gripped his heart to think of them, and he wondered whether this was one of those houses.

The path turned and Olav and Ingunn saw the huge grey mass and pale leaden roof of Christ Church and the stone walls of the Bishop's palace above the trees a little way in front of them. Olav stopped and turned to the girl.

"Tell me, Ingunn—did you hear what Brother Vegard said—and the smith?"

"What mean you?"

"Brother Vegard asked if Steinfinn had sent for the armourer to Frettastein," said Olav slowly. "And Jon smith asked if we made ready our axes now."

"What meant they? Olav—you look so strangely!"

"Nay, I know not. Unless there is news at the Thing—folk are breaking up from the Thing these days, the first of them—"

"What mean you?"

"Nay, I know not. Unless Steinfinn has made some proclama-tion—"

The girl raised both hands abruptly and laid them on Olav's breast. He laid both his palms upon them and pressed her hands against his bosom. And as they stood thus, there welled up again in Olav more powerfully than before that new feeling that they were adrift—that something which had been was now gone for ever; they were drifting toward the new and unknown. But as he gazed into her tense dark eyes, he saw that she felt the same. And he knew in his whole body and his whole soul that she had turned to him and clutched at him because it was the same with her as with him—she scented the change that was coming over them and their destiny, and so she clung to him instinctively, be-cause they had so grown together throughout their forlorn, neg-lected childhood that now they were nearer to each other than any beside.

And this knowledge was unutterably sweet. And while they stood motionless looking into each other's face, they seemed to become one flesh, simply through the warm pressure of their hands. The raw chill of the pathway that went through their wet shoes, the sunshine that poured warmly over them, the strong blended smell that they breathed in, the little sounds of the after-noon—they seemed to be aware of them all with the senses of one body.

The pealing of the church bells broke in upon their mute and tranquil rapture—the mighty brazen tones from the minster tower, the busy little bell from Holy Cross Church—and there was a sound of ringing from St. Olav's on the point.

Olav dropped the girl's hands. "We must make haste."

Both felt as though the peal of bells had proclaimed the consummation of a mystery. Instinctively they took hands, as though after a consecration, and they went on hand in hand until they reached the main street.

The monks were in the choir and had already begun to chant vespers as Olav and Ingunn entered the dark little church. No light was burning but the lamp before the tabernacle and the little candles on the monks' desks. Pictures and metal ornaments showed but faintly in the brown dusk, which gathered into gloom under the crossed beams of the roof. There was a strong smell of tar, of which the church had recently received its yearly coat, and a faint, sharp trace of incense left behind from the day's mass.

In their strangely agitated mood they remained on their knees inside the door, side by side, and bowed their heads much lower than usual as they whispered their prayers with unwonted devotion. Then they rose to their feet and stole away to one side and the other.

There were but few people in church. On the men's side sat some old men, and one or two younger knelt in the narrow aisle—they seemed to be the convent's labourers. On the women's side he saw none but Ingunn; she stood leaning against the farthest pillar, trying to make out the pictures painted on the baldachin over the side altar.

Olav took a seat on the bench—now he felt again how fearfully stiff and tired he was all over. The palms of his hands were blistered.

The boy knew nothing of what the monks sang. Of the Psalms of David he had learned no more than the *Miserere* and *De profundis*, and those but fairly well. But he knew the chant—saw it inwardly as a long, low wave that broke with a short, sharp turn and trickled back over the pebbles; and at first, whenever they came to the end of a psalm and sang "*Gloria Patri, et Filio, et Spiritu Sancto,*" he whispered the response: "*Sicut erat in principio et nunc et semper et in sæcula sæculorum. Amen.*" The monk who led the singing had a fine deep, dark voice. In drowsy well-being Olav listened to the great male voice that rose alone and to the choir joining in, verse after verse throughout the psalms. After all the varied emotions of the day peace and security fell upon his soul as he sat in the dark church looking at the white-clad singers and the little flames of the candles behind the choir-screen. He would do the right and shun the wrong, he thought—then God's might and compassion would surely aid him and save him in all his difficulties.

Pictures began to swarm before his inner vision: the boat, Ingunn with the velvet hood over her fair face, the glitter on the water behind her, the floor-boards covered with shining fish-scales—the dark, damp path among nettles and angelica—the fence they had climbed and the flowery meadow through which they had run—the golden net over the bottom of the lake—all these scenes succeeded one another behind his closed and burning eyelids.

He awoke as Ingunn took him by the shoulder. "You have been asleep," she said reprovingly.

The church was empty, and just beside him the south door stood open to the green cloister garth in the evening sun. Olav yawned and stretched his stiff limbs. He dreaded the journey home terribly; this made him speak to her a little more masterfully than usual; " 'Twill soon be time to set out, Ingunn."

"Yes." She sighed deeply. "Would we might sleep here to-night!"

"You know we cannot do that."

"Then we could have heard mass in Christ Church in the morning. We never see strange folk, we who must ever bide at home—it makes the time seem long."

"You know that one day it will be otherwise with us."

"But you have been in Oslo too, you have, Olav."

"Ay, but I remember nothing of it."

"When we come to Hestviken, you must promise me this, that you will take me thither some time, to a fair or a gathering."

"That I may well promise you, methinks."

Olav was so hungry his entrails cried out for food. So it was good to get warm groats and whey in the guest-room of the convent. But he could not help thinking all the time of the row home. And then he was uneasy about his axe.

But now they fell into talk with two men who also sat at meat in the guest-house. They came from a small farm that lay by the shore a little to the north of the point where Olav and Ingunn were to land, and they asked to be taken in their boat. But they would fain stay till after complin.

Again Olav sat in the dark church listening to the deep male voices that chanted the great king's song to the King of kings. And again the images of that long, eventful day flickered behind his weary eyelids—he was on the point of falling asleep.

He was awakened by the voices changing to another tune; through the dark little church resounded the hymn:

> *Te lucis ante terminum*
> *Rerum Creator poscimus*
> *Ut pro tua clementia*
> *Sis præsul et custodia.*
>
> *Procul recedant somnia*
> *Et noctium phantasmata;*
> *Hostemque nostrum comprime,*
> *Ne polluantur corpora.*
>
> *Præsta, Pater piissime,*
> *Patrique compar Unice,*
> *Cum Spiritu Paraclito*
> *Regnans per omne sæculum.*[7]

He knew this; Arnvid Finnsson had often sung it to them in the evening, and he knew pretty well what the words meant in Norse. He let himself sink stiffly on his knees at the bench, and with his face hidden in his hands he said his evening prayers.

It had clouded over when they went down to the boat; the sky was flecked with grey high up and the fiord was leaden with dark stripes. The wooded slopes on both sides seemed plunged in darkness.

The strangers offered to row, and so Olav sat in the stern with

[7] Ere daylight be gone, we pray Thee, Creator of the world, that of Thy mercy Thou wilt be our Guide and Guardian.

May the visions and spectres of the night be far from us; hold back our enemy, lest our bodies be defiled.

Hear our prayer, O Father most holy, and Thou, only-begotten Son, equal to the Father, who with the Holy Ghost, the Comforter, reignest for ever and ever.

(Ambrosian hymn, seventh century)

Ingunn. They shot forward at a different pace now, under the long, steady strokes of the two young peasants; but Olav's boy-ish pride suffered no great injury nevertheless—it was so good to sit and be rowed.

After a while a few drops of rain fell. Ingunn spread out the folds of the heavy cloak and bade him come closer.

So they both sat wrapped in it and he had to put an arm around her waist. She was so slender and warm and supple, good to hold clasped. The boat flew lightly through the water in the blue dusk of the summer night. Lighter shreds of mist with scuds of rain drifted over the lake and the hills around, but they were spared the rain. Soon the two young heads sank against each other, cheek to cheek. The men laughed and bade them lie down upon their empty sacks in the bottom of the boat.

Ingunn nestled close to him and fell asleep at once. Olav sat half up, with his neck against the stern seat; now and again he opened his eyes and looked up at the cloudy sky. Then his weari-ness seemed to flow over him, strangely sweet and good. He started up as the boat grounded on the sand outside Aud's cabin.

The men laughed. No, why should they have waked him?— 'twas nothing of a row.

It was midnight. Olav guessed that they had rowed it in less than half the time he had taken. He helped the men to shove the boat up on the beach; then they said good-night and went. First they became two queerly black spots losing themselves in the dark rocky shore of the bay, and soon they had wholly disappeared into the murky summer night.

Olav's back was wet with bilge-water and he was stiff from his cramped position, but Ingunn was so tired that she whimpered— she would have it they must rest before setting out to walk home. Olav himself would best have liked to go at once—he felt it would have suppled his limbs so pleasantly to walk in the fresh, cool night, and he was afraid of what Steinfinn would say, if he had come home. But Ingunn was too tired, he saw—and they both dreaded to pass the cairn or to be out at all in the dead of night.

So they shared the last of the food in their wallet and crept into the cabin.

Just inside the door was a little hearth, from which some warmth still came. A narrow passage led in, which divided the earthen floor into two raised halves. On one side they heard Aud snoring; they felt their way among utensils and gear to the couch that they knew was on the other.

But Olav could not fall asleep. The air was thick with smoke even down to the floor and it hurt his chest—and the smell of raw fish and smoked fish and rotten fish was not to be borne. And his worn limbs twinged and tingled.

Ingunn lay uneasily, turning and twisting in the darkness. "I have no room for my head—surely there is an earthen pot just behind me—"

Olav felt for it and tried to push it away. But there was so much gear stowed behind, it felt as if it would all clatter down on them if he moved anything. Ingunn crawled farther down, doubled herself up, and lay with head and arms on his chest. "Do I crush you?" In a moment she was fast asleep.

After a while he slipped from under the warm body, heavy with sleep. Then he got his feet down on the passage, stood up, and stole out.

It was already growing light. A faint, cold air, like a shudder, breathed through the long, limber boughs of the birches and shook down a few icy drops; a pale gust blew over the steel-grey mirror of the lake.

Olav looked inland. It was so inconceivably still—there was as yet no life in the village; the farms were asleep and fields and meadows and groves were asleep, pale in the grey dawn. Scattered over the screes behind the nearest houses stood a few spruce-firs as though lifeless, so still and straight were they. The sky was almost white, with a faint yellow tinge in the north above the black tree-tops. Only high up floated a few dark shreds of the night's clouds.

It was so lonely to be standing here, the only one awake, driven out by this new feeling which chased him incessantly farther and farther away from the easy self-confidence of childhood. It was about this hour yesterday that he had risen—it seemed years ago.

He stood, shy and oppressed at heart, listening to the stillness. Now and again there was the clatter of a wooden bell; the widow's cow was moving in the grove. Then the cuckoo called, unearthly clear and far away somewhere in the dark forests, and some little birds began to wake. Each of the little sounds seemed only to intensify the immense hush of space.

Olav went to the byre and peeped in, but drew his head back at once before the sharp scent of lye that met him. But the ground was good and dry under the lean-to roof; brown and bare, with some wisps from the winter's stacks of hay and leaves. He lay down, rolled up like an animal, and went to sleep in a moment.

He was awakened by Ingunn shaking him. She was on her knees beside him. "Have you lain out here?"

" 'Twas so thick with smoke in the cabin." Olav rose to his knees and shook the wisps and twigs from his clothes.

The sun came out above the ridge, and the tops of the firs seemed to take fire as it rose higher. And now there was a full-throated song of birds all through the woods. Shadows still lay over the land and far out on the deep-blue lake, but on the other side of the water the sunshine flooded the forest and the green hamlets on the upper slopes.

Olav and Ingunn remained on their knees, facing each other, as though in wonder. And without either's saying anything they laid their arms on each other's shoulders and leaned forward.

They let go at the same time and looked at each other with a faint smile of surprise. Then Olav raised his hand and touched the girl's temples. He pushed back the tawny, dishevelled hair. As she let him do it, he put his other arm about her, drew her toward him, and kissed her long and tenderly on the sweet, tempting pit under the roots of the hair.

He looked into her face when he had done it and a warm tingling ran through him—she liked him to do that. Then they kissed each other on the lips, and at last he took courage to kiss her on the white arch of her throat.

But not a word did they say. When they stood up, he took the empty wallet and his cloak and set out. And so they walked in silence, he before and she behind, along the road through the village, while the morning sun shed its light farther and farther down the slopes.

On the higher ground folk were already astir on all the farms. As they went through the last of the woods, it was full daylight. But when they came to the staked gate where the home fields of Frettastein began, they saw no one about. Perhaps they might come well out of their adventure after all.

Behind the bushes by the gate they halted for a moment and looked at each other—the dazed, blissful surprise broke out in their eyes once more. Quickly he touched her hand, then turned to the gate again and pulled up the stakes.

When they entered the courtyard, the door of the byre stood open, but no one was to be seen. Ingunn made for the loft-room where she had slept the night before.

All at once she turned and came running back to Olav. "Your brooch—" she had taken it off and held it out to him.

"You may have it—I will give it you," he said quickly. He took off her little one, which he had worn instead, and put it in her hand that held the gold brooch. "No, you are not to give me yours in exchange. I have brooches enough, I have—"

He turned abruptly, blushing, ran from her grasp, and strode off rapidly toward the hall.

He drew a deep breath, much relieved after all to find that the rooms beyond were empty. One of the dogs got up and came to meet him, wagging its tail; Olav patted it and spoke a friendly word or two.

He stretched himself and yawned with relief on getting off his tight clothes. The coat had chafed him horribly under the arms—he could not possibly wear it again, unless it was altered. Ingunn could do that.

As he was about to fling himself into his sleeping-place, he saw that there was already a man lying there. "Are you all come home now?" asked the other drowsily. Olav knew by the voice it was Arnvid Finnsson.

"No, it is but I. I had an errand in the town," he said as calmly as if there were nothing strange in his going to Hamar on business of his own. Arnvid grunted something. In a moment they were both snoring.

3

WHEN Olav awoke, he saw by the light in the hall that it was long past noon. He raised himself on his elbow and found that Ingunn and Arnvid were sitting on the dais. The look on the girl's face was so strange—at once scared and thoughtful.

She heard him get up and came rapidly to his bed. She wore the same bright-red kirtle as the day before; and with the new vision with which he looked on her, Olav turned hot with joy, for she was fair to see.

"Now methinks we shall soon know what Brother Vegard meant—and the smith—with that they said about the axes," she said, greatly moved. "Arnvid says that Mattias Haraldsson was at the Thing and fared northward to the manor he has at Birid."

"Ah," said Olav. He was bending down to tie his shoestring. Then he straightened himself and gave Arnvid his hand in greeting: "Now we shall see what Steinfinn will do when he hears this."

"He *has* heard it," replied Arnvid. "It is for that he has ridden north to Kolbein, says Ingebjörg."

"You must go out and fetch me some food, Ingunn," said Olav. As soon as the girl was out of the hall, he asked the other: "Know you what thoughts Steinfinn has now?"

"I know what thoughts Ingebjörg has," replied Arnvid.

"Ay, they are easily guessed."

Olav had always liked Arnvid Finnsson best of all the men he knew—though he had never thought about it. But he felt at ease in Arnvid's company. For all that, it would never have occurred to him to call the other his friend; Arnvid had been grown up and married almost as long as Olav remembered him; and now he had been two years a widower.

But today it was as though the difference in their ages had vanished—Olav felt it so. He felt that he was grown up and the other was a young man like himself; Arnvid was not settled and fixed in his ways like other married men. His marriage had been like a yoke that was laid upon him in his youth, and since then he had striven instinctively to outgrow the marks of it—all this Olav was suddenly aware of, without knowing whence he had it.

And in the same way Arnvid seemed to feel that the two young ones had shot up much nearer to him in age. He spoke to them as to equals. While Olav was eating, Arnvid sat shaving fine slices, no thicker than a leaf, from a wind-dried shoulder of reindeer, which Ingunn was so fond of chewing.

"The worst of it is that Steinfinn has let this insult grow so old," said Arnvid. " 'Tis too late to bring a suit—he must take a dear revenge now, if he would right himself in folks' eyes."

"I cannot see how Steinfinn could do aught ere now. The man

took pilgrim's fancies—fled the country with his tail between his legs. But now that we have gotten two unbreeched children for kings, a man may well use his own right arm and need not let the peasants' Thing be judge of his honour—so I have heard Steinfinn and Kolbein say."

"Ay, I trow there is many a man now who makes ready to do his pleasure without much questioning of the law of the land or the law of God," said Arnvid. "There's many a one is growing restive now, up and down the land."

"And what of you?" asked Olav. "Will you not be with them, if Steinfinn and Kolbein have thoughts of seeking out Mattias and—chastening him?"

Arnvid made no answer. He sat there, tall and high-shouldered, resting his forehead in his slender, shapely hand, so that his small and ugly face was completely shaded.

Arnvid Finnsson was very tall and slight, of handsome build— above all, his hands and feet were shapely. But his shoulders were too broad and high, and his head was quite small, but he was short-necked; this did much to take the eye away from the rest of his handsome form. His face too was strangely ill-featured, as though compressed, with a low forehead and short, broad chin, and black curly hair like the forelock of a bull. In spite of this, Olav now saw for the first time that Arnvid and Ingunn bore a likeness to each other—Arnvid too had a small nose, as though unfinished, but in the man it seemed pressed in under the brow. Arnvid too had large, dark-blue eyes—but in him they were deep-set.

Arnvid did not belong to the Steinfinn stock, but Tore of Hov had married his father's sister. And the likeness between his heavy, dark ugliness and Ingunn's restless charm was not to be mistaken.

"So I see you have little mind to go with your kinsmen in that which is now brewing?" said Olav rather mockingly.

"Be sure I shall not hang back," answered Arnvid.

"What will he say to it, Bishop Torfinn, your ghostly father, if you make common cause with us in what Steinfinn has on foot?" asked Olav with his little mocking smile.

"He is in Björgvin now, so he cannot hear aught of it till the thing be done," said Arnvid shortly. "I can do naught else, I must go with my cousin."

"Ay, and you are not one of his priests either," said Olav as before.

"No, the more the pity," replied Arnvid. "Would I were. This matter between Steinfinn and Mattias—the worst of it is, I ween, that it is grown so old. Steinfinn *must* do something now to win back his honour. But then, you may be sure that all the old talk will be chewed over again, and foully will it stink. I hold myself not more fearful than other men—none the less do I wish I could have held aloof from these doings."

Olav held his peace. Now they were touching again on a matter that was no clearer to Olav than it was to the Steinfinnssons. Arnvid had been put to book-learning in his childhood. But then both his elder brothers had died, and his parents took him home again and married him to the rich bride who had been promised to his brother. But it seemed Arnvid did not count it as good fortune to be called to the headship of his family and to possess the manor in Elfardal, instead of being made a priest.

The wife he got was fair and rich and only five or six years older than he; yet the young couple seemed ill suited to each other. In some measure this may have come from their having little say in the house so long as Arnvid's parents were alive. Then Finn, Arnvid's father, died; but just after that his young wife, Tordis Erlingsdatter, died in childbirth. From that time Arnvid's mother took control, and they said she was somewhat masterful. Arnvid let her have charge both of the estate and of his three little sons and submitted to her in all things.

In former times many men of the Steinfinn kin had been priests, and even if none of them had made a special mark in the service of the Church, they had yet been good priests. But when it became the rule that priests in Norway must live unmarried, as in other Christian lands, the Steinfinnssons sought no more after book-learning. It was by prudent marriages that the kin had always extended its power, and that a man might make his way in the world without support in his marriage they could not believe.

Summer heat had come in earnest the day Olav and Ingunn had stolen away to Hamar.

From the crag above the outlying barn the fiord could be seen far below, beyond the waves of forest and patches of meadow in the hollows. On clear mornings Lake Mjösen lay reflecting the headlands, scored with light stripes, which betokened fine weather. As the day went on, all nature was bathed in heat haze, the land on the other side in blue mist, through which the green paddocks around the farms shimmered brightly. Far to the south on Skrei Fell there was still a glitter of snow high up, gleaming like water and cloud, but the patches of snow grew smaller day by day. Fair-weather clouds were piled up everywhere on the horizon and sailed over forest and lake, casting shadows below. Sometimes they thinned out and spread over the sky, making it a dull white, and the lake turned grey and no longer reflected the land. But the rain came to nothing—it was blown away, and all the trees glittered with leaves flickering in the sunshine, as though the very land panted for heat.

The turf roots began to look scorched and the cornfields yellowed in patches, where the soil was thin; but the weeds flourished and grew high above the light shoots of young corn. The meadows burst into purple with sorrel and monk's-hood and St. Olav's flower.[8]

There was little to do on the farm now, and nothing was done—the few who were left at home spent their days in waiting.

Olav and Ingunn idled among the houses. Separately and as though by chance they wandered down to the beck that ran north of the farm. It flowed between high banks worn in the turf; the water rushed over great bedded rocks that stretched from bank to bank, and fell into a pool below with a strangely soothing murmur.

The two found a place under a clump of quivering aspens above the stream. The ground was dry here, with fine, thin grass and no flowers.

"Come and lay your head in my lap," said the girl, "and I will clean it for you."

Olav shifted a little and laid his head on her knees. Ingunn turned his fair, silky hair over and over, till the boy dozed, breathing evenly and audibly. She took the little kerchief that covered the throat of her dress and wiped the sweat from Olav's face; then sat with the kerchief in her hand fanning off the flies and midges.

From the higher ground she heard her mother's sharp, im-

[8] A name given to several wild-flowers of the Geranium family.

petuous voice. The lady Ingebjörg and Arnvid Finnsson were walking on the path at the edge of the corn.

Every day Ingebjörg Jonsdatter went up and sat on the crag above the manor, gazing out as she talked and talked—of her old deadly hatred of Mattias Haraldsson and of her and Steinfinn's long-hatched plans of revenge. It was always Arnvid who had to go with her and listen and give ever the same answers to the lady's speech.

Olav slept with his head in Ingunn's lap; she sat with her neck against the stem of an aspen, staring before her, thoughtlessly happy, as Arnvid came down, wading through the long grass of the meadow.

"I saw you two sitting here—"

" 'Tis cool and pleasant here," said Ingunn.

"It seems high time to begin haymaking," said Arnvid; he looked up the slope as a gust of wind swayed the grass.

Olav awoke and turned over, laying the other cheek in Ingunn's lap. "We shall begin after the holy-day—I spoke to Grim this morning."

"You do Steinfinn no little service here, Olav?" asked Arnvid, to draw him.

"Oh—" Olav paused. "But 'tis ever the same here, everything is left undone; 'tis of little use to take a hand. For all that—*now* there must come a change; Steinfinn will surely be more minded to look to his affairs. But this is my last summer here."

"Are you to leave Frettastein now?" asked Arnvid.

"I trow I must go home and see to my own property some time," said Olav with a wisdom beyond his years. "So when Steinfinn has made an end of this matter, there will be talk of my going home to Hestviken. Steinfinn will be glad enough to have Ingunn and me off his hands."

" 'Tis not so sure that Steinfinn will have peace to settle such matters at present," said Arnvid below his breath.

Olav shrugged his shoulders, putting on a bold air.

"All the more need for him that I take over the charge of my own estate. He knows I am no shirker, but will back my foster-father."

"You two are young yet to take over the charge of a great manor."

"You were no older, Arnvid, when you were married."

"No, but we had my parents to back us—and yet I was the youngest. But they feared our line should die out, when my brothers were dead."

"Ay, and I am the last man of my race, I too," said Olav.

"That is so," replied Arnvid. "But Ingunn is very young."

All this Olav had thought out since the journey to Hamar. After that first sweet and frenzied day, when he was plunged from one bewilderment to another with his playmate, he calmed down as soon as they were back at Frettastein. None there had so much as noticed their flight. And this had a strangely cooling effect on his mental tumult. Then there was this too, that change and great events were in the air at the very moment when he himself felt that he was grown up—and this seemed to make it more natural that he too should feel an inward change.

He left off playing with the other boys of the place; and none was surprised at this, for the tension that now prevailed at Frettastein had spread to all their neighbours on the hills.

Thus it seemed now quite natural that he should think seriously of his marriage. And in these long, sunny days of summer that he spent with Ingunn he felt a kind of tangible satisfaction in that he now had a much better understanding of the future that was in store for him than he ever could have had in his more childish years.

Instead of uneasiness and timid shame there was come a joyful and inquiring expectation. Something must happen now. Steinfinn would no doubt seize the opportunity—strike a blow. Of the consequences that might follow if Steinfinn struck his blow, Olav had little thought—instinctively he had absorbed the Steinfinnssons' ideas of their own power and glory; there was none to touch them. But neither had he any other thought than that Steinfinn would at once consent when, after the deed was done, he asked leave to go home and hold his wedding. That would be next autumn or winter. And his new-born desire to possess her became one with his new-born ambition—to be his own master. When he took her in his arms, it was as though he held a pledge of his maturity. When they came to Hestviken, they would sleep together and rule together, indoors and out, and there would be none to

49

give orders but they two. Then they would come into their full rights.

It was not often, however, that Olav caressed his betrothed now. If he no longer was so shy and afraid, nor had gloomy thoughts, as when he felt the first breath of desire, he now had a clear view of what was manly and seemly. Only, when they parted for the night, he would often seek an occasion to bid her good-night alone, in the manner he deemed proper to two lovers who were soon to be married.

That Ingunn's eyes betrayed far too much whenever they chanced to look at each other seemed to Olav a part of the good fortune fate had prepared for him. He noted how she watched for a chance of looking at him, and her glance was strange, heavy, and full of delightful darkness. Then she met his eyes—a little sparkle was kindled in hers; she looked away, afraid she might smile. She stole a chance of stroking him with her hand when they met—was fond of playing with his hair whenever they were left alone for a moment. She was very eager to do things for him— offered to mend his clothes, brought in his food if he came to a meal a little later than the rest of the men. And when he said good-night to her, she clung to him as though hungry and thirsty for his caresses. Olav took this to mean that she too longed for their wedding, and he thought that natural—time must be long for her too in this house; she must look forward eagerly to being mistress of her own home. It never occurred to him that there might be young people who did not care for one another although they were betrothed.

But the journey to Hamar remained a dream to Olav. He thought of it most often when he lay down at night, and he lived it again till he felt the strange, sweet tremor in body and mind. He recalled how they had knelt at dawn behind the widow's byre, leaning breast to breast, and he had dared to kiss her on the temple, under the hair that smelt so warm and good. And then this unaccountable melancholy and dread settled on him. He tried to think of the future—and for them the path of the future was a straight one, to the church door and the high seat and the bridal bed. But his heart seemed to grow weak and faint when in these night hours he tried to rejoice in all that awaited them—as though, after all, the future could have nothing in store for them so sweet as that morning kiss.

"What is it?" asked Arnvid crossly. "Cannot you lie still?"

"I am going out awhile." Olav got up, dressed again, and threw a cloak about him.

There was already less light in the sky at night; the thick foliage of the trees looked darker against the misty blue of the hills beyond. The clouds to the northward were streaked with yellow. A bat flittered past him, black and swift as lightning.

Olav went to the bower where Ingunn slept. The door was left ajar for coolness' sake—and still it was close inside, with a smell of sun-baked timber, of bedding, and of human sweat.

The maid who lay next the wall snored loudly in her sleep. Olav knelt down and bent his face over her who lay outside. With cheek and lips he gently touched Ingunn's breast. For an instant he kept quite still so as to feel the soft, warm bosom that lightly rose and fell as she breathed in sleep—and he heard her heartbeats under it. Then he drew his face up to hers and she awoke.

"Dress yourself," he whispered in her ear. "Come out awhile—"

He waited outside on the balcony. Soon Ingunn appeared in the low doorway and stood awhile, as though surprised at the stillness. She took a few deep breaths—the night was cool and good. They sat down side by side at the top of the stairway.

And now they both felt it so strange that they should be the only ones awake in the whole manor—neither was used to being out at night. So they sat there without moving, scarce venturing to whisper a word now and then. Olav had thought he would wrap his cloak around her and put an arm about her waist. But all he did was to place one of her hands on his knee and stroke her fingers; till Ingunn withdrew her hand, threw her arm about his shoulder, and pressed her face hard against his neck.

"Are not the nights darker already?" she asked in a hushed voice.

"The air is dense tonight," he said.

"Ay, haply there will be rain tomorrow," she wondered.

There was a blue-grey mist over the strip of fiord they could see from where they sat, and the hills were blotted out on the far side. Olav looked vacantly before him, pondering: "That is not so sure—there is an easterly set in the wind. Can you not hear how loud the stream sounds above tonight?"

"We had best go to bed," he whispered a little later. They

kissed each other, a quick and timid little kiss. Then he stole down again and she went in.

Inside the hall it was pitch-dark. Olav undressed and lay down again.

"Have you been out talking to Ingunn?" asked Arnvid, wide awake at his side.

"Yes."

Soon after, Arnvid asked again: "Have you found out, Olav, what are the settlements about your estate and Ingunn's?"

"No, I have not. You know, I was so young when I was betrothed to her. But surely Steinfinn and my father must have made an agreement about that—what we are to bring to each other.—Why do you ask me this?" said Olav, with sudden surprise.

Arnvid did not answer.

Olav said: "Steinfinn will take good care that we get what we are to have according to the settlement."

"Ay—he is my cousin." Arnvid spoke with some hesitation. "But you are soon to be our kinsman by marriage—I may well speak of it to you. They say Steinfinn's fortunes are not so good as they were. I have lain awake thinking of what you spoke of—I believe you are right. You will be wise to hasten the marriage—so that Ingunn may get what comes to her as soon as may be."

"Ay, we have nothing to wait for, either," said Olav.

The next day was a holy-day, and the day after they began to cut the grass at Frettastein. Arnvid and his man helped in the haymaking. Early in the day the sky turned pale and grey, and by afternoon big, dark clouds began to drift up from the south and spread over the hazy sky. Olav looked up as they stood whetting their scythes; the first drop of rain fell on his face.

"Maybe 'twill be but a shower or two tonight," said one of the old house-carls.

"Tomorrow is Midsummer Day," answered Olav. "If the weather change on that day, 'twill rain as many days after as the sun shone before, I have always heard. I trow we shall have no better hay crop this year, Torleif, than we had last."

Arnvid was standing a little farther down the field. Now he laid down his scythe, came up quickly toward the others, and pointed. Far down the hillside rode a long line of armed men across a little glade in the forest.

"It is they," said Arnvid. "It seems they are set upon another kind of mowing. And now, by my troth, I wonder how it will go with the haymaking at Frettastein this year."

Late in the evening the rain came down, with a thick white mist that drifted in patches over the fields and wooded slopes. Olav and Ingunn stood under the balcony of the loft where she slept; the lad stared angrily at the pouring rain.

Arnvid came running across the mud of the courtyard, darted in to the couple, and shook himself.

"How is it you are not in the men's councils?" asked Olav with a sneer.

Olav would have followed them when the men went into Inge-björg's little house—they chose it for their meeting, out of ear-shot of the servants. But Steinfinn had bidden his foster-son stay in the hall with the house-carls. Olav was angry—now that in his own thoughts he reckoned himself Steinfinn's son-in-law, he forgot that the other did not yet know their alliance was about to be welded so fast.

Arnvid stood leaning against the wall, glaring before him mournfully. "I shall not shirk my duty, but shall follow my kins-men as far as Steinfinn may call upon me. But I will have no part in their councils."

Olav looked at his friend—the boy's pale, finely arched lips curled lightly in a scornful smile.

4

On the evening of the second day the men went down to the lake. The rain had held off that day, but it had been cold, with a high wind and much cloud.

Kolbein rode with five of his men, Steinfinn had with him seven house-carls and Olav Audunsson; Arnvid followed with one henchman. Kolbein had provided boats, which lay concealed in a cove of Lake Mjösen a little to the northward.

Ingunn went early to rest in her loft. She did not know how long she had slept when she was awakened by a touch on her chest.

"Is it you?" she whispered, heavy with sleep—expecting only to find Olav's soft locks; but she awoke to see a coifed head. "Mother—" she cried in astonishment.

"I can get no sleep," said Ingebjörg. "I have been walking outside. Put on some clothes and come down."

Ingunn got up obediently and dressed. She was surprised beyond measure.

It was not so late after all, she saw on coming out. The weather had cleared. The moon, nearly full, rose due south above the ridge, pale red like a sunset cloud, giving no light as yet.

The mother's hand was hot as fire as she took her daughter's. Ingebjörg drew the girl along, roving hither and thither beyond the houses, but saying scarcely a word.

At one moment they stayed leaning over the fence of a cornfield. Down in the field was a water-hole surrounded by tall, thick rushes, which were darkly mirrored in it, but in the middle of the smooth little pond the moon shone—it had now risen high enough to give a yellow light.

The mother looked into the distance, where the lake and the farms surrounding it lay in a pale, calm mist.

"Have you the wit to see, I wonder, what we have all at stake?" said Ingebjörg.

Ingunn felt her cheeks go white and cold at her mother's words. She had always known what there was to know of her father and mother; she had known too that great events were now at hand. But here by her mother's side, seeing how she was stirred to the depths of her soul, she guessed for the first time what it all *meant*. A feeble sound came from her lips—like the squeaking of a mouse.

Ingebjörg's ravaged face was drawn sideways in a sort of smile.

"Are you afraid to watch this night with your mother? Tora would not have refused to stay with me, but she is such a child, gentle and quiet. That you are not—and you are the elder, I ween," she concluded hotly.

Ingunn clasped her slender hands together. Again it was as though she had climbed a little higher, had gained a wider view over her world. She had always been clear that her parents were not very old folk. But now she saw that they were young. Their love, of which she had heard as a tale of old days, was ready to be quickened and to burn with a bright flame, as the fire may be revived from the glowing embers beneath the ashes. With wonder and reluctance she suspected that her father and mother loved each other even yet—as she and Olav loved—only so much the more strongly as the river is greater and fuller near its mouth than it is high up in the hills. And although what she guessed made her ashamed, she felt proud withal at the uncommon lot of her parents.

Timidly she held out both hands. "I will gladly watch with you all night, Mother."

Ingebjörg squeezed her daughter's hand. "God can grant Steinfinn no less than that we may wash the shame from us," she said impetuously, clasping the girl and kissing her.

Ingunn put her arms round her mother's neck—it was so long since she had kissed her. She remembered it as part of the life that was brought to an end on the night Mattias came to the house.

Not that Ingunn had felt the want of it—as a child she had not been fond of caresses. Between her and Olav it was like something they had found out for themselves. It had come as the spring comes—one day it is there like a miracle, but no sooner is it come than one feels it must be summer always. Like the bare strip of sod that borders the cornfield—so long as it lies naked with its withered grass after the thaw, it is nothing but a little grey balk amongst the sown; but then there comes a forest of tangled wild growth that makes it wellnigh impassable.

Now the springlike bareness of her child's mind was overgrown with a summer luxuriance. She laid her cool, soft cheek against her mother's wasted face. "I will *gladly* share your watching, Mother!"

The words seemed to sink into herself—for *she* had to watch for Olav. It was as though her thoughts had been astray when he set out with the others in the evening—she had not thought of the dangers the men were to face. A fear thrilled through her—but it was only as a flutter at the root of her heart. She could not fancy in earnest that anything could happen to one of *hers*.

For all that, she asked: "Mother—are *you afraid*?"

Ingebjörg Jonsdatter shook her head: "No. God will give us our right, for right is on our side." When she saw her daughter's look she added, with a smile Ingunn did not like—there was a queer cunning in it: "You see, my girl, it is on this wise—'tis a lucky chance for us that King Magnus died this spring. We have kinsmen and friends among those who will now have most power —so says Kolbein. And there are many of them who would fain see Mattias—do you mind what manner of man he is? Oh no, you cannot—he is short of stature, is Mattias; yet there are many who think he might be shorter by a head. Queen Ingebjörg never liked him. You must know, but for that, he would not lie at Birid at this time, when knights and barons are gathering at Björgvin and the young King is to be crowned."

She went on talking as they walked along the fences. Ingunn fervently desired to speak to her mother of Olav Audunsson, but she guessed that she was so wholly lost in her own thoughts that she would not care to hear of aught else. Yet she could not help saying: "Was it not an ill chance that Olav could not fetch his axe in time?"

"Oh, your father will have seen that they are as well armed as there is need, all the men he has taken with him," said the mistress. "Steinfinn would not have had the boy with him, but he begged leave to go—"

"But you are cold," said her mother a moment later. "Put on your cloak—"

Ingunn's cloak still hung in her mother's room; she had not fetched it in all these fourteen days, but had worn Olav's fine mantle when she needed an outer garment. Her mother went in with her. She stirred the fire on the hearth and lighted the lantern.

"Your father and I were wont to move into the great loft in summer—had we been sleeping there the night Mattias came, he could not have taken Steinfinn unawares. It will be safer for us to sleep there till Steinfinn be made free of the law."

The great loft-room had no outside stairway, for it had been used for storing household goods of value. From the floor below, a ladder led up into the loft. It was not often that Ingunn had been up there; the very smell of the place gave her a solemn feeling. Bags of strong-smelling spices hung among bedcovers of fur and leather sacks—there was almost an uncanny look about all the things that hung from the roof. Against the walls stood great chests. Ingunn went up to Olav's and let the light fall on it; it was of pale limewood, and carved.

Ingebjörg opened the door to the balcony. She emptied the bedstead of all that was piled upon it and began searching in chests and coffers, making her daughter hold the light for her; then she dropped on the floor all she had in her hands and went out on the balcony.

The moon was now so far to the westward that its light lay like a golden bridge over the water. It was about to sink into a bank of heavy blue cloud, some shreds of which floated up toward the moon and were gilded.

The mother went in again and turned over more of the chests. She had come upon a woman's gown of silk—green with a woven pattern of yellow flowers—the light of the lantern gave the whole kirtle the tint of a fading aspen.

"This I will give to you now—"

Ingunn curtsied and kissed her mother's hand. A silken gown she had never owned before. From a little casket of walrus ivory her mother took a green velvet ribbon, set all over with silver gilt roses. She put it over the crown of her daughter's head, pushed it a little forward, and brought the ends together at the back of the neck under the hair.

"So. Fair as you looked to be when you were small, you are not—but you have grown fairer again this summer. 'Tis time for you to wear the garland—you are a marriageable maid now, my Ingunn."

"Yes; Olav and I have spoken of that too," Ingunn took courage to say. She strove instinctively to speak as naturally as she could.

Ingebjörg looked up—they were both crouching before a chest. "Have Olav and you spoken of *that*?"

"Yes." Ingunn spoke as calmly as before, dropping her eyelids meekly. "We are old enough now to expect that you will soon see to the fulfilment of this bargain that was made for us."

"Oh, that bargain was not of a kind that cannot be undone again," said her mother; "if you yourselves have no mind to it. We shall not force you."

"Nay, but we are well pleased with what you have purposed for us," said Ingunn meekly. "We are agreed that it is well as our fathers have disposed."

"So that is the way of it." Ingebjörg stared thoughtfully before her. "Then I doubt not some means will be found— Do you like Olav *well*?" she asked.

"What could I do else? We have known each other so long, and he has always been good and kind and has shown himself dutiful toward you."

Her mother nodded thoughtfully.

"We knew not, Steinfinn and I, whether you two remembered aught of that bargain or thought more of it. Ay, some means must be found, one way or another. At your age you two cannot be so closely tied. Handsome he is, Olav. And Audun left wealth behind him—"

Ingunn would fain have said more of Olav. But she saw that her mother was far away in her own thoughts again.

"We went by desert paths, your father and I, when we crossed the fells," she said. "From Vors we took to the moors, and then we passed through the upper dales. There was still much snow on the fells. In one place we had to stay a whole week in a stone hut. It stood beside a tarn and a snow-field came down into the water—we heard the flakes of ice break off and splash into the lake as we lay at night. Steinfinn offered a gold ring from his finger at the first church we came to below—it was a holy-day. The poor folk of the fells stared at us agape—we had ridden from the town as we stood, in our Sunday clothes. They were much the worse for wear, but, for all that, no such clothes had ever been seen in that dale.

"But a weary bride I was, when Steinfinn brought me home to Hov. And already I bore you under my heart—"

Ingunn stared at her mother as though spellbound. In the faint light of the lantern that stood on the floor between them she saw so strange a smile on her mother's face. Ingebjörg stroked her daughter's head and drew her long plaits through her hand.

"—And now you are already a grown maid."

Her mother rose and gave her the great embroidered bedcover, bidding her shake it out over the balcony.

"Mother!" the girl cried loudly from outside.

Ingebjörg ran out to her.

It was almost daylight and the sky was pale and clear high up, but clouds and mist lay over the land. Straight across the lake in the north-west a great fire was blazing, shedding a ruddy light on the thick air far around. Black smoke poured out, drifted away, and mingled with the fog, thickening and darkening it far over the ridge. Now and again they saw the very flames, when they rose high, but the burning homestead lay hidden behind a tongue of the woods.

The two women stood for a while gazing at it. The mother said not a word, and the girl dared not speak. Then the mistress turned into the loft—a moment later Ingunn saw her running across the yard to her little house.

Two women servants rushed out in their bare shifts and ran down to the courtyard fence. Then came Tora, with her fair hair fluttering loose, her mother leading her two young sons, and all the women of the place. Their cries and talk reached Ingunn.

But when they began to swarm up into the loft, she stole out. With her head bent and her hands crossed under the cloak that she held tightly about her—she would have wished to be quite invisible—she crept up to her own loft and lay down.

A violent fit of weeping came upon her—she could not make out what it was she wept like that for. It was just that she was too full of all that had crowded in upon her that night. She could not bear others to come near her—it made her tears run over. Tired she was too. It was morning now.

When she awoke, the sun was shining in at the door. Ingunn started up and pulled on her shift—she heard there were horses in the yard.

Four or five of their own strayed about grazing, unsaddled. Olav's dun Elk was among them. And there was a neighing from the paddock. The maids ran between the cook-house and the hall—they were all in festival clothes.

She threw her cloak over her and ran to the eastern bower. The floor was strewed with brier-roses and meadowsweet—it almost took her breath away. She had not seen festivity in her home since she was a little girl. Drinking-bouts in the hall and banquets on high days—but not such as they strewed the rooms with flowers for. Her silken kirtle and the gilt circlet lay on Olav's chest. Ingunn fetched them and ran back.

She had no mirror, but she did not feel the want of it as she stood ready dressed in her bower. She felt the weight of the gilt garland over her flowing hair, looked down at her figure wrapped in the green and yellow silk. The kirtle fell in long folds from her bosom to her feet, held in slightly by the silver belt at her waist. The gown was ample and long, so she had to lift it with both hands as she stepped over the grass of the courtyard. Full of delight, she knew that she looked like one of the carven images in a church: tall and slender, low-bosomed and slight of limb, gleaming with jewels.

At the door of the hall she stopped, overwhelmed. The long fires were burning on the central hearth, and the sunshine poured in through the smoke-vent, turning the smoke sky-blue as it drifted under the rafters. And lighted torches stood on the board before the high seat, facing the door. There sat her mother by her father's side, and her mother was dressed in red silk. Instead of the kerchief that Ingunn was used to seeing on her, she wore a starched white coif; it rose like a crown above her forehead and left the back of her head uncovered; her knot of hair gleamed golden within a net.

The other women were not seated at table; they went to and fro, bearing meat and drink. Ingunn then took up a tankard; she carried it in her right hand and held up her gown with her left, making herself as lithe and supple as she could—she thrust her hips well forward, dropped her shoulders to make herself look more narrow-breasted, and bowed her neck, leaning her head to one side like a flower on its stalk. Thus she moved forward, gliding as lightly as she could.

But the men were already half-drunken, and maybe tired too after the night's exploit; none paid any great heed to her. Her father looked up with a laugh when she filled his beaker. His eyes were bright and stiff, his face blazed red under his tousled tawny hair—and now Ingunn saw that one arm was bound up over his chest. He had on his best cloak over the tight leather jerkin that he wore under the coat of mail. Most of the men seemed to have sat down to table just as they came from the saddle.

Her father signed to her to pour out for Kolbein and his two sons, Einar and Haftor; they sat at Steinfinn's right hand.

On Steinfinn's left sat Arnvid. He was red in the face, and his dark-blue eyes shone like metal. A tremor passed over his features as he stared at his young kinswoman. Ingunn could see that he, at any rate, thought her fair this evening, and she smiled with joy as she filled his cup.

She came where Olav Audunsson sat on the outer bench, and squeezed in between him and his neighbour as she poured out for those sitting on the inner bench. Then the boy caught hold of her down by the knees and pressed her toward him, screened by the table, making her spill the drink.

Ingunn saw at once that he was drunken. He sat astride the bench with his legs stretched far out, his head supported in one hand, with the elbow on the table among the food. It was so unlike Olav to sit thus that she could not help laughing—they used always to tease him for keeping just as steady and quiet, no matter what he drank. God's gifts did not bite on him, said the others.

But this evening the ale had plainly got the better even of his stiffness. When she was going to pour out for him, he seized her hands, put the tankard to his lips, and drank, spilling the drink over himself, so that the breast of his elkskin jerkin was all befouled.

"Now take a drink yourself," he said, laughing up in her face—but his eyes looked so queer and strange; they gleamed with a wanton wildness. Ingunn was flustered a little, but she filled his beaker and drank; then he clutched her again under the table and came near to making her fall into his arms.

The man by Olav's side took the tankard from them. "Bide awhile, you two—you must leave a drop for the rest of us—"

Ingunn went out to fill the tankard again—and then she saw that her hands trembled. With surprise she found that she was shaking all over. It was almost as if she had been scared by the boy's violence. But she was drawn toward him in a way she had never known before—a sweet and consuming curiosity. She had never seen Olav in this state. But it was so joyous—this evening nothing was as it was wont to be. As she went about filling the cups she could not help trying to brush past Olav, that he might have a chance of stealing those rough and furtive caresses of his. It was as though they drew her on.

None had marked that it was growing dark outside before the rain spurted through the smoke-vent. They had to close the ventil; then Ingebjörg bade bring in more lights. The men rose from the board; some went to their places to sleep, but others sat down again to drink and talk to the women, who now began to think of food.

Arnvid and Einar Kolbeinsson, her cousin, sat down by Ingunn, and Einar was to tell her more of the raid:

They had sailed under the eastern shore right up to the river, and there they went across to Vingarheim, so that they came riding down upon Mattias's manor from the north. This proved unnecessary, however, as Mattias had set no watch.

"He never believed Steinfinn would strike in earnest," said Einar scornfully. "None can wonder at that—after so much prating and waiting he would be apt to think that, could Steinfinn bear his shame in patience for six years, the seventh would not be too great a burden for him."

"Meseems I heard a tale of Mattias—that he fled the country for fear of Steinfinn," said Olav Audunsson, who had joined them. He squeezed in between Arnvid and Ingunn.

"Ay, and Steinfinn is lazy too; he is one to sit under the bush and wait till the bird falls into his hand—"

"You would have had him take to lawsuits and wrangling like your father?"

Arnvid interposed and made them keep the peace. Then Einar took up his story:

They came into the courtyard unopposed and some men were posted to guard those houses in which folk might be sleeping, while Steinfinn and the sons of Kolbein went with Arnvid, Olav, and five of the house-carls to the hall. Kolbein stayed outside. The men within started up from sleep when the door was broken down—some naked and some in their shirts, but all reached for their weapons. There were Mattias and a friend of his, the tenant of the farm and his half-grown son, and two serving-men. There came a short struggle, but the drowsy house-folk were quickly overpowered. And then it was Steinfinn and Mattias.

"This was unlooked for—are *you* abroad thus betimes, Steinfinn?" said Mattias. "I mind me you were once so sound a sleeper, and a fair wife you had to keep you to your bed."

"Ay, and 'twas she who sent me hither with her greeting," said Steinfinn. "You surely won her heart when last you came to us—she cannot put you out of her mind.—But don your clothes," he said; "I have ever thought it a dastard's deed to set on a naked man."

Mattias turned flaming red at those words. But he made light of it and asked: "Will you give me leave to buckle on my coat of mail too, since it seems you would make a show of chivalry?"

"No," cried Steinfinn. "For I have no thought that you shall come off with your life from this our meeting. But I am nothing loath to meet you unharnessed."

While Steinfinn unbuckled his coat of mail, Kolbein came in and he and another man held Mattias. This he liked ill, but Steinfinn said with a laugh: "Methinks you are more ticklish than I was—you cannot bear a man's hand near your skin!" After that Steinfinn let Mattias put on his clothes and take a shield. Then the two set upon each other.

In his youth Steinfinn had been counted most skilful in the use of arms, but of late he had fallen out of practice; it was quickly seen that Mattias, small and slight as he was, would be more than a match for the other. Steinfinn had to give ground, foot by foot; his breath came heavily—then Mattias made a cut at him and disabled his right arm. Steinfinn changed his sword over to his left hand—both men had long since thrown away the wreckage of their shields. But now Steinfinn's men thought it looked badly for their master: on a sign from Kolbein one of his men sprang to Steinfinn's side. Mattias was somewhat dazed at this, and now Steinfinn gave him his death-blow.

"But they fought like two good lads, we all said that," said Arnvid.

Meanwhile, as ill luck would have it, some of the strange men-at-arms whom Steinfinn had with him bethought them of pillage, and others tried to stay them from it. And in the tumult some man set fire to a stack of birchbark which stood in the narrow gangway between the hall and one of the storehouses. It was doubtless that Tjostolv who did it, a man none thought well of, and he must have carried bark into the storehouse too, for it burst into flames on the instant, though timbers and roof were wet from the rain. And then the fire took hold of the hall. They had to bear out Mattias's corpse and loose the other men.

Now folk came up from the neighbouring farms, and a number of these peasants came to blows with them. Some were hurt on both sides, but 'twas unlikely that more were slain.

"Ay, we need not have had the fire and the brawling on our hands," said Einar, "had not Steinfinn been set on showing prowess and chivalry."

Olav had never liked Einar Kolbeinsson. He was three years

older than himself and had always loved to tease the younger boys with his spite. So Olav answered him, pretty scornfully: "Nay, no man will charge your father or you brothers with *that*—none will accuse Kolbein Borghildsson of goading on his half-brother to ill-timed high-mindedness."

"Have a care of yourself, young sniveller—Father's name has always stood next to Tore of Hov's. Our stock is just as good as Aasa's offspring—mind that, Olav; and don't sit there fondling my kinswomen—take your paw out of her lap, and quick about it!"

Olav jumped up and they were at each other. Ingunn and Arnvid ran to part them. Then it was that Steinfinn rose and called for silence.

The house-folk, men and women, and the strangers drew toward the table. Steinfinn stood leaning on his wife's shoulder—he was no longer red in the face, but white and sunken under the eyes. But he smiled and held himself erect as he spoke: "Now I will give you thanks, all you who were with me in this deed—first will I thank you, brother, and your sons, and then my dear cousin, Arnvid Finnsson, and you others, good kinsmen and trusty men. If God will, we shall soon have peace and atonement for these things that have befallen this night, for He is a righteous God and it is His will that a man shall hold his wife in honour and protect the good name of women. But I am weary now, good friends, and now we will go to bed, I and my wife—and you must forgive me that I say no more—but I am weary, and I have gotten a small scratch too. But Grim and Dalla will have good care of you, and now ye may drink as long as ye list, and play and be merry as is fitting on a joyful day such as this—but now we go to rest, Ingebjörg and I—and so you must forgive us that we leave you now—"

Toward the close his speech had become thick and halting; he swayed slightly on his feet, and Ingebjörg had to support him as they went out of the hall.

Some of the house-carls had raised a cheer, hammering on the tables with their knives and drinking-cups. But the noise died away of itself, and the men stood aside in silence. Not a few of them guessed that Steinfinn's wound might be worse than he would have it thought.

All followed them out—stood in silent groups watching the tall and handsome couple as they went together to the loft-room in the rain-drenched summer evening. Most of them marked how Steinfinn stood still and seemed to speak hastily to his wife. It looked as though she opposed him and tried to hold his hand; but he tore off the bandage that bound his wounded arm to his breast and flung it impatiently from him. They heard Steinfinn laugh as he went on.

The house-folk were still quiet when they came in again, though Grim and Dalla had more drink brought in and fresh wood thrown on the fire. The table and benches were cleared out of the way. But most of the men were tired and seemed most inclined for sleep. Yet some went out into the yard to dance, but came in again at once; the shower was just overhead and the grass was too wet.

Ingunn still sat between Arnvid and Olav, and Olav had laid his hand in her lap. "Silk," he said, stroking her knee; "silk is fine," he went on saying again and again.

"You are bemused and know not what you say," said Arnvid with vexation. "You're half-asleep already—go to bed!"

But Olav shook his head and laughed softly to himself: "I'll go when I please."

Meanwhile some of the men had taken their swords and stood up for dancing. Haftor Kolbeinsson came up to Arnvid and would have him sing for them. But Arnvid declined—he was too tired, he said. Nor would Olav and Ingunn take part in the dance; they said they did not know that lay—the *Kraaka-maal*.[9]

Einar headed the chain of dancers with his drawn sword in his right hand. Tora held his left and had placed her other hand on the next man's shoulder. Thus they stood in a row, a man with drawn sword and then a woman, all down the hall. It was a fine sight with all the blades held high. Einar began the singing:

"Swiftly went the sword-play—"

[9] The reader will find this old lay, with a literal translation, in Vigfusson and Powell: *Corpus Poeticum Boreale*, Vol. II, p. 339. The song is supposed to be sung by the famous Ragnar Lodbrok (Shaggy-breeks) after he had been thrown into the snake pit by Ælla, King of Northumberland. The editors remark: "The *story* of the poem is the one legend which has survived in Norway of the great movement which led to the conquest and settlement of half England by the Danes in the ninth century." Skarpa-skerry is Scarborough.

The AXE

The chain moved three paces to the right. Then the men stepped to the left, while the women had to take one place to the rear, so that the men stood on a line before them; and then they crossed swords in pairs and marked time with their feet, as the women ran under their weapons and re-formed the chain. Einar sang on:

> *"Swiftly went the sword-play—*
> *Young was I when east in*
> *Öresound I scattered*
> *Food to greedy grey-legs—"*

There was none among the dancers who was quite sure of the steps, it was seen. When the women were to leap forward under the swords, they made a poor shift to keep time with the men's tramping. The place was too narrow and constrained, between the long hearth and the row of posts that held up the roof and divided the sleeping-places from the hall.

The three on the dais at the end had risen to have a better view. And when the game threatened to break up even in the second verse, people shouted again for Arnvid and bade him come in. They knew that he could sing the whole dance, and he had the finest of voices.

So when he took his sword, drew it, and placed himself at the head of the row of dancers, the game at once took better shape. Olav and Ingunn stepped in just below him. Arnvid led as surely and gracefully as anyone could look for who saw his high-shouldered, stooping figure. He took up the song in his full, clear voice, while the women swayed in and out under the play of the swords.

> *"Swiftly went the sword-play—*
> *Hild's game we helped in*
> *When to halls of Odin*
> *Helsing-host we banished.*
> *Keenly did the sword bite*
> *When we lay in Iva—"*

Then all was confusion, for there was no woman between Olav and Einar. The dancers had to stop and Einar declared that Olav must stand out; they quarreled over this, until one of the older house-carls said that he had as lief go out. Then Arnvid set the game going again:

"Swiftly went the sword-play—

.   .   .   .

Cutting-iron in battle
Bit at Skarpa-skerry—"

But all the time the ranks were in confusion. And as they came farther on in the lay, there was none but Arnvid who knew the words—some had a scrap of one verse, some of another. Olav and Einar were bickering the whole time; and there were all too few who sang the tune. Arnvid was tired, and he had got some scratches that began to smart, he said, as soon as he stirred himself.

So the chain broke up. Some went and threw themselves on their sleeping-benches—some stood chatting and would have more to drink—or they still wished to dance, but to one of these new ballads the steps of which were much easier.

Olav stood in the shadow under the roof-posts; he and Ingunn still held each other's hands. Olav thrust his sword into the scabbard: "Come, we will go up to your loft and talk together," he whispered.

Hand in hand they ran through the rain over the dark and empty yard, dashed up the stair, and stopped inside the door, panting with excitement, as though they had done something unlawful. Then they flung their arms about each other.

Ingunn bent the boy's head against her bosom and sniffed at his hair. "There is a smell of burning on you," she murmured. "Oh no, oh no," she begged in fear; he was pressing her against the doorpost.

"No—no—I am going now," he whispered: "I am going now," he kept repeating.

"Yes—" but she clung to him closely, dazed and quivering, afraid he would do as he said and go. She knew they had lost their senses, both of them—but all thoughts of past and present seemed swept away on the stream of the last wild, ungoverned hours—and they two had been flung ashore in this dark loft. Why should they leave each other?—they had but each other.

She felt her gilt circlet pushed up on her crown—Olav was rumpling her loosened hair. The garland fell off, jingling on the floor, and the lad took fistfuls of her hair and pressed them to his face, buried his chin in her shoulder.

Then they heard Reidunn—the serving-maid who slept with Ingunn—calling to someone from the yard below.

They started apart, trembling with guilty conscience. And quick as lightning Olav shot out his arm, pulled the door to, and bolted it.

Reidunn came up into the balcony, knocked, and called to Ingunn. The two children stood in pitch-darkness, shaken by the beating of their hearts.

The maid knocked awhile—thundered on the door. Then she must have thought Ingunn had fallen asleep and soundly. They heard the stairs creak under her heavy tread. Out in the yard she called to another maid—they guessed she had gone off to sleep in another house. And Olav and Ingunn flew to each other's arms, as though they had escaped a great danger.

5

Olav awoke in pitch-darkness—and in the same instant he remembered. He seemed to sink into the depths as he lay. He felt a chill on his brows—his heart shrank suddenly, as a small defenceless creature makes itself smaller when a hand is groping for it.

Against the wall lay Ingunn, breathing calmly, as a happy, innocent child breathes in its sleep. Wave after wave of terror and shame and sorrow broke over Olav—he lay still, as though the very marrow were blown out of his bones. He had but one burning desire—to fly from Frettastein; he was utterly unequal to facing her accusation, when at last she rose from the happy forgetfulness of sleep. But he knew obscurely within himself that the only way to make this terrible thing yet worse would be to steal away from it now.

Then it struck him that he must contrive to slip out of this loft before anyone was awake. He must find out what time of night it was. But he lay on as though all power were taken from him.

At last he broke out of his torpor with a jerk, crept out of bed, and opened a crack of the door. The clouds above the roofs were tinged with pink—it would be an hour to sunrise.

As he dressed, it came back to him that the last time he had

shared Ingunn's bed was last Yule, and then he had been very
angry that he had to give up his place in the hall to a guest and
crawl in among Steinfinn's daughters. He had pushed Ingunn
roughly when he thought she was taking up too much room, and
had jostled her crossly when in her sleep she dug her sharp elbows
and knees into him. The memory of their former innocence
wrung him as the memory of a lost paradise.

He *dared* not stay here longer, he *must* go now. But when he
bent over her, caught the scent of her hair, faintly descried the
outline of her face and limbs in the darkness, he felt—in spite of
his remorse and shame—that this too was sweet. He bent quite
down, almost touched her shoulder with his forehead—and again
that strange divided feeling ensnared his heart: joy at the frail
daintiness of his bride, and torment at the very thought that anyone could touch her roughly or ungently.

Never, he swore to himself, never again would he do her any
ill. After making this resolve he gained more courage to face her
awake. He touched her face with his hand and softly called her
name.

She started up and sat for a moment, heavy with sleep. Then
she threw her arms about him, so that he fell on his knees, with
head and shoulders in the bed.

She wormed herself about him, drew him up in her slender
arms; and as he knelt thus, burying his face in her strangely soft
and yielding flesh, he had to clench his teeth to keep from bursting into tears. He was so relieved and humiliated that she was so
good and kind and did not raise a lament or reproach him. Full
of tenderness for her and of shame and sorrow and happiness, he
knew not what he should do.

Then there came a howl from the yard below—the long-drawn,
uncanny howl of a dog.

"That is Erp," whispered Olav. "He yelped like that last night
too. I wonder how he has got out again"—and he stole to the door.

"Olav—you are not going from me?" she cried in fear, as she
saw he was dressed and ready to go out.

"I must watch my chance—to slip down unseen," he whispered
back. "That hell-hound will wake the whole place soon."

"Olav, Olav, don't go from me—" she was kneeling in bed. As
he sprang back and bade her hush, she threw her arms about him

and held him fast. Instinctively he turned his head aside as he loosened her hold on his neck; he drew up the coverlet and spread it over her.

"Cannot you see that I must go?" he whispered. " 'Tis bad enough as it is."

Then she burst into a fit of weeping—threw herself down on the bed and wept and wept. Olav spread the clothes over her up to her chin and stood there at his wit's end in the dark, begging her in a whisper not to cry like that. At last he knelt down and put an arm under her neck—that stilled her weeping a little.

The dog out in the yard was howling as though possessed. Olav began to rock the girl backwards and forwards. "Do not weep, my Ingunn—do not weep so sorely—" but his face was hard and stiff with tension.

No dog could howl like that except for a corpse or some disaster. And as he knelt there in the chilly morning with the weeping girl in his arms, growing more and more pitilessly sober the while, one thought after another came into his mind.

He had given no great thought to the price that might be paid for their raid on Mattias Haraldsson's house—nor had any of the others, so far as he could guess. And that was just as well; for Steinfinn had no choice.—But he misliked that cursed howling in the yard. Steinfinn's wounds were not so slight; he knew that, for he had held his arm as Arnvid bound it up. And he recalled Steinfinn's face—once in the boat, as they were coming back—and as they rode up the hillside: Kolbein had to dismount and support his brother, leading his horse. And then last evening, when he bade them good-night.

Now he saw all at once how fond he was of his foster-father. He had taken Steinfinn as part of his everyday life—liked him well enough, but looked down on the man a little too, without knowing it, all these years. Such as Steinfinn was, casual, a dawdler, easy and careless through and through, with the painful burden of sorrow and shame that had been thrust upon him and that seemed so ill suited to the shoulders of this thoughtless lord—his foster-son had felt in his heart a slight contempt for what was so unlike his own nature. And now, when Steinfinn had risen up and shown what manner of man he was in the hour of trial; now that Olav felt in his heart of hearts that he loved Steinfinn after all—now he had done this thing to him. And disgraced him-

self and brought ruin upon Ingunn.—His forehead grew icy cold
again and his heart thumped with a dull throbbing—if indeed the
worst misfortune was already past.

He pressed his forehead against her bosom—and could not that
dog be quiet outside?—A kind of sob went through his soul—of
homesickness for his childhood, which was now inexorably past.
He felt his youth and his loneliness so terribly.—Then Olav
straightened himself, stood erect, and shut his mouth firmly on
his sighing: now he had dealt in such wise that he had taken a
grown man's responsibility upon himself. Useless to whine after
the event. And there must surely be a way out.

At last someone came and scolded the dog, tried to get him in,
he could hear. As far as he could guess, Erp ran up into the paddock. All was quiet outside.

Olav took the girl in a protecting embrace, kissed her forehead
at the roots of the hair before he let her go. Then he grasped his
sword and put the belt over his right shoulder. It seemed to put
heart into him to feel the weapon on his hip. He went to the door
and glanced over the balcony.

"There is no one in the yard—now I must slip away."

Ingunn stopped him with a wail: "Oh no, oh no, don't go—
'twill make me so afraid to be left here alone."

Olav saw at once that it was vain to try to reason with her.

"Get up, then," he whispered, "and dress yourself. If they see
us walking together outside, none will suspect."

He went out, sat down on the stairway, and waited. With both
hands on his sword-hilt, and his chin resting on them, he sat
watching the rosy reflection in the western sky fade away as the
light in the east grew stronger and whiter. The grass of the fields
was grey with dew and rain.

He called to mind all the late evenings and early mornings of
that summer with Ingunn—and the memories of their games and
frolics hurt him now and filled him with bitter disappointment
and wrath. A betrayer he had become—but it was as though he
himself had also been betrayed. They had been playing on a
flowery slope and had not had the wit to see that it ended in a
precipice. They had tumbled over before they knew of it. Well,
well, there they lay, 'twas no use whining over it now, he tried
to console himself.

Once they were married, they would get back their honour as

before, and then they would forget this secret humiliation, which was what the fall was. But now he had looked forward with such joy to his wedding—that day when all should make for his and Ingunn's honour, which should confer full maturity upon them. Now there must be a secret bitterness at the bottom of the cup—a sense that they were not worthy the honour.

This thing that he had done was reckoned the mark of the meanest. 'Twas a hind they had gotten for son-in-law, a man who would prove no trustier than that, folk would say, when it came out. For a boat and a horse and a bride a man should pay the right price before he took and used them—unless he had great need.

For folk of their condition he had thought three months the shortest time they could fitly wait from the day when the settlement of their estate was proclaimed here at Frettastein before he held his wedding at Hestviken. But perhaps, now that Steinfinn had this case of arson and manslaughter on his hands, it would not look so unreasonable if he hastened on the marriage—so that instead of the guardianship of two minors he would have a well-to-do son-in-law whose help he had a right to claim, in fines and suchlike.

So when Ingunn came out to him and whispered, not daring to look at him: "If my father knew this of us, Olav, I ween he would kill us—" Olav laughed a little and took her hand in his.

"For that he would need be far duller than he is. He will have enough gear to unravel, Ingunn, without this—he may have more use for a living son-in-law than for a dead.—But you know well 'twould be the worst mischance," he whispered dejectedly, "if he—or any—came to know of this."

The sun was just rising, it was icy cold outside and wet everywhere. Olav and Ingunn huddled together on the stairway and sat there nodding sleepily while the pale yellow light in the east mounted higher and higher in the sky, and the birds twittered louder and louder—their singing was almost over for the year.

"There he is again!" Olav started up. The dog had come back into the yard and posted himself howling before the great house. They both ran down and Olav called to Erp and tried to entice him away. The dog had always obeyed him, but now he would not let himself be caught.

Arnvid Finnsson came out of the hall and tried, but the dog would not come to him either. Each time one of the men came near him, he slipped away, ran a short space, and began howling again.

"But have you two not been out of your clothes tonight?" Arnvid asked presently, looking from one to the other.

Ingunn turned red as fire and turned away hastily. Olav answered: "No—we sat talking up in the loft, and then we fell asleep as we sat, and slept on till this dog waked us."

More people came out now, both men and women, wondering at the dog. Last of all came Kolbein.

All at once there was one who cried: "Look—!"

Up in the balcony of the great bower they saw a glimpse of Steinfinn Toresson's head—his face was so changed that they scarce knew him. He called something—then vanished, as though he had fallen inward.

Kolbein dashed to the house, but the door was barred within. Arnvid sprang to his side and they helped Kolbein onto his shoulders; from there he swung himself onto the balcony. A moment later he bent over the rail—his face was utterly distorted: "He has bled—like a slaughtered ox—some of you must come up. Not his maids—" he said, and a shiver of frost seemed to go through him.

In a moment he had opened the door from inside. Arnvid and some of the house-carls went in, while Tora and the serving-maids ran to get water and wine, linen cloths and unguents.

Arnvid Finnsson appeared in the doorway—and all the dread and horror that had gathered in those waiting outside found relief in a groan when they saw him. Arnvid came forward like a sleep-walker—then his eye fell upon Olav Audunsson and he beckoned him aside: "Ingebjörg—" his lower jaw trembled so that his teeth chattered. "Ingebjörg is dead. God have mercy on us poor sinners!—You must take Ingunn—and Tora and the boys—into the hall. Kolbein says that I must tell them."

He turned and walked on in front.

"What of Steinfinn?" asked Olav in hot haste. "In God's name—it cannot be that he—has he *killed* her?"

"I know not—" Arnvid looked ready to drop. "She lay dead in the bed. Steinfinn's wound has opened—the blood has poured from him in streams. I know no more—"

Olav turned quickly to face Ingunn, who was coming up—put

73

out his hand as though to stop her, as he repeated Arnvid's words: "God have mercy on us poor sinners! Ingunn, Ingunn—now you must try—you must try to trust yourself to me, my dear!"

He took hold of her arm and led her with him—she had begun to weep, softly and sorely, like a child that fears to let its terror have full sway.

As the day wore on, Olav sat in the hall with the girls. Arnvid told them what they had gathered from Steinfinn about his wife's death, and Olav kept his arm openly on Ingunn's shoulder the while—he scarce knew himself that he did so.

Steinfinn knew but little of what had happened. Before they lay down, Ingebjörg had tended his arm. He had slept uneasily and had been wandering in fever during the night, but he seemed to remember that his wife had been up now and again; she had given him to drink. He had been waked by the dog's howling— and then she lay dead between the wall and him.

Ingebjörg had been troubled by fits of swooning in her last years. Maybe her joy at the restoration of their honour had been too much for her, Arnvid thought. Ingunn abandoned herself, weeping, in Olav's embrace, and he stroked her on the back. There was this, that he himself, and doubtless the others too, in their first horror had thought of yet worse things. Though God alone could know why Steinfinn should have wished his wife dead. For all that, Arnvid's words released them from a horror-struck suspense. Beneath it all a thought lay at the bottom of Olav's mind, striving to come forth; he tried to banish it, 'twas shameful but— Steinfinn had said he firmly believed he should follow his wife. However things might go, there was a chance that neither Steinfinn nor Ingebjörg would ever know that he had betrayed them. Olav could do naught else than feel relieved now, strangely exhausted, but safer.

There had been a moment when he thought he must go under. Just after Ingebjörg was borne out, he had met some women coming from the loft-room. They stopped, after the fashion of serving-women, to show him the bloody garments they were carrying out, making loud lamentation the while. One of them had swept up the flowers from the floor into a fur rug—the meadowsweet was smeared all over with blood, and above them lay the strips Arnvid had cut from his and Olav's shirts to bind

Steinfinn's arm—they were soaked and shining with blood. Against his will all that had happened since yesternight, when they assembled in the meadow below the burning homestead, was crowded within him into one vision. And he had not the strength to bear such a horror as this. The disaster to his foster-parents, and then his sin against them— It was as though he had violated his own sister. The boy's whole world was shattered to pieces about him.

It seemed as though his mind could not contain it—and then it slipped away from him again. And when Steinfinn's children clung to him, since no one else in the place had leisure to bestow on them, he found a kind of refuge for himself in watching over them as an elder brother.

Tora wept much and talked much. She had always been the most intelligent and thoughtful of the children. She said to Olav that it seemed hard her parents had not been allowed to enjoy their happiness together after all these years of undeserved sorrow and shame. Olav thought it would have been much worse if Ingebjörg had died before Steinfinn had taken his revenge. That their rehabilitation might be dearly bought in other ways was quite clear to Tora. She was also troubled about the welfare of her mother's soul and the future of herself and her brothers and sister, if this were in Kolbein's hands. She had no great belief in her uncle's judgment.

Olav thought that toward Steinfinn, at any rate, Kolbein had acted the part of a trusty kinsman; Mattias's slaying was not unprovoked, and the burning had been the work of chance. And it must be said that Ingebjörg had lived a pious and Christian life in her last years. She had been given a fair burial. No one told the children what some folk were saying: that had Bishop Torfinn been at home, 'twas doubtful if the lady had been committed to the earth in such great honour, until it had been made clear whether the dead woman had had any say in planning the deed or no.

Olav's best consolation came from Arnvid Finnsson. They shared a bed, and when Arnvid was not watching by his sick kinsman, the two young men lay talking far into the night.

And it sustained Olav, as it comforted all the household, that Steinfinn bore his lot in so noble and manly a way. He had lost much blood; yet his wounds were not such as were like to prove the death of so strong and big a man. But Steinfinn said he knew he was to die, and he seemed to waste away and be drifting toward an early dissolution. And in a way Olav deemed this to be the fittest ending to all that had befallen at Frettastein. It would indeed have been still stranger if Steinfinn and Ingebjörg had taken up again the old carefree life of riot and revelry and idleness that they had once led—after all they had gone through.

And this new shame that had come upon them in their daughter they would never know. That reckoning he would escape.

So it was chiefly anxiety for Ingunn that tortured him. It was an everlasting uneasiness—her sorrow was perfectly still and mute. She sat there silent as a stone, while he and Tora were talking. Now and again her eyes filled with tears, her lips began to quiver feebly—her tears ran over, but never a sound was there in her; it was a picture of despair, so far away and so lonely that he had not the strength to look at it. Why could she not speak her sorrow and let herself be consoled together with them? Sometimes he felt that she was looking at him; but when he turned his head to her, he caught a glimpse of a look so pained and helpless—and instantly she looked away from him. His ears rang and rang with one of these new dancing-lays he had heard down by the church last winter—he tried not to think of it, but it came—"or is it thine honour thou mournest for so? . . ." Often he was near being angry with her for not letting him be rid of these dark night-thoughts that had taken such a hold of his throat in his first remorse and sorrow over his fall.

But he had a care of himself now, strove to be like a good brother to her. He had avoided being alone with her ever since the first morning. And he felt safer and had a better conscience since he had got Tora to persuade Ingunn to go back and sleep with her sister in the little house. He thought that in Tora's keeping she would be safe from him too.

6

ONE evening Olav came riding down through the wood; he had been on an errand to the sæter for Grim. The evening sun was sinking behind the tops of the pines as he came where the path skirted the marshy side of the tarn a little to the north of the manor. The forest rose steeply around the little brown lake, so that darkness came early here. Then he saw Ingunn sitting in the heather close to the path.

He pulled up his horse as he came up beside her. "Are you sitting here?" he asked in surprise. It was thought to be unsafe hereabouts after sundown.

She was a sorry sight—she had been eating bilberries and was all blue about the mouth and fingers, and then she had wept till her face was swollen, and dried her tears with her berry-stained hands.

"Is it worse with Steinfinn?" asked Olav earnestly.

Ingunn bent forward and wept much louder than before.

"He is not dead?" asked the lad in the same tone.

Ingunn stammered amid her sobs that her father was better today.

Olav held back Elk, who wanted to go on. He had left off being surprised at her constant fits of weeping, but they annoyed him somewhat. It had been better had she been as Tora, who had now got over her mourning for her mother and spared her tears—soon enough they might have other cause for weeping.

"What is it, then?" he asked, a little impatiently; "what do you want with me?"

Ingunn looked up with her befouled and tear-stained face. When Olav showed no sign of dismounting, she flung her hands before her eyes and wept again.

"What ails you?" he asked as before, but she made no answer. Then he leaped to the ground and went up to her.

"What is it?" he asked in fear, taking her hands from her face. For a long time he could get no answer. He asked again and again: "What is it—why do you weep thus?"

"Should I not weep," she sobbed, breaking down completely, "when you have not a word for me any more?"

"Why should I not have a word for you?" he asked in wonder.

"I have done no other sin than that you would have me do," she complained. "I begged you to be gone, but you would not let me go. And since then you have not counted me worth a word. —Soon I shall have lost both father and mother, and you are hard as flint and iron, turn your back on me, and will not *look* at me—

77

though we were brought up as brother and sister. For naught else but that I loved you so well that I forgot honour and honesty for the nonce—"

"Now I never heard the like! I trow you have lost the little wit you had—"

"Ay, when you cast me off as you have done! But you know not, Olav," she shrieked, beside herself. "You cannot tell, Olav, whether I be not with child to you already!"

"Hush, shriek not so loud," he checked her. "You cannot tell that either as yet," he said sharply. "I cannot guess what is in your mind—have *I* not spoken to *you?*—methinks I have done naught else these last weeks than talk and talk, and never did I have three words of answer from you, for you did but weep and weep."

"You spoke to me when you were forced to it," she snapped between her sobs; "when Tora and the others were by. But me you shun, as though I were a leper—not once have you sought me out, that we might talk together alone. Must I not weep—when I think on this summer—every night you came to me in my bower—"

Olav had grown very red in the face. "Meseems that would be unwise now," he said shortly. He spat on the corner of his cloak and began to wipe her face—it availed but little. "I had most thought of what was best for you," he whispered.

She looked up at him, questioning, intensely sorrowful. Then he took her in his arms. "I wish you naught but well, Ingunn."

They both gave a start. Something had stirred in the scree on the far side of the tarn. Not a soul was to be seen, but the solitary young birch growing on the scree trembled as though a man had just pulled its stem. It was still daylight, but the little lake was shadowed by the forest; a mist was rising from the tarn and from the marsh at its eastern end.

Olav went to his horse.

"Let us come away from here," he said in a low voice. "You must get up behind."

"Can you not come out to me in the bower, so that we may talk?" she implored him as he picked up the reins. "Come after supper!"

"You may be sure I shall come, if you wish it," he said after a pause.

She held her arms around him as they rode down to the manor. Olav felt in a way strangely relieved. He guessed that he might fling aside his good resolutions of avoiding fresh temptation—when she took it thus. But it humiliated him none the less that she rejected the sacrifice he had wished to offer her.

That thing she had said—how she had begged him be gone, but he would not let her go—it was not true, he suddenly recalled. But he banished the thought as disloyal. If she said so— He had not been so sober that he could swear he remembered aright.

Next evening Olav went to the bower in which Steinfinn lay. Arnvid opened the trap and let him into the loft. Arnvid was alone with the sick man.

It was dark inside, for Steinfinn had grown so cold that he could not bear them to open the door to the balcony. A few rays of sunlight found their way in through chinks between the logs, cleaving the dust-laden darkness and throwing golden patches of light on the furs that hung from the roof. There was a heavy, stifling smell in the room.

Olav went over to the bed to greet his foster-father—he had not seen him for many days, he grudged coming up here now. But Steinfinn slept, moaning a little in his sleep. Olav could not see his face in the darkness by the wall.

There was no change, either for the worse or for the better, said Arnvid. "Will you stay here awhile? Then I will lie down for a space."

He would do that willingly, said Olav, and Arnvid threw some clothes on the floor and lay down. Then Olav spoke: " 'Tis not easy for me, Arnvid—'twere ill to trouble Steinfinn, sick as he is—yet methinks before he dies, Ingunn and I must hear what is his will concerning our marriage."

Arnvid held his peace.

"Ay, I know the time fits ill," said Olav hotly. "But with the weighty concerns that hang over all our heads, I think 'tis now time to settle all that *can* be settled. Nor do I know whether there be any other than Steinfinn who knows what he and my father agreed about our moneys."

As Arnvid made no answer, Olav said: "To me it is of great moment that I receive Ingunn from her own father's hand."

"Ay, I can guess that," said Arnvid.

Soon after, Olav heard that he had fallen asleep.

The little shafts of sunlight were gone. Olav alone was awake in the darkness and he felt his anxiety as a pain about his heart.

He *must* retrieve what had gone amiss. He had now learned that his good resolutions were vain—there was no turning back from the erring road into which he and Ingunn had strayed. And he felt himself that this new knowledge had coarsened his soul. But to stand by Steinfinn's bier as his secret son-in-law was beyond his power. Secret shame was a heavy burden to bear, he knew now.

Before Steinfinn passed away, he must give him Ingunn. "I can guess that," Arnvid had said. Olav felt hot all over: what was it that Arnvid guessed? When he came back at daybreak to his place in the hall, he did not know whether Arnvid was asleep or only feigning.

He started up as the trap in the floor was raised. It was the women with lights and food for the sick man. Vaguely Olav recalled the shadowy visions of his light-headed sleep: he was walking with Ingunn by the swamp above; they followed the beck that ran out of the tarn—then he was with her in the loft-room. Memories of fervid caresses in the dark were blended with pictures of the scree in the rugged glen. He lay holding Ingunn in his arms, and at the same time he thought he was lifting her over great fallen trees. Last of all he had dreamed they were walking on the path in the dale, where it opened out to the cultivated land with the lake far below.

This was surely a foreboding that he and Ingunn would soon leave the place together, he tried to believe.

Steinfinn pleaded when the women woke him to tend his wound: it booted not, and he would be left in peace. Dalla feigned not to hear him; she raised his great body and changed the bedclothes as though he had been an infant. She asked Olav to hold the candle for her—Arnvid was sleeping soundly, dead-tired.

Steinfinn's face was scarcely to be recognized, with some weeks' growth of reddish beard mounting to his cheek-bones. He turned his face to the wall, but Olav could see by the straining of his throat that he was struggling not to moan, as Dalla took off his bandages; they had grown fast to the wound.

The secret disgust that Olav had always felt at the sight and smell of festering wounds came upon him with sickening strength. Proud flesh had formed; the wound no longer looked like a gash; it was full of matter and grey, fungous patches, with raw red holes oozing blood.

Ingunn had appeared at his side—pale, with great eyes full of fear she stared at her father. Olav had to nudge her; she absently forgot to give Dalla the fresh bandage when she held out her hand for it. Again Olav felt his shame and sorrow like a stab at the heart—that they could have forgotten her sick and suffering father as they had done. Ah, but—the dark bower and they two alone, in close embrace—dimly he saw how hard it was to keep in mind charity and loyalty to one who was absent.

"Stay here," he said to her, as the other women were going. "This evening I will speak to your father," he explained. He saw that this made her more frightened than glad, and he liked it not.

Steinfinn lay in a doze, worn out by his pain. Olav asked Ingunn to fetch him a little food meanwhile.

She had filched all the good things she could find, she showed him with a laugh when she came back. Presently, as Olav sat eating, with the bowl between his knees, she blew down his neck. She seemed bursting with wantonness and affection this evening. Once more it cut Olav to the heart—here they sat, scarce out of her sick father's sight—and he knew not whether he liked or disliked her caresses most.

Arnvid stirred—Ingunn started up from Olav's knee and busied herself with his food. Suddenly Steinfinn asked from the bed: "Who is it you have with you, Arnvid and Ingunn?"

"Olav is here, Father," said the girl.

Olav braced his heart within him; he went up to the bed and said: "There is a matter of which I would fain speak with you, Foster-father—it is for that I stayed behind when we had done tending you."

"Were you here then? I saw you not." Steinfinn made a sign for the young man to come nearer. "You may sit awhile and talk to me, Olav foster. You have been drawn into our troubles; now we must talk of what you are to do when I die. You ought to go home to Hestviken, methinks, and seek support among your own kinsmen."

"Yes, Foster-father. It is of that I had thought to ask you. Myself I thought it were best so—and that I get Ingunn ere I go. Thus you kinsfolk will be spared the long journey, now that you have feuds upon you."

Steinfinn's eyes flickered irresolutely.

"It is so, Olav, that I mind me well what was spoken between Audun and me. But you must see yourself, boy—'tis not my doing that my fortunes have shaped themselves otherwise than we then foresaw. Now it will fall to Kolbein and Ivar to marry off my daughters—"

Arnvid had joined them:

"Do you remember, kinsman—I was with you that summer at the Thing, and I stood by in the hall when you and Audun betrothed the children?"

"You were a little boy," said Steinfinn hastily; "—no legal witness!"

"No," said Arnvid. "But listen to me, Steinfinn. It has happened before, in case of need, when called to arms or setting out on a long voyage, that a man has given his daughter to him to whom she had been promised before witnesses, without wedding, but only in such wise that he declared before trustworthy witnesses what had been agreed as to the dowry and the bridegroom's gift, and that it was his will that the betrothal should hold as binding wedlock from that day."

Steinfinn turned his head and looked at the three young people. Arnvid went on, eagerly: "Brother Vegard came hither today—and here am I, your cousin, and the old house-folk of yours who know of the compact between Audun and you. You could declare the marriage, with the monk and me for chief witnesses. Then the young couple could dwell in the little house till such time as may be fitting for Olav to fare south with her. Brother Vegard could bless the bridal cup and the bed for them—draw up writings as to their estate—"

Steinfinn reflected awhile. "No," he said shortly, and seemed very weary at once. "A daughter of mine shall not go to bed with her betrothed unfeasted like cottars' children. And there might arise contentions in after time whether she were a duly wedded wife. I marvel that you can think of such things," he went on hotly, "young as these two children are withal. Olav may have coil enough when he meets these kinsmen whom he knows not—without my sending him from me with such a burden on his neck, an outlawed man's daughter, and she smuggled away with no kinsmen of his or mine to stand by when he took her in marriage. Had but Olav been of age, we might have thought of it; but now I scarce believe it would be lawful marriage, should a child such as he is take a wife to himself—"

"It must be right enough that my father let me plight troth with the maid," said Olav. "And you have been my guardian since—"

"Oh, you know not what you talk of. You begged leave to be in the raid with us, but if Mattias's heirs think to bring that against you, 'twill not avail them much, since your kinsmen can make the defence that you were under age and in my service. Were you a married man, answerable at law and my son-in-law, 'twould be another matter. Nay, I owe it to Audun, my friend, to give you no warrant for such folly—now that perchance I am soon to meet him."

"Listen to me, Steinfinn—I am too old, for all that, to obey others after you are dead—these kinsmen of mine whom I have neither seen nor heard of. Rather will I be married and my own master, and take my hazard of the danger."

"You prate like a little child," said Steinfinn impatiently. "It shall be as I have said. But let me rest now—I can no more tonight."

Before Arnvid and Olav went to bed, the former laid the matter before Brother Vegard. But the monk would by no means take upon himself to speak to Steinfinn and try to alter his decision. He held that Steinfinn had judged rightly and wisely—and he as a priest was not allowed to have a hand in a wedding unless the banns had been proclaimed in the parish church on three mass-days. Here it was even doubtful whether Olav himself could conclude the contract so that it would be lawful marriage, seeing he was under age. And besides, he never liked folk to hold weddings without the blessing of the Church. He would in no wise have anything to do with drawing up writings or the like, but he would depart from Frettastein if they concluded such a bargain on doubtful conditions.

Steinfinn grew worse in the days that followed, and Olav could not bring himself to speak again of his marriage when he was up with his foster-father. Nor did he say more to Arnvid about the matter.

But then Ivar Toresson, Steinfinn's full brother, came to Frettastein, and Kolbein with both his sons; they had had word that Steinfinn was now near his end. The day after the coming of these men Olav asked Arnvid to go out with him, that they might speak in private.

He had not dared to speak to Arnvid before—he was afraid of what the other would say. Several nights in the last week he had been with Ingunn in the loft-room. She too was downcast and disappointed that her father had raised such unlooked-for difficulties to giving them to one another. But she can never have thought this would do more than delay their wedding at Hestviken somewhat. She grieved greatly for her father's misery and her mother's death—and in all her sorrows she clung fast to Olav; it seemed she was quite destroyed with grief when she could not hide herself in his embrace. And after a while Olav gave up all thoughts of holding back; he let himself be drawn deeper and deeper into love's rapture—she was so sweet withal. But his disquietude and qualms of conscience were a constant torment. When she fell asleep, clasped tightly to his breast, he suffered pain; it pained him too that she was so innocent in her love, she seemed utterly without fear or remorse. When he stole from her at early dawn, he was weary and dejected.

He was afraid that it might end in her misfortune; but he could not bring himself to speak of this to the girl. Still less had he the heart to tell her that he feared far worse difficulties. It had never before come into his mind that aught could be said against the validity of their betrothal. But now a new light had suddenly fallen upon his position in Steinfinn's household in all these years. He had never stood otherwise than Steinfinn's own children; but, little care as the parents had bestowed on them in these last years, it was strange nevertheless that they had never said a word of his and Ingunn's marriage, nor had Steinfinn taken any steps to find out how his son-in-law's estate was administered. That Kolbein had never heeded him was perhaps no great matter— Kolbein was arrogant and unfriendly toward most men. The coxcombs his sons Olav had never got on with; but he had always thought that this came simply from their counting themselves grown men and him a child. But now it all struck him as very strange—if they had looked upon him all the time as one who was to be their brother-in-law. "In my service," Steinfinn had said—he had never been paid wages here at Frettastein, so that meant nothing—'twas a means to clear him of the manslaughter that his foster-father had hit upon.

Olav led the way through the fields northward to the woods. On reaching the bare rocks he stopped. From there they looked down upon the houses with the steep-sloping fields below them and the forest around.

"We can sit here," said Olav. "Here we shall be safe from eavesdroppers." But he himself remained standing. Arnvid sat with his eyes on the young man.

Olav stood there contracting his white eyebrows—his fair forelock was now grown so long that it almost reached them; this made his face look yet broader, shorter, and more glum. The firm, pale lips were tightly compressed—morose and quarrelsome he looked, and he was become much older in these last weeks. The frank and childlike innocence that had become him so well— since with it all the boy was fully grown and grave of mien— had vanished like the dew. There was another kind of seriousness now upon his wrathful, tormented face. And his paleness and fairness were not so fresh—he was dark under the eyes and had a tired look.

"You have never told me before that you were there when Ingunn and I were given to each other," said Olav.

"I was but fourteen," replied Arnvid, "so it mattered not that I was there."

"Who were the others?" asked Olav.

"My father and Magnus, my brother, Viking and Magnhild from Berg, Tore Bring of Vik and his wife—I know not who the others were. The hall was full of folk, but I cannot call to mind that there were others I knew."

"Was there none in company with my father?" asked Olav.

"No, Audun Ingolfsson was alone."

Olav was silent awhile. Then he said, as he sat down: "Then there are no others alive to bear witness than Magnhild and Tore of Vik.—But maybe they can show us the way to some more."

"That they surely can."

"If they will—" said Olav in a low voice. "But you, Arnvid? Mayhap your testimony goes for little, since you were a child—

85

but what is your *judgment*? Were we *affianced* that night, In-gunn and I?"

"Yes," said Arnvid firmly. "That I have always held for sure. Do you not remember, they made you plight her with a ring?"

Olav nodded.

"Steinfinn must have that ring somewhere.—Think you you would know it again? That must be a good proof, I trow?"

"I mind me the ring well. 'Twas my mother's signet-ring, with her name and an image of God's Mother on a green stone. Father had promised it to me—I mind me I was ill pleased to give it to Ingunn." He laughed a little.

They sat in silence for a while. Then Olav asked slowly: "How liked you the answer Steinfinn gave me when I spoke to him of the matter?"

"I know not what I shall say," replied Arnvid.

"I know not what assurance I may have," said Olav still more slowly, "that Steinfinn has spoken in such wise to Kolbein that he holds it for a binding bargain between Steinfinn and my father that I was to have Ingunn."

"Kolbein will not be the only one to dispose of the children," said Arnvid.

Olav shrugged his shoulders, smiling scornfully.

"As I said to you," Arnvid went on, "I have always held it a valid betrothal that was made that night."

"Then the new sponsors cannot set aside the bargain?"

"No. That I remember is what I heard when I was at the school. If two children be betrothed by their fathers, it cannot be broken, except the children themselves, when they come to years of discretion—fourteen winters, I think it is—declare to their parish priest that they will have the bargain undone. But then they must both make oath that she is a virgin undefiled of him."

Both the young men's faces turned red as fire; they avoided each other's eyes.

"But if they cannot swear such an oath?" asked Olav at last, in a very low voice.

Arnvid looked down at his hands. "Then it is *consensus matri-monialis*, as it is called in Latin—in their deeds they have already conformed to the counsels of their parents, and if after that either of them marries another, willingly or by constraint, then it is whoredom."

Olav nodded.

"I wonder whether you could help me," he said after a moment, "to find out what Steinfinn has done with that ring."

Arnvid muttered something. Without saying more they got up and walked back.

"Autumn will be early this year," said Olav after a while. The birches already showed yellow leaves among the green, and the ears of corn were turning white among the tall thistles and ragwort. The blue air was full of drifting down—the floating seed of traveller's-joy.

The evening sun fell right in Olav's face, making him blink; and his eyes shone keen and blue as ice under the white lashes. The thick, fair down on his upper lip had a golden look against the boy's milk-white skin. Arnvid felt a drawing as of pain in his chest that his friend was so fair to look upon—he saw himself, dark, ugly as a troll, high-shouldered, and short-necked, against the other's strong and handsome youth. 'Twas not to be wondered at that Ingunn loved him as she did.

How much of right or wrong there was in those two he left others to judge. He would help them as far as he could. He had always liked Olav—believed him to be steadfast and trusty. And Ingunn was so weak—it must have been for that he had always been so fond of the little maid; she looked as though a hand could break her in two.

The air was so heavy in the loft that night that the holy candle which they burned nightly by the dying man could scarcely live. It gave a faint and drowsy light.

Steinfinn was dozing, utterly worn out. The fever was not so high that night, but he had talked at length with his brothers during the evening, and that had told on him. Afterwards, when his wounds were tended, he had been so overspent that the tears poured down into his beard when Dalla had to go roughly to work to get away some matter.

At last, in the course of the night, Steinfinn seemed to be sleeping more easily. But Arnvid and Olav sat on—till they felt so weary in the heavy air that they could scarce keep awake.

"Ay—" whispered Arnvid at last. "Is it your wish that we seek for that ring?"

"We must do so, I ween." Everything within him shrank from

the act—and he saw it went much against the grain with Arnvid too, but— Still as a pair of thieves they ransacked Steinfinn's clothes and emptied his keys out of the pouch of his belt. It dawned on Olav the while that he who has once left the straight path of honour soon finds himself in broken ground, where he may be forced to many a crooked leap. But he could see no other way.

None the less, as he knelt by Steinfinn's clothes-chest, he thought he had never felt so ill. Now and again they threw a glance at the bed. It was like robbing a corpse.

Arnvid found the little casket, bound all over with meshwork of wrought iron, in which Steinfinn kept his most costly jewels. Key after key they tried before they found one to fit the lock.

Sitting on their haunches, they rummaged among brooches, chains, and buttons. "This is it," said Olav, drawing a deep breath, unspeakably relieved.

Together they looked at the ring against the light. It was of gold, with a great green stone in it. Arnvid made out the inscription around the image of God's Mother and the Child, with a roof above and a woman kneeling at the side: *Sigillum Ceciliæ Beornis Filiæ.*

"Will you keep it?" asked Arnvid.

"No. It cannot serve—as proof—except it be found among Steinfinn's hoard?" Olav thought.

They locked the casket and put all in order again. Arnvid asked: "Will you sleep now, Olav?"

"No, you may sleep first. I am not tired."

Arnvid lay down on the bench. After a while he said, in a wide-awake voice: "I could wish we had not been forced to do this—"

"I am with you in that wish," replied Olav with a quiver in his voice.

A *great* sin it was not—could not be, he thought. But it was so ugly. And he was afraid of it as of an evil omen—for the life that lay before him; would a man be forced to do many things that—that irked him so unspeakably as this?

They watched by turns till morning. It made Olav glad whenever he was able to do some little thing for his foster-father—give him to drink or arrange the bedclothes. At last, early in the day, when Steinfinn awoke out of a doze, he asked: "Is it you two who are still here?" His voice was weak, but he was clear in his senses. "Come hither, Olav," he bade.

Both the young men came forward. Steinfinn put out his sound hand to Olav. "You are not so wroth with me, foster, that I would not give you your will in what we spoke of that evening, but that you would watch with me all this night? You have ever been obedient and good, Olav—God keep you all your days. As surely as I need His mercy, I tell you, had I had the ruling of it, I should have kept my word to Audun. Were it granted me to live, I should be well pleased to have you as my son-in-law."

Olav knelt down and kissed his foster-father's hand. He could say nothing—inwardly he besought Steinfinn to speak the words that could rescue him from all his difficulties. But shame and guilt kept his lips closed.

This was the last time he spoke with Steinfinn Toresson. He and Arnvid were still sleeping in the afternoon when Haftor Kolbeinsson came and woke them. Steinfinn's death struggle had begun, and all the people of the house went up to be with him.

7

BROTHER VEGARD had given Steinfinn absolution *in articulo mortis;* so he had a fair burial. Steinfinn's kinsmen and friends spoke big words at the funeral feast; they swore that Mattias Haraldsson should lie unatoned. As yet the dead man's next of kin had made no sign—but they all lived in other parts of the country. There was also trouble in the air—rumours were abroad of great events that were brewing. And Steinfinn's kinsmen boasted that the men who would now have most power in the land, while the King and the Duke were children, were their friends.

Only a small part of Steinfinn's debts and dues were settled at the division of his estate among his under-aged children. The kinsmen made as though there were immense riches—but between man and man many a hint was dropped.

Arnvid Finnsson was to stay at Frettastein with the children until Haftor Kolbeinsson had held his wedding at the New Year.

Then Haftor was to move to the manor and have charge of it for Hallvard, Steinfinn's elder son, till the boy came of age.

Steinfinn's brothers stayed behind at Frettastein some days after the funeral guests had departed. The evening before they were to ride away, the men sat as usual drinking ale after the supper had been cleared away. Then Arnvid stood up, making a sign to Olav that he was to come forward.

"It is so, Ivar and Kolbein, that here is my friend, Olav Audunsson, who has bid me lay a matter before you. Steinfinn declared before he died that Olav ought to go home to his own house and speak with his kinsmen of a portion and a morning-gift for Ingunn, when he now takes her to wife. But now we have thought that, as matters stand, 'twill be easier that we conclude this matter at once and that Olav's wedding be held here—thus both we and his kinsmen will be spared the long road, while winter is at hand and our fortunes are so uncertain. Therefore Olav has bid me tell you that he offers to give surety—and I am willing to be his surety as far as sixteen marks of gold—that he will put to what he gets with Ingunn so much that she shall own the third part of his estate, besides her bedclothes, apparel, and jewels according to their condition. He also offers to give surety that he will make full restitution of its cost to him of you who shall provide his wedding—whether you will have ready money, or that he shall sell you for a fair price Ingunn's share in Hindkleiv and make amends to her of his lands in the south—"

Arnvid spoke on for a while about the terms that Olav offered his wife's kinsfolk, and these were unwontedly good. Olav promised masses for the repose of Steinfinn and Ingebjörg, and he pledged himself that the Steinfinnssons should always find in him a trusty and compliant son-in-law, who would hearken to the counsel of his elders as was fitting for a young man of his age. Finally Arnvid asked the Steinfinnssons to receive this offer as it was put forward—with goodwill and in a loyal spirit.

Steinfinn's brothers listened as though the matter gave them no little trouble. While his friend was speaking, Olav had stood before him, on the outer side of the table. He stood erect, with his calm, pale face turned toward Ingunn's uncles. Now and again he nodded assent to Arnvid's words.

At last Kolbein Toresson made reply: "It is true, Olav, that we know there was once talk between your father and our brother that you should marry one of his daughters. And you must not think we do aught but esteem your goodwill in desiring to order this matter so that we might all have been well pleased. But the thing is whether your kinsmen would *now* be so set upon this marriage of our niece to you that they would consent to your offer. But what weighs most is that we now have greater need to ally ourselves by marriage with men who have power and powerful kinsfolk, and these you have not. We must now seek support rather than riches—we look to you to acknowledge this, since you have shown by your offer that you have foresight far beyond your age. But because of the promise Steinfinn once made to your father that he would help you to a good marriage, we will gladly help you in this matter. For Steinfinn's daughters we have other designs—but you must not be dejected on that account: with God's help we shall find you a match as good in every way and better fitted to your age—for young as you are, Olav, you were ill served with a bride as young; you ought either to take a wife who is older and more discerning, or betroth yourself to a maid who is younger and let your wedding wait till you yourself be fully grown."

Olav had turned red in the face while the other was speaking. Before he could make answer, Arnvid said quickly: "Hereabouts all have held Olav and Ingunn to be betrothed—and I myself stood by when Steinfinn handselled him his daughter—"

"Nay, nay," said Kolbein. "I have heard of that, it was a game they played—afterward they spoke of it, Steinfinn and Audun, saying it might be fitting if they turned the jest to earnest one day. And that might well have been, had not our brother fallen into these misfortunes. But since this betrothal has never been concluded—"

"The ring I pledged her with—Steinfinn has it in his coffer, I know it," Olav broke in hotly.

"You may know it; Steinfinn is not like to have made away with any of your goods, my Olav, but your kinsmen shall witness that not a button is missing when they come to receive them on your behalf."

Olav's breath came quick and short.

Kolbein went on: "You must see plainly, Olav, no man of sound mind gives away his children thus, in his drink—"

"Steinfinn did it— I know not whether he were a man of sound mind—"

"—except all covenants about marriage portions and the like were made beforehand. You must know, had Steinfinn thus bound himself to Audun Ingolfsson, he would have said no straight out when I spoke to him this spring of Ingunn for the son of a friend of mine—"

"What said he then?" asked Olav breathlessly.

"He said neither yes nor no, but promised to listen to the man; we spoke of it again when we conferred about this other matter— that it might profit us greatly if Ingunn were married into that kindred. But I stand by what I have said to you, Olav: gladly will we kinsmen help you to a good match—"

"I have not asked you that; I was promised Ingunn—"

Arnvid interposed: " 'Twas one of the last words Steinfinn spoke, Ivar—on the morning of his death—that had he himself been able to give away Ingunn, he would have chosen Olav for son-in-law."

"Ay, that is likely enough," said Kolbein, rising from his seat and coming forward; "but now it falls out, Arnvid, that Steinfinn *could* not do it. *You* should be old and wise enough to see that we cannot turn away the man who can give us most support in our troubles, because Olav has taken for earnest a game they played with him once when he was a little boy. *You* went unwilling enough to your bridal bed, Arnvid—'tis strange you should make such haste to push your friend into his. Belike Olav will thank us one day that we did not let him have his will in such childish fancies—"

With that he and Ivar went to the closed bed in which Steinfinn had been used to sleep before the raid; they lay down and shut the door.

Arnvid went up to Olav; the young man had not moved and his eyes were fixed on the floor; his face twitched again and again. Arnvid bade him come and lie down.

" 'Twas lucky you curbed yourself so that it came not to angry words between Kolbein and you," said Arnvid as they undressed in the dark behind the pillars.

A sound like a snort came from Olav.

Arnvid went on: "Else it would have been hard to bring this matter to a good ending—Kolbein could have claimed that you should leave the house at once. Let him not mark that your heart is so set upon getting Ingunn and none other—then 'twill be easier."

Olav said nothing. He was used to sleeping on the outer side, but as they were getting into bed, Arnvid asked: "You must let me sleep outside tonight, friend—that ale tonight was not good; I feel sick from it."

"I had no good of it either," said Olav with a short laugh.

But he lay down on the inside against the wall. Arnvid was just falling asleep when he felt Olav get up and try to step over him.

"Where are you going?" asked his friend, taking hold of him.

"I am thirsty," muttered Olav. Arnvid heard him grope his way over to the tub of whey and water; he ladled some out and drank.

"Now come and lie down," Arnvid bade him.

And indeed Olav soon came pattering back, crept into the bed, and lay down.

"It were much best you say nothing to Ingunn of the answer we have had, till we have taken counsel what course to pursue," whispered Arnvid earnestly.

Olav lay quiet a good while before he answered: "Ay, ay." He sighed deeply. "So be it, then."

Arnvid felt a little easier after that. But he dared not abandon himself to sleep before he heard that the young man was in a deep slumber.

8

THE SNOW was falling thickly when Olav came out into the yard at dusk on St. Catherine's Eve.[1] It was the first snowfall of the year; his footprints showed black on the ground as he ran across to the stable.

He stood for a moment before the stable door, watching the whirling mass of white. His eyes blinked as the snowflakes fell on his long lashes; they felt like a light caress against his skin. The forest below the manor on the north and east, which in the

[1] November 24.

autumn nights had been full of gloom and desolation, now seemed near and shone like a white and friendly wall through the driving snow and the gathering darkness. Olav felt glad at the snow.

Someone within the stable was speaking in a loud voice—the door flew open behind him, and a man dashed out as if he had been thrown. He pitched against Olav, and both went to the ground. The other got onto his feet and shouted back to someone standing in the doorway, a vague black figure in the pale gleam of the lantern: "Here is one more for you to show your manhood on, Arnvid"—with which he ran off into the snow and the darkness.

Olav shook himself and dived in under the doorway. "What was that with Gudmund?"—when in the shadow behind Arnvid he caught sight of a girl in tears.

"Out with you, foul slut," Arnvid said to her, furious. The woman slunk crouching past the men and out. Arnvid barred the door behind her.

"What is it?" asked Olav again.

"Oh—no great thing, as you may think," said Arnvid hotly. He picked up the little lantern and hung it on the hook; Olav saw that he was trembling with agitation. "Naught else but that now every whoreson who serves about the place seems to think he dare scorn me because—because— I have said I will not have womenfolk in the stables; 'tis unfitting. Gudmund answered me that I should rather keep a watch on the bowers here and on my kinswomen."

Olav turned away. In the darkness beyond, the horses could be heard crunching their fodder and stamping their feet. The nearest stretched its neck and snorted at Olav, and the flame of the lantern was reflected in its dark eyes.

"Did you hear?" Arnvid insisted.

Olav turned to the horse and did not answer. He felt in agony that he was blushing violently.

"What have you to say to that?" asked Arnvid hotly.

"What would you have me say?" answered Olav in a low voice. "As my case stood—after the answer Kolbein gave me— you cannot well be surprised—that I followed your advice."

"My—advice!"

"The advice you gave me that day we spoke together up in

the woods. You said that when two persons under age have been betrothed by their lawful guardians, none has the right to part them, but if they agree to follow the designs of their parents, there is no need of more; they can come together as married folk—"

"That I have never said!"

"I mind me not how the words went. But such I guessed to be your meaning."

"My meaning!" whispered Arnvid, deeply moved. "Nay, Olav—what I meant—I—I thought you knew—"

"No. What meant you, then?" asked Olav point-blank, turning toward the other. Driven by a sense of utter shame, he hardened himself, looked his friend defiantly in the eyes, while his face was on fire.

But Arnvid Finnsson dropped his eyes before the younger man and blushed in his turn. What he had thought he could not say. And he found it hard to undeceive himself now. Confusion and shame made him speechless. That he had kept up familiar friendship with a man whom he himself believed to be the seducer of his kinswoman—how ill it looked he seemed not to have guessed till now. It was as though he had not seen its ugly, dishonourable side before—because Olav seemed so honourable all through, he had been blind to the dishonour—when it was Olav.

Nor could he believe it now—that Olav stood there lying to him. He had always held Olav to be the most truthful of all men. And he clutched at it now—Olav's words must be worthy of belief. He himself must have wronged his friend with his suspicion in the summer—so it must be. There had been nothing unseemly between the two, though they had been together at night in the summer.

"I have ever thought well of you, Olav," he said. "Believed you jealous of your honour—"

"Then you could not well expect," Olav broke in hotly, still staring the other in the face, "that I should lie down tamely and let the Toressons trample on my honour and cheat me of my right. I will not go home to my own country in such guise that every man may mock at me and say I let these men defraud me of the marriage I should have made. You know that they use fraud against me, Kolbein and those—you remember how I got back my ring?"

Arnvid nodded. When the property was divided, Kolbein had given back to Olav the chests of movables which Steinfinn had taken charge of for his foster-son. But then Olav's mother's signet-ring was among these goods, threaded on a ribbon together with some other rings. And Olav could not say a word about his having lately seen the ring lying among Steinfinn's own treasures.

"And in *my* eyes it concerns my father's honour too," Olav continued excitedly, "if I am to let strangers set at naught his last will and the promises given to him before he died! And Steinfinn—you heard yourself what he said; but he knew well enough, poor man, that he had not the power to carry it against those overbearing brothers of his. Are Ingunn's father and my father to have so little respect in their graves that they are not to be allowed the right to dispose of their own children's marriage?"

Arnvid reflected, a long time.

"None the less, Olav," he said slowly, "you must not now do such things as—go to her in her bower and meet her secretly so that all the house-folk know of it. God knows, I should not have kept my counsel so long—but it seemed to me an ill thing to speak of. You have not been afraid to show *me* disrespect."

Olav made no answer—and Arnvid felt sorry for him when he looked at him. Arnvid said: "I deem, Olav, since it has come to this between you and her, that *you* must take charge of the manor here."

Olav looked up with a question in his eyes.

"Declare to the house-folk here that you will not give way to the new sponsors, but hold them to the bargain Steinfinn and your father made and take your wife to yourself. Step into the master's bed with Ingunn and declare that now you think that *you* are next of kin to have charge for Hallvard and Jon, so long as you and Ingunn stay here in the north."

Olav stood biting his lip; his cheeks were burning. At first Arnvid's advice tempted him—unspeakably. This was the plain road out of all the furtive dealings by night and by stealth which, he felt, were making him a meaner and weaklier man. Take Ingunn by the hand and boldly lead her to the bed and high seat left by Steinfinn and Ingebjörg. Then let them talk about *that*, all these folk about the place who giggled and muttered behind his back—though as yet they had not dared to come out with it before him.

But then his courage sank when he thought of carrying it out. It was their sneers, their nasty little words. They were so apt at that, the people hereabout—with an innocent look, making it hard for a man to return an answer and defend himself, they dropped a few sly words with a sting in them. Many a time the malice in their speech was hidden so cunningly that it was a little while before he guessed what the men were smiling at, when one of them broke off, with too unconcerned an air, or gave a start.— Without being aware of it he had striven in all his doing at Frettastein so to conduct himself as to give them no occasion to make that sort of game of *him*. Until now he had succeeded in some measure—he knew that his fellow servants liked him well enough, and stood in a sort of awe of him, as happens when a man is sparing of words, but is known not to be a fool; thus he may easily be accounted wiser than he is. As yet none had dared to hint at what all knew of him and Ingunn—no word, at least, had come to his ears.

But he flinched at the thought—the laughter and the jesting would break out sure enough when he himself made no secret of the matter and offered to take over the stewardship of the farm, where he had been reckoned a young lad until this year. Insensibly Olav's view of himself and of his position on Steinfinn's estate had changed—he no longer counted Frettastein as the home to which he had belonged as one of the children of the house. The chance words that had trickled into his mind, the fact that Ingunn's kinsmen disregarded him, the stings of an evil conscience and the sense of shame at all he had done in secret, made him see himself in a meaner light than before.

And then there was this—that he was so young; all the other men of the place were much older than he. He was well used, indeed, to their counting him and Ingunn as not yet fully grown. And he blushed at the thought of having to own that he was living with a woman—when no grown man had led him forward and accepted him in the ranks of husbands. Without that he could not feel that it was *real*.

At length he replied: " 'Tis not to be done, Arnvid. Think you either man or woman here would obey me if I tried to command?

Grim or Josep or Gudmund? Or would Dalla willingly give up her keys to Ingunn?"

"No; Ingunn would have to be content to wear the coif—" Arnvid gave a little laugh—"till you can give her the keys of Hestviken."

"Nay, Arnvid; they go in fear of Kolbein, every mother's child here—what you counsel is impossible."

"Then I know of only one other way—and this counsel I should have given you long ago, God forgive me. Go to Hamar and put your case in the Bishop's hands."

"In Bishop Torfinn's? I trow not *I* can look for much mercy of *him*," said Olav slowly.

"Your right you may look for," replied Arnvid. "In this question it is only Holy Church that can judge. You two *can* only be married to each other."

"Who knows if the pious father will not order us to be monk and nun, send us to the cloister to expiate our sin?"

"He will assuredly make you do penance to the Church for going to your bride without banns or wedding. But if you can bring forward witnesses that the betrothal is valid—and that I think we can surely do—he will demand of the Toressons that they accept offers of honourable atonement—"

"Think you," Olav broke in, " 'twill avail much if the lord Torfinn demand it? Before now the Bishop of Hamar has had to give away to the Steinfinnssons."

"Ay—in questions of property and the like. But for all that, they are not so ungodly as to deny that in this matter none has the right to judge but the fathers of the Church—whether marriage be marriage or not."

"I wonder. Oh no—then I have more mind to take Ingunn with me and fare south to my own country."

"Ah, not so long as I can wield a sword. In the devil's name, Olav, do you expect, because I have—lacked counsel so long— that I should sit here and shut my eyes while you steal my kinswoman out of my ward?" He saw that Olav was on the point of flaring up. "Be calm," he said curtly; "I know you are not afraid of me. And I am not afraid of you either. But I reckoned we were friends. If you feel yourself that your conduct to me has been something short of a trusty friend's, then do as I say, seek to make an end of this matter in seemliness and honour.

"I shall go with you to the Bishop," he added, seeing that the other still hesitated.

"Against my will I do this thing," said Olav with a sigh.

"Is it more to your liking as things are now," Arnvid rejoined hotly, "to let the talk go on, here on the manor and among the neighbours—of you and me and Ingunn? Can you not see that the womenfolk smirk and whisper behind her back wherever she goes—stare at her slyly? They look to see if she treads as lightly as ever—"

"There is no danger on that score," muttered Olav angrily; "so she says." His face was crimson again. "Ingunn must stay with us, then," he said reflectively. "Else it might be difficult even for Bishop Torfinn to get her out of Kolbein's clutches."

"Ay, I shall take Tora and Ingunn with me. Think you I would let her fall into Kolbein's hands after this?"

"So be it, then," answered Olav; he stared gloomily before him.

Two days later they rode down and reached the town late in the evening. The maids were long abed next morning, and Olav said he would go seek the smith and fetch his axe, while the others made ready to hear the last mass that was sung in Christ Church.

They had already set out when he came back to the inn. He hurried after them along the street, and the snow crunched under him—it was fine, frosty weather. The bells rang out so sweetly in the clear air, and the southern sky was so finely tinged with gold above white ridges and dark-blue water. He saw the others by the churchyard gate and ran up to them.

Ingunn turned toward him, flushing red as a rose—Olav saw that under her hood she wore a white coif about her face like a young wife. He turned red too, and his heart began to hammer—this was dead earnest; 'twas as though he had not known it till now. Young as he was and lacking friends and kinsmen, he had taken this upon himself—to face it out that she was his wife. And it made him terribly bashful to walk beside her thus. Straight as two candles, gazing fixedly before them, they strode side by side across the churchyard.

After the morning meal Olav accompanied Arnvid to the Bishop's palace. He was ill at ease during the walk, and it was no better when he had to sit waiting by himself in the Bishop's stone hall, after a clerk had taken Arnvid up to Lord Torfinn in the Bishop's bedchamber.

The time dragged on and on. Olav had never been in a stone hall before and there was much to look at. The roof was also of stone and vaulted, so that no light came in except from a little glazed window in the back wall; but in spite of that it was not so very dark, as the room was whitewashed within, and the walls were painted with bright flowers and birds in place of tapestries and to the same height. The room was without any sort of fireplace, but as soon as he had entered, two men came in bearing a great brazier, which they placed in the middle of the floor. Olav went up and warmed his hands over it, when he grew tired of sitting and freezing on the bench. He was left to sit alone most of the time, and he was ill at ease in this hall; there was something churchlike about it which unsettled him.

After a while three men came in, clad in furs; they placed themselves around the charcoal brazier and took no notice of the boy on the bench. They had come about a case they had—of fishing-rights. The two old ones were farmers from somewhere about Fagaberg, and the younger one was a priest and stepson of one of the farmers. Olav was made to feel very young and inexperienced—it would surely not be easy for him to assert himself here. Soon one of the Bishop's men came and fetched them away. Olav himself would have been glad to go out into the palace yard too—there were many things to look at. But he judged that this would be unbecoming; he would have to stay where he was.

At last Arnvid came in great haste, snatched his sword, and buckled it on, saying that the Bishop was to ride out to a house in Vang and had bidden him go with him. No, he had not been able to say much about Olav's case—folk had been coming and going in the Bishop's chamber the whole morning. No, the Bishop had not said much, but he had invited both Arnvid and Olav to lodge in the palace, so now Olav must go back to the inn and bring his horse and their things.

"What of the maids—they cannot be left behind in the inn?"

"No," said Arnvid. They were to lodge in a house in the town, with two pious old women who had boarders. In a day or two they would be joined by Magnhild, Steinfinn's sister from Berg; the Bishop would send a letter tomorrow, bidding her come: "He says you and Ingunn ought not to meet until a reconcilia-

tion be made in this affair—except, as you know, you may see
each other in church and speak together there." Arnvid dashed
out.

Olav hurried to the inn, but one of these women from the
guest-house was there before him, and Ingunn and Tora were
ready to go with her. So he was not able to speak to her. She
looked sorrowful as he gave her his hand in farewell. But Olav
said to Tora, so that her sister might hear, that the Bishop had
received them well; it was a great mark of favour that all four
were to be his guests.

But when he came back to the Bishop's palace, he was met by
a young priest, who said they were to be *contubernales*. Olav
guessed that this meant he was to sleep in this priest's room. He
was a tall, lean man with a big, bony, horse's head, and they
called him Asbjörn All-fat. He got a man to take charge of
Olav's horse, and himself showed the young man to the loft where
he was to sleep. Then he said he must go down to the boat-hithe;
a vessel had come that morning with goods from Gudbrandsdal—
maybe 'twould amuse Olav to go with him and look on? Olav
was glad to accept.

There was much shipping at Hestviken, Olav knew; and yet
no man could know less of ships and boats than he, so strangely
had his life been ordered. He used both eyes and ears when aboard
the trading vessel, made bold even to ask about one thing and
another. He took a hand with the men and helped to discharge
the freight—'twas a better pastime than standing by with idle
hands. Most of it was barrels of salt herrings and sea-trout, but
there were also bales of hides and a quantity of furs, butter, and
tallow. While the priest kept the tally, Olav helped him, notching
the stick; in this he had had practice at Frettastein, as he had
often done it for Grim; the old man was not very good at reckoning now.

He kept with Asbjörn Priest the whole day—followed him to
prayers in the choir of the church and to supper, which Olav
was to take at the same table as the Bishop's household. And
when at night he went to the loft with Asbjörn and another
young priest, he was in a much better frame of mind. He no
longer felt such a stranger in the palace, and there were many
new things to see.—Arnvid was not yet come home.

But in the course of the night Olav awoke and lay thinking of all that had been told him of Bishop Torfinn. He was afraid of the Bishop after all.

Rather let ten men lose their lives than one maiden be ravished, he was reported to have said. There was a case that had been much talked about in the country round, a year before. A rich man's son in Alvheim had set his mind on a poor peasant's daughter; as he could not tempt the woman with promises and gifts, he came one evening in springtime, when the girl was ploughing, and tried to use force. Her father was below in the wood, busy with the mending of a fence; he was old and ailing, but on hearing his daughter's cries he took his woodcutter's axe and ran up; he cleft the other's skull. The ravisher was left unatoned; his kinsmen had to be content with that. But, as was natural, they tried to get the slayer to leave the country. First they offered to buy him out, but when he would not have it, they fell upon him with threats and overbearing treatment. Then Bishop Torfinn had taken the poor peasant and his children under his protection.

Then there was that case of the man at Tonstad who had been found slain in his coppice. His wife and children charged the other tenant of the farm with the murder; the man had to flee to save his life, and his wife and young children suffered affliction and cruelty without end at the hands of the murdered man's relatives. Then it came about that the dead man's own cousin confessed that he was the one who had killed his kinsman—they had quarrelled about an inheritance. But it was said that Biship Torfinn had forced the murderer to avow before the people what he had confessed to the Bishop—saying that no priest had power to absolve him of the sin before he had shown sincere repentance and rescued the innocent who might be suffering from his misdeed.

Arnvid said that to the poor and sorrowing this Bishop would stoop with the gentlest kindness, praying them to turn to him as to a loving father. But he never bowed his neck the least jot when faced with self-willing or hard-hearted men, whether they were great folk or small, clergy or laity. Never would he excuse sin in any man—but if any sinner showed repentance and will to make amends, he received him with both hands, guided, consoled, and protected him.

This was nobly done, Olav had thought—and much of what he had heard of the lord Torfinn he had liked very well—a fearless man this monk from Trondheim must be, and one who knew his own will. But then he had never thought that he himself would have a case to submit to the Bishop's judgment. And what Arnvid said about the Bishop's being no respecter of persons seemed to Olav to be stretching his goodness somewhat far—he could see naught else but that it did make some difference whether it were a lowly peasant who killed his neighbour for a small matter, or Steinfinn revenging himself upon Mattias. In any case, he would not like anyone to think he had turned to the Bishop and sought his protection against the Steinfinnssons because—ay, because he felt himself in a way their inferior. Then there was this other thing, that Bishop Torfinn was so strict on the point of chastity. With all other men he might hold to his assertion that this life he and Ingunn had led since the summer was wedlock in a way. But he did not feel it so himself.

Next morning he sat waiting again in the little hall. It was so called because there was a larger hall or court-house beside it. There was no door between; none of the rooms in the stone building had more than one door, and that led into the courtyard. Olav had sat there awhile when a little young man came in, clad in a greyish-white monk's frock which was a little different from that of the preaching friars. The monk closed the door behind him and advanced rapidly to Olav—and the young man got up in great haste and knelt upon one knee; he knew at once that this must be the lord Torfinn. When the Bishop held out his hand, Olav meekly kissed the great stone in his ring.

"Welcome to Hamar, Olav Audunsson! 'Twas not well that I should be absent yesterday when you came—but I hope my house-folk have had good care of our guests?"

He was not so young after all, Olav saw—his thin wreath of hair shone like silver, and his face was shrunken, wrinkled, and grey as his frock almost. But he was slim and wonderfully lithe in all his movements—scarce so tall as Olav. It was impossible to guess his age—his smile took away the look of age; a brightness came into his great yellow-grey eyes, but upon his pale and narrow lips the smile became the faintest shadow.

Olav mumbled his thanks and stood in embarrassment—the zealous Bishop looked so utterly different from what he had expected. He remembered dimly that he had seen the former Bishop

—a man who filled a room with his voice and his presence. Olav felt that this one could also fill the room, slight and silver-grey as he was—in another way. When Lord Torfinn sat down and bade him be seated beside him, he modestly withdrew to the bench at a little distance.

"There is great likelihood that you must be content to bide here a part of the winter," said Bishop Torfinn. "You are a man of the Vik,[2] I hear, and all your kinsmen dwell far away, save only the Tveits folk out in Soleyar. It will take time ere we can receive their answer as to what their testimony may be in this matter. Know you if they have resigned their guardianship of you in lawful wise?"

"My father did so, lord—was it not he who had the right to that?"

"Yes, yes. But he must have spoken of it to his kinsmen and had their consent that Steinfinn should enjoy the payment for your wardship in place of them?"

Olav was silent. This case of his did not seem so simple a matter —ay, he had guessed as much of late. No wardship payment from his estate had ever been made to Steinfinn—so far as he knew.

"I know nothing of this—I know little of the law; none has ever taught me such things," he said dejectedly.

"Nay, I supposed that. But we must be clear about this question of guardianship, Olav—first on account of your share in the deed of arson—whether you accompanied Steinfinn as his son-in-law or as a man in his pay. Kolbein and those have got their freedom now, but you were not included in it.[3] I shall speak with the Sheriff about this matter, so that you may be safe here in the town. But then there is that saying of Steinfinn before he died— that he desired the marriage between you and his daughter, as Arnvid tells me. Whether *he* were your guardian at that time, or these kinsmen of yours, who are so now."

"I thought," said Olav, turning red, "that I was come to man's estate. Since she was betrothed to me in lawful wise, and I have taken her to me as my wife."

The Bishop shook his head. "Can you suppose that you two

---

[2] *Vik:* the great bay in the south of Norway, of which the Oslo Fiord is the northern extremity.

[3] That is, Kolbein and the rest had been declared free to remain in the country, safe from outlawry.

children have acquired any right in law because you have gone to bed together, as seemed good to yourselves, without the presence of your kinsfolk and without banns in church? A duty you have taken upon yourselves, since you acted in the belief that it was binding wedlock—you are now bound under pain of mortal sin to live together till death shall part you, or to remain single if we cannot bring about a reconciliation between her sponsors and yours. But you have not come to man's estate through a marriage of this sort, and your spokesmen can demand no dowry on your behalf until you have fallen at the feet of the Toressons and made amends to them—and 'twould be unlike them if they should be willing to grant you such dowry with Ingunn Steinfinnsdatter as a man of your condition might otherwise look to get with his wife. This game may cost you dear, Olav. To the Church you must do penance, for making your marriage in secret, as she has forbidden all her children to do, since matters of matrimony are to be conducted in the light, in prudent and seemly fashion. Were it not so, too many young folk might deal as you have dealt; you and this woman are bound by the promises you have made to God, but no man is bound to grant you rights or afford you support, since no men were present, to make promises to you and for you, when you bound yourself."

"My lord!" said Olav; "I had thought that you would defend our rights—since you yourself deem that we are bound to keep the faith we gave to each other—"

"Had you submitted the case to the judgment of the Church as soon as you saw that the maid's uncles were minded to oppose the validity of the betrothal—that would have been the right way. You could have claimed of my official, Sir Arinbjörn Skolp, that he should forbid Kolbein under threat of ban to betroth Ingunn to another man, before it had been made clear whether you had already a right to this marriage."

"How much, trow, would Kolbein have cared for that?"

"Hm. *So* much you know, for all that. You have not learned law, but you have seen unlawfulness—" The Bishop moved his hands in his lap under the scapular. "You must bear in mind, Kolbein and Ivar have already so much on their hands that perchance they will not be so eager to have a matter of excommunication added."

"I thought 'twas held good enough," Olav began again ob-

stinately, "that her father had handselled the maid to my father
for my wife."

"No." The Bishop shook his head. "As I told you, guilt and
duties you have gained, but no rights. Had you come to Sir Arinbjörn with the matter while the girl was yet a maid, you had
gained more than the best you can win now. Either they would
have been forced to give you both the woman and her goods, or
she and you could have parted and been free to make another
marriage. As the matter now stands, my son, you must pray God
to help you, that you may not repent by daylight and in your
manhood that you bound yourself hand and foot blindly and
in darkness, before you were yet wholly out of your childhood."

"That day will never come," said Olav hotly, "when I repent
me that I did not let Kolbein Borghildsson cheat me of what was
mine by right—"

The Bishop looked at him searchingly, as Olav went on: "Oh
no, my lord—Kolbein was resolved to upset this bargain, and
small scruple will he have of the means he uses—that I know!" He
told the Bishop of the betrothal ring.

"Are you sure," asked Lord Torfinn, "that Steinfinn had not
replaced the ring in your coffer before he died? He may have
thought it safer, so that you should surely receive again all that
was yours and that he had in charge for you."

"No, for it was on the morning of his death-day that I saw
Ingunn's betrothal ring; then it lay in the casket in which Steinfinn kept his own and his children's most costly jewels."

"Was it Steinfinn himself who brought out the casket—did he
show you this?"

"No, 'twas Arnvid did it."

"Hm. Ay, then it looks as though Kolbein—" The Bishop
paused for a moment, then turned to Olav. "As you two young
people are placed, the best way will be—I do not say it is a perfect way, but the best—that your kinsmen and hers assent to a
marriage according to the law of the land, and that you be allowed to enjoy one another and all that you possess and are to
bring to one another. Otherwise life will be very difficult for you,
and your feet will be beset with temptation to worse sins than
this first sin, if you be parted. But you understand, I ween, that,
even if we can bring witnesses to the validity of the betrothal,

the Toressons may make such conditions for reconciliation that you will be poorer by your marriage than you were before?"

"Ay, that is all one to me," said Olav defiantly. "The word that was given to my father shall not be broken because he is dead. I will have Ingunn home with me, if I have to take her in her bare shift—"

"And what of this young Ingunn," said the Bishop quietly; "are you sure that she is of the same mind as you—that she would rather hold fast to the old bargain than be given to another man?"

"Ingunn was minded as I—we should not set ourselves up against our fathers' will because they were dead and strangers would minish their right to dispose of their own children."

Bishop Torfinn did his best not to smile. "So you two children stole into the bridal bed simply to be obedient to your fathers?"

"My lord!" said Olav in a low voice, turning red again, "Ingunn and I are of even age, and we were brought up as brother and sister from the time we were small. From my seventh year I have lived far from all my kinsfolk. And when she lost both mother and father, she betook herself to me. Then we agreed that we would not let them part us."

The Bishop nodded slowly; Olav said passionately: "My lord—meseems 'twould be a great dishonour both to me and to my father were I to ride brideless from Frettastein, where all have held us to be betrothed for ten years. But I also had the thought that, when I come home to my native place, where no man knows me, I could have no better wife than the one with whom I have been friends from childhood."

"How old were you when you lost your parents, Olav?" asked the Bishop.

"Seven years old I was when my father died. And I was motherless in my hour of birth."

"—And my mother is still living." Lord Torfinn sat silent awhile. "I see, 'tis natural you should not wish to lose your playmate." He rose and Olav sprang up at once. The Bishop said: "You know well, Olav, that motherless and friendless you are not—no Christian man is that. You, as we all, have the mightiest brother in Christ, our Lord, and His Mother is your mother—and with her, I trust, is she, your mother who bore you. I have always thought that the Lady Sancta Maria prays yet more to her Son for those children who must grow up motherless here below than for us others.—True it is that none should forget who are our nearest and mightiest kin. But it ought to be easier for you to bear this in mind. You will not so lightly be tempted to forget what power of kindred you have in the God of peace—since you have no brothers or kinsmen in the flesh who might draw you with them to deeds of violence and arrogance or egg you on to revenge and strife. You are young, Olav, and already others have drawn you into blood-guiltiness—you have thrust yourself into strife and litigation. God be with you, that you may become a man of peace, when you are answerable for yourself."

Olav knelt and kissed Bishop Torfinn's hand in farewell. The Bishop looked down at his face and smiled faintly.

"You have a headstrong look—ay, so it is. God and His gentle Mother preserve you, that you grow not hard-hearted."

He raised his hand and gave the young man his blessing. On reaching the door Lord Torfinn turned with a little laugh: "One thing I had forgot—to thank you for your help. My Asbjörn, All-fat they call him, spoke of how you had already lent him a hand since you came here. I thank you for it."

Not till the evening, when he was in bed and about to fall asleep, did the thought cross Olav's mind like a chill breath: what he had said to Bishop Torfinn about himself and Ingunn—it was not altogether truthful. But he banished the thought at once—now of all times he had no desire to think upon last summer and autumn, the nights in the bower and all that.

He felt at home in the Bishop's palace, and every day the life seemed better to him, with only men around him, all older than himself and all with their regular tasks to perform, hour by hour.

Olav followed on the heels of Asbjörn All-fat wherever the priest went. They were four men in the loft-room where Olav and Arnvid slept; there was a young priest who had been at the school with Arnvid, besides Asbjörn, who was a good deal older than the others—close on thirty. Arnvid went to church and sang the daily office with the clergy, and he had borrowed the book from which he had learned when he was a pupil in the school, and sat amusing himself with it in the leisure hour after breakfast. He sat on the edge of the bed reading aloud the first pieces that were written in it: *De arte grammatica* and *Nominale*.

Olav lay listening to him: 'twas strange how many names these men of Rome had had for a single word; *sea*, for instance. At the end of the book were some leaves on which to practise the art of writing. Arnvid diverted himself by engrossing letters and sentences after the old copies. But it was chilly work in the cold loft— and his fingers had lost their cunning for such things. One day he wrote at the end of his copy:

"Est mala scriptura quia penna non fuit dura." [4]

But when he had put away the book and gone out, Asbjörn Priest took it and wrote in the margin:

"Penna non valet dixit ille qui scribere nescit." [5]

Olav smiled quietly when he was told what it meant.

Asbjörn All-fat said his mass early in the morning, and Olav usually went with him to the church; often he did not go there again on week-days. At most times Asbjörn Priest was exempted from service in the choir and read his hours from a book, wherever his duties might call him. He had much to do with the incomings and outgoings of the see, received rents and tithes in kind, and spoke with people. The priest taught Olav to inspect goods and judge their quality and how each kind should best be stored; he explained to him the laws of buying and selling and of tithes and showed him how to use the abacus. Mjösen was not yet frozen over off the town, and folk came rowing and sailing thither. Asbjörn Priest took Olav with him several times on short journeys. He also bought two brooches of Olav, so now the boy had ready money in his belt for the first time in his life.

In this way it was not much that he saw of Ingunn. He kept his word to the Bishop and sought no meeting with her except at church, but she seldom came there before one of the later masses, and Olav was usually at the first. Arnvid often visited the house where Steinfinn's daughters were lodged. From him Olav heard that the lady Magnhild had been far from gentle with her niece— in her words Ingunn had let herself be seduced; and Ingunn had replied to her aunt in great wrath. The lord Torfinn had been very friendly when he spoke with Ingunn and Tora—he had

[4] " 'Twas badly written, for the pen was lame."
[5] "Who knows not how to write his pen will blame."

sent for them to see him one day. But Olav was not at home when the maids came to the Bishop's palace—he had accompanied Asbjörn All-fat on an errand to Holy Isle that day.

Nor could they have much speech together those times when they met in church and he afterwards walked with her the little way down to the house by Holy Cross Church. But he himself deemed it best so. At times, indeed, he would remember how it felt to hold her in his arms—so soft and slight, so warm and loving. But he thrust the thought from him—now was not the time for such things. They had all the years before them to live together as good and loving friends. He was so sure that Bishop Torfinn would help him to get his rights.

And besides this he felt as it were a dislike to thinking of the life of the last months. Now that it was over, it seemed so unreal, wellnigh unnatural, in his memory. Those nights in the bower with Ingunn in black darkness—he lived and felt with all his senses wide awake, except his sight; ay, 'twas so dark he might as well have been blind. All day long he went about half-asleep and caring for nothing—feeling only the strain and uncertainty of all that threatened him from without, like a booming inside his dazed and empty head. Somewhere deep down within him he was always uneasy—even when at the moment he could not tell what was the newest thing that afflicted his conscience, he knew that there was something wrong and that soon he would feel its urge. Even when he was alone with Ingunn, he could not forget it quite—that something was out of gear. And then she irked him a little, because she never seemed to be tormented by either fear or doubt, and he grew tired of her, because she would always have him gay and wanton and ready to caress her.

It distressed him not the least that he was now forced for a while to lead a life in which there was no place for women and secret love.

The Bishop himself was seldom seen by Olav. So far as his office permitted, the lord Torfinn lived according to the rule of the order he had entered in his youth. His bedchamber was over the council hall, and there he worked, said his hours, and took most of his meals. From this room a stair led down to the chapel in which the Bishop said his mass in the morning, and from the balcony, which ran outside the rooms of the upper story, a covered bridge led across to one of the chapels of Christ Church. Many of those who dwelt in the Bishop's palace were little pleased that they had gotten a starveling monk for their lord: the late Bishop, Gilbert, had kept house like a great noble, and yet he had been a devout priest and an able and zealous father of the Church. Asbjörn Priest said that he liked this Bishop well, but he had liked the old one better: Bishop Gilbert had been a man of cheer, a great saga-man and the boldest of horsemen and hunters.

Olav thought he had never seen a man who sat his horse more freely and handsomely than the lord Torfinn. And in every way a lordly house was kept, though the Bishop himself lived so strictly—every guest who came to the palace was sumptuously entertained; every serving-man was given strong ale every day and mead on holy-days. At the table in the Bishop's guest-hall wine was served, and when the lord Torfinn himself ate with the guests he specially wished to honour, he had a great silver tankard set on the board before him. During the whole meal his cup-bearer stood by his high seat and filled the tankard as often as the Bishop gave him a sign. It was a fine sight, thought Olav, to see Lord Torfinn take the cup, sip it, bowing with graceful courtesy toward him with whom he drank, and give it to be borne to him whom he honoured thus.

On the evening that Tore Bring of Vik was there, it fell to Olav's lot that the lord Torfinn drank with him. After supper the Bishop had him summoned from his seat far down the table; he had to come forward and stand before the Bishop's chair. Lord Torfinn raised the tankard to his lips and handed it to Olav: it felt icy cold in his hand, and the wine had a pale greenish look in the bright silver vessel. It was sharp and sour and pricked the boy's palate, but he liked the taste for all that, 'twas fresh, a drink for men, and afterwards it warmed his whole body with a rare, festal glow. He shook his head when Bishop Torfinn smiled and asked: "Maybe you like mead better, Olav?" Then he asked what Olav had thought of the service that day—there had been a festival mass and procession in the morning; and then he bade Olav drink again: "You are happy now, I dare say? I think we may be well content with what Tore has spoken."

The Bishop had not been able to get any satisfaction from the lady Magnhild—she would give no opinion as to what had happened at the Thing that time. She was inclined, indeed, to believe

that her brother had thought of a marriage between Olav Audunsson and one of his daughters—at one time, in any case—but never
that the match was made and settled. But Tore Vik declared that
he was sure of it—Steinfinn and Audun concluded a bargain about
their children that evening. They had given each other their hands
on it, and Tore himself was the one who had struck the bargain;
he named three or four men who had witnessed the taking of
hands and who were still living, so far as he knew. What agreement was made as to settlements he knew not, but he had heard
the men discuss it on a later day; he even remembered that Audun
Ingolfsson would not hear of an equal division of property, unless Steinfinn increased his daughter's dowry a good deal; "My
son will be much richer than that, Steinfinn," Audun had said.

During Advent, Arnvid went home to his farm in Elfardal for
a space, and Olav went with him. Olav had not been there since
he was a little boy. Now he came as the master's friend and equal,
looked about him with discerning eyes, and put in his word as a
man who himself had one thing and another on his hands. Here
Arnvid's mother ruled supreme, and she received Olav with both
hands, since he had upset Kolbein's plans for Ingunn; for she sin-
cerely hated Kolbein and all the children her brother-in-law had
had with his leman. Mistress Hillebjörg was a proud and handsome woman, old as she was; but there seemed to be a coolness
between her and her son. Arnvid's children were three pretty,
fair-haired boys. "They take after their mother," said Arnvid.
Olav was well pleased with the thought that he would be a master
himself when he came home to Hestviken.

Just before Yule the friends returned to the town; Arnvid
wished to keep the feast there.

9

THE EVENING before Christmas Eve Olav was sent for to the
Bishop.

A candle was burning on the reading-desk in the deep window;
the little stone-walled chamber looked cosy and comfortable in
its faint light. There was no other furniture but a chest for books
and a bench against the walls. The Bishop slept and ate there; he

used neither bed nor table. But there was a low stool on which his secretary could sit with his writing-board in his lap, when the Bishop dictated letters to him. At other times when Olav had been up, the lord Torfinn had bidden him sit on the stool, and Olav had liked to crouch at the Bishop's knee; it made it easy to speak to him, as to a father.

But this evening Lord Torfinn came straight up to him and stood with his hands under his scapular. "The Toressons will be here on Twelfth Night, Olav; I have summoned them hither and they have promised to appear. Now we shall have an end of this matter—with God's help."

Olav bowed in silence and looked anxiously at the Bishop. Lord Torfinn pursed his lips and nodded once or twice.

"To tell the truth, my son, they show no great mind to be reconciled. They spoke to my men about my having accepted penance of you for your share in the slaughter and suffered you to go to mass. They would have had me free them also from the ban before Yule; but that is another matter of which we must speak at our meeting. But you can guess, they are wroth that I did not receive you as though you had been a robber and a ravisher—" he gave a short and angry laugh.

Olav looked at the Bishop and waited.

"*You* have done wrong, never must you think aught else—but you are young and far from your kinsfolk and guardians—and these incendiaries seek to abate the rights of two fatherless children.—You will not be down-hearted, I trust," he said, giving Olav a little slap on the shoulder, "if you are forced to bow somewhat low to Ingunn's uncles? You know, boy, you have injured them. You shall not have to suffer wrong at their hands, if I am able to hinder it."

"I shall do as you say, my lord and father," said Olav, a little downcast.

The Bishop looked at him with a fleeting smile.

"You will not like it—having to bow your neck a trifle—no, no.—If you are going to church now, you may go by the balcony."

Bishop Torfinn nodded and held out his hand to be kissed, in token that the audience was at an end.

The Brothers of the Cross were in the middle of singing vespers. Olav knelt down in a corner with his fur cloak well spread under his knees and held his cap before his eyes, that he might the better collect his thoughts.

He was on the strain—but it was a good thing nevertheless that the decision was now at hand. He longed to escape from uncertainty. It had been like walking in the dark on a road where at any moment he might stumble and plunge both feet into the mire. *That* he had feared—of Kolbein and the rest he was not afraid. An end was to be made of all doubtful and—and half-concealed conduct; his case was to be brought to a conclusion. He would soon be seventeen years old—he liked to feel that he was the chief person in a suit. And he felt as though his bones had hardened within him in these weeks he had lived in the Bishop's palace—after all the slothful years at Frettastein among lazy house-carls and cackling women, joining in children's games. His pride in himself had grown with every day he spent here, where there were neither women nor frivolity, but only grown men who had taught him much and to whom he had taken a liking with all his youthful desire of meeting equals and superiors. It warmed his soul through and through to think that Asbjörn Priest had the greatest use for his help and that Bishop Torfinn bent over him with fatherly kindness.

When he had finished his prayers, he seated himself in a corner to hear the singing to the end. He thought of what Asbjörn Allfat had told him one day of the art of reckoning—how the nature of God was revealed in figures, through the law and order that reigned in them. *Arithmetica*, he thought it had such a fine sound; and all that the priest had expounded about the harmony of figures—how they swelled and cleft one another according to mystic and immovable laws; it was like being given an insight into one of the heavenly kingdoms; on golden chains of numbers the whole of creation was suspended, and angels and spirits ascended and descended along the links. And his heart was exalted in longing that his life also might rest in God's hand like one of these golden links—a reckoning in which there was no fault. When that which now weighed upon him should be effaced like false notches upon a tally-stick.

The midnight mass—the mass of the angels—was more beautiful than anything Olav had imagined. The whole great body of the church lay in pitch-darkness, but in the choir around the high altar so many candles, high and low, were burning that they seemed like a wall of living flame. There was a soft sheen of gold-embroidered silk and a brightness of white linen: tonight all the priests wore cantor's vestments of cloth of gold and silk, and the other singers were clad in linen surplices and held candles in their hands as they stood and sang from the great books. Arnvid Finnsson was among them, and other men of repute from the country round who had been at the school in their youth. The whole church was heavy with the scent of incense from the evening procession, and the grey clouds of perfume still ascended from the altar. When the whole choir of men and boys joined in the great Gloria, it was as though angels took up the song and swelled the music from the gloom of the roof.

Bishop Torfinn's face shone like alabaster as he sat on his throne with mitre and staff, in golden vestments. Now all the mass bells pealed out, and now all who had been standing or sitting knelt down, waiting in breathless silence for the transubstantiation, which tonight became one with God's birth in the world of men. Olav waited in eager longing; his prayers became one with his yearning for righteousness and a good conscience.

He had had a glimpse of Ingunn over on the women's side, but he did not go out after mass, when he saw her go. While they were singing the *Laudi* in the choir, he found a place to sit on the base of one of the pillars, and there, wrapped in his cloak, he shivered and nodded by turns till the priests left the choir.

On the ground outside the graveyard, there was still a glow of burned-out bonfires where the church folk had thrown down their torches in a heap as they came in. Olav went up to warm himself—he was chilled and numb from the many hours in church. The snow was melted far around, down to the bare earth, and the red and black embers still gave out a good strong heat. Many people were standing about. Olav caught sight of Ingunn—she was standing with her back to him; she was alone. He went up and greeted her.

She turned half round, and a reflection of the fire shown red upon the white linen wimple that showed under the hood of her cloak. She still seemed a little strange to him in this woman's dress—he could not grasp the thought that she should go about looking old and dignified because he for his part was determined to win his rights and to be respected as a grown man.

They took hands and wished each other a blessing on the feast.
Then they talked a little about the weather; the cold was not too
bad and the sky was half clear, with a few stars, but not many,
for there was some mist, since the lake was not yet frozen over
here.

Tora came up to them, and Olav greeted her with a kiss. He
could never bring himself to kiss Ingunn now when they met—
she was both too near and too far for him to embrace her as a
foster-brother.

Tora went again at once, over to some friends she saw. Ingunn
had scarcely spoken and had looked away the whole time. Olav
thought perhaps he would have to go—it could not look well, their
standing here together. Then she put out her hand and timidly
took hold of his cloak.

"Can you not go with me, so that we may talk?"

"I can surely. Do you take the south road?"

The dark street was alive with heavy, fur-clad figures, swaying
black against the snow—folk were going to rest awhile in their
houses before the mid-morning mass. The drifts were banked
high against houses and fences and trees—walls and branches were
but little restless spots of black in the snow. Christmas Night lay
close and dark upon the little town, and folk moved about silently
as scared shadows, hurrying in where a door was opened and a
faint light fell upon the snowdrifts in yard and street. But smoke
issued from the louvers and there was a smell of smoke everywhere—the women were putting on the pots for the Christmas
meal. Outside Holy Cross Church a gleam of light fell on the
snow from the wide-open doors, and some old inmates of the
spital dragged themselves in; there was to be mass now.

They tramped along the narrow alley behind the church. Here
they did not meet a soul; it was very dark under the trees and
heavy going, as the snow had been little trodden.

"We had no thought, when we came here that day last summer, that it would be so difficult for us," said Ingunn with a sigh.

"Nay, we could not know that."

"Can you not come in with me?" she asked as they stood in the
yard. "The others were going to Holy Cross—"

"I can surely."

They entered a pitch-dark room, but Ingunn stirred the fire on
the hearth and put fresh wood on it. She had taken off her cloak,

and as she knelt forward to blow the fire, the long white wimple lay over her shoulders and down to her hips.

"Tora and I sleep here," she said, with her back to him. "I promised to do this for them—" she hung the pot on its hook. Olav guessed that this was the kitchen of the house; round about were things used in cookery. Ingunn busied herself to and fro in the glare of the fire, tall and slight and young in her dark dress and white coif. It was like a game, something unreal. Olav sat on the edge of the bed and looked on; he did not know what to say—and then he had grown so sleepy.

"Can you not help me?" asked Ingunn; she was cutting up meat and bacon on a platter by the hearthstone. There was a piece of back that she could not sever with the knife. Olav found a hatchet, chopped it, and broke it apart.

While they were busy with this, she whispered to him, as they knelt among the pots: "You are so glum, Olav! Are you unhappy?" As he only shook his head, she whispered yet lower: "It is so long since we were alone together. I thought you would be glad—?"

"You know that surely.—Have you heard that your uncles are coming on Twelfth Night?" he asked. Then it struck him that she might take that for an answer to her question, whether he were unhappy. "You need not be afraid," he said firmly. "We shall have no fear of *them*."

Ingunn had risen to her feet and she was staring at him, as she opened her mouth in a little gasp. Then she made as though she would throw herself into his arms. Olav showed his hands—they were smeared with fat and brine.

"Come here—you can wipe them on the bedspread." She moved one of the pots. "We can lie down a little, while we wait for it to boil."

Olav drew off his boots and unfastened his cloak. When he had lain down by her side, he spread it over them both. The next instant she had him in a close embrace, with her face pressed hotly against his cheek, so that her breath tickled his neck.

"Olav—you will not suffer them to take me away with them and part me from you?"

"No. But they will have no power to do that either. But you know that it is no trifling matters Kolbein will claim before he will be reconciled with me."

"Is it for that?" she whispered, clinging to him yet tighter. "Is it for that you are less fond of me now?"

"I am just as fond of you as I have ever been," he muttered thickly, groping to get an arm under her neck, but it was so tangled in the wimple.

"Shall I take it off?" she whispered eagerly.

"Oh no, 'twill give you trouble to put it on again."

"It will soon be a month since—we have scarce seen each other all this time," she complained.

"Ingunn—you know I only wish for your good," he pleaded—and recalled at once that he had said this before; when, he could not remember. "To think she has so little wit," he reflected sadly, "that she cannot see she is tempting me this moment—"

"Ay, but—I long so for you. They are kind, these women here, but, for all that, I long to be with you—"

"Ay. But—'tis so holy a night, this—we must go to mass again in a little while—" He turned red with shame in the dark at his own words. Such things should not even be *spoken.*—Quickly he rose in the dark, kissed her eyelids, and felt the eyeballs move and quiver under his mouth, while the tears trickled down and wet his lips.

"Be not angry," he whispered imploringly. Then he moved to the foot of the bed and lay with his face to the room, looking at the fire. Tormented by the tumult in his heart and in his blood, he listened for any sign of movement or weeping in her. But she kept as still as a mouse. At last he heard that she had fallen asleep. Then he stood up, put on his boots, and took his cloak, wrapping her in the bedcover instead. He was freezing, and felt sleepy and giddy and empty from his long fast. The cauldron of meat was boiling and smelt so good that it gave him a pain in his chest.

Outside, it had turned colder; the snow cried under his feet and there was more frost in the air, he could see that in spite of the darkness. Folk were beginning slowly to go up to the church again; Olav shivered a little under his fur cloak. He was so tired that he had no great mind to go to mass now—would rather have gone home and slept. And he had looked forward so much to this Christmas Night with its three services, each more beautiful than the last, they said.

· · ·

In the days that intervened before that of the meeting Olav stayed for the most part within the palace and scarcely went beyond the church. Day after day there were splendid services, and the palace was full of guests for the feast; both priests and laymen had their hands so full with all kinds of duties that Olav was left mostly to himself. With the Bishop he had only once had speech—when he thanked him for his new-year's gift. Lord Torfinn had given him a brown cloth kirtle, reaching to the feet and bordered with fine black otter-skin. It was the first garment Olav had possessed which was altogether handsome and fit for one who would pass for a grown young man, and it added not a little to his self-respect that he could now feel perfectly well dressed—for Arnvid had lent him money to buy a handsome winter cloak, lined with marten, with hose, boots, and other things to go with it.

From Asbjörn All-fat Olav heard that the Bishop had now received an answer from the men he had charged to inquire of Olav's own kinsmen what they thought of the case. The Bishop was by no means pleased with their answers. So much was certain, that Steinfinn had never taken over the guardianship of Olav in a proper, binding way—and yet none of the men of the family had asked after the child or claimed his return from Frettastein.

" 'Tis no little trouble and expense our reverend father is put to for your sake, Olav," said Asbjörn Priest with a little laugh. "Now he has summoned hither these kinsmen of yours from Tveit—it seems he of Hestviken is palsied and in poor case. But the men of Tveit must give consent to your marriage, I trow, before it can be lawful. And they let fall to the parish priest, who spoke with them on Lord Torfinn's behalf, that if the Toressons would have this marriage, then they must offer you the seduced maid—ay, 'twas their word, not mine—with such dowry as you may be pleased to accept. But they would never consent to your making more amends to her kinsmen than the law allows for fornication. And you know that Kolbein and Ivar cannot accept an atonement on such terms; 'twould be to their shame as long as they live."

"Methinks 'twould be to my shame and—and to hers," said Olav angrily. " 'Twould be the same as were she a—leman—"

"Yes. Therefore the Bishop hinted of another way, which might be the last resort—that you leave the country and stay

abroad four winters, till you be of full age and can parley on your
own behalf. Lord Torfinn thought you could betake you to Denmark and seek refuge with your mother's kin—you know that in
that land your mother's kinsmen are among the mightiest? Your
uncle, Sir Barnim Eriksson of Hövdinggaard, is said to be the
richest knight in Sealand."

Olav shook his head. "My mother's father was called Björn
Andersson of Hvitaberg, and her only brother was Stig.—'Twas
in Jutland, I have been told—"

"The lady Margrete was twice married; Björn was her second
husband, and first she had a son named Erik Eriksson; he owned
Hövdinggaard in Sealand. Think you, Olav, 'twould be the worst
mischance if you had to live some years in foreign lands and could
see something of other folks' manners and customs—and could
associate with right wealthy and powerful kinsfolk to boot?"

The priest's words turned Olav's thoughts in a new direction.
Since he came to the Bishop's see, he had indeed found out that
it was a very small and narrow piece of the world he knew. These
churchmen, they sent letters and messengers north, south, east,
and west; in less than six weeks they managed to get word from
folk whom it would have been impossible for Olav to reach—
they might as well have lived in Iceland or in Rome. And now the
Bishop knew more of Olav's own mother's kindred than he himself had ever done. In the church were books and candlesticks
from France, silk curtains from Sicily sent hither by a pope,
woven tapestries from Arras, relics of martyrs and confessors who
had lived in Engelland and Asia. Asbjörn All-fat told him of the
great schools in Paris and Bologna, where a man might learn all
the arts and wisdom in the world—in Salerno one could learn the
Greek tongue and how to become proof against steel or poison.
Asbjörn was a farmer's son from the Upplands, and the longest
journey he had ever made was north to Eyjabu church, but he
talked very often of travelling in foreign lands—and he would
surely be sent abroad in time, for he was an able man and useful
in many ways.

On most days Olav spoke to Arnvid Finnsson only when they
went to bed at night and when they got up. The friends had become strangers to each other since they came to the Bishop's
palace. Arnvid was occupied with so much that Olav did not

understand. And then Arnvid's presence reminded the young man of so many things that were difficult and humiliating. Olav felt a kind of remorse or shame when he remembered all the things of which Arnvid had been a half-willing, half-reluctant witness—though Olav himself could not understand how he had been able to compel a man who was so much older than he, a rich and powerful landowner, when one came to think of it. But it was as though he had used force upon his friend in one way or another, both in that matter of the ring—and afterwards when Arnvid held his peace about what he knew of Olav's nightly visits to his young kinswoman. This last would be judged harshly not only by the Toressons but by all others; Arnvid had gotten an ugly stain on his honour there—and for that he was too good. And Olav knew that Arnvid took things greatly to heart. Therefore he was not quite at his ease with Arnvid now.

With Asbjörn Priest he felt safe and easy. He was always the same, a steady, strenuous worker, whether he were saying his hours or passing salted hides. His long, thin, horse's face was just as unmoved and his voice just as dry and precise when he was saying his mass or when he stood by while goods were being weighed, or tested whether it were true that the supports of a cow-house were rotten on one of the farms of the Bishop's estate. Olav went with him, thinking of his own future; when he came to Hestviken and would go about in his own boats, among his own quays and byres and storehouses—unconsciously it was this friend he dreamed of imitating.

The memory of those hours alone with Ingunn on Christmas Night had reawakened his longing for her. He thought of the slender, girlish young wife in her woman's dress, on her knees blowing at the embers, moving in and out of the flickering light, and busying herself between the benches and the hearth. Thus he would lie at home in his own bed at Hestviken on dark winter mornings and look on while Ingunn made a fire on his hearth. He recalled her warm and affectionate embraces when they lay resting in the dark—when they came to Hestviken, they would sleep together in the great bed, as master and mistress of the house. Then he would be able to take her in his arms as often as he would, and every evening he could lie and talk to her of all that had happened to him that day, take counsel with her as to what he should do next. And he would no longer be forced to fear what he had hitherto dreaded as a misfortune—it would only increase their joy and their repute to have children. Then he would no longer be the last slender twig of a dying race; he would himself become the stem of the new tree.

Then it was that Asbjörn's words suddenly threw this new, unimagined thought into his mind. He had never thought it might fall to his lot to roam abroad and see the world. Far, far away—Valland,[6] Engelland, Denmark—they were all one to the boy, who, as long as he could remember clearly, had travelled no longer road than that between Frettastein and Hamar, had never dreamed of farther voyaging than out from Hestviken and back again with his trading craft. He had been willing to accept the fate prepared for him and had been content therewith—but that was before he had had any thought that it might be different. Now— It was as though he had been offered a gift—four years to look about him in the world and try his fortunes, see peoples and countries, and this just as he had found out what a small and out-of-the way corner of the world they were, these places which he had believed were all he was destined to see. And then there was this other thing, that he was said to come of such great folk on his mother's side—and they told him that now, just as the Steinfinnssons sought to make him a lesser man than they, and when it appeared that his kinsmen on his father's side either did not care or were not strong enough to defend his rights. But in Denmark he need only ride straight to the richest and mightiest knight's castle there was in the land and say to its master: "I am your sister Cecilia's son."—One evening Olav took out his mother's signet-ring and put it on his finger; he might as well wear it himself, till he was reconciled with Ingunn's kinsmen. And the little gold cross with the gilt chain he hung around his neck and hid on his breast under the shirt; he had heard his mother brought it with her from her home. Just as well to take good care of those things he had which might serve as tokens in case of need. Come what might, he would not be at a loss, even if his enemies set hidden snares for his feet, and his kinsmen in Norway availed him little.

The Steinfinnssons came to Hamar a few days later than they had been summoned. There were Kolbein with both his sons, Ivar Toresson, and a young nephew of the Toressons, Hallvard

6 Northern France.

Erlingsson. Hallvard's mother, Ragna, was full sister to Kolbein; she too was one of old Tore's children by his leman; and Hallvard had been but seldom at Frettastein, so Olav scarcely knew him. But he had heard it said that Hallvard was very stupid.

Olav was not allowed to be present at their audience with the Bishop; Arnvid said it was because his spokesmen had not come, and therefore Olav could not appear himself. It was not on *his* behalf that the Bishop was acting, but on that of the Church, which alone had the right to decide whether a marriage was valid or not. Olav did not like this, nor did he see the difference clearly. But both Arnvid and Asbjörn Priest had been present at the interview. They said that at first Kolbein and Ivar had been very headstrong. What angered them most was that the lord Torfinn had sent Ingunn out of the town, to a farm near Ottastad church. Kolbein said that here in the Upplands it had never been the custom to let the Bishop of Hamar rule like a petty king—'twas easy to see that the man came from Nidaros,[7] for there the priests did as they pleased in everything. Nevertheless it was surely an unheard-of thing that the Bishop should harbour a seduced maid who had run from her kinsmen to hide her shame and escape chastisement, or should throw his shield over the ravisher.

Bishop Torfinn answered that so far as he knew, Ingunn Steinfinnsdatter had neither run away nor been ravished by Olav Audunsson; but Arnvid Finnsson had brought the two young people hither and requested the Bishop to search out a matter that came under the jurisdiction of the Church and to retain Olav and the girl in the meantime. It was the brothers themselves who had asked Arnvid to stay at Frettastein and take charge of the estate and the children; when therefore he found out that Olav had outraged the elder daughter, he had called the man to account for his conduct. Then it came out that these two childish people had fancied that because their fathers had made a bargain about them when they were small, and both Steinfinn and Audun were now dead and gone, they themselves and none else were now to see that the agreement was kept and the bargain accomplished: wherefore they had cohabited as a married couple ever since Steinfinn's death, believing that they did no wrong in this. Arnvid had then taken the course of bringing these two to Hamar, in order that learned men might inquire how the case stood.

[7] The old name for the town of Trondhiem.

Tꜧe Aꝗe

One thing was certain: since Olav and Ingunn had given themselves to each other in the belief that they were fulfilling a marriage agreement, neither of them was now free to marry anyone
else. Equally certain was it that such a wedding was against the
law of the land and the commandments of the Church, and the
woman had forfeited her right to dowry, inheritance, and support of kinsfolk for herself and her child or children, if it should
prove that she had conceived. But from the man her sponsors
could claim fines for his infringement of their rights—and both
were under an obligation to do penance to the Church for not
having kept her commandments as to the proclamation of banns
and the due celebration of matrimony.

But now the Bishop bade the woman's uncles remember that
Olav and Ingunn were very childish, ignorant, and unlearned in
the law, and that they had grown up in the belief that they were
destined to be married. Tore Bring of Vik and two good franklins
besides had deposed before him, the Bishop, that Steinfinn Toresson had handselled his child Ingunn to Audun Ingolfsson as a wife
for Audun's son—they would make oath of this on the book. And
Arnvid testified that just before his death Steinfinn had spoken of
the agreement to Olav and said it was his wish that it should
hold good. Therefore he asked Ingunn's kinsmen to accept atonement on such terms as might be agreeable to all: that Olav and
Ingunn should fall at the feet of the Toressons and beg their
forgiveness, and that Olav should make amends for his self-willed
conduct according to the judgment of impartial men. But, this
being done, Bishop Torfinn deemed that it would best become the
Toressons if they were reconciled to Olav as good Christians and
great-minded men—let him possess the woman with such dowry
that the affinity would bring no shame to themselves, and Olav
would suffer no disgrace in his native place for having made a
marriage that did not add to his power and fortune. Finally the
Bishop bade the brothers bear in mind that it is a good deed and
specially pleasing in the eyes of God to care for fatherless children, but that to deprive such of their rights is one of the worst
of sins, a sin that cries aloud for vengeance even here on earth—
and it was the dead man's wish that their children should be given
to each other in marriage.

But if it were as they sought to prove, that Olav and Ingunn
had never been affianced in legal wise, and they could not agree

with Olav's guardians on the course to adopt, then it was clear
that they must bring a suit for fornication against the lad. And
in that case the Bishop would hand Ingunn over to them, that they
might punish her as they thought she deserved and divide her
part of the inheritance among her brothers and sister, and afterwards her kinsmen would have to support her as seemed fit to
them. But he himself would cause it to be published in all the
bishoprics of Norway that these two were not free to marry any
others, so long as both were alive—lest any third party, man or
woman, might fall into the sin of adultery by taking a husband
or a wife who was already bound in wedlock according to God's
ordinances.

This last hit the mark, both Arnvid and Asbjörn thought. Neither of the uncles had a mind to receive Ingunn if they were to
feed her and could never get her married off. Kolbein spoke at
length to the effect that Olav Audunsson had well known how
he and his brother regarded the betrothal and that they intended
to dispose of Ingunn in another way; but he promised at the last
that for the Bishop's sake he would make atonement with Olav.
As to the conditions, however, he would say nothing until all was
made plain about the old agreement and he had made tryst with
Ingolf Helgesson of Tveit or whichever of Olav's kinsmen it
might be who had authority to act on the boy's behalf. The
Bishop hinted that so much at least was certain, that *sponsalia de
futuro* had been made at that time at the Thing, so if only the
Toressons gave their consent to what was already accomplished,
Olav could act for himself; and then they would surely find him
very compliant. But to this Kolbein gave a flat no: they would
not take advantage of the boy's ignorance, but they claimed to
deal with Olav's kinsmen, that the case might end in honourable
and seemly fashion for them and their kinswoman.

10

THE NEXT evening Arnvid and Olav agreed to go down to the
convent. Arnvid had promised the brothers a gift of wool, and
Olav wished to speak to Brother Vegard about making confession to him one day. It was very dark outside, so they each took

a weapon. Olav had his axe, Kinfetch, which he carried whenever he had an opportunity.

When they came into the courtyard, they found it was later than they had thought; one of the monks, who had come out to look at the weather, said that the lay brother had already gone to ring the bell for complin. But Arnvid would fain have a word or two with Brother Helge. Ay, he would find him in the guest-room, said the monk. So they went thither.

The first they saw on entering were the sons of Kolbein and their cousin, Hallvard, with three other men; they sat on the inner bench, eating and drinking. Brother Helge and another monk stood on the outside, talking and laughing with them—the strangers were already very merry.

Olav stayed by the door while Arnvid went forward to Brother Helge. At that moment the convent bell began to ring.

"Sit down," said Brother Helge, "and taste our ale; 'tis uncommon good this time—then I will ask leave of the Prior to go and visit you after service. Sit down meanwhile, Arnvid!"

"Olav is with me," whispered Arnvid; he had to repeat it louder a couple of times, for Brother Helge was hard of hearing. When at last he understood, he went up to Olav and greeted him, bidding him sit down too and drink; and now the sons of Kolbein saw who was with Arnvid.

Olav answered the monk that he would rather go with him to the church and hear the singing, but Haftor Kolbeinsson called to him: "No, come here, Olav, and keep us company! We have not seen you since you were our brother-in-law. Come, Arnvid, sit down and drink!"

As Arnvid seated himself on the outer bench, Olav put away his axe and threw back his hood. As he came forward to take his seat. Einar clapped his hands together with a smile such as one gives to little children:

"Nay, how big you are grown, boy! Truly you begin to look like a married man already!"

"Oh, we were all as much married as Olav, I trow, when we were his age," sneered Hallvard.

Olav had turned red as fire, but he smiled scornfully.

Brother Helge shook his head, but he gave a little laugh. Then he bade them keep the peace. Haftor answered that they would do that sure enough, and the monks went out. Olav followed them

with his eyes, murmuring that after all he was more minded to go
to church.

"Oh no, Olav," said Einar. "That is discourteous—you must
not show so little zeal to make acquaintance with your wife's kin-
folk. Now let us drink," he said; he took the bowl that the lay
brother had placed on the table and drank to Olav.

"That was a heavy thirst you had on you," said Olav under his
breath. Einar was already half-drunken. Aloud he said: "Oh, acquainted we are already. And as to drinking to our closer kinship—methinks we could as well wait for that till I am agreed with
your father."

"It must be good enough when Father has agreed with the
Bishop," said Einar, bland as butter, "—since he has adopted you.
But 'tis a fine thing to see young people so quick to learn: do you
see now, sometimes it is proper to wait? They say Lord Torfinn
was so eloquent on patience in his Advent preaching—is that
where you learned your lesson?"

"Yes," replied Olav. "But you know 'tis a new word to me,
therefore I am so afraid I might forget it."

"Be sure I shall remind you," laughed Einar as before.

Again Olav made as though he would rise, but Arnvid pulled
him back onto the seat.

"Is that how you keep your promise to the good brothers?" he
said to Einar. "In this house we must keep the peace!"

"Nay, am I not peaceful? There is no harm in a little jesting
among kinsfolk, kinsman!"

"I knew not that I was among kinsfolk," muttered Arnvid with
vexation.

"What say you?"

Arnvid did not own kinship with Tore of Hof's offspring by
Borghild, his leman. But he checked himself—turned his eyes upon
the serving-men of the sons of Kolbein and upon the lay brother,
who was listening inquisitively as he moved about.

"There are many here who are not kinsmen—"

Haftor Kolbeinsson told his brother to keep his mouth shut:
"—though I think we all know Einar, all of us here, and are used
to his teasing ways when he is in drink. But now, Olav, 'tis time
you showed yourself a grown man—if you mean to set yourself
up and play the master, it will not do to let yourself be provoked
by Einar as when you were a little lad—crying with temper—"

"Crying—" Olav puffed with wrath; "I never did so! And playing the master—I trow there will be no play in it, when I go home and take over my property—"

"Nay, that's sure," said Haftor quietly.

Olav had a feeling that he had said something foolish; he turned scarlet again.

" 'Tis the chief manor in that country, Hestviken. 'Tis the biggest farm in all the parish."

"Nay, is it so?" said Haftor, imperturbably serious. "You will have much to answer for, young Olav—but you will be the man for it, sure enough. You know, brother-in-law, 'twill be worse with Ingunn, methinks. Can she cope with a mistress's duties on a great farm like that, think you?"

"We shall find a way. My wife herself will have no need to drudge," said Olav proudly.

"Nay, that's sure," said Haftor as before. "She is coming into great abundance, Ingunn, I see that."

"Oh, that may be saying too much—though Hestviken is no such small place. The shipping and fishery are the main things."

"Nay, is it so?" said Haftor. "Then you own much shipping too, down there in the Vik?"

Olav said: "I know not how it is with that—'tis so many years since I was at Hestviken. But in old days it was so. And now I mean to take it up again—I have followed Asbjörn Priest here and learned not a little of ships and trading."

"Meseems you could not possibly want *that*," said Einar with a smile. "With such great shipping as we saw you deal with—in Ingebjörg's goose-pond."

Olav rose and left the bench. They had only been making fun of him—Haftor too—he saw that.—That about shipping in the goose-pond was a game he had got up for Hallvard and Jon last summer, when the children of Frettastein were left so much to themselves.

"I cannot see that I demeaned myself in that," he said hotly, "if I carved some little boats for the children; none could think I was playing myself—" then he heard how silly and childish this sounded, and stopped suddenly.

"Nay, 'tis true," replied Einar; "that would be a very childish game for a boy who was already grown enough and bold enough to seduce their sister—'twas more manly work when you played with Ingunn in the outhouse and got her with child in the barn—"

" 'Tis a lie!" said Olav furiously. "The thrall's blood shows in you, when you use such foul talk of your own kinswoman. I know naught of a child either—but if 'tis as you say, you need not be afraid we shall ask your father to bring it up. We know that it is not to his liking—"

"Be silent now," said Arnvid; he had jumped up and gone to Olav's side. "And do you shut your mouths too"—he turned to the others. "Man's work, you said—do you call it man's work, after Kolbein has accepted atonement, that you sit here snarling like dogs? But you, Olav, should have more respect for yourself than to let them egg you on to barking with them."

But now the sons of Kolbein and Hallvard were on their feet—beside themselves with wrath at the last words Olav had spoken. Kolbein in his young days had freed himself by oath from the fathering of a child, but ill things had been said about the matter at the time, and as the boy grew up to manhood, 'twas thought he bore an ugly likeness to Kolbein.

"Hold your jaw yourself, Arnvid," said Haftor—he was fairly sober. " 'Tis true your share in this business is such that you had rather it were not talked about. But Olav must brook it, though I do not begrudge him atonement instead of the reward he deserves—he cannot expect us to embrace him as if he were *welcome* in our kin."

"Nay, *welcome* to our kin you will never be, my Olav," sneered Hallvard.

"Answer for yourselves, not for the kin," said Arnvid. "If that were so, think you Kolbein would have offered Olav your sister Borghild to wife instead of Ingunn, Hallvard?"

" 'Tis a lie!" shouted Hallvard.

"That may be," answered Arnvid. "But he told me that he meant to do so."

"Hold your jaw, Arnvid," Einar began again; "we all know of your friendship for Olav—'twill do you no good if we inquire into *that*. You keep nothing from this minion of yours—not even your own childish kinswoman for his leman—"

Arnvid leaned threateningly toward the other. "Have a care of your mouth now, Einar!"

"Nay, devil take me if I care for a rotten clerk. 'Tis a fine story, methinks, this friendship of yours for the lily-white boy. We have heard a tale or two, we have, of the kind of friendship you learn in the schools—"

Arnvid took Einar by both wrists and twisted them till the other fell on his knees with an oath and a groan of pain and rage. Then Haftor came between them.

The Kolbeinssons' house-carls sat as before, seeming little minded to meddle in the quarrel between the masters. Einar Kolbeinsson got on his feet again and stood rubbing his hands and arms, swearing heartily below his breath.

Olav stood looking from one to the other. He did not understand it quite, but felt as though a hand squeezed at his heart: he had brought Arnvid into a worse slough than he had guessed; they fell upon his friend with grievous insults, flayed him mercilessly. It hurt him to look into Arnvid's face, chiefly because he could not interpret what he saw in it. Then his anger flared up hotly, and all other feelings were burned up in its flame.

Einar found his voice again, now that he had his brother and cousin at his back. He said something—Olav did not hear the words. Arnvid's face seemed to knit together—then he drove his fist at Einar and caught him below the chin, so that the man fell backward at full length and crashed against the bench.

The lay brother had rushed in among the men; he helped Einar Kolbeinsson to his feet and wiped the blood from him, as he shouted to the others: "'Tis a banning matter, you know that, to break the peace in our house—is this fitting conduct for nobles?"

Arnvid recovered himself and said to Haftor: "Brother Sigvald is right. Now we will go, Olav and I—that is safest."

"Shall *we* go?" asked Olav sharply. "'Twas not we who started the quarrel here—"

"Let them end it who have kept their wits," said Arnvid curtly. "I shall give Einar his answer in a fitter place. To you, Haftor, I say that I can answer fully for my conduct in this matter—I *have* answered both the Bishop and Kolbein, and *you* are not concerned in it."

"You said you saw nothing of it," said Einar with a grimace; "and that may well be true, if 'tis as folk say—that you were a married man yourself for a full year before you guessed what your mother had given you a wife for—"

Olav saw Arnvid's face quiver—as when a man has a sudden knock on an open wound; he ran back and snatched his spear, which he had left standing by the door. Seized with insensate wrath on the other's behalf, Olav sprang between them—saw Einar swing an axe in the air and himself raised Kinfetch in both hands. He struck Einar's axe aside so that it rang and flew out of his hands, grazed Hallvard, who stood behind him, and fell to the floor. Olav raised Kinfetch once more and struck at Einar Kolbeinsson. Einar ducked to avoid the blow—it caught him on the back below the shoulder-blade, and the axe sank in deeply. Einar dropped and lay doubled up.

Now Kolbein's men had come to life—all three staggered out from the bench and thrust at the air with their weapons, but they were very drunken and seemed to have no great heart for a fight, though they yelled bravely. Hallvard sat on the bench holding his wounded leg, rocking to and fro and groaning.

Haftor had drawn his sword and made for the two; it was a rather short weapon and the others had axe and spear, so at first they only tried to keep Haftor from coming to close quarters. But soon they found this as much as they could do—the man was now quite sober and plied his sword with great skill; with a sullen determination to avenge his brother he took his aim, supple, swift, and sure in every muscle, with senses wide awake.

Olav defended himself, unaccustomed though he was to the use of arms in earnest—but there was a strange voluptuous excitement in this game, and in a vague way he felt acutely impatient every time Arnvid's spear was thrust forward to protect him.

Though aware in a way that the door had been opened to the night, he was yet overwhelmed with surprise when the Prior and several of the monks rushed in. The whole scene had not lasted many minutes, but Olav had a feeling of being roused from a long dream when the fight came to an end without his clearly knowing how.

It was fairly dark in the parlour now, as the fire on the hearth had burned low. Olav looked about him at the band of black and white monks—he passed his hand across his face once, let it drop, and stood leaning on his axe. He was now filled with astonishment that this thing had actually occurred.

Someone lighted a candle at the fire and carried it to the bench, where Brother Vegard and another of the friars were busy with

Einar. There was still life in him, and a sound came from him like the retching of a drunken man—Olav heard them say that the bleeding must be mostly *within*. Brother Vegard gave him such a queer look once—

He heard that the Prior was speaking to him, asking if it were he who first broke the peace.

"Yes, I struck first and cut down Einar Kolbeinsson. But the peace was but frail in here the whole evening—long before I broke it. At the last Einar used such shameful speech to us that we took to our weapons—"

"'Tis true," said the lay brother. He was an old countryman who had entered the convent only lately. "Einar spoke such words that in old days any man would have judged he died an outlaw's death by Olav's hand."

Haftor was standing by his brother; he turned and said with a cold smile: "Ay, so they will judge the murder in this house—and in the Bishop's. Since these two are the Bishop's men, body and soul. But mayhap the nobles of this land will soon be tired of such dishonour—that every priest who thinks he has authority uses it to shelter the worst brawlers and law-breakers—"

"That is untrue, Haftor," said the Prior; "we servants of God will not protect any evil-doer farther than he has protection in the law. But we are bound to do our best that law-breaking be punished according to law, and not avenged by fresh unlawfulness, which begets fresh vengeance without end."

Haftor said scornfully: "I call them dirty laws, these new laws. The old were better suited to men of honour—but 'tis true the new are better for such fellows as Olav there, who outrage the daughters of our best houses and strike down their kinsmen when they call them to account for their misdeeds."

The Prior shrugged his shoulders. "But now the law is such that the Sheriff must take Olav and hold him prisoner until the matter be brought to judgment. And here we have these men whom I sent for," he said, turning to some men-at-arms who, Olav knew, lived in the houses next the church. "Bjarne and Kaare, you must bind this young lad and carry him to Sir Audun. He has struck a man a blow that may give him his death."

Olav handed Kinfetch to one of the monks.

"You need not bind me," he said sharply to the strange men; "nay, lay no hands on me—I will go with you unforced."

"Ay, now you must go out in any case," said the Prior. "You can see that we cannot let *you* stay here—they are coming with Corpus Domini for Einar."

Outside, it had begun to snow again and there was much wind. The town had gone to rest more than an hour ago. The little band tramped heavily in the dark through drifts and loose snow between the churchyard wall and the low, black, timber houses of the canons; everything looked dreary and lifeless, and the wind howled mournfully about the walls and whistled shrilly in the great ash trees.

One of the watch went in front, and then came an old monk who was a stranger to Olav, but he knew him to be the subprior. Then walked Olav, with a man on each side of him and one behind, so close that he almost trod on his heels. Olav's mind was full of the thought that now he was a *prisoner*—but he was sleepy and strangely blunted and inert.

The Sheriff's house lay east of the cathedral. For a long time they had to stand in the drifts hammering on the locked door, while the snow worked through their clothes and turned the whole band white. But at last the door was opened and a sleepy man with a lantern in his hand came forward and asked what was the matter. Then they were admitted.

Olav had never been inside this gate. He could distinguish nothing in the darkness but driven snow between black walls. The Sheriff was away—had ridden out of town about midday in company with the Bishop, Olav heard in a half-dazed way—he was almost asleep as he stood. Reeling with tiredness, he let himself be led into a little house that stood in the yard.

It was bitterly cold inside and pitch-dark, with no fire on the hearth. In a few minutes some men came with a candle and bed-clothes, which they threw down upon the bedstead within. They bade him good-night, and Olav replied half-asleep. Then they went out and barred the door, and Olav was alone—suddenly wide awake. He stood staring at the little flame of the candle.

The first thing he felt was a kind of chill. Then his rage boiled up, with a defiant, voluptuous joy—so he had paid out that unbearable Einar Kolbeinsson—and God strike him if he rued it. He cared not, whatever his hastiness might cost him! Kolbein and those—how cordially he hated them! Now for the first time he saw how he had fallen off in these last months: his dread, his gnawing pains of conscience, all the humiliations he had been exposed to, while he was trying to find a way out of the slough in which he was sunk—it was Kolbein who had barred the way for him wherever he tried to get a firm foothold again. Had not that Kolbein crew stood in his path, he might long ago have been out of all this evil, free and safe, able to forget the painful feeling that he had been a false deceiver. But Kolbein had kept him under his thumb.—And now it was avenged—and he *thanked* God for it with all his heart. It mattered not that Bishop Torfinn and all these new friends of his said it was sinful to have such thoughts. A man's flesh and blood were not to be denied.

Olav's mind rose in revolt against all these new doctrines and thoughts he had come under in this place—ay, they were fine in a way, he saw that even now, but—no, no, they were unnatural, impossible dreams. *All* men could never be such saints as to consent to submit all their concerns, great and small, to the judgment of their even Christians, always being satisfied with the law and with *receiving* their rights—never *taking* them for themselves. He remembered that Haftor had said something of the same sort this evening—that these new laws were only good for the common people. And he felt at once that he was one with such as Kolbein and his sons, if only in this—he would rather take his case against them into his own hands, set wrong against wrong, if need were. His place was among such as Kolbein and Steinfinn and Ingebjörg —and Ingunn, who had thrown herself into his arms without a thought of the law, in the warmth of her self-willed love—not among these priests and monks, whose life was passed in clear and cool regularity, who every day did the same things at the same times: prayed, worked, ate, sang, lay down to sleep, and got up again to begin their prayers. And they inquired into the laws, copied them out and discussed their wording, and disagreed among themselves and came into conflict with laymen about the laws—all because they loved this law and dreamed that by its means all folk might be tamed, till no man more would bear arms against his neighbour or take his rights by force, but all would be quiet and willing to listen to our Lord's new and gentle tidings of brotherhood among all God's children.—He felt a kind of distant, melancholy affection for all this even now, a respect for the men who thought thus—but *he* was not able always to bow beneath the law, and the very thought that they would slip these bonds about *himself* filled him with violent loathing.

It added to his rebellious feeling that he was dimly sure they now must look upon *him* as an outlaw. Bishop Torfinn could not possibly have any more love for him after the way he had repaid his fatherly kindness. And all the preaching friars had looked on him with such eyes—they must be full of resentment at his defiling their parlour with a man's blood. The old subprior had said something about repentance and penance before he went out just now. But Olav was not in any mood for repentance.

It must cost what it might. He ought never to have listened to Arnvid, never come hither, never let himself be parted from Ingunn.

Ingunn, he thought, and his longing for her came up in him as an incurable torment—she was the only one on earth whom he really knew and was allied to. Ingunn, such as she was and not otherwise, weak and obstinate, short of wit, alluring and tender and warm—she was the only one in the knowledge of whom he was quite secure; the only one of all his possessions that he could take and feel and see and own as something apart from unreal dreams and words and uncertain memories. But *she* was actually as his own body and his own soul, and now he cried out with her, silently, as he bent double, gnashed his teeth, and clenched his hands till the nails ran into the flesh. At the thought of how far he was from her now, and what chance he now had of getting her, all his desire blazed up, so that he moaned aloud and bit his own clenched fists. He would go to her, he would have her now at once, he was ready to tear her to pieces and eat her up in terror lest anyone should drag them apart.—"Ingunn, Ingunn," he groaned.

He *must* find her. For he must tell her what had happened—find out how she would take it, that he had killed her cousin. Ay, for Einar would die, of that he was sure, there was blood between them now, but, Holy Mary! what could that do, when they two were already one flesh? She was not fond of these sons of Kolbein, but kin is kin, and so she would weep and mourn, his poor darling—and yet he could not wish it were undone. And then he must find out whether it were with her as Einar had said—ah, then she would suffer cruelly indeed.—Olav was shaken by a short, dry sob. Kolbein, who had demanded that she be handed over to him for punishment—but if she fell into his hands, and if she proved with child by his son's slayer—then they would surely torture her to death.

He must speak with Arnvid about this—Arnvid would surely seek him out in the morning. Arnvid must get her away to some place where Kolbein could not reach her.

The candle was but a thin wick wound about an iron spike. Olav was not afraid of the dark at most times, but now he dreaded the light's going out and leaving him in the dark with his thoughts. With a cautious hand he trimmed the wick.

In a moment he threw off his cloak, his boots, and the fine kirtle and leaped into the bed. He buried himself in the icy-cold bedclothes and dug his face into the pillow, moaning for Ingunn. He remembered Christmas Night and felt a sort of resentment against providence: was this his reward for having done what was right that evening!

He drew the skins right over his head—so he would be spared seeing when the light burned out. But soon he threw them off again, rested his face in his hand, and lay staring at the little flame.

Ay, Arnvid was the only one he could ask to protect Ingunn, when he could not do so himself.—And all at once he had such a strange dislike of the thought of Arnvid.

He had not understood what Einar meant by the insults he flung at Arnvid, but so much he saw, that Arnvid felt them like a kick on an open wound; and whenever he thought of it, it turned him sick at first, then beside himself with rage; it was as though he had been witness to a nameless piece of brutality.

He had gradually become aware that he was very far from knowing Arnvid thoroughly. He relied on him, more than on any other person he had met—on his generosity, his loyalty; he knew that Arnvid would fear nothing when it was a question of helping a friend or kinsman. But there was something about Arnvid Finnsson which made him think of a tarn with unfathomable deeps.— Or—Asbjörn All-fat had told a story one evening, of a learned doctor in the southern lands who wooed a lady, the fairest in that country. At last she made as though he should have his will; she led him secretly into her bower, loosened her clothing, and let him see her breasts. One of them was white and fair, but of the other naught was left but a putrid sore. The other hearers praised this tale greatly and called it good and instructive—for Raimond, the learned man, turned his heart altogether from the world after this sight and betook him to a cloister. But Olav thought it the most loathsome story he had ever heard, and he lay awake till far into the night and could not get it out of his head. But there was something about Arnvid which made him afraid—that one day he would see something like this in his friend, some hidden sore. But in secret he had always shrunk most painfully at the sight of sickness and suffering—could scarce bring himself to do anyone a hurt. And Olav had a vague suspicion that it might be the fear of being touched on a sore point that had paralysed Arnvid so strangely in the autumn. Now he came near to wishing that Arnvid had not been so meek, but called him to account earlier. He did not like the thought that he had taken advantage of a man's defencelessness. And here he lay, with the knowledge that he would be forced to ask Arnvid to have a care of Ingunn and protect her, whatever consequences his rash deed might involve; since God alone knew when he would be in a position to do so himself.

In a way Olav saw something of what ailed Arnvid. Arnvid had never made it a secret that his most heart-felt wish had always been to devote himself to the service of God in holy orders. And after this time he had spent in Hamar Olav guessed better than before that a man could wish that. But he suspected that there were more windings in Arnvid's brain than—well, than in Asbjörn All-fat's or Brother Vegard's, for instance. Arnvid longed to submit himself, to obey and to serve—but at the same time he had a sort of fellow-feeling with the men who demanded that the other law should hold: the law for men with fleshly hearts, hot blood, and vengeful minds. It was as though at some time Arnvid had been badly crushed between the two laws.

It had impressed Olav that Arnvid never spoke of the years he had been married. From other quarters he had heard this and that about Arnvid's marriage: Tordis, his wife, had first been promised to the eldest of the Finnssons, Magnus—a scapegrace, but of merry disposition, well liked and a remarkably handsome man. She had certainly been bitterly disappointed with the one she got instead—but there was no doubt Arnvid had had no great love for his wife either. Tordis was proud and quarrelsome; she made no secret of despising her husband because he was so young, quiet-mannered, and rather shy among folk. With the mother-in-law she lived in open conflict. Arnvid must have had a joyless youth between these two imperious, quarrelling women. Doubtless it was for that he now seemed to avoid all women—except Ingunn. Of her he was intensely fond, Olav saw, and this must have been because Ingunn was so weak, had need of men to defend and support her, and had never a thought of ruling over them and giving them orders. Often Arnvid would sit lost in thought, looking at her with such strange sadness, as though pitying her.—But that was a weakness of Arnvid, that he seemed too much given to pitying— animals, for instance. Olav was kind to animals himself—but the way Arnvid could nurse and tend a sick creature— 'Twas strange, too, how often it mended and thrived when Arnvid took in hand a sick animal. Even his dead wife—the two or three times Olav had heard Arnvid speak of her, it struck him that the man felt pity for her.

But lately Olav had felt a growing ill will toward Arnvid for being so ready to show compassion. Olav knew he was not free from this weakness himself, but now he saw it to be a fault: it might so easily make a man soft and cause him to give way before those who were harder of heart.

Olav sighed, weary and at a loss. It made him so sad to think of all those he had loved—Bishop Torfinn, Arnvid, Ingunn. But when he called to mind Einar Kolbeinsson and his enemies, he was *glad* he had done it, in spite of it all—nay, repent he *could* not. But he could not bear being parted from Ingunn now.—He had reached an utter deadlock.

The candle was almost burned out; Olav crept up and carefully wound the last of the wick. He went to the door and scanned it closely—not that he had any hope of being able to escape, but he felt he must.

It was a heavy, solid door, but it did not shut tight—a deal of snow had drifted in. He brought the light: there seemed to be a big lock on the outside and a wooden bar, but there was no part of the lock on the inside, only a withy handle nailed on. Olav drew his dagger and tried it in the crack of the door. Then he noticed that the key had not been turned in the lock; the door was only bolted with the wooden bar, and he could move that a little with his dagger—only a little, for the bar was big and heavy and the blade of his dagger was thin.

But he was all on fire—his hands were trembling as he put on his boots and outer garments. He could not give up, when once he had found he was not locked in. He took his dagger in both hands and tried to force the bolt upward. At the first attempt the blade broke off in the middle. Olav clenched his teeth and thrust the rest of the blade into the crack right up to the handle. Then there was not room to work the dagger in the narrow crack. Sweating with excitement he coaxed it till he found how far in he could get the dagger—and then to bend it up and lift the bar. Several times he knew he had got it out of the catch, but it fell in again when he let go with one hand to pull the door-handle. But at last he did it.—The snow burst in upon him; he stepped quietly across the threshold and looked out into the night.

No sign of dogs—they must have shut them indoors for the weather. Not a sound but the infinitely fine whistling of dry, powdery snow blown by the wind. Slowly and cautiously Olav worked his way in the dark across the unknown courtyard. In a heap of snow by one of the houses stood a number of skis. Olav chose a pair and went on.

The gate to the street was shut, but close beside it a load of timber had been left. From that he could slip over the paling. He began to believe a miracle was taking place. He climbed the pile and dropped the skis over the fence—heard the soft sound as they fell into the snowdrift outside. "Mother!" he thought—"perhaps it is my mother who is praying for me, that I may get away."

It was awkward with his loose cloak and long kirtle, but he succeeded in getting over and dropped into the snow out in the street. He kilted up his kirtle as high as he could with the belt and bound the skis fast to his feet; then he threw his body forward and set out against the driving snow, which flecked the darkness with streaks of white.

As soon as he reached the end of the town, the road was lost in drifts. Only here and there he made out the tops of the fences, now that his eyes were used to the dark. But he kept on, with the snow in his face almost all the time. It was perfectly impossible to distinguish any road-marks on a night like this, though he knew the farm where she was; he had ridden past it many times on the highway in company with Asbjörn, but that would not help him in this weather. He was as good a ski-runner as the best, but the going was very heavy. Nevertheless he was undaunted and toiled on blindly—he was so certain of being helped tonight. It scarcely crossed his mind that he was quite unarmed—the dagger was useless now—and that he had no more than five or six ducats in money. But he was altogether dauntless.

He did not know what time of night it might be when at last he dragged himself into the yard of the farm where Ingunn lay. Here indeed the dogs were awake—a whole pack of them rushed out at him, barking ferociously. He kept them off with a pole he had picked up on the way, and shouted the while. At last someone appeared in a doorway.

"Is Ingunn Steinfinnsdatter within? I must speak with her instantly—I am Olav Audunsson, her husband."

The short winter day was already sinking and the grey dusk gathering over the snow-covered land as two sledges with worn-out horses drove into the little farm near Ottastad church. The three fur-clad strangers stood awhile talking to the master of the house.

"Ay, she sits within in the room," he said. "Her man is yet in bed, I wis—he came hither at early morn, and then they lay and talked in whispers—our Lord and Saint Olav know what there may be between them, the way they bore themselves—I fell asleep and left them to it—" he scratched his head and looked at the three with shrewd inquiry. Asbjörn Priest he knew well, and the others were Arnvid Finnsson from Miklebö, the woman's kinsman, who had been here more than once and spoken with her, and his old henchman.

The three strode into the room. Ingunn was sitting on the step below the farther bed; she held some sewing work in her lap, but it was too dark for her to sew in that corner. She rose at once on seeing who had come, and went toward them, tall and slender in her black garb, pale and dark-eyed under her woman's coif.

"Hush," she bade them in a low voice, "go quietly—Olav is asleep!"

"Ay, then 'tis time you wake him, little woman," said Asbjörn Priest. "Too much wit I never thought the boy was burdened with, but this is worse than the worst. Can he not guess they will search for him here first of all?—and here he lies asleep!" The priest neighed in his anger.

Ingunn posted herself in the men's way. "What would you with Olav?"

"We wish him no ill," said Arnvid; "but the way he has marred all— You must come with me now, Ingunn, and stay with me at Miklebö, for you can guess that now the lord Torfinn can hardly refuse to give you back to your kinsfolk."

"And what of Olav?" she asked as before.

The priest gave a despairing groan: "She there—is't not the very mischief that he should fly straight hither? She there will never keep a close mouth with what she hears."

"Oh yes, she will. When she sees it is for Olav's good. Ingunn, you must know that this priest here, and I too, we run no small risk in concealing a homicide and helping him to get away."

"I shall know how to hold my peace," said Ingunn seriously. She stepped aside and went up to the bed, where she stood for a moment looking at the sleeper like a mother who has not the heart to wake her child.

The priest thought: "Ah yes, she is fair after all." It seemed to him that these women for whom young boys committed folly and sin were seldom such that a sober and sapient man could see anything goodly in them. And for her here he had had uncommonly little liking: this Ingunn Steinfinnsdatter had the look of a slothful, loose-minded woman, feeble and cosseted, useful for nothing but to make trouble and strife among men. But now, he thought, perchance she was better after all than he had deemed her, she might even make a good wife, when she grew older and steadier of mind. In any case she had conducted herself like a person of sense, and she looked on her friend as though she loved him faithfully. And fair she was, he had to admit they were right who said so.

Olav looked very young and innocent as he lay asleep with his white, muscular arms under his neck and his fair hair spread over the brown woollen pillow. He slept as soundly as a child. But the moment Ingunn took hold of his shoulder and woke him, he started up wide awake, drew up his feet, and sat up in the bed with his arms clasping his knees as he looked calmly at the two men.

"Have you come hither to fetch me?"

"Arnvid has come to take your wife home with him. I—" The priest looked round at the others. "I think you must let me speak with Olav alone first."

Arnvid took Ingunn by the hand and led her to a seat at the farther end of the room. Asbjörn All-fat sat down on the bed beside Olav. Olav asked earnestly: "What says Lord Torfinn to this? An ill chance it is that I should repay his hospitality so badly."

"Ah, there you spoke a truer word than you know yourself. And therefore you must now see that you betake yourself yet farther, out of the land."

"Shall I fly out of the land?" asked Olav slowly. "Uncondemned—? Does Lord Torfinn say I must do this?"

"Nay, I say it. The Bishop and the Sheriff can scarce have heard of the slaying yet—ay, Einar is dead—we look not to see them home before tomorrow. And I made Audun's folk understand that, since they could not hold you better, they ought to keep Kolbein ignorant of your flight till the Sheriff himself could tell him. They are out searching for you now, but with this heavy going they cannot have come so far out as this, and now it will soon be night. Whatever betide, we must venture it, in God's name—we stay here till the moon is up, a little after midnight—'tis clearing up outside and freezing. Old Guttorm will go with you and show the way. Swift ski-runners such as you are should reach Solberga by the evening of the third day. There you must stay with my sister no longer than is necessary and keep in hiding till Sven Birgersson finds you a lodging somewhere in the neighbourhood."

"But can this be wise, to fly the country before I have been condemned to it?" asked Olav.

"Since you have taken wings, you must fly on," said the priest. "Will you have folk say of you that you broke out of prison merely to come hither and fondle your wife? Nay, you need not look at me so madly because I say this to you.—Young you are and bull-headed, and little thought have you beyond your own affairs; such is the nature of your age. And maybe you have not thought that a man like Lord Torfinn may have many matters on hand of greater moment than that you should enjoy your Ingunn and her goods in peace. And you came with this suit of yours at an inconvenient time—hardly could you have found a worse time to trouble the Bishop with your concerns—"

"Ay, 'twas Arnvid's counsel, not mine," Olav interrupted.

"Oh, Arnvid! He is as ill-timed as you, when it is a question of this frail wisp of a woman. But as I told you, Olav, we must now order it so that the Bishop shall not have to deal with this case of manslaughter too; here your kinsmen must come forward, and it will be their affair to obtain leave for your return, so that you may buy your peace in the lands of Norway's King."

"I wonder," said Olav pondering. "I scarce think Bishop Torfinn will like it that I go off in this way."

"No, he will not," said the priest curtly. "And it is for that I will have you do it. These new men, who rule the realm for our little King, are making ready for open war against Holy Church—and the lord Torfinn must have his hands free of such suits as yours. Had you been shut up in Mjös Castle, he would have leaped into the saddle for your sake—because you have sought his help and because you have few friends, and the lord Torfinn is so saintly and a true holy father to all the fatherless—and withal he is obstinate and headstrong as a he-goat; that is his chief fault. But I expect you to understand this: you have sought his protection *once*, and you were given it, and after that you disgraced yourself as you have done. 'Twould not be very manly of you to ask more of him now, knowing that you add to his difficulties thereby."

Olav nodded in silence. He stood up and began to dress.

"It will be more difficult for us now," he said quietly, "for Ingunn and me—to be brought together."

"At the last I trow her kinsmen will tire of having to keep her—when she is neither rightly married nor unmarried," said the priest. "But you two can surely wait a few years now."

Olav contracted his brows, looking straight before him. "That we have promised each other last night—we shall keep the troth we plighted to each other, and I shall come back to her, alive or dead."

"That was an ungodly promise," said Asbjörn dryly. "But 'tis as I thought.—It is an easy matter, Olav, to be a good Christian so long as God asks no more of you than to hear sweet singing in church, and to yield Him obedience while He caresses you with the hand of a father. But a man's faith is put to the test on the day God's will is not his. But now I will tell you what Bishop Torfinn said to me one day—it was of you and your suit we were speaking. 'God grant,' he said, 'that he may learn to understand in time that whoso is minded to do as he himself wills will soon enough see the day when he will find he has done that which he had never willed.' "

Olav looked earnestly before him. Then he nodded: "Ay. That is true. I know it."

They took some food, and awhile after, they lay down in their clothes, all but Arnvid; he offered to watch. He sat beside the hearth, reading softly from a book he had brought in his travelling-wallet. Now and again he went out of doors to see the time. It had cleared now and the stars sparkled densely over the whole vault of heaven—it was freezing hard. Once he knelt down and prayed with his arms stretched out in the form of a cross.

At last he saw that the light of the rising moon was growing over the top of the ridge. He turned and went in, to the bed where Olav and Ingunn slept together, cheek to cheek. He roused the man: "Now it is near time you were gone."

Olav opened his eyes, gently freed himself from the woman's arms, and at once got out of bed. He was fully clad, all but his boots and outer garment. He now drew on his footgear and a coat of reindeer-skin; Arnvid had provided clothing more suited to a long journey on skis than the kirtle and the red cordwain boots, which had suffered badly on the night before.

"This Guttorm of mine knows his way everywhere about here on both sides of the border," said Arnvid. This was Arnvid's old henchman, his foster-father he might be called, who was to act as guide for Olav. Arnvid handed Olav his own sword, a spear, and a purse of money. "We will say that you have sold me your horse Elk—you know I have always wished he was mine."

"So be it."

"That foul talk Einar came out with—" muttered Arnvid hesitatingly as he looked down into the fire. "He was always ill-natured and a liar— And a lecherous goat himself, and never guessed that other men may—may turn sick at what he—"

Olav cast down his eyes, mortally embarrassed. He understood not a word.

"I was fain you should have Ingunn, for I believed you would be good to her.—Will you swear, Olav, never to desert my kinswoman?"

"Yes. And I may rely that you will hold your hand over her? Did I not know that I can feel safe leaving her in your care, I would never in this world do as Asbjörn says and fly to Sweden. But I know you are fond of her—"

"I am." Arnvid burst out laughing. He struggled against it, but could not stop; he trembled with suppressed giggling till the tears ran down his cheeks. At last he sat doubled up and laughed till he shook, with his arms on his knees and his head buried in them. Olav stood by, profoundly uncomfortable.

"Nay—now you and Guttorm must be gone." Arnvid pulled himself together, wiped the tears of laughter from his face, and stood up. He went and called the three others.

Olav and old Guttorm stood out in the yard, with their skis bound fast to their feet, well armed, and furnished with all they required. The three others stood before the door of the house as Ingunn went up to Olav and gave him her hand. He shook it hard, and they spoke together, a few words, in low tones. She was calm and altogether self-possessed.

The waning moon had soared up into the sky high enough to cast long, uncertain shadows across the heaped-up drifts of the snow-field.

"In the forest the going will be fine, I trow," the priest encouraged them.

Olav turned and glided back to his two friends who stood at the door. He shook hands with them too and thanked them handsomely for their help. Then he faced about. Arnvid Finnsson and Asbjörn stood watching the two, Olav Audunsson and his guide, as they glided over the long stretch of fields toward the forest with powerful, dogged strokes. Then they passed into the shadow at the edge of the woods.

"Ay, *laus Deo*," said the priest. "So ill is it that this is the best. I was afraid Ingunn would break out into a fit, shriek and howl at the last minute."

"Oh no," said Arnvid. He looked up at the moon with a strangely frolicsome smile. " 'Tis only in trifles that she takes on like that. When serious matters are at stake, she is as good as gold."

"Say you so?—ay, you should know her better than I," said Asbjörn Priest unconcernedly. "Now it is we two, Arnvid. This may prove a dear jest for us, that we have helped Olav Audunsson to get away."

"Ay, but there was no other way."

"No." The priest shook his head. "But I wonder whether Olav has any notion that you and I have risked *much* by helping him in this?"

"Nay, have you lost your wits?" said Arnvid, and the waves of laughter heaved up in him again. "You surely know he has no notion of what *anything* costs, at his age."

Asbjörn All-fat gave a little laugh; then he yawned. And the three, the priest, the other man, and the woman, went in and lay down again.

PART TWO

Ingunn Steinfinnsdatter

FTER Olav Audunsson's flight Bishop Torfinn said he no
longer had the right to keep back Ingunn Steinfinnsdatter
from her uncles. But Arnvid Finnsson answered that the
woman was sick and he could not send her away. Lord Torfinn
was very angry when he learned that Arnvid too refused to bow
to the law further than it suited himself. And now the Bishop
sought to order matters so that Ingunn should go to her father's
sister at Berg; but Arnvid said that she was utterly unfit for any
journey.

On their side Kolbein Toresson and Haftor were beside themselves with wrath that Olav had escaped, and they said the Bishop
certainly had had a finger in it—though the lord Torfinn had been
away from the town when the slaying was done and did not return home till after the slayer had fled—and though Arnvid Finnsson made known that it was he who had helped Olav over to
Sweden. When it came out that Asbjörn All-fat had been privy
to the matter and that the fugitive had been received by the
priest's sister, who was married in Sweden, Lord Torfinn was so
indignant that he sent Asbjörn away from him for a time, after
the priest had bought his peace for his part in the affair. But although no man seriously believed that the Bishop had been a party
to Olav's flight, there were many who counted him to blame in
that one of his priests had broken the law, connived with an outlaw, and helped him to safety.

The Sheriff proclaimed Olav's outlawry, and then at last Helge
of Tveit and his sons came forward and offered on Olav's behalf to make amends for the slaying according to the judgment
of good men and true at the Thing. However, these men were not
Olav's nearest kinsmen; they were descended from a brother of
his great-grandfather, and the two branches, that of Tveit and

that of Hestviken, had held little intercourse through the years.
The old man at Hestviken was Olav's true guardian. It was therefore a long and difficult matter for Olav's spokesmen to accom-
plish anything in his case, and as Bishop Torfinn had to journey
to Björgvin on another errand in the course of the spring, he let
Jon Helgesson of Tveit go thither in his company, in order that
he might beg permission of the King for Olav to return to the
country.[1]

Kolbein demanded that Olav should be declared a felon. What
could it be but a felony? he maintained—Olav had debauched
Kolbein's niece in her father's house and afterwards struck down
the girl's cousin when he called Olav to account for his misdeed.
As his spokesmen at Björgvin, Kolbein chose the knight Gaut
Torvardsson and his son Haakon. Sir Gaut was a kinsman of
Baron Andres Plytt; Lord Andres sat in the council that was to
govern Norway while the King was under age, and he was one of
the leaders of those nobles who were now determined to join issue
with the prelates over the rights and liberties of the Church. It
appeared that these were the men on whose support the Toressons
had relied, and Haakon Gautsson was to have had Ingunn to wife.

Then once more the Bishop of Hamar took upon himself to
plead Olav's cause. He insisted that it was impossible to charge
Olav with rape if he had taken Ingunn to himself in good faith
in an old betrothal, and Ivar and Kolbein had already promised
to grant Olav atonement on this score when the man had the misfortune to kill Einar in a brawl, as they sat drinking with several
other men in the preaching friars' guest-house at Hamar. He said
it would be the direst injustice if Olav were not accorded the
same mercy as any other man who became a homicide—be given
grace to remain at home and security for his possessions, if he was
willing to pay weregild to the King and blood-fine to Einar Kolbeinsson's heirs. Although, for that matter, in every parish of
Norway might be found men who had manslaughters or other
outlawry charges hanging over them sitting safely on their estates with royal letters of grace—nay, those who thought them-

---

[1] "When a man had committed any offence punishable with outlawry
(such as manslaughter or the abduction of a woman), he might, on making
a payment to the Crown, be given leave to remain at his home under the
protection of the law till his case was judged."—(Note to *The Mistress of
Husaby*.)

selves powerful enough stayed calmly on without such letters. But then it must be plain to every man that it was beyond measure unjust if harsher treatment were meted out to Olav, who was so young that, had it not been for the last amendment of the law under their late lord, King Magnus, none could have done him any worse thing than order him to leave the country and stay abroad until he was of age. And Olav had at once sent word to Kolbein through Arnvid Finnsson and Asbjörn All-fat that he was quite willing to pay the fine for the slaughter.

Olav had entered Norway again at Whitsuntide down in Elvesyssel, near Mariaskog convent. He owned a small farm there which he held on udal tenure, and some shares in other farms; this estate had come to the men of Hestviken with the wife of Olav's grandfather, Ingolf Olavsson. Here no one attempted to seize him, but the King's officers let him stay in peace till far on in the autumn—it was a long way from the parts frequented by Olav's enemies. But when proclamation was made in the autumn that Olav Audunsson's goods in the north had been attached—the movables he had left behind him in the Upplands and his estate in the Vik, save only his udal lands—Olav left the country for the second time, and now he sailed southward to Denmark.

At Miklebö, Mistress Hillebjörg had given Ingunn Steinfinnsdatter a good reception. She had liked Olav, the little she had seen of him, and she liked him no less for having made an inroad on the brood of Tore's leman. She treated her son with more kindness than she was wont, and when a suit of outlawry was brought against Arnvid for having helped Olav, she laughed and patted him on the shoulder. " 'Twas none too soon either, my son, that you too had a taste of the law; I never liked your meek ways."

She was gentler with the sick young woman than Arnvid had ever seen her with anyone. Ingunn was no more than moderately well; she was so troubled with giddiness that when she got out of bed in the morning, she had to stand a long while holding on to something, for the room turned round with her, and dark mists came before her eyes, so that she could not see. If she had to stoop and pick up anything from the floor, this mist came on and blinded her for a long time. She could not take food, and she fell away and grew thin, till she was pale to the very corners of her eyes. Hillebjörg brewed drinks for her, which were to remedy her affliction—but Ingunn could not keep these either. The old woman laughed and consoled her—'twas known such sickliness endured but for its time, and soon she would feel better. Ingunn made no reply when the mistress jested in this way, but bent her head and tried to hide the tears that filled her eyes. Otherwise she never wept, but was very quiet and patient.

She was not fit to perform the smallest piece of work, but sat with a ribbon in her hand, sewing a border of fine flowers and animals. Or else she was making the linen shirt she had cut out while she was at Hamar. She had always been skilful at fine needlework, and she put all her art and industry into this shirt, which Olav was to have when he came home; but the work went but slowly. Or she made playthings for Arnvid's sons, wove them breastplates of straw, feathered their arrows, and made bats and balls that were better than any they had had before. It was because she had always played with boys that she could do this so well, she told Arnvid. Olav had taught her this. She sang to the children and told them stories and rhymes, and she seemed to be of better cheer when caring for these three little lads—she would gladly have had one of the children on her knees always. Magnus was five years old now, and the twins, Finn and Steinar, nearly four. Magnus and Finn were strong, romping little fellows and did not care so much to be fondled by women, but Steinar was weaker and took a fancy to Ingunn. So she led the boy with her wherever she went, carried him in her arms, and took him to her bed at night. Steinar was also his father's favourite, and Arnvid often sat with Ingunn in the evening, while the child played on her lap, and he sang to them till the little one fell asleep with his head resting on Ingunn's bosom. Then she whispered to him to be quiet, and sat in silence, gazing before her and down at the sleeping child, kissed the boy's hair softly, and gazed into vacancy again.

But as it drew on toward summer, it became clear that there was no natural cause for Ingunn's disorder, and no one could guess what ailed her.

Arnvid wondered whether it could be sorrow alone that had broken her down so completely—for she grew no better, but rather worse: the fainting-fits gained upon her, and often she fell into a swoon, all the food she tried to eat came up again, and she complained of constant pains in the back across her hips, as though she had had a heavy blow with a stick—and there was such a queer feeling in her legs, as though they were withered; she was scarcely able to walk any more.

She longed for Olav day and night, Arnvid could see that, and then there was her sorrow over her parents, which had now come upon her again; for a while she had half forgotten it on Olav's account. But now she accused herself bitterly for this, saying she had thrown away by her fault a happiness that bade fair to be hers: "The night that mother died I became Olav's wife!"

A strange look came over Arnvid's face as she said this, but he held his peace.

She grieved also at being parted from her brothers and sister. Tora was at Berg with her aunt, and though there had never been any very warm affection between Ingunn and Tora, she now longed for her sister. But it was far sadder to think of her two young brothers; with them she had always been good friends, but now they were at Frettastein with Haftor and his young wife—and now of course Hallvard and Jon would be brought up in hatred of Olav Audunsson and anger with her.

She spoke of all this to Arnvid, without many tears—but it was almost as though she were too hopeless and heavy of heart to be able to weep. Arnvid wondered whether she would die of grief.

But Mistress Ingebjörg hinted that this sickness that had fallen upon Ingunn was so strange as almost to persuade her it was the work of some *guile*.

One evening at the beginning of summer Arnvid was able to coax Ingunn to walk down with him to look at the corn that was coming up so finely in the fair weather. He had to support her as she walked, and he saw that she moved her feet as though they were hindered by invisible fetters. He had got her as far as the edge of the wood when she suddenly sank to the ground and lay in a swoon. At long last he succeeded in bringing her back to life; so long he thought her fits had never lasted before. She could not stand on her feet, so he had to carry her in as one carries a child. She was so thin and weighed so little that he was quite scared.

Next morning it proved that she could not move her legs—the lower part of her body was quite paralysed. At first she lay moaning softly—the pains in her back were so grievous. But as the days went by they passed off, and now her body seemed to be entirely without feeling, from the waist downward. In this state she remained. She never complained, spoke but little, and often seemed absent from all around her. The only thing she asked for was to have Steinar with her, and when he crept up into the bed and played and frolicked over her half-dead body, which was now wasted to a skeleton, she appeared to be content.

During this time none knew where Olav was. Arnvid thought that Ingunn must surely die, and he could send no word to Olav of how matters were with her.

But Mistress Hillebjörg now said aloud to everyone she spoke with that it was certain someone had put the sickness upon Ingunn by witchcraft. She had stuck pins into the woman's thighs and calves and burned her with red-hot irons, but Ingunn felt nothing; she could bring witnesses to this, men and women of good repute and her parish priest and her son. But there was none beside Kolbein and Haftor who could be suspected of this misdeed. And here lay the unhappy child, wasting away and slowly dying. Now therefore she charged her son that he should call upon the Bishop to take up the matter and inquire into it.

Arnvid came near believing his mother had guessed rightly, and he promised to go to the lord Torfinn, as soon as the Bishop came home from his visitation. Meanwhile he made Ingunn speak to the priest and make her confession, and he had masses said for her. Thus the time passed till the birthday of our Lady.[2]

That day Arnvid had confessed and taken *corpus Domini*, and during mass he had prayed for his sick kinswoman so long and so earnestly that he was all in a sweat. It was past noonday before the church folk from Miklebö came home. Arnvid stood talking to Guttorm about his horse Elk, which had fallen lame as he rode homeward, when he heard loud cries for help from the room in which Ingunn lay.

He and Guttorm dashed headlong to the room. There they saw Ingunn, running barefoot and in her shift and tramping on the floor—the room was full of smoke and the straw was alight among the rugs she had thrown upon it. She held Steinar in her arms; he was wrapped in the bedspread, shrieking and wailing.

When the others came in, she sank down on the bench, kissing

[2] September 8.

and fondling the boy and trying to lull him: "Steinar, Steinar, my darling, now you will soon be better, now I will make you so well, my little one!" She called to the others that Steinar had burned himself and they must bring her cloths and ointment at once.

She had been lying alone, and Steinar was in the room with her; he had been sitting by the hearth, where a tiny fire was burning, and although the woman in the bed told him he must not, he had played with it, sticking dry twigs into the fire and letting them burn. The day was warm, and the boy had nothing on but a shirt—all at once the fire caught it. Then Ingunn knew no more till she was standing by the hearth with the child in her arms; she had put out the fire in his shirt by throwing the coverlet about him; but now she saw that the rushes with which the floor was strewed were burning, and so she threw down the cushions from the benches and trampled the fire as she cried for help.

The boy had been burned about the body, but Ingunn too had ugly burns on her legs and on the under side of both arms. But she heeded nothing but Steinar; they were not allowed to bind her wounds until the child had been tended, and then she laid him in her bed and lay watching over him, fondling and wheedling the poor little thing. And as long as the boy had fever and pain from his burns, she gave no thought to other things.

The palsy had slipped from her—she herself seemed scarce aware of it. She ate and drank what they brought her, greedily and unthinking, and the terrible vomiting and dizziness had altogether ceased. Arnvid sat by Steinar day and night, and, cruelly as it hurt him to see the boy suffer so, he nevertheless thanked God for the miracle that had happened to Ingunn.

From now on she quickly grew better, and when Steinar was well enough to be carried out into the sun to look at the snow that had fallen in the night, Ingunn had got back a little of her delicate roundness of face and form, and her cheeks flushed pink in the frosty air. She stood with Steinar on her arm waiting for Arnvid, who was away among the rocks collecting frozen haws in his hat—Steinar had said his father *must* find some berries for him.

The prospects of a reconciliation between Arnvid and the rest of Ingunn's kinsfolk had not been improved by these rumours Mistress Hillebjörg had spread abroad about Kolbein—that he had had spells cast upon his niece to bring her to her death. And when the betrothal ale was drunk at Frettastein, for Haakon Gautsson and Tora Steinfinnsdatter, a short time before Advent, no one from Miklebö was present at the ceremony. The wedding was held at the New Year in 1282, and afterwards the newly married pair went round visiting the young wife's kinsfolk, for Haakon was the youngest of many brothers and had no house of his own in the westland. It was intended that he should settle in the Upplands.

But now there came word from the lady Magnhild of Berg that she wished to take Ingunn. Ivar and Kolbein had promised that they would leave the girl in peace if she would stay there quietly and live in chastity. Arnvid swore horribly when Brother Vegard told him this, but he could not deny that he had no legal right to dispose of Ingunn. And Mistress Hillebjörg was beginning to be tired of her guest: now that Ingunn was well she had no patience with the young woman, who was only for show and no use at all. And the message Lady Magnhild had sent was no more than was reasonable: she had her old mother with her, Aasa Magnusdatter, the widow of Tore of Hov; the old lady was infirm and had need of her granddaughter for help and pastime.

Just before Easter, then, Arnvid went to Berg with Ingunn.

Lady Magnhild was the eldest of all Tore's true-born children; she was now a woman of two score years and ten—the same age as her half-brother Kolbein Toresson. She was the widow of the knight Viking Erlingsson. Children she had never had; in order to do good, therefore, she took to herself young maids, the daughters of kinsmen or friends, and taught them courtesy and such attainments as were suited to women of good birth; for Lady Magnhild had seen much of the King's court while her husband was alive. She had also offered to receive her nieces from Frettastein, but Steinfinn—or Ingebjörg—had been unwilling to send the little maids to her, and Lady Magnhild had been exceeding angry thereat. So when it came out that Ingunn had let herself be ensnared by her foster-brother, she said it had turned out as she expected: the children had been ill brought up, and their mother had been disobedient to her father and false to her betrothed, so it seemed most likely that Steinfinn's daughters would bring shame on their race.

Ingunn was tired and low-spirited as she sat in the sledge on the last stage of the journey through the forest. They had been several days on the road, for the weather had set in mild, with snow, as soon as they left Miklebö. Now toward evening it froze hard, and Arnvid walked beside the sledge and drove, as the road was bad—in places over bare rock, slippery with ice, in others through deep snowdrifts, for no one had passed this way since the last snowfall.

When they came out of the woods, the sun was low above the ridge facing them; it was an orange ball behind the mist, and the dark, rugged ice of the bay had a dull and coppery gleam. The mist had frosted the snow-covered woods and fens, so that all was grey and ugly as evening drew on. Down in the fields Arnvid's men struggled on; they and the sledge with the baggage went straight ahead through the snow. The manor lay down by the water, at some distance from the other houses of the parish—the woods formed a barrier, so that from Berg one could not see any of the other great farms about.

Ingunn had not seen her aunt since she came to Hamar, well-nigh a year and a half ago, and then the lady of Berg had been harsh toward her. She did not expect much good of the lady Magnhild this time either.

Arnvid hoisted himself onto the edge of the sledge, as it dipped into the first hollow.

"Look not so sorrowful, Ingunn," he begged her. " 'Twill be hard parting from you, if you are so faint-hearted."

Ingunn said: "Faint-hearted I am not; you know that I have not complained. But I shall not be in the hands of friends here. Pray to God for me, kinsman, that I may keep a firm mind, for I look to be sorely tried, so long as I must bide here at Berg."

But as they drove into the courtyard the lady Magnhild herself came out and received Ingunn in friendly fashion. She led her niece into the women's room and bade the maids bring warm drinks and dry footgear. She herself helped the young woman to take off her fur-lined boots and coat of skins. But then she said, taking hold of a corner of Ingunn's coif: "This you must now put off."

Ingunn turned red. "I have worn the coif ever since I was at Hamar. The Bishop bade me cover my hair—he said no virtuous woman goes bareheaded when she is no longer a maid."

"*He!*" sneered Lady Magnhild. "He has so many fancies— But now so much time has passed that the gossip has died down hereabouts. I will not have you blow fresh life into the rumours of your own shame by going here like a fool in married woman's attire. Take off the kerchief and turn your belt again. 'Twas a mercy at least that you were never *forced* to buckle it at the side."

Ingunn wore a leather belt around her waist, set with little silver studs and handsomely mounted at the end that hung down. Lady Magnhild took hold of it and pulled it straight, so that the buckle came in front. Again she ordered Ingunn to take off her headcovering.

"All *know* this about me," said Ingunn hotly. "If I do this, folk must think worse of me and deem me an immodest woman—if I am to go bareheaded when I have no right to that—as the wantons do."

Lady Magnhild said: "There is your grandmother too, Ingunn; she is old now. She remembers well enough all things that happened in her youth, but new tidings she forgets as soon as she hears them. Every day we should have to tell her afresh why you were to go in matron's dress."

" 'Twould be easy to answer her that my husband is gone away."

"And soon it will come to Kolbein's ears that you stand by the old claims, and his hatred of Olav will never cool down. Be reasonable now, Ingunn, and cease these follies."

Ingunn unbound her coif and began to fold it together. It was the finest she had—four ells long and sewed with silk. Hillebjörg had given it her the year before, saying she could use it for a church-going coif and wear it the first time she went to mass with Olav, when he came home.

She drew the pins out of her hair and let the heavy yellow locks fall about her shoulders.

"And such goodly hair you have," said Lady Magnhild. "Most women would be glad to make boast of it awhile longer, Ingunn— if they could have no joy of their man, and the coif brought them no power or authority. Let it hang loose this evening, I pray you."

"Oh no, aunt," begged Ingunn, almost in tears. "*That* you must never ask me!" She divided her mass of hair and bound it in two plaits, stiff and unadorned.

Arnvid was already sitting at the table when Lady Magnhild and Ingunn came into the room. He looked up, and his eyes clouded over.

"Is it thus they will have it here?" he asked later, when they said good-night to each other. "You are not to be allowed the honour of a married woman?"

"Nay, you may see that," was all Ingunn said.

Aasa Magnusdatter had a house to herself at Berg with a loft-room and two maidservants to do the housework and cooking, and to spin and weave all the flax and wool that fell to her share. Grim and Dalla, the old bailiff and his sister from Frettastein, looked after her beasts, which stood in Lady Magnhild's byre; these two had been given a little cot to dwell in, close by the cow-house, but they were counted as part of Aasa's household.

Ingunn then had nothing to do at Berg but to be, as it were, at the head of her grandmother's little household and to be a solace to the old woman. She mostly sat with her grandmother when the maids were at their work.

As Lady Magnhild had said, Aasa was now grown somewhat childish, she remembered little of what was said to her, but asked again and again about the same things day after day. Sometimes she asked after her youngest son, Steinfinn, whether he had been there lately or whether they expected him soon. Often, however, she remembered that he was dead. Then she would ask: was it not four children he had alive? "And you are the oldest? Ah yes, I know that very well; your name is Ingunn—after my mother, for Ingebjörg's mother was still living when you came, and she had cursed her daughter for running away with Steinfinn. Ay, he was simple-minded and glad of heart, my Steinfinn, and it came to cost him dear that he was so nice in his choice of a leman that he carried off a knight's daughter by force. . . ." Aasa had never liked Ingebjörg, and she used often to talk of Steinfinn and his wife, without remembering that it was their daughter she spoke to. "But how was it now—did not a great misfortune befall one of these little maids of Steinfinn's? Nay, that cannot be so—they cannot be so old yet?"

"Dear Grandmother," Ingunn begged in her embarrassment, "you should try to get a little sleep now."

"Oh ay, Gyrid, perchance that were best for me—" Aasa often called her granddaughter Gyrid, taking her for a Gyrid Alfs-datter, a kinswoman who had been at Berg some fifteen winters before.

But all that had happened in her young days Mistress Aasa re-membered clearly. She spoke of her parents and of her brother Finn, Arnvid's father, and of her sister-in-law, Hillebjörg, whom she both loved and feared—although Hillebjörg was much younger than Aasa.

When fourteen winters old she had been given to Tore of Hov. Before that he had lived with that Borghild for over ten years, and very loath he was to send away his leman—she did not depart from Hov until the morning of the very day when Aasa was brought there as a bride. Borghild continued to have great power over Tore as long as she lived—and that was for twenty years after the man's marriage. He consulted her about all matters of importance, and he often took his true-born children to her, that she might foretell their future and judge whether they seemed promising. But Tore bestowed his greatest efforts and his love chiefly on the four children he had had by his leman. Borghild was the daughter of a woman thrall and a nobleman—some said, one of those kings that Norway was full of at that time. She was fair and wise, and a bold schemer, but haughty, rapacious, and cruel to folk of low degree.

Meanwhile Aasa Magnusdatter was mistress of Hov. She bore her husband fourteen children, but five died in the cradle, and only four lived to grow up.

Aasa remembered all her dead children and used to speak of them. She mourned most for a daughter, Herdis, who became pal-sied from having slept out on the dewy ground. She died four years afterwards, when she was eleven winters old. A half-grown son had been kicked to death by his horse, and Magnus had lost his life in a brawl on board the ship, when coming home across the lake from a banquet in Toten together with other drunken young men. Magnus had just been married, but there was no child after him, and the widow married again in an-other part of the country. Aasa had liked her best of her daugh-ters-in-law.

"But tell me, Grandmother," asked Ingunn, "have you had naught but sorrow in your life? Have you no good days to think upon now?"

Her grandmother looked at her and seemed not to understand. Now, as she lay waiting for death, she seemed to take as much pleasure in recalling her sorrows as her joys.

Ingunn did not thrive ill in this life with the old woman. Weak she was, even now when she had her health, and she had never liked to have to do anything that demanded hard work or continued thought. She would sit with some fine needlework that there was no need to finish in a hurry, lost in her own thoughts, while she listened with half an ear to her grandmother's talk.

In her growing years she had been restless and had found it hard to sit still for long at a time. But now it was different. The strange sickness that had fallen upon her after the separation from Olav seemed to have left behind a shadow that would not give way; it was as though she were always in a half-dreaming state.— At Frettastein she had had all the boys, and Olav first and last, and they had brought games and excitement and life to her, who herself lacked enterprise to undertake anything. Here at Berg there were only women, two old ladies and their servants, and a few elderly house-carls and workmen; they could not rouse her from the torpor into which she had sunk while she lay paralysed in bed, expecting to wither away altogether from among the living.

When Olav was whisked away, she seemed to have no strength to believe he would ever come back. All too many great events had overwhelmed her in the short time between her father's departure to seek out Mattias Haraldsson and Arnvid's taking her to Hamar. She felt she had been carried away by a flood, and the time at Hamar was like an eddy, in which she and Olav had been churned round in a ring, slowly but surely passing farther and farther from each other. There all had been new and strange, and Olav had changed till even he seemed to have become a stranger. She could understand indeed that it was right of him never to seek an opportunity for meeting her in secret while they were there. But that he should have taken it as he did when she brought about that meeting with him on Christmas Night—that had frightened her into a corner; she had felt so shamed and abandoned afterwards that she dared not even *think* of him as she had done before, lingeringly, with a sweet, hot desire for his love. She was like a child that has been corrected and punished by a grown-up—she herself had never guessed there could be anything wrong in it.

Then he had come to her that last night, out of the darkness and the driving snow, worn out and agitated, shaking between tiredness and suppressed ferocity—an outlawed man with her cousin's blood yet warm on his hands. She had been self-possessed in a way. But when he left her, it was as though all the waters closed over her.

At first, when she was so sick, she too had thought that it was with her as Mistress Hillebjörg said. But as time went on and it became clear that she was not to have a child, she scarce had the strength to feel disappointed. She was so worn out that it would have seemed too much if she had had more to look for, of either good or ill. She bore it with patience that she was so sick and that none could tell what ailed her and that there seemed to be no cure for her. If she tried to look forward into the future, she saw naught but black, waving mists like the darkness that whirled before her eyes when she had her swooning-fits.

Then she plunged deep into the memories of all that had been between Olav and her that last summer and autumn. She closed both eyes and kissed her own plait of hair and hands and arms and made believe it was Olav. But the more she abandoned herself to dreams and desires, the more unreal it seemed to her that these things had happened in truth. That the end of the matter would be that they were united at last, in peace and with full right, she had indeed believed, but never been able to imagine— just as she believed, but was little able to imagine all that she had heard of the priests about a blissful state in the other world.

So she lay powerless, not expecting ever to regain the use of her limbs. With it the last rope was broken that still held her to the everyday life and occupations of other men and women. She no longer hoped that she would ever be lawfully married to Olav Audunsson, would be mistress of his house and mother of his children. Instead she allowed herself to drift as the sport of dreams which she never looked to see fulfilled.

Every evening, when the candle was extinguished and the fire raked out, she played that Olav came and lay down with her.

Every morning, when she awoke, she played that her husband
had risen and gone out. She lay listening to the sounds of the
great farm, playing that she was at Hestviken; and she played that
it was Olav who had the hay carted in, that they were his horses
and sledges, and that it was he who set his folk to their work.
When Steinar lay still for a moment in her bed, she laid her thin
arm about the boy, pressed his fair head against her breast, and
to herself she called the boy Audun, and he was her son and
Olav's. Then he wanted to get up and out, struggled to free himself from her embrace. Ingunn coaxed him to stay by giving him
dainty morsels of food she had hidden in her bed, telling him
stories, and playing at being a mother who was talking to her
child.

The first thing that waked her out of her dreams and play when
she came to Berg was Lady Magnhild's taking the coif from her.
Never before had she looked upon it as a shame that she had become Olav's own. At Frettastein she had thought so little, only
loved. Only when both Olav and Arnvid were suddenly so ur-
gent to go to Hamar and have Olav's right to her acknowledged
had anything like confusion been aroused in her. But when the
good Bishop sent her the modest white linen and bade her bind
up her hair, she grew calm again. Even if she had wronged her
uncles, who should have been her sponsors after her father's death,
the lord Torfinn would surely make all well again, and then she
would be as good a wife as all other married women.
She was chilled with humiliation in the unwonted feeling of
being bareheaded, after wearing the married woman's garb for a
year and a half. It was as though she had been immodestly bared
by violent hands—as they did with women thralls in the slave
market in former times. She excused herself from going across
to Magnhild's house when strangers were there. She did not willingly show herself abroad among folk except in church—there *all*
women had to cover their heads. Ingunn drew the hood of her
cloak over her face so that not a hair was seen. To make some
small amends for having to clothe herself as was unfitting for her,
she put away all jewels, wore none but dark, plain kirtles, and
did her hair in two hard, stiff plaits without ribbons or other
adornment.

. . .

163

Then came the spring. One day the ice sank in the bay, the water lay open and clear and reflected the green hills on both shores. Now Berg was at its fairest. Ingunn led her grandmother out on the sunny side and sat with her, sewing the shirt for Olav Audunsson. Olav had told her that Hestviken lay on the fiord.

She found some trifles to busy herself with in the loft-room that belonged to Aasa. Morning after morning she spent up there, rummaging and tidying. Ingunn took the shutter from the little window and leaned out.

A boat was rowing under the opposite shore—the dark reflection of the wooded hill was broken by long streaks. Ingunn played at its being Olav and the boy who were in the boat. They were rowing this way—Ingunn could *see* it. They put in at the hard and Audun helped his father to make the boat fast. The father stood up on the wooden pier and the boy was busy in the stern of the boat, collecting their things. At last he took his little axe, Olav held out his hand and helped him up—ay, the boy was now as big as Jon, her youngest brother. The two came up the path toward the house, the father first and the son following.

She also had a little daughter, whose name was Ingebjörg. She was out in the yard—she was just coming from the storehouse, carrying a great wooden tray full of bannocks. She broke one of them up and scattered the crumbs to the hens—no, the geese. Ingunn remembered that they had had geese at Frettastein when she was a little child, and there was something grave and imposing about the heavy white and grey-flecked birds. They would have geese at Hestviken.

Softly, as though she were doing something wrong, she stole to the door and shot the bolt. Then she took a coif from her chest and wound it about her head. Ingunn turned her belt, so that the buckle was at the side; she hung on it all the heavy things she could find—a pair of scissors and some keys. Thus adorned she sat on the edge of the empty bedstead that was in the loft; with her hands in her lap she turned over in her mind all the things that had to be done before her husband and children came in.

At Berg it was only now and then that they heard anything of the remarkable events which took place in Norway that year. Almost no news reached Ingunn, shut up as she was in her grandmother's house. So it was like a bolt from the blue when she heard one day that Bishop Torfinn had been declared an outlaw and was said to have left the country.

It was their parish priest who brought this news to the house, one day at the beginning of winter. For some months the lord Torfinn had been on a visitation in Norddalen, and from thence it seemed he had intended to meet the Archbishop somewhere in the outer islands. But before he could do so, these barons, who now possessed all the power in the realm, had outlawed the Archbishop and several of the other bishops and persecuted them till they fled the country in all directions. Bishop Torfinn was said to have gone on board a ship, but none knew what had become of him since, or when he might return to his see. The parish priest did not grieve for this—the Bishop had reproved him for indolence and for neglecting to punish the sins of great folks as they deserved; but the priest thought himself a good shepherd enough, and there was no need to treat *his* flock in the Bishop's way; he had been very angry with that stiff-necked monk, as he called him.

It was clear that the conflict between the bishops and the young King's advisers was concerned with great matters of state, and this marriage suit of Olav Audunsson was a trifle of no account—although it was brought forward as an instance of the Bishop of Hamar's intolerable obstinacy and desire to upset the ancient laws of the land. But the parish priest wished to remain good friends with the rich lady of Berg—and perhaps he had no idea how little this affair of the marriage of two children meant outside the parishes where the families of the young people were known. From the way he talked, it might be thought Bishop Torfinn had been outlawed mainly because he had held his hand over the Steinfinnssons' worst enemy.

Ingunn was seized by a terrible dread. Scared into wakefulness, she saw again her position as it was in reality, and all her dreams collapsed suddenly, as a flowery meadow is blighted by a frosty night. She realized with a shiver that she was but a defenceless and deserted orphan, neither maid nor wife; she had not a friend to maintain her rights—Olav was away, none knew where, the Bishop was gone, Arnvid was far off and she could not send him a message. She had no one on whom to lean, except her old grandmother, who was in second childhood, if her ungentle kinsmen were minded to take revenge on her.—She clung, a little trembling, quivering creature, to the only firmness in her weak, in-stinct-governed soul—she would hold fast to Olav and be true to him, even if they were to torture her to death for his sake.

At about this time—during Advent—Tora Steinfinnsdatter and her husband, Haakon Gautsson, came to Berg. Haakon had not yet found a place where he cared to settle for good, and now Tora was expecting a child before Yule. So it was the intention of the young people to stay at Berg that winter. Ingunn had not seen her sister for two years, and her brother-in-law she had never met till now. He did not look amiss—he was a powerfully built young man, with handsome features and curly chestnut hair, but he had little brown eyes placed close together at the high root of his hooked nose, and he squinted not a little.

From the first day he met his wife's sister with ill will. In words and bearing he plainly showed that he counted Ingunn naught else than a seduced woman who had disgraced herself and her whole family. He was intensely pleased with his marriage, proud of Tora's beauty and of her good understanding, proud that she was soon to bear him an heir to all the riches he boasted of possess-ing; he allowed himself to be guided by his wife in all things—which was well for Haakon. But though this was so, and though poor Ingunn had been ignorant of the honour and good fortune she missed in giving herself to Olav Audunsson—when she might have been married to Haakon Gautsson—Haakon had conceived a hatred for her, since she had preferred a young lad, her father's serving-man and one of whose family and fortune none here in the Mjösen country knew anything certain, to him, the knight's son from Harland.

And the younger sister went about in her fruitfulness, gleaming pink and white, proud of her matronly dignity, though she owned neither house nor farm to rule over. The white wimple, which she wore with honour and by right, reached nearly to her feet; a heavy bunch of keys jingled at her belt—though God alone knew what the houseless man's wife was to lock or unlock with them. But Tora bore herself so that every mother's child at Berg, and even the lady Magnhild, would do anything to honour her and her husband, and the women made all preparations to receive the child they expected with such pomp as became the son of so great a man.

Through all the time of their growing up Ingunn had known
well enough that Tora was seldom pleased with her conduct—
thought her elder sister wanting in affection to their parents,
thoughtless and lazy, and that she should have sat quietly with
their mother and the maids in the women's room instead of always running out to play with Olav and his friends. But Tora
never said anything—she was two years younger, and that is a
great deal in childhood; Ingunn cared very little what Tora
might *think*. And the last autumn at Frettastein Tora had kept
silence about what Ingunn knew she must have guessed and been
dismayed at. But only when they were in the guest-house at
Hamar had her sister spoken of the matter, and then Tora had
judged her and Olav's conduct with unexpected leniency and had
been kind to Ingunn while they stayed there. One thing was that
Tora had always been fond of her foster-brother with true sisterly
affection—she liked Olav better than her own brothers and sister,
because he was quieter and more natural—and then the Bishop
had given some countenance to Olav and Ingunn, and all the
people the sisters met in the town followed the lord Torfinn in
their judgment; even if Olav had returned wrong for wrong, they
had nevertheless done a greater wrong who had sought to break
a handselled betrothal because the bridegroom was young and
lacked powerful spokesmen. No one doubted that the Bishop in
the end would force such a settlement of the suit as would be
honourable to Olav. So at that time Tora had not thought that
Ingunn's rashness might prove a disgrace to them all.

Now it was otherwise. She could not forgive Olav for having
slain her near kinsman, and she spoke harsh words of the way he
had rewarded them all for having taken him up, a friendless child,
and fostered him in the Steinfinn kindred. Toward Ingunn she
was not unfriendly—but, for all that, Ingunn guessed what Tora
thought of her: that from a child she had been such that her
younger sister was not surprised at her ending in misfortune—
but Tora wished to be kind and not to make it harder for the
poor thing to bear the fate she had brought upon herself.

Ingunn bowed in silence beneath Tora's gentle little words of
pity, but when the talk turned to Olav's misdeeds, she tried to
raise her voice in opposition. It availed but little; the other held
such an advantage; that she was the elder was of no weight now,
since Tora was the married woman. Tora had experience and the

right of judging between other grown people. Ingunn was left with her experiences to which she had no right: of a love for which all seemed minded to punish her, of household management and bringing up of children, at which she had played in her dreams, but never set her hand to in reality. She felt poor and down-hearted as she sat in her corner and saw how Tora and Haakon filled the whole house with their life. In her dark, penitential garments, with the two smooth, heavy plaits hanging over her shoulders, as though it were their weight that bowed her head and bent her back, she looked like a poor maidservant beside the young, richly clad wife.

Tora had a son, as no doubt had been the hope of her and Haakon—a big, promising child, as all said who saw the boy. Ingunn was set to stay by her sister, while Tora was lying in, and thus she was occupied in tending her nephew. She had always been very fond of little children, and now she conceived a great affection for this young Steinfinn Haakonsson. When she had to take him into her bed at night to give the mother better rest, she could not help it—she *had* to play at the boy's being her own. She had to warm herself awhile at her old fancies that she was at Hestviken, in her own house, and that she was living there with Olav and their children, Audun, Ingebjörg, and the new little one. But now she felt with bitter truth that it was but a poor web of dreams that she had to wrap herself in, while she saw her sister well and warmly enfolded in her tangible wealth, with husband and infant son and all the crowd of their servants, who took up so much room in the place, and the chests and sacks of their goods that were stacked up in the lofts and storehouses.

Haakon wished to hold a great christening ale, and Lady Magnhild offered to bear half of the cost. Not only Haftor Kolbeinsson, who had become a great friend of Haakon, but the uncles, Kolbein and Ivar, came to the feast, and these stayed for some days after the other guests had left.

One evening the kinsfolk were sitting over the supper-table in Lady Magnhild's room; Aasa Magnusdatter was there too and sat in the high seat, with Ingunn by her side to help her with her food and drink, for the old lady's hands were very shaky. Otherwise she had been in much better health this winter; it had rejoiced her greatly to be a great-grandmother; this last piece of news she never forgot, but often asked after the child and wished to see it.

This evening the men's talk turned upon the conflict between the barons and the bishops, and the Toressons pretended it was certain which side would win. It was the bishops who would have to give in, content themselves with the power that was theirs by right as the spiritual fathers of the people, but let the old laws regarding laymen's dealings with one another stand unshaken. As to Bishop Torfinn, many of the priests here in his own diocese now thought he had gone too far: "I have spoken with three parish priests, good and learned men of God," said Kolbein, "and all three answered me that they were willing to say the bridal mass on the day we give away Ingunn here."

Lady Magnhild answered: "It is clear that the Bishop's interpretation cannot possibly be right. It cannot be God's commandment that His priests should hold with loose-minded and self-willed young people, or that Holy Church should help wicked children to force through their will against their parents—"

"Nay, indeed," said the others.

Ingunn had turned scarlet in the face, but now she straightened herself and defiance struggled with fear in her look—her eyes seemed unnaturally large and dark as she turned them upon her uncles.

"Ay, 'tis of you we are speaking," Kolbein answered back. "You have been a burden to your kinsfolk long enough now, Ingunn. It is time you had a man who can bridle you."

"Can you find a man who will take me?" asked Ingunn scornfully. "So wretched a wife as you would make me to be?"

"We shall not speak of *that*," said Kolbein furiously. "I thought you had had time to find your wits again. So shameless you cannot be, I ween, that you lust after living with a man who has stained his hands with the blood of your cousin—even if you could get him?"

" 'Tis not the first time a man has come to grief through his wife's kinsfolk," said Ingunn in a low and faltering voice.

"Say no more of that," replied Kolbein angrily. "Never will we give you to Einar's slayer."

"Ay, that you have power to refuse—maybe," said Ingunn. She felt that all around the table were staring at her. And she was strangely fired by the thought that she had thus stepped out of

169

the shadow of subjection. "But if you would give me to any other
—you will find *that* is not in your power!"

"In whose power think you that you are?" asked Kolbein scornfully.

Ingunn's hands grasped the bench she was sitting on. She felt
her cheeks go white. But this was herself—she was not dreaming.
It was herself who spoke, all were staring at her. Before she could
get out her answer, Ivar put in a conciliatory word: "In God's
name, Ingunn—this Olav—no man knows where he may be. You
yourself know not whether he is alive or dead. Will you pass all
your days as a widow, waiting for a dead man?"

"I *know* that he is alive." She thrust her hand into her bosom
and drew out a little silver-mounted sheath-knife which hung
by a string around her neck. She drew the knife and laid it before
her on the table. "Olav gave me this for a talisman, before we
parted—he bade me wait so long as the blade was bright, he said—
did it rust, then he was dead—"

She breathed hard once or twice. Then she became aware of a
young man sitting lower down the table, who stared at her excitedly. Ingunn knew that his name was Gudmund Jonsson and
that he was the only son of a great house in the neighbouring
parish; she had seen him once or twice here at Berg, but never
spoken to him. Now she guessed at once—this was the bridegroom
her uncles intended for her; she was quite certain of this. She
looked the young man straight in the eye; her own glance was
firm as steel, she felt.

Then said the conciliatory Ivar Toresson, scratching his hair:
"Such talismans—oh ay, I know not how much one may believe
in such things—"

"I trow, my Ingunn, you will soon see who is to decide your
marriage," Kolbein broke in. "So you will oppose us if we give
you to a man whom we reckon to be an equal match for you?
Whom will you turn to then—since your friend the Bishop has
taken to his heels, out of the country, so that you cannot crawl
under his cloak?"

"I will turn to God my Creator Himself," said Ingunn; her face
was white as a sheet and she half rose from the bench. "Relying
on His mercy, if you drive me to commit *one* sin to avoid a
greater. Ere I let you force me to be an adulteress and enter the

bridal bed with another man while my true husband lives, I will throw myself into the fiord out there!"

Both Kolbein and Ivar were about to answer her, when old Aasa Magnusdatter put her hands on the table, raised herself with difficulty, and stood up, tall and thin and stooping; she blinked at the men about her with her old red and running eyes.

"What is it you would do to this child?" she asked threateningly, laying her bony claw of a hand on Ingunn's neck. "You wish her ill, I know. Ivar, my son, will you do the work of this bastard brood of Borghild? They would harm Steinfinn's children, I see that—are you to lend them a hand in it, Magnhild and Ivar? Then I fear I have too many left to me in you two!"

"But, Mother!" entreated Ivar Toresson.

"Grandmother!" Ingunn nestled close to the old lady, creeping in under her fur cloak. "Ay, Grandmother, you must help me!"

The old lady put her arm around her.

"Now we will go," she whispered. "Come, my child, we will go."

Ingunn rose and helped her grandmother to reach the floor. Groping before her with her stick, and with the other arm round her granddaughter's shoulder, Aasa Magnusdatter staggered toward the door, muttering the while: "Lending a hand to Borghild's brood—my children—I have lived too long, I have—I mark that!"

"Nay, nay, Mother—" Ivar came after them, took the stick from his mother, and offered his shoulder to support her. "Now I have said the whole time that it were better they accepted an atonement from Olav, but— And now that he is clean gone—"

They had reached the door of Aasa's house. Ivar said to his niece: "I wish you no ill, you must know. But meseems it must be better for yourself—that you were married and mistress in your own house. Better than tarrying here to fade away—"

Ingunn gently pushed him aside as she almost lifted her grandmother over the threshold and barred the door after her, shutting Ivar out.

She undressed the old woman and laid her down, said the evening prayer with her, kneeling by her grandmother's bed. Mistress Aasa was now quite exhausted after her unwonted exertion. Ingunn busied herself for a while longer in the room before she began to prepare for bed.

She stood in her shift and was just about to jump into bed when there was a soft knock at the door. Ingunn went and drew the bolt—and saw a man standing outside in the snow, a dark bulk against the starry sky. Before he opened his mouth, she knew it was her wooer, and she felt a strange festal thrill, while at the same time she was a little afraid. After all—something was happening.

It was, as she thought, Gudmund Jonsson. He asked: "Had you lain down already? I wonder if I could say a word to you tonight. There is some haste in it, you can guess."

"Ay, you may come in. We cannot stand here in the cold—"

"But lay you down," he said as he came in and saw how thinly clad she was. "Maybe you will let me lie here by the bedpost, so that we may talk better?"

At first they talked a little of the weather and of Haakon Gautsson, who now seemed minded to settle at Frettastein, and so Haftor would go home to his father's. Ingunn liked Gudmund's voice and his quiet, pleasant manner. And besides, she could not help liking to lie here in the dark, chatting with a wooer, in cosy comfort. It was so long since anyone had sought her out or cared to talk to her for her own sake. In spite of her having to tell him that his wooing was useless, it was some reparation that a man of Gudmund's condition should have cast his eyes upon her, although her own kinsmen had declared her a worthless woman.

"Ay, there was a thing I wished to ask you," said her guest at last. "Were you in earnest in that you said this evening?"

"I was in earnest."

"Ay, then it is best I tell you," said Gudmund, "my father and mother would fain have me married this year, and we have agreed to ask Ivar Toresson for you."

Ingunn was silent. Gudmund began again: "But if I ask my father to seek elsewhere, he will do so. If it is so that you mean all that you said this evening?"

As he still got no answer, he said: "For you must know, if we once ask Ivar or Kolbein, we shall not get nay. But if you like it not, I will make it so that you shall not be troubled with the matter any more."

Ingunn said: "I cannot understand, Gudmund, how you and

your kinsfolk should think of such a one as I—seeing what a good match you have the right to expect. You must know all that is said of me."

"Yes. But we must not be too strict or too hard. Your kinsmen would admit you to full inheritance with your brothers and sister if this match could be made between us two—and for myself I think you look well—and are right comely—"

Ingunn made no haste to reply. It was so good to be able to lie thus talking with such a pleasing young man, to feel the warmth of his presence and his living breath against her cheek in the dark. There had so long been a cold, empty space about her. Then she said very gently: "Now you know my mind—I cannot let myself be married to *any* man but to him who owns me. But for that, you must know, I would prize aright the good fortune which you would offer me."

"Ah," said Gudmund. "Think you not, Ingunn, that we two might have agreed well together?"

"Indeed I think so. The woman would needs be a troll who could not live happily with you. But now you must see that I am not free—"

"Nay, nay," said Gudmund with a sigh. "Then I will take care that you have no more torment for our sake. I would fain have had you. But now I wis I shall have another."

They lay chatting awhile yet, but at last Gudmund thought it time he was away, and Ingunn said it might be so. She followed him to the door to bar it after him, and they parted with a clasp of the hand. Ingunn felt strangely warmed and exhilarated as she came back and went to bed for good. Tonight she would be able to sleep so well—

In Lent Ingunn was allowed to ride into the town, that she might make her confession to Brother Vegard—he had been her father confessor since the day she was confirmed, at the age of eight, until Arnvid took her with him to Miklebö.

It was no easy matter for her to tell the monk all about her difficulties. Until now she had always been able in confessing to give each sin its name: she had prayed without reflecting, had answered her parents discourteously, been angry with Tora or the maids, taken things without leave, spoken untruthfully—and then this last sin with Olav. Now she felt that it was mostly thoughts she had to speak about—and she herself found it hard to grasp them and put them into words. There was especially this thought, that she was afraid she might let herself be scared or threatened into breaking the troth she had given Olav Audunsson under God's eyes.

Brother Vegard said she had done right in refusing to let herself be given to any other man, so long as she had not received true tidings of Olav's death. The monk had judged her and Olav's self-will far more strictly than the Bishop; but he too said they were bound to each other, so long as both were alive. But she must pray to God to save her from such thoughts as that she would take her own life; that was a deadly sin, no less than if she let herself be forced into a marriage without being a widow. And he cautioned her, in serious terms, against thinking too much, as she had said, of life with Olav and of the children she was to have by him. Such thoughts could only serve to weaken her will, to provoke lasciviousness and defiance of her kinsmen—and she must have learned by now that she and Olav had themselves brought about their misfortunes by their fond self-indulgence and by their disobedience toward those whom God had set over them in their youth. It would be far better now that she should aim at the virtue of patience, bear her fate as the chastisement of a loving father, apply herself to a life of prayer, almsgiving, and ministering affection toward her kinsfolk, so long as they did not ask her to obey them in what was sinful. Finally Brother Vegard said that he believed it would be better for her if she could be admitted to a convent of nuns and dwell there as a pious widow while waiting to hear whether Olav could come home to his native land and take her to himself, if it were God's will that such happiness should be theirs. If she received certain tidings of his death, then she could choose whether she would return to the world or whether she would take the veil, devote herself to prayer for the souls of Olav and her parents and for all souls that had been led astray by self-will and by over-great love of the pomps and joys of this world. The monk offered himself to speak with her kinsfolk of this, and himself to conduct her to a convent, if she had a mind to it.

But Ingunn was frightened; she feared that if once she were inside a convent, it would not be easy for her to slip out—although Brother Vegard said that, so long as Olav lived, she could not take the veil without his consent. So Ingunn replied that her grand-mother was old and weak and needed her, and Brother Vegard then agreed with her that so long as Aasa Magnusdatter had need of her, she must stay with her grandmother.

When she came back to Berg after Easter, Haakon and Tora had left with all their train; it had been settled that they were to live at Frettastein. The place was very quiet after them. With the old women one day was so much like another that for that matter Ingunn might as well have been living in a convent.

And then she could not resist it—after a while she took up again her imaginary life with husband and children in a dream-manor that she called Hestviken. But now and again they came up in her, those feelings which Gudmund Jonsson's wooing had called to life—fear, but with it a sort of satisfaction. So after all she had not misbehaved herself so badly but that a rich and well-born young man could think of wooing her. And she dreamed of hand-some and mighty suitors whom her uncles would seek to force on her—and she showed her courage and her firm will, and no tor-ments and humiliations they could think of would prevail against her fidelity to Olav Audunsson.

2

AT Berg one day passed like another. Time flew so fast that In-gunn could not guess what became of it. But when she saw how much had happened in the others' lives, how everything about them grew and spread, she felt a sting of anxiety—was it so long ago already!

Tora came down from Frettastein and brought both the chil-dren with her. Steinfinn romped high and low like a whirlwind—he was big and forward for his age, two years and a half. His little sister could already push herself along the floor till she reached a bench, when she would catch hold of it and stand on her feet. Tora insisted that Ingunn must come with her to Frettastein. In-gunn had such a way with children—and as Tora expected her third before Olav's Mass,[3] she thought it no more than reasonable

July 29.

that her sister should come to live with her and help to bring up all these children. But Ingunn said her grandmother could not manage without her. In her heart she thought she had no wish to see Frettastein again—unless she came there together with Olav.

She did not know where he was now. The only time she had heard news of him was last summer, when Arnvid was a guest at Berg. Asbjörn All-fat, the priest, had returned to Norway the same spring—he had followed Bishop Torfinn in his exile, accompanied him to Rome, and been with him when he died, in Flanders. On his way home Asbjörn had sought out Olav in Denmark; he was then with his mother's brother and was well. Asbjörn had afterwards become a parish priest somewhere in the Trondheim district. On his journey up through Österdal he had looked in on Arnvid at Miklebö and brought him greetings from his friend.

Arnvid had Steinar with him to give pleasure to Ingunn. But the boy had grown so big that she could not play with him as of old. His father said to Steinar that Ingunn had once rescued him from being burned up. But this did not seem to make much impression on the child.

Ingunn took him out in a boat on the lake—they were to fish. She paddled about near the shore, without the strength to row the heavy boat any distance, and Steinar had never been in a boat before. But they had a great deal of fun in this way, though their fishing did not come to much.

Gudmund Jonsson was married long ago and had a son by his wife. He came to Berg now and then and borrowed a boat there, when he had to go to his grandfather's on the other side of the bay.

There was only herself about the place, day in, day out, with the two old women, and now she was already twenty winters old. Fade away, Uncle Ivar had said that time—vaguely she knew that she was fairer than she had ever been. The shut-in life with her grandmother had paled her cheeks, but her skin was as clear as a flower. And she was no longer so thin; her flesh had grown firmer —and she did not hold herself so loosely and stoopingly. She had learned to walk gracefully, and she carried her tall, slender figure with a soft and supple charm of her own. On the rare occasions when she mixed among people, she felt that many men had their eyes on her; she noticed this, though she never returned their gaze, but always moved quietly, with eyes modestly lowered and a gentle melancholy in her look.

One evening, when some strangers had been at Berg on some business with Lady Magnhild, one of the men forced his way into the room after she had gone to bed. He was far gone in drink. Ingunn got him out again; old Aasa had not so much as noticed that anyone had come in. The man turned almost sober as he slunk out—like a whipped dog under the lash of her icy, low-voiced anger.

But when she had got the fellow out of doors, she collapsed altogether—she trembled and her teeth chattered with fright. And what frightened her most was—she herself had felt so strangely—though he could not have noticed anything, of that she were sure. While she was defending herself against him, cool and collected, far too angry and outraged to be afraid, she had felt deep down within herself, as it were, a temptation to let go, to give up.—She was so tired, so tired—it seemed to her all at once that she had been defending herself for years. She was tired of waiting.—Olav should have been here—he should have been here *now!* She did not get a wink of sleep that night; shaken and miserable she lay sobbing and weeping, buried beneath the bedclothes; it seemed to her she could no longer bear this life.—But next day, when this man came to make his excuses, she received his stuttering speech with a few words of gentle dignity, looking him straight in the face; the glance of her great dark eyes was so full of sorrowful scorn that the man crept rather than walked away from her.

Olav—she now knew nothing more of him. And oftener and oftener she lay weeping till far into the night, tortured by disquietude and longing and a dull dread: how long would it be—! She pressed his sheath-knife with both hands against her bosom. The blade was still as bright as ever. And that was all she had to cling to.

Then came a Sunday, toward the end of summer. Only Ingunn had gone to mass from Berg, together with some of the servants. She was on horseback; old Grim walked by her side, leading the dun. They came into the courtyard, the old man was just about to

help her off her horse—when she saw a young, fair-haired man
stooping his head as he came out of the low door of Magnhild's
house. It seemed a strangely long and stubborn moment before
she recognized the man—it was Olav.

He came to meet her, and in the first flash Ingunn thought
everything turned queerly grey and lustreless—as when one has
been lying on the ground face-downward on a scorching summer
day, and then opens one's eyes and looks around: the sunshine
and the whole world seem to have faded and all the colours are
much paler than one expected.

She had always remembered Olav as much taller, bigger in
every way. And handsomer—she remembered his fair colour as
something radiant.

He came up, lifted her out of the saddle, and set her on the
ground. Then they took hands in greeting, walked side by side
toward the house; neither said anything.

Ivar Toresson appeared in the doorway; he greeted Ingunn
with a great smile: "Are you pleased now, Ingunn—with the guest
I have brought to the house this time?"

Ingunn's whole face awoke—she turned pink right down to her
neck, a radiant smile broke out in her eyes and on her lips. "Have
you two come *together*?" She looked from her uncle to Olav.
Then he too smiled—the quiet brightening that she knew so in-
timately: the pale, handsome mouth moved gently, the lips were
not even parted; he dropped his eyelids slightly, and under the
long, silky white lashes his glance was blue and happy.

"So at last you have come home too?" she asked smiling.

"Yes, I thought I must look in at home some time," he said in
the same tone.

She sat on the threshold with her hands in her lap, looking up
at Olav, who stood talking to Ivar. With a strange suddenness all
became calm within her. Happiness, that was the same as allow-
ing rest to descend upon her—perfect rest.

Ivar had something to show to Olav—the men walked away.
Ingunn watched him and recognized his walk: she had never seen
a man who walked so well, carried himself with such easy grace.
He was not very tall, she well remembered that now; she was
herself perhaps a trifle taller than he—but he was so wonderfully
well built, with just the right breadth of shoulder, narrow in the

waist, well knit, and firm of muscle, though he was so slender,
erect, and delicately limbed.

He had grown thinner in the face, his complexion was dry and
hard. And his hair had darkened a little—it was not so bright a
yellow—more the colour of ashes. But the longer she looked at
him, the better she knew him again. There was only this, that
when they parted, there was still a touch of childish softness in
his good looks. Now he was a grown man—but a remarkably
handsome young man withal.

Lingering over her deep happiness Ingunn sat at the supper-
table and saw with glad surprise that both Ivar and Magnhild were
so friendly toward Olav. Olav had come back to Norway a week
ago—to Oslo.

"Methinks you ought to have seen to your own home first,"
said Ivar. "There could scarcely have been any danger in that—
now that you are the Earl's man."

"Oh no, I might well have ventured *that*. But I had said to myself that I would not come home to Hestviken before I got back
the control of my own estate. Time enough, I thought," he smiled,
"when I can make all things ready there in the south to bring Ingunn home with me."

Ingunn guessed from their talk that Olav had not yet been given
safe-conduct and leave to remain in Norway. But neither Ivar
nor Olav himself seemed to count that any great matter. The
Earl, Alf Erlingsson of Tornberg, was now the mightiest man
in the land, and Olav had met him in Denmark and become his
liegeman. The Earl had promised to obtain for him a bought peace
and it was with leave from the Earl that he had journeyed up-
country to find a man who could negotiate on his behalf concerning the atonement with Einar's kinsmen. Then he had thought
that boldness pays best—he had ridden straight to Ivar Toresson
at Galtestad. And they were soon agreed.

"Ay, you know I remember you since you were as high as
that," said Ivar; "and I have always liked you. You know I was
angry that time, when we heard you had helped yourself to your
bride, as was natural enough—"

"Surely it was natural." And Olav laughed with him.

Ingunn asked timidly: "Then you have not yet come home to
stay, Olav?"

"In Norway I shall stay—maybe. But here in the north I cannot stay many days. By Bartholomew's Day [4] I must be with the Earl at Valdinsholm."

Ingunn did not know where in the world Valdinsholm might be, but it sounded far away.

It was easy to see that Olav had learned to conduct himself among folk. The glum and silent country lad had become a mannerly young courtier, who knew how to choose his words: Olav could be lively and hold his own when he opened his mouth, but he listened readily to his elders, and most of what he said was in answer to Ivar's and Magnhild's questions. He rarely addressed his words to Ingunn, and never tried to have speech with her alone.

He said the times were very troubled in Denmark—the great nobles were discontented with their King in every way, although they had much greater liberties and rights in that land than here at home—but perhaps that was what made them open their mouths wide for more. His own uncle, Barnim Eriksson, did as he pleased in everything, Olav thought, and he had never seen that the knight paid any attention to the laws, which must hold good in that country too.

"You have not been able to lay your hands on any of the inheritance of your mother's kinsmen?" asked Ivar. "Surely you could claim that now?"

"Uncle says no," said Olav with a little mocking smile. "And that may well be true.—It was the first thing he made plain to me when I came to Hövdinggaard, that my grandmother had divided Sir Erik's estate with her children, before she married Björn Andersson. And my mother had lost all right of inheritance from her kinsfolk in Denmark when she left the country and married in Norway without asking their advice—that was the second thing. And the third was that the King has declared my mother's own brother, Stig Björnsson, an outlaw, and he is dead and his sons dwell in a foreign land; and the King has laid hands on the manor of Hvidbjerg. Now Duke Valdemar has taken up the cause of Stig's sons, and if he can get the estate back for them, Uncle Barnim thought that I ought to come forward: there might be a slice of the cake for me too." He laughed. "Ay, 'twas after uncle and I were better acquainted, that—we have been good

[4] August 24.

friends always, and he has kept me in seemly fashion and has been right generous with me. Only he will not have it that I should claim anything as my right."

Olav spoke with a smile. But Ingunn saw that a new look had come over his countenance; a touch of loneliness, which had been there always, but now appeared much more strongly, and something hard, which was new. She suspected that he had not fallen into unmixed joy and splendour when he sought shelter, a poor outlaw, among his mighty Danish kinsmen.

"But in all else I must say that Barnim Eriksson has treated me well.—For all that, I was a happy man the day I met with Earl Alf —when I took the oath to him on the hilt, I almost thought I had come home."

"You like him?" asked Ivar.

"Like—!" Olav beamed. "Had you met the Earl you would not say such a word. We would follow him—if he bade us sail across the smoking lake of hell—every man he looks at when he laughs. Those yellow eyes of his shine like gems. Small he is, and low— I am a head taller, I wis—and broad as the door of a house, shaggy and brown and curly-haired; ay, the Tornberg race comes of a king's daughter and a bear, they say. And Earl Alf has the strength of ten men and the wits of twelve. And there are not many men, I ween, who are not glad and thankful to obey him—nor many women either—" said Olav with a laugh.

"Is it true, think you, what they say of our Queen—that she would marry him?" asked Ivar inquisitively.

"How should I know that?" laughed Olav. "But if they say truly that she is so wise a woman—though there will be an end of the lady's rule in the land if she comes under the bear's paws—"

But Ivar thought it was in Queen Ingebjörg's service that Earl Alf lay in the Danish waters, harrying the coasts there and taking up the German merchant ships that tried to slip northward through the sounds.

Olav said it was true enough—the Earl sought to win for Queen Ingebjörg her fathers' inheritance in Denmark, while at the same time he chastised the German merchants for their late encroachments in Björgvin and Tunsberg. But no doubt he did it of his own will and not because the Queen had bidden him. Now there was certainly an agreement between the Earl and the Danish nobles—he was to support them in their feud with the Danish

King, and in return Count Jacob and the other lords were to rap the King so hard over the knuckles that he would take his hands off the Lady Ingebjörg's estates in Denmark.

They had sat drinking after supper, and Ivar already talked of going to rest, when Olav stood up and drew the great gold ring with the green stone from his finger. He showed it to Ivar and Lady Magnhild. "I wonder if you know this again? With this ring my father let me betroth her. Think you not it were fitting Ingunn had it now and wore it herself?"

Ingunn's uncle said yes to this, and Olav set the ring on her finger. Next he took from his saddle-bag a gilt chain with a cross hanging to it and silver plates for a belt and gave these also to Ingunn. Then he produced good gifts for Ivar and Magnhild, and three gold rings, which he asked Ivar to give to Tora, Hallvard, and Jon. Both the lady and Ivar were well pleased with this, praised the gifts, and were now very bland with Olav; Lady Magnhild had wine brought and all four drank together from the Yule horn.

When Lady Magnhild said that now Ingunn must go across to her grandmother and go to bed, Olav stood up—he said he was going over to Grim's and Dalla's house to talk with them awhile. Magnhild made no objection.

The sky was overcast, but between rifts in the clouds the sunset glow shone through, cold and brassy. The evenings were already beginning to be chilly and autumnal.

Olav and Ingunn strolled down between the outhouses. They came to the fence of a cornfield; the man rested his arms on the rail and stood looking out. The corn was thin, it shone white under the heavy grey sky; down below, the bay lay in a dead calm, reflecting the gathering darkness; under the opposite bank the image of the blue-black woods merged with the land.

" 'Tis as I remember it," said Olav softly. "As it used to be in autumn. In Denmark it blows almost always."

He turned half round to the girl, laid an arm about her shoulder, and drew her toward him. With a long breath of happiness she leaned heavily against him. At long last she felt she had come home; now she was in his arm.

Olav took her face in both his hands, pushed up her hair, and kissed her on the temples. "It used to curl here, where the hair begins," he whispered.

"It is because I comb it down so hard," she said softly. "I have combed away the curls. When they took the coif from me, I plaited it as flat as I could."

"Ah, now I remember it—you went in a coif that winter at Hamar!"

"Are you angry with me for letting them force me—to put it off?"

Olav shook his head with a little laugh. "I had almost forgotten it—when I thought of you, 'twas always as you were before that."

"Do you think I am like myself as I was then?" whispered Ingunn anxiously; "or have I fallen off?"

"No!" He squeezed her tightly in his arms. For a while they stood in close embrace. Then he let go. "Nay—we must go in. 'Twill soon be dark—" but he drew her plaits through his hands, twined them about his wrists, and shook her gently to and fro, standing at arm's length.

"How fair you are, Ingunn!" he said warmly. Again he let go, with a queer, short laugh. Then he asked abruptly: "Then it is more than a year since you saw Arnvid last?"

Ingunn replied that it was so.

"I would fain have met him this time. He is the only friend I had in my youth—he and you. The folk one meets later, when one is getting on in years, are not the same."

He was one-and-twenty and she twenty, but neither of them thought they were too young to talk thus. Far too much had happened to them both before they were quite out of their childhood.

When he had said this, Olav turned and began to walk back; Ingunn followed behind him up the narrow alley between the cattle-sheds. Grim and Dalla were sitting on the stone before the door of the byre. The two old people were delighted when Olav stopped to speak to them. Presently he took some money out of his belt and gave it to them—then there was no end to their joy.

Ingunn stood waiting by the wall of the byre, but no one spoke to her; and when she saw that Olav wished to stay here awhile with the old bailiff and his sister, she bade them good-night and went back to her grandmother's house.

. . .

Olav stayed five days at Berg, and on the morning of the sixth he said he must ride to Hamar that evening, for he had been promised a boat to take him to Eidsvold, if he could be ready early next morning.

He was now very good friends with Ivar and Magnhild, and all about the place thought that Olav had become much more of a man in these years he had spent abroad. But Ingunn and he had not had much talk together.

The day he was to ride away she asked him to go with her up into the loft where Aasa's and her own things were. She unlocked her chest, took out a folded linen garment, and handed it to him, turning her face away as she did so.

"This is your wedding-shirt, Olav. I wished to give it you *now*."

When at last she looked at him, he was standing with the shirt in his hands; he had turned red and his features were strangely discomposed. "Christ bless you, my Ingunn—Christ bless your hands for every stitch you have sewed here—"

"Olav—do not go!"

"You know I must go," he said quietly.

"Oh no, Olav! I never thought, when once you came home, that you would straightway go from me again. Stay here, Olav—only three days—only *one* day more!"

"Nay." Olav sighed. "Cannot you see, Ingunn—I am still an outlaw; 'twas rash of me to *come*, but I thought I must *see* you and talk with your kinsfolk. I own nothing in Norway today that I may rightly call mine. It is my lord the Earl who has promised me— And if it were not so—when *he* summons me to be with him on a certain day, I cannot stay away. I must make haste, as it is, to reach him at the right time—"

"Can you not take me with you?" she whispered almost inaudibly.

"You must surely see that I cannot. Whither should I carry you? To Valdinsholm, among the Earl's men—!" He laughed.

"I have had such evil days here at Berg," she whispered as before.

"I cannot see that. For they are kind, Lady Magnhild and Lady Aasa— While I was out there in the south—many a time I thought: what if Kolbein carried it so that *he* had you in his charge? And I feared for you, my dear. But here you have been as well off as you could be."

"I cannot bear to be here any more. Can you not take me with you—find me a lodging otherwheres?"

"I can find you no lodging so long as I have not been given control of my own estate," said Olav impatiently. "And how think you Ivar and Magnhild would like it if I took you away—Ivar, who is to be my spokesman with Kolbein? Be not so unreasoning, Ingunn. And Mistress Aasa cannot make shift without you."

They were both silent a good while. Ingunn went to the little window. "I have always thought, as I stood here looking out, that this must be like Hestviken."

Olav came up to her and laid a hand caressingly on her neck. "Oh no," he said absently; "the fiord is much broader at Hestviken, you must know. It is the salt sea there. And the manor stands higher, as far as I remember."

He went back, picked up the shirt, and folded it. "This must have been a great task, Ingunn—with all the stitches you have put into it."

"Oh—I have had four years to work at it," she said in a hard voice.

"Come, we will go out," said Olav hotly. "We will go out and talk!"

They walked together over the fields till they came to a meadow that sloped to the water. Junipers and other bushes grew on the dry, rocky ground, and here and there were patches of short, sun-scorched grass.

"Come, sit down here!"—He lay on his stomach facing her and gazed fixedly as though far away in his own thoughts.

In a way she thought they were brought nearer to each other merely by his losing himself in thought and remaining silent as soon as he had got her alone; she was so used to this from their childhood. She sat looking affectionately at the little scattered freckles over the root of his nose—they too were intimate, it seemed to her.

Great clouds drifted across the sky, throwing shadows that turned the forests dark blue—the patches of green meadow and white cornfield showed up so strongly between. And the fiord was grey with smooth dark currents farther out, which reflected scraps of the autumnal land. Now and again the sun came out, and its sharp, golden light baked them—but the next moment a cloud came by and the warmth was gone—and the ground was bleak.

At long last the girl asked: "What are you thinking of so, Olav?"

He sighed, as though awaking; then he took her hand and laid his face against the palm. "If you could be less unreasonable—" he answered, taking up again their talk in the loft. He paused a moment. "I ran off from Hövdinggaard without saying a word of thanks—"

Ingunn gave a little terrified cry.

"Ay," Olav went on. " 'Tis ill done—'twas not seemly, for uncle had been a good man to me in many ways—"

"Did you quarrel?"

"Not that either. It came about that he did a thing I liked not. He had one of his house-carls punished—I cannot say it was more than the man deserved. But uncle was often cruel, when he was beside himself with rage—and you know I have never liked to see man or beast tortured needlessly—"

"And so you quarrelled?"

"Not that either. This fellow had turned traitor— They had been sitting drinking in the hall, uncle and some kinsmen and friends—ay, they were *my* kinsmen too—they had come to us to keep Easter—it was the evening of Easter Day. They spoke of the King, and there was none there who wished him well—and so they let out something of their plans against King Eirik. They weave many strange plots there now, you see—and we were all drunken and careless of our mouths. This Aake had been waiting at table, and he ran off to the King's captain at Holbekgaard and sold him the tidings he had heard; and this came to uncle's ears. So uncle had the man led out into the pleasance and bound to the biggest oak, and then he stretched up the traitor's right hand, the hand that had sworn fealty to Barnim, and nailed it to the trunk with a knife.

"Ay, 'tis not that 'twas undeserved, I say naught of that. But as the night wore on. I thought that Aake might have stood there long enough. So I went out and freed him and lent him a horse— I bade him send it back to a house in Kallundborg, where I was known, when he had found a chance to escape from Sealand.— But I thought that uncle would be mighty wroth with me for playing him this trick, and that 'twould boot me little to speak with him. I had heard that the Earl lay to the northward off the point—so I gathered together what I could of my goods and rode northward the same night. And so it came about that I was in England with the Earl this year.

"Ay, 'twas no fitting thanks I gave uncle—and I pray to God every day that he may not have more trouble through my setting Aake free. You know, I made him swear, but an oath and a belch are all one to such a fellow— Had uncle had him hanged, I should have said 'twas well done. But as he stood there by the oak, with his hand nailed fast— 'Twas just after Easter, you know; we had been to church every day, and I had crept to the cross and kissed it on Good Friday.—So it came over me that the man standing there was like one crucified—"

Ingunn nodded quietly. " 'Twas surely a good deed."

"God knows. Would I could believe it. And you know that if I go back to Denmark in the Earl's company, I can send uncle a message—maybe find occasion to visit him and beg his forgiveness. For I showed him gross ingratitude."

He gazed longingly over the dark-blue forests. "You say you are not in good case here, Ingunn. It has not been like keeping Yule every day with me either. I make no complaint of my rich kinsmen—but they are rich and proud men, and I came to them poor and a stranger, an outlawed man—a boy they counted me and no true-born scion of their race, since 'twas not they who had given mother in marriage. I will not say they might have received me better than they did—things being as they were.

"You must not be deaf to reason," he bade her again. He pushed himself forward and let his head fall heavily in her lap. "Gladly would I stay here now, or take you with me—were there any means to do it. Would you rather I had not come, since I could not come to stay?"

Ingunn shook her head, drew her hands through his hair, and ruffled it caressingly.

"But 'tis strange," she said in a low voice, "that your uncle would not do more for you—when he has no children living, other than that nun?"

"Had I been willing to stay in Denmark. But I always said I would not. And he must have seen that I yearned to be home again."

After a while Ingunn asked: "These friends of yours—in that town you spoke of—what kind of folk are they?"

"Oh, nothing," replied Olav a little crossly. "A tavern. I was

often in that town for uncle—selling bullocks and such errands—"
Ingunn stroked his hair again and again.

"A kiss you may give me for all that!" He rose on his knees, clasped her tightly in his arms, and kissed her on the mouth.

"You may have as many as you will," she whispered close to him. The tears came trickling from her eyelids as she felt his strong, hot kisses all over her face and down her neck. "As many as you will— You might have had kisses every day!"

"Then I fear I should have been far too greedy!" He laughed low in his throat. "My Ingunn!" He bent her head back till her neck nearly touched the ground. "But now 'twill not be long—" he muttered.

"We must go up," he said, letting her go. " 'Tis long past dinner-time. I wonder how Lady Magnhild will like it that we left the house in this fashion!"

"I care not," muttered Ingunn defiantly.

"Nay, nor I either!" Olav laughed as he took her hand and raised her. He dusted her and himself with his cap. "But now we must go home, for all that."

He walked on with her hand in his, until they came to the path where they could be seen from the house.

3

INGUNN went about her daily life, after Olav had gone, unable to conquer a trace of disappointment. It was as though his visit had been to *her* least of all.

She knew it was wrong to take it thus. Olav had behaved prudently in letting it seem that he had given up his old claim on her: that she was his to possess and enjoy. In any case they could never have carried that through here at Berg. And he had gained the assent of both Ivar and Magnhild to her staying here as his lawful betrothed.

Lady Magnhild gave her gifts for her bridal chest—it had been sadly empty till now. A cloak of green velvet, lined with beaver-skin, as good as new; a tablecloth and a towel with a blue pattern;

two shifts of linen and one of silk; the full furnishing of a cradle; three bench covers in picture weaving; a brass pot, a drinking-horn with silver mounts, and a great silver tankard—all this she received in the course of the next two months. And she got Aasa Magnusdatter to give her granddaughter the good bedding she had in store, with curtains and rugs, bolster, skin coverlets, and sheets of stuff. "Is Ingunn to be married?" the grandmother asked in surprise, each time her daughter begged some of her possessions. She forgot it from day to day.

Ivar promised to give her a horse and saddle, and money to buy six good cows—it would be too heavy a task to drive cattle from the Upplands to the Vik. And he bade her come south to Galtestad, so that she might choose from among the wearing-apparel left by his dead wife: "I would rather you had it than Tora—she is grown so high and mighty since she got this Haakon Thunder-guts and became the royal mother of his sons."

He went so far as to find out what had become of Olav's clothes-chest, which was sold at Hamar when the boy was proclaimed outlaw. The chest was of white limewood, an unusually handsome piece of work, with the finest carving on the fore side. Ivar bought it back and sent it to Ingunn at Berg.

The axe Kinfetch had been with the Dominicans at Hamar the whole time. Brother Vegard hid it away when the Sheriff took possession of Olav's personal property. The monk said it was no great sin; for this axe, which had descended in the same family for more than a hundred years, ought not to come into the hands of strangers so long as Olav was alive. When Olav now came back to Hamar, Brother Vegard was in Rendalen preaching to the peasants there on the Paternoster and the Angel's Greeting—he had made up four excellent sermons on these subjects, and with these he travelled about the diocese in the summer. But Olav had sought out the Prior and had done public penance in church for the manslaughter in the convent. After that the Prior had given him back the axe. But when he set out again for the south, he left it behind in charge of the monks.

Kolbein was beyond measure furious when Ivar applied to him to treat of an atonement on Olav's behalf. Never would he accept fines for Einar's slaying—Olav Audunsson should be an unatoned felon, and Ingunn could stay where she was, without honour and without inheritance, unless she would accept such a match as her kinsmen could provide for a debauched woman—a serving-man or a small farmer.

Ivar merely laughed at his half-brother. Kolbein must be mad if he knew so little of the times he lived in: if the King granted Olav leave to dwell in the land, then Kolbein might, if he pleased, refuse to accept the fines—let the silver lie by the church door for crows and vagabonds to pick up; Olav would sit just as safely at Hestviken for all that. And as to his betrothal with Ingunn, 'twas nothing but folly to seek to deny that the bargain had been made of old. That Olav had forestalled them, at the time they thought of giving the bride to Haakon Gautsson, Ivar now thought a good thing: he was well pleased that this nephew by marriage had shown while still so young that he was a man who would not be cheated of his lawful rights.

Haakon Gautsson was now engaged in litigation with his wife's kinsmen about an inheritance that he claimed on Tora's behalf; but Ivar had little thought of praising *this* nephew on this account; it was for this he had given Haakon his pretty nickname. Thus Haakon and Tora kept away this autumn, while Ivar and Magnhild were working to arrange Ingunn's marriage.

Haftor Kolbeinsson had a meeting with Ivar at Berg to treat of the matter. Haftor was a hard, cold man, but upright in a way, and much shrewder than his father. He saw full well that if Olav Audunsson had made powerful friends who would advance his cause, it was useless for his father to raise difficulties about the atonement. The only way in which they could gain was by demanding that the fines be fixed as high as possible.

All this kept up Ingunn's spirits. She accepted every gift as a pledge that now she would soon have Olav back, and then he would take her home with him. She yearned so for him—and when he was here last, he had spoken so little to her. It was natural, she saw, that he must now think above all of winning over her kinsmen and securing their joint estate. And when she was once his, she believed full surely that he would love her as in old days. Although he was no longer so blind and hasty as he had been then. The change in him was that he was now grown up—it was in him that she first became fully aware how many years had gone by since they were children together at Frettastein.

.   .   .

It was Haftor Kolbeinsson who brought news to Berg, when he came thither after Whitsuntide next spring to receive the second part of the blood-money for Einar.

Olav had made payment of one half at mid-Lent in Hamar—a German merchant from Oslo had brought the silver, and Ivar had appeared with him; Haftor received the money for his father. A part of the sum should now have been paid after Whitsuntide, and the remainder Olav himself was to hand over to the dead man's representatives at the summer Thing, which was held every year at Hamar after the conclusion of the Eidsiva Thing. After that he was to have received Ingunn at the hands of her kinsmen.

But this time no man had come from Olav; on the other hand, Haftor had strange tidings to tell of the Earl, Olav's lord. Queen Ingebjörg Eiriksdatter had died at Björgvin early in the spring, and Earl Alf must then have feared that the days of his mastery in Norway were over. The young Duke Haakon had hated his mother's counsellors heartily ever since he was a little boy. Now he sent word to the Earl bidding him send to Oslo the mercenaries he had hired in England the summer before—it had been done in the name of the Norwegian King, but Earl Alf had kept them with him at Borg, to the great annoyance and mischief of the folk of the country round. The Earl obeyed the command in this manner, that he came sailing in to Oslo with a whole fleet and went up into the town with more than two hundred men; he himself lodged with his following in the King's palace with Sir Hallkel Krökedans, the Duke's captain. One evening some of these Fi'port wights,[5] as the English hirelings were called, broke into a homestead near the town, plundered it, and maimed the master of the house. Sir Hallkel demanded the surrender of the malefactors, and when the Englishmen refused to give up the culprits, he had a number of them made prisoners, took out five men at random, and hanged them. Thereupon the Englishmen made an attack on the King's palace and it came to an open fight between the Earl's men and the townsmen, the town was plundered, and the whole of that part which lies from St. Clement's Church and the river down to the King's Palace and the quays was burned. The end of it was that the Earl sailed out of Folden [6] with his whole host,

[5] The Earl's mercenaries were drawn from the Cinque Ports.
[6] The Oslo Fiord.

and he carried Sir Hallkel with him as a prisoner—he sought to throw the whole blame of the disaster upon him. But these tidings were brought to the Duke while he lay under the coast in the south, on his way home from his mother's funeral, and now he collected a force in haste and got his brother, the King, with him. They sailed across to Borgesyssel; Sarpsborg and Isegran were taken by storm, and about three hundred of the Earl's men were said to have fallen or were slain afterwards by the peasants of the district; Alf's seneschal at Isegran and several men of his body-guard were executed by the Duke—folk said in revenge for Hall-kel Krökedans, who had been put to death in the castle there by order of the Earl. Alf himself and the remnant of his host were said to have saved themselves by flight to Sweden, and King Eirik had made him an outlaw in Norway with all the men who were in his following.

They were very silent, the Berg folks, when Haftor had told this story, dryly and calmly. Olav's name he never mentioned, but after a long pause Ivar asked in sheer despondency if Haftor had heard any news of him—if he were among the fallen.

Haftor hesitated a moment and answered no. It chanced that the men from whom he had first heard this—two white friars from Tunsberg—could give him special news of Olav Audunsson, because he had been at the sister convent, Mariaskog, when the fire of Oslo took place; Olav had been given leave by the Earl before the move upon Oslo, and he had fared south to Elvesyssel to sell some of the land he owned there to the monks of Dragsmark. They said further that, when tidings came to him there of how the Earl's greatness had been brought to an end, Olav had declared that he owed Lord Alf all that he now possessed and had won back, and he would not part without leave from the first lord to whom he had sworn fealty. Thereupon he had set out into Sweden to seek the Earl.

" 'Tis odd how unlucky he is, Olav, in the men he chooses to back him," said Haftor dryly. "They end as outlaws, first the Bishop and now the Earl.—But I trow 'tis in his blood; 'twas a Baglers' nest, Hestviken, in his forefathers' time, I have heard."

"Ay, Baglers' nest and Ribbungs' den [7] were the names folk

---

[7] The Baglers (or "crozier men") were the party of the Church and the old nobility, opposed to Sverre and his followers, the Birchlegs (see

gave in old days to Hov and Galtestad and many another manor of our kin, Haftor," Ivar protested, but his voice was very tame.

Haftor shrugged his shoulders. "Ay—Olav may be a good enough man, for all it seems his fate ever to be on the side of the loser. *My* friend he can never be, but, I will say, 'tis plain enough that his friends like the man. But if Ingunn is to wait for him, she will have to practise patience."

Ivar objected that this time it might well be that his affairs could quickly be set in order. Haftor merely shrugged again.

It was Ivar who told Ingunn there was but little hope that Olav could take her home this summer. It did not enter his mind to speak at length of Earl Alf's revolt to a young woman whom he counted somewhat simple and light-minded—so that at first Ingunn did not know that Olav was in as evil a plight as before he had found a helper in Alf Erlingsson.

All she knew was that nothing more was said about her marriage.

Ivar and Lady Magnhild felt somewhat at a loss. They had taken up this affair with both hands and had received Olav with such favour that they could hardly turn against him, now that he had been plunged so unexpectedly into a new strait. So they chose to be perfectly silent about the whole matter.

Kolbein Toresson was at his own home and lay abed for the most part—he had had a stroke. So Ingunn did not hear much of what he said. And Haftor held his peace. He had received one half of the blood-money in excellent English coin and judged it unprofitable to try whether the atonement could be upset after that. Moreover he had some pity for Ingunn, and he thought it might be just as well in the end if Olav got her and carried her off to another part of the country—her kinsfolk had neither honour nor profit of her. When old Lady Aasa was gone, she would only be a burden to her sister and brothers. And he was now foster-father to Hallvard and Jon, Steinfinn's sons, and good friends with the boys—Haakon Gautsson had also quarrelled with his young brothers-in-law.

.   .   .

note, p. 4). The Ribbungs (named after their leader) were a remnant of the Bagler party, the champions of a lost cause, and thus went down to history with the stigma of the under dog.

So Ingunn was left once more to herself, to sit brooding in her corner with her grandmother.

The first autumn she still went on as she was wont—she span, weaved, and sewed her bridal garments. But by degrees she lost heart for the work. No one ever said a word of her future. She left off hoping that Olav would come *soon*—and immediately it was as though she had never believed it in earnest. Their meetings during the days he had last been here had left behind a vague disappointment in her heart—Olav had been half a stranger to her.

She did not seem able to make his image fit into her old dreams of living with him in his house, where they were master and mistress and had a flock of little children about them—and yet they were the same two who had loved each other at Frettastein.

So she seized upon the memory of the only hour they two had been alone together, face to face and lips to lips—that last day, when they sat together in the meadow. She let her thoughts weave fresh pictures from their talk and from his one ardent, passionate caress—when he burned a kiss upon her and bent her neck backward to the ground. She dreamed that he had yielded to his own desire and her prayers—and had taken her with him. She called to mind what her mother had told her the night before her death —of her bridal ride over hill and dale—the daughter now had this to feed her fancies.—Next summer, the second since Olav's visit, she chanced to go with Lady Magnhild far up into the Gudbrandsdal, to a wedding at Ringabu. They stayed some weeks there with their kinsfolk at Eldridstad, and these took them up to their mountain sæter, that Lady Magnhild might see their wealth of cattle. For the first time in her life Ingunn went up a mountain, so high that she was above the forests: she looked out over bare wastes with osier scrub and stunted birches and greyish-yellow bogs, and in the distance rose hill after hill, as far as the northern horizon, where snow mountains closed the view, with clouds about their sides.

At this great wedding she had been made to wear brightcoloured clothes, a silver belt, and floating hair. At the time she had been only shy and confused. But it left its mark in her. When she was back in her grandmother's room at Berg, new images floated before her mind—she saw herself walking with Olav, jewelled and glorious—it might be in the palace of some foreign king; this seemed to compensate her for all these years she had sat in the corner. And in her dreams she wandered over the fells with her outlawed man—they rode through mountain streams, which foamed swifter and clearer than the rivers in the lowlands—there was more music in their sound, less roar—and their beds shone with white pebbles. Every sound under heaven, the light, the air, were different on the mountains from what they were in the fields below. She was journeying with Olav toward the distant blue fells, through deep valleys and over wide moorlands again; they rested in stone huts like the Eldridstad sæter.—At the thought of these fells a wildness was born within her. She who had longed in such meek abandonment to fate, who had only wept quietly under the bedclothes now and then, when she seemed too bitterly oppressed—she felt an unruly spirit quicken within her. And her dreams became chequered and fantastic—she wove into them such incidents as she had heard of in ballads and stories, she imagined all those things which she had never seen; stone castles roofed with lead, and warriors in blue coats of mail, and ships with silken sails and golden pennants. This was all more gorgeous and splendid than the old pictures of the farmstead with Olav and their children—but it was far more airy and confused and dreamlike.

Arnvid Finnsson had been at Berg once or twice in the last years, and they had spoken of Olav, but he knew no more of his friend than that Olav was said to be alive and in Sweden. But the winter after her journey to the fells—it was New Year, and men wrote 1289 after God's birth—Arnvid came to Berg, very cheerful. Arnvid was wont to go almost every year to a fair at Serna, and there he had met Olav that autumn; they had been together for four days. Olav said that the Earl had himself released him from his oath; he would have Olav think now of his own welfare—and he had given him tokens to Sir Tore Haakonsson of Tunsberg, who was married to Lord Alf's sister. Olav had now entered the service of a Swedish lord in order to provide himself with means against his home-coming, but he intended to go home to Norway at the New Year—perhaps he was already at Hestviken.

Ingunn was made happy; at least so long as Arnvid stayed at Berg, she felt her courage awaken once more. But afterwards her hope seemed to pale again and fade away; she dared not abandon herself to the expectation that something was really going to happen. Nevertheless there was a brighter background to her thoughts and dreams that winter, while she watched the approach of spring—and perhaps Olav would come, as Arnvid had said.

In summer the women of Berg, when they had to smoke meat or fish, used to take it out of doors. In the birch grove north of the homestead there were some great bare rocks; they lighted a fire in a crevice of the rock and covered it with a chest without a bottom, within which they hung what was to be smoked; and then a woman had to sit and tend the fire.

One day before Hallvard's Eve,[8] Aasa Magnusdatter wished to have some fish smoked, and Dalla and Ingunn went out with it. The old woman lighted a fire and got it to burn and smoke as it should; but then she had to go home to tend a cow, and Ingunn was left alone.

The soil was almost bare here in the grove, brown and bleak, but the sun on the rocks was warm—fair-weather clouds drifted high up in the silky blue sky. But the bay, of which she could see a glimpse between the naked white birch-trunks, was still covered with rotten, thawing ice, and on the far shore the snow still glared white among the woods, right down to the beach. Here on the sunny side there was a trickling and gurgling of water everywhere, but the thaw had not yet given its full roar to the voice of spring.

Ingunn was happy and contented as she sat in the sunshine watching the smoke. She had already been there some hours and was just wondering whether she would have to go and look for more juniper when she heard someone come riding along the path above where she had been sitting. She looked up—it was only a man on a little shaggy, ill-kept dun pony.—In doing so she pushed against her water-bucket; it stood unsteadily on the rocks and upset.

She saw with annoyance that she would have to go and fetch water—and Dalla had taken the wooden bucket; the one she had was of stone, with two ears and a stick thrust through them to lift it by. She picked it up; then the man called from the path above—he had jumped off his pony and came running down through the withered heather: "Nay, nay, fair maid—I will do that for you!"

[8] St. Hallvard's Day is May 15.

He threw his arms around her waist to check himself, pressing her to him in his haste, took the bucket from her, and set off again briskly down to the burn. Ingunn laughed with him in spite of herself as she stood watching him—he had shown such a mass of white teeth when he laughed.

He was dark-complexioned and curly-haired—the hood of his cloak was thrown back and he was bareheaded. He was very tall and slight and active, but rather loose-jointed in all his movements, and his voice had been so merry—

He came back with the water, and she saw he was very young. His swarthy face was narrow and bony, but not ugly—the eyes were large, yellow or light brown, merry, and clear. His mouth was big, with its arched row of teeth, but the curve of his nose was fine and bold. The man was dressed in a proper moss-green kirtle and an ample brown cloak; he wore a short sword in his belt.

"There!" he said laughing. "If you would have more help, you need but to ask me!"

Ingunn laughed too; she said she had no need of more, and it was much that he had already done for her—the bucket was heavy.

"Far too heavy for so fine and young a maid. Are you from Berg?"

Ingunn answered yes.

"'Tis thither I am bound—I have a message and a letter from my lord to your lady. But now I shall stay here and help you—then I shall be so late that Lady Magnhild must house me for the night. And then you will let me sleep with you?"

"No doubt I shall." Ingunn had no other thought but that the boy was jesting—he was no more than a boy, she saw, and she laughed with him.

"But now I will stay here and talk with you awhile," he said. "'Tis a tiresome task you have, and lonely it must be for you to sit here alone in the wood, young and fair as you are."

"It were worse to sit here, I trow, if I were old and ugly. And 'tis not lonely in this wood. I have sat here but four hours, and already you have come this way."

"Ay, then I doubt not I was sent to pass the time for you—stay, I will help you; I am better at this work than you!" Ingunn went about it rather awkwardly, for she did not like to get the smoke in her eyes and throat. The boy dipped the juniper sprays in the water and laid them on the embers, jumping aside when the smoke blew out toward him. "What is your name, fair lass?"

"Why would you know that?"

"Why, for then I will tell you mine. It might be useful for you to know it—since I am to sleep with you tonight?"

Ingunn only shook her head and laughed. "But you are not from these parts?" she asked; there was such a strange tone in his speech, she heard.

"Nay, I am an Icelander. And my name is Teit. Now you must tell me yours."

"Oh, I have no such queer name as yours. I am called naught but Ingunn."

"That may be good enough for you—for the present; 'tis as fine a name as the finest I wot of. If I find a better, I will write it in golden letters and give it to you, Ingunn rosy-cheeks."

He helped her to take out the smoked fish and put in fresh. Lying on the ground, he picked out a trout, split it, and began to eat.

"You take the fattest and best," said Ingunn with a laugh.

"Is she so grudging of her food, Lady Magnhild, your mistress, that she would refuse us poor folks a fish-bone?" Teit laughed back at her.

Ingunn guessed he took her for a serving-maid. She was clad in a brown homespun dress with a plain leather belt at her waist, and she wore her hair as usual, in two plaits without ornament, simply bound with blue woollen knots.

Teit seemed disposed to stay with her for good. He tended the smoke for her, dipped juniper, and laid it on; between whiles he stretched himself on the ground by her side and talked. She learned that he was now clerk to the Sheriff's officer in these parts. He was the son of a priest whose name was Sira Hall Sigurdsson, and he had been at the school in Holar; but Teit had no mind to be a priest, he chose rather to go out into the world and seek his fortune.

"Have you found it, then?" asked Ingunn.

"I will give you an answer to that tomorrow"—he smiled darkly.

She could not help liking this merry boy. And then he asked if he might take a kiss. It came over her—there could be no harm. So she said neither yes nor no—simply sat still and laughed. And

Teit took her round the waist and kissed her full on the mouth. But after that he would not let her go—and he slipped his hands in under her clothes, grew somewhat indelicate in his advances. Ingunn tried to defend herself, she was near being afraid—and she bade him cease.

" 'Tis unmanly of you, Teit," she begged—"I sit here and must tend my work—I cannot run, you know that well!"

"I had not thought of that!" He let her go at once, rather shame-facedly. "I must go and see what has become of my jade," he said a moment later. —"We shall meet at Berg?" he called to her from the bridle-path above.

When Ingunn and Dalla came down to the house in the evening, there was no one in the courtyard, but when the door of Lady Magnhild's living-room was opened, they heard laughter and loud voices within. Lady Magnhild had guests, two young maids, Dagny and Margret, the twin daughters of one of her foster-daughters, and this evening a number of young people had come to Berg, the girls' kinsfolk and their friends.

Ingunn went into her grandmother's house. Taking the bowl on her knees, she sat by the bedside and gave the old lady porridge and milk, taking a spoonful herself now and then, after that she took a knife and a basket and went out. The evenings were already fine and bright, and cummin and other wild herbs had come up on the sunny slope facing the bay, below the Bride's Acre, as they called the best and largest cornfield on the place. She wished to dig up a basketful and make broth for her grandmother—the old lady must need to cleanse her body of rheum and unwholesome humours after the winter.

The plants were so small and young, before she had filled her basket the grey-blue dusk of the spring evening had fallen upon the land. As she came up toward the house she was met by a tall, slight man coming down in the twilight—Teit, the Icelander.

"Is it so—must you go out and toil and swink so late?" he asked kindly. He put his hand into her basket, took up a handful of the green herbs, and smelled them. Then he took hold of her wrist and stroked it gently up and down.

"There is frolic and dance in the hall. Will you not join in it, Ingunn? Come—and I will sing the best I can."

Ingunn shook her head.

"Surely she cannot be so hard on you, your mistress? All the others are within, the whole household—"

" 'Twould surprise them if I came," said Ingunn quietly. " 'Tis long since I was seen in the young folks' dance. Dagny and Margret would wonder, if I went in to them and their friends."

" 'Tis only that they are jealous of your beauty. They like it not that the maid is fairer than—" He clasped her, crushing the basket she held before her. "I shall come to you by and by," he whispered.

Ingunn stood for a while before the door, looking out into the grey spring night and listening to the sound of song and harping which came faintly from Magnhild's hall. She would not go in there—they were young and wanton. But there could not be any harm in it if she let Teit in tonight. She too had a mind to talk with a stranger once again. She left the door ajar and lay down fully clad.

The time dragged on, and she tried to deny to herself that she was disappointed at his not coming after all. At last she must have fallen asleep—she was awakened with a start by the man's jumping into her bed and lying down beside her, in no very seemly fashion. But when she thrust him roughly from her, he was tame at once.

He excused himself, saying there had been so much noise and revelry in the hall. But when Ingunn lay so still and answered so coldly to all he told her of their merry-making, Teit grew more and more subdued. At last he said meekly: "You must know, what rejoiced me most was that I was to speak with you—and now you are angry with me, I wis? My sweet, what would you that I should say to you that will give you pleasure in the hearing?"

"Nay, that you must find for yourself," said Ingunn; she fell to laughing again. "If you have come a-courting, you must not ask me how to set about it!"

"How so? Could I then win your heart—would you not gladly leave Berg, Ingunn?"

"Oh—oh—that may well be—"

"Would you have a mind to flit over to Iceland and dwell there?"

"Is it very far to Iceland?" asked Ingunn.

Teit said yes. But it was a good land to live in, better than Norway—in any case better than the Upplands, for here the winter was so horridly cold. At home where he came from there was many a winter with no snow on the ground—the sheep were out all year round and the ponies.—This sounded tempting to Ingunn, for she too thought the winter was horrid—when the beast starved in the byre, and the bedcover was frozen fast to the wall in the morning, and one's feet were always cold, and one had to break a hole in the ice for every drop of water wanted in the house.

Teit waxed eloquent as he spoke of his native land. Ingunn thought it must be beautiful—those heaths, where they herded sheep and goats in the autumn, must be like the mountain she had climbed, when they were north in the dale. The world was wide and great—for the men, who could roam afar in it. She fell to thinking of Olav, how he had roamed abroad—to England and Denmark and Sweden—Teit had seen no other lands but Iceland and Norway. She wished Olav had been one who would tell her something of all he had seen—but Olav was always so silent about the things that had happened to him. But it might be because Teit had great learning—she had never thought that a learned man could be so young and frank and full of life. But then she had never before met a layman who was a clerk—save Arnvid, and he was so much older and so serious-minded.

At last they grew sleepy, both of them—several times their talk came to a standstill. Then the boy crept closer to her and began to fondle and caress her. Ingunn repelled him, at first rather sleepily and half-heartedly—but then she took fright, Teit was so wild. She bade him remember that Lady Aasa slept in the other bed; were she to wake and find that Ingunn had a bedfellow, it would go ill with her.

Teit made some show of wailing and lamenting, as if in jest—but then he mended his manners, wished her good-night, and thanked her. Ingunn followed him to the door and barred it—then she saw that it was already past midnight.

She was up late next morning and it was the middle of the day before she was out in the courtyard. She caught sight of the Icelander, who was hovering by the stable door, looking as if he had sold butter and not been paid for it. Ingunn went up to him, wished him good-morning, and thanked him for their last meeting.

Teit feigned not to see her outstretched hand; he gazed gloomily before him.

" 'Twas a good jest you thought to play on me, that—I was such a dullard that you could cozen me to your heart's content?"

"I know not what you mean!"

"Was it not a fine conceit to lead on a poor young lad to woo you—the daughter of Berg?"

"I am not the daughter of Berg, Teit—the niece am I. That makes a great difference."

Teit looked at her suspiciously.

"I thought it was *you* who jested—when you spoke of wooing, and when you would fondle—I took it not for earnest. But I did not believe you would mock me—for my simplicity, I mean. And you must know that I, who have never been beyond these parts, where I was born, have little wit or knowledge; I thought it solace to speak with you, so wise and learned and far-faring a man as you are."

She smiled at him with gentle entreaty. Teit looked down. "That you surely do not mean."

"Yes, I mean it. I had thought perhaps you would stay here some days—and that I should be cheered by hearing and learning more of you."

"Nay, I must go home now. But I expect that Gunnar Bergsson will send me hither again after the holy-days," he said, a little annoyed.

"Then you will be welcome!" Ingunn gave him her hand in farewell and went back to her house.

4

ARNVID FINNSSON came down at John's Mass to see to his aunt—it was up and down with Mistress Aasa now; she might go out at any moment, but she might also live a good while yet, if it was God's will. Arnvid had heard no more news of Olav since his last visit.

The day after he came, he and Ingunn were walking together in the courtyard. Then Teit Hallsson came in, ran past them, and went into Magnhild's house. Arnvid stopped and followed the young man with his eyes: "He has errands here day after day, that clerk?"

Ingunn said yes.

"I know not whether you ought to talk so much with him, Ingunn—"

"Why so?—know you aught of him?" she asked after a moment.

"I heard of him at Hamar," said Arnvid curtly.

"What was it?" asked Ingunn rather uneasily. "Do they charge him with—any *vice*?"

"A double one," said Arnvid quietly, as though with reluctance. It was Master Torgard, the cantor, who had first had the knave in his service, and he praised him too. The Icelander wrote the fairest hand, and he wrote quickly and correctly; he also knew how to illuminate, so Master Torgard had entrusted him with drawing and colouring the initials in an antiphonal and in a copy of the law of the land, and the work was fairly done. And when the book-binder's wife, who usually helped her husband, fell sick, Teit had assisted the man in her place, and he proved to be as skilful a book-binder as the Bishop's own man. So Master Torgard had been loath to send the lad away. But his weakness was that he went clean out of his wits when he touched dice or tables. And there was a good deal of such play in the town. He was a man who could play away hose and shoes, this Teit, and then he would come home to his master in borrowed clothes. In short, he had no sense to take care of his own welfare—he was in debt to ale-wives and chapmen. Unwilling as he was to be rid of so skilful a writer, Master Torgard thought that for the boy's own sake he must get him disposed where so many temptations would not beset his feet. He was in other ways a likable fellow, the cantor had said. But when the Sheriff at Reyne required a clerk who was good at reading and writing, Master Torgard had got the Icelander the place.

That he had also been involved in some irregularities with women Arnvid thought there was no need to mention to Ingunn; he was loath enough to spread rumours about the boy in any case. But he thought he must tell her this other thing about Teit—the Icelander had borrowed money from Master Torgard's old sisters and the like.

The day before John's Mass the people of Berg had been to morning mass—it was Sir Viking's anniversary—and as they were on their way home from church, a terrible thunderstorm broke.

It rained so that one would have thought the world had not seen the like since the days of Noah. The church folk sought shelter under some great overhanging rocks; for all that, they were drenched to the skin when they reached home late in the day.

Tora Steinfinnsdatter was visiting her aunt for the holy-day and had brought her two eldest children with her. She had been very friendly with her sister this time, and in the course of the afternoon she came into Aasa's house to get Ingunn to come over to them—they had several guests today.

Ingunn sat crouching by the fire on the hearth; she had let down her hair to get it to dry quicker. She objected at first that she could not leave her grandmother. Tora thought Dalla might well sit with the old lady. Then Ingunn said she had no fitting gown to wear—her only Sunday kirtle had been soaked that day on the church road.

Tora walked about the room, humming to herself. She was still a very handsome young wife, though she had grown very stout with years. But she was bravely clad, in a blue velvet kirtle and a silken coif—and her brooches and gilt belt made a goodly show on her broad figure. She had opened Ingunn's clothes-chest.

"Can you not put on this?" Tora came forward into the light of the fire carrying the green silk gown that her mother had given Ingunn for the feast after Mattias Haraldsson's slaying.

Ingunn bent her head shyly. Tora went on: "You have not worn it many times, sister. I mind me I grudged it you a little when Mother gave it you. *Have* you worn it more than that one evening?"

"I wore it to the wedding at Eldridstad."

"Ay, I heard say you looked so bravely there." Tora sighed. "And I lay abed and was vexed I could not be there too—the greatest wedding there has been in the dale these twenty years. Come now, sister," she begged. "Oh, I have such a mind to dance and play tonight—'tis the first summer I have been free to do the like since I was wed. Come now, my Ingunn—we have Arnvid to sing for us, and that Icelander, your friend—I know not which has the finer voice!"

Ingunn got up hesitatingly. With a laugh Tora took the gown, cast it over her head, and helped her to arrange the folds under the silver belt.

"My hair is still half wet," murmured Ingunn in embarrassment, as she gathered it in her hands.

"Then let it hang loose," laughed Tora. She took her sister's hand and led her out.

"Nay, look at Aunt Ingunn, look at Aunt Ingunn!" screamed Tora's little daughter as she came into the light. Ingunn picked up the child in her arms. The little maid threw her arms about her neck and sniffed at her half-dried hair, which enshrouded the woman like a mantle of some dark golden texture and reached below her knees. "Mother," she cried, "I will have hair like that when I am a grown maid!"

"Ay, you may well wish that."

Ingunn put the little one down. She was conscious of her own beauty tonight, it even dazzled herself. Olav, she thought, and her heart beat with a heavy thump—he *must* be here tonight. She passed her hand over her face, pushing the hair from it, and looked about her; she met Arnvid's strange, dark glance; and Teit's yellow-brown eyes blazed at her like torches. But the one she sought was not there. She clasped her hands crosswise over her bosom—*he* was not here who ought to have seen that tonight she was the fairest woman present. For an instant she felt she would rather run back to her grandmother, pluck off her finery, and give way to her tears.

As the evening wore on, there was talk of dancing—they called for the *Kraaka-maal*, the stately old sword-dance. Arnvid admitted that he had known it, and Tora said both she and her sister had learned the steps. Teit cut in, flushed and keen—he knew the *whole* lay, would gladly sing for them. Lady Magnhild laughed and said that if it would amuse the young people to see the old dance once more, she could bear a part—"And you, Bjarne?" She turned to an old knight, the friend of her youth. Then two or three of the older house-folk came forward, somewhat bashfully. It was easy to see that they were eager to essay their youthful exercise once more.

Arnvid said that Teit must lead the dance—he doubtless knew it best—and then Lady Magnhild and Sir Bjarne ought to stand next. But the old people would not have this. The end of it was that

THE AXE

Teit came first in the chain, then Ingunn, and Arnvid with Tora. There were in all seven men with drawn swords and six women.

The dance went right well—Teit was an excellent leader. His bright, full voice was a little sharp, but it could be heard that he was a trained singer. Arnvid's fine, rich voice supported him well in the lower part, and Sir Bjarne and two of the old house-carls still had very good voices—and they all warmed to it, so well did Teit carry on the lay and the dance. None of the women joined in the song—but thereby the old sword-dance seemed to gain in seriousness and force: it was the weapons that were to the fore, the men's rhythmical tramp and the rising fire of their singing; the women only glided silently in and out beneath the clashing play of the swords. Ingunn danced as though in a dream—she was tall and limber, had to stoop lower than the other women; and she turned pale and breathed heavily, keeping her eyes half-closed. As she sprang forward under the blades, her loose mantle of hair fluttered out, as though she were rising on heavy wings. One of its strands swept across Teit's chest and caught in a buckle; it gave her a wrench each time she crossed over, but she did not think of stopping the dance to free herself.

They had danced fifteen or sixteen of the verses when Lady Magnhild gave a loud cry that brought the whole chain to a standstill. The sweat was pouring down her red face—she clutched herself with both hands below the breast—now she could do no more, she cried with a laugh.

Arnvid signed to Teit with a fling of his compact little head; his eyes glistened wildly and he called out something, as he took up the strain, and all the men with him:

> "Swiftly went the sword-play—
> Aslaug's sons would quickly
> Rouse up Hild with weapons
> Keen, if they could see me—"

the men *would* have the last stanzas, even if they had to skip over ten or twelve verses between—

> "Strong meat gave I my sons,
> Strengthening their manhood!"

The men dancers were so wrought up by the game that they glowed with excitement and their voices boomed in chorus:

"Swiftly went the sword-play!—
Fain am I now for the end!
Home the bright ones call me,
Whom from Herjan's halls
Odin has sent out.
Gladly shall I in the high seat
Drink ale with the Æsir;
Gone are the hopes of life:
Laughing I go to my death!"

Then they broke the chain and reeled back to the benches, while the men laid aside their swords and wiped the sweat from their faces, laughing with delight. And the young people who had looked on cried out—so fine it had been! Lady Magnhild held her sides, panting with exhaustion: "Ay, 'tis another sort of dance than the way you hop and jump nowadays—'tis your turn now, Margret; dance one of these sweet love-ballads you young ones like so well:

'It was the King Lord Eirik
Rode north upon the hill—'

for they are dainty and sweet as honey, and I trow the old lays must be too rough for such silken dolls as you are!"

The young ones did not wait to be asked twice—most of them had thought rather that the old people kept the floor too long, though 'twas a rare sight to have the old sword-dance for once.

Teit came over to where Ingunn was sitting, crouched against the wall, wrapped in her own lovely hair. The dance had not flushed her, but her face was bedewed with a waxy pallor.

"Nay, I have no more strength to dance. I will sit here and look at you."

Teit rushed back to the others. He was unwearying and seemed to know everything, both the old lays and these new ballads by the score.

Ingunn paused in the courtyard—she had left the dancing to cross to her grandmother's house and go to rest.

It must be nearly midnight, she thought; the sky was pale and clear all round the horizon with a white sheen that deepened to yellow in the north. Only upon the ridge on the far side of the bay was there a grey-blue veil of thin clouds, and among them the moon was setting in a trail of moist vapour.

THE AXE

Although the night was so clear, it was darker over the land than was usual at this time of year—meadows and cornfields and groves were still soaked from the storm earlier in the day; a cold, damp mist was rising everywhere. Over the water floated thin wisps of brownish smoke, but all the bonfires had now died down, save one which blazed fiercely on a headland far away and threw its reflection like a narrow, glowing blade upon the steel-blue water.

Teit came out to look for her—she had known he would do so. Without looking back she walked out toward the cornfield that stretched down to the fiord. When she reached the gate and stood pulling up the stakes, he came up with her.

They did not speak as they walked on, she in front and he following, along the narrow path through the tender young corn. At the end of the cornfield ran a burn, and the path followed it through a thicket of alders and osiers down to the manor hard.

Ingunn stopped as soon as she entered the shadow of the foliage. It was so dark in there—she was afraid to go on.

"Ugh—'tis so cold tonight," she whispered almost inaudibly, shivering a little. She could barely make out the man's figure in the darkness, but she felt the warm breath of his body as something mild and sweet amid the cold and acrid scent of wet leaves and raw mould. He said not a word, and his silence seemed all at once to loom threateningly and terrifyingly—with a sudden uncontrollable dread she thought she must get him to say something; then the danger would pass.

"That verse you sang in the hall," she whispered; "of the willow —say it again!"

In a low, clear voice Teit repeated in the darkness:

> "Blest art thou, willow,
>   Standing out on the shore;
>   Fair is thy garment of leaves.
>   Men shake from thee
>   Dews of the morning.
>   And my longing is to Thegn
>   By night and by day!" [9]

Ingunn reached up and drew down an armful of the bitter-scented foliage—rain and dew showered over her in the darkness.

[9] *Aan Bogsveig's Saga.*

"You will spoil your fine clothes," said Teit. "Are you wet?—let me feel—"

But as his hands lightly brushed her bosom in the dark, she darted quick as lightning under his outstretched arms; with a low scream of fright she rushed along the path—catching up her gown in both hands, she ran as though for her life through the cornfield.

Teit was so surprised at the turn things had taken that it took him a moment to collect himself and follow her. And then she had such a start that he did not catch her up till they were at the gate. From there they could be seen and heard from the yard, where the guests were now passing to seek their quarters. So he stopped and let her go.

He showed a black and offended look when they met next day. Ingunn greeted him almost humbly; she murmured shyly: "I trow we had both lost our wits last night—to think of going down to the lake at midnight."

"Oh, was it that you thought of?" asked the Icelander.

"And yet there were no more bonfires than we could see from the house. So it had been waste of time to go down to the hard."

"Nay, I doubt not we could have had more pleasure of each other if we had stayed together within doors," said Teit bitterly. He bowed and went his way.

5

THEN there came an afternoon in the autumn—three months after Midsummer Night. Ingunn went through the gate, from which the stakes were now removed, as the cattle had been brought in from the sæter and were grazing freely over all the home fields.

Today the cows were in the meadow below the cornfield—no fairer sight could be seen than these fat sæter-fed beasts glistening in the sun; they were of every hue that cattle can be—and the after-grass was so green and thick that it seemed in a ferment of plenty, with masses of shimmering dog-fennel among the grass. The sky was blue, and blithe little fine-weather clouds drifted high up; the fiord was blue and reflected the autumnal brightness of the land, the red and yellow woods surrounding the home fields. Farther off stood the dark, blue forests, where each single fir tree stood out by itself, as they stood drinking in light in the strong, cool air.

The glad radiance of the day forced her to shrink beneath her own desperate dread and misery. She dared not fail, when he had trysted her. She was in mortal fear of being alone with him; but she dared do naught else. For if she did not come, he might seek her out up at the homestead and others would hear.

The stubble shone like pale gold on either side of the path—now there was a wide view over the open, reaped fields. His little dun jade was grazing in the coppice by the burn.

Ingunn prayed in her heart, a wordless prayer that was but a groan of her deep distress. As she had prayed that night when he stood outside her door, knocked softly, and called her by name. In the darkness she had knelt at the head of the bed, clasping the carved horse's head of the bedpost, and called for help, sound-lessly within herself, shaking with terror. For if the disaster *had* happened, if she had sunk into the worst that could befall—she would no more, she would not sink yet deeper. But it came over her that he could force her against her will, so that she *must* cross the floor and let him in.

When she guessed that he had gone from her door, she had sobbed from very gratitude. For it seemed that not her own tiny spark of will had held her back, but an invisible power, strong and stern, had filled the darkness between her and the terror at the door. As she huddled exhausted beneath the bedclothes, humbly thankful for her deliverance, she had thought that no punishment for her sin could be so hard that she would not accept it with gratitude, if only she might never more fall into Teit's power.

And when they met next day and he jested at her sleeping so heavily that he had to go unsolaced from her door, she had an-swered: "I was awake, I heard you." She was quite calm, for she was sure that the good powers that had kept her back last night would not suffer him to compel her any more.

When he asked why she had not opened, whether she had not dared, or someone had been within, she made bold to answer: "No; but I would not. And you must not come here any more, Teit. Be good, do not come after me any more!"

"Now, I have never heard the like—be good, you say! The other night—"

"Ay, ay," she had interrupted him, with a groan of suffering. " 'Tis ill enough, sin enough—"

"*Sin?*" he exclaimed, overwhelmed with astonishment. "Is it *that* you think of!"

She had remembered it then, and she remembered it now as she walked here, and she felt a sort of pity for the lad. *He* could not know how great a sin had been committed when she let herself be his: that she had broken a troth of which she could not even bear to think in this outpost of hell where now she had her dwelling.

Six weeks—six weeks it was already since that day and that night which she had begun to hope, deep down below her conscious thoughts, might be forgotten—some day; she could do penance and be shriven, and then she could let herself forget this matter of Teit. For she had neither seen nor heard anything of him since. Until today he came to Berg—had found himself an errand to Lady Magnhild. And he had made this tryst with her—and she dared do naught but go.

Now she could see the man; he was sitting on a rock within the thicket. And silently she cried within her: "Help me, let him not affright me, so that I do his will again!"

Where he sat was almost the same spot on which they had stood together in the dark on Midsummer Night, when he had repeated the verse about the willow for her. But she did not think of that— it was now a light and airy bower under the fading trees. Sunshine and blue sky reached them through the half-stripped branches; a glitter of light danced on the burn behind the bushes, dewdrops glistened on pale blades of grass and on the coarse weeds that were already touched and browned by the frost. The patch was bright with fallen leaves.

Even the moss-grown rock on which he had been sitting was so fair to see, with the wealth of green cushions clinging to it, that she was in sheer despair at being so alone with her terror and hopelessness in this fair and glorious world.

"Christ save me! What has come to you?" He had leaped up and stood looking at her. Then he made as though he would clasp her to him—she raised her hands with a little blunted gesture, weakly warding him off, as she shrank away. Quickly he set her on the rock and stood looking at her. "You seem not to have been right merry all these weeks that I have not seen you!—Has anyone got wind of it?" he asked quickly.

Ingunn shook her head. She trembled as she sat.

" 'Tis best I tell you my good news at once," he said, smiling a little at her. "I have been at Hamar, Ingunn, and spoken with Master Torgard about the matter. He has promised that he himself will speak for me with your kinsmen—he and Gunnar Bergsson. So I am not so badly off for spokesmen to my suit, how think you?"

She felt as if she had once been carried away by a landslide—and had crawled out, bruised and bleeding. And now this fresh fall came and buried her.

"What say you to that?"

"I have never thought any such thing," she whispered, wringing her hands. "That you could—ask for me—"

"I have thought of it before, I have—last summer, sometimes. I liked you from the first time I saw you—and as you made no secret of your liking for me— But 'tis not certain"—he looked down at her with a crafty laugh—"that I should have bestirred myself so speedily had you not barred your door to me even the second night. Nay, I saw myself afterwards that 'twould have been too perilous had we carried on with that game at Berg. And to lose you I am loath.—So now you may cease to mourn for your *sin*, if 'tis that has troubled you!" He smiled and stroked her cheek —Ingunn cowered away, like a dog that expects to be whipped. "I had scarce thought you would take *that* so sadly— But haply you can take comfort now, my poor one?"

"Teit—'tis impossible we two can come together—"

"Neither Gunnar nor Master Torgard seemed to think so."

"What is it you have told them?" she whispered almost inaudibly.

"I have told them all there has been between us—save the thing you wot of," he laughed. "But I have told them that we two have gotten such a heart-felt kindness for each other. And now at last you had let me know for certain that you would fain we should be wed.—But you must know I have said naught that may let them guess I have had more of you than your *word*." He gave a wanton laugh, took her by the chin, and tried to make her look up. "My Ingunn?"

"I have never meant that."

"How so?" Teit's face darkened. "Do you mean perchance I am too poor a match for you? Gunnar and Master Torgard did not think that, I ween. You must know I have no thought of staying in Gunnar's service after I am married—we are agreed that I shall leave him even now, after Yule. 'Tis not my purpose to stay longer in this part of the country either—unless you wish it and your kinsfolk will give us land to live on, but haply they will not do that. Nay, but Master Torgard will give me letters to the Archbishop himself, Ingunn, and to certain friends of his in the chapter there—and he will write in them that I am a most skilful clerk and painter of images on vellum. I can support you much better by my handicraft, when I come to such a place as Nidaros, than any of you country folk think. There I might find many roads to wealth, Ingunn—when I get woods that I can trade in.—And then we can sail home to Iceland. You spoke of that many a time in the summer, and said you were so fain to come to Iceland. I think I can promise you that I shall be able to take you thither, and that right handsomely."

He looked down at her white, terror-stricken face and it made him angry. "You ought to think of it, Ingunn—you are not so young either: you have entered on the second score of years. And your suitors have not worn down the grass of your kinsmen's courts lately, I have heard—" he looked away, a little ashamed of his own words.

"Teit—I *cannot!*" She twisted her hands violently in her lap. "There is another—another to whom I have given my troth—long years ago—"

"I marvel whether he would deem you have kept it well, if he knew all," said Teit dryly. " 'Tis not I would be content with such a troth if 'twere *my* betrothed that gambolled with a strange man and jested with him so freely—as you have shown me that you liked the game we two have played last summer. Nay, the troll trounce me if I would—not even if you had kept back that which you parted with the first day we chanced to be alone in the house!"

Ingunn put her hand to her face as though he had struck her. "Teit—'twas against my will!"

"Nay—I know that!" He gave a sneering laugh.

"I did not believe—I could not think you would do such a thing."

"Nay, how could you?"

"You were so young—you are younger than I am; I thought it was but wanton frolic, for you were so young a boy—"

"Ay, that was it."

"I resisted—and tried to defend myself—"

Teit gave a little laugh. "Ay, 'tis the way with most of you—but I am not so young but that I have learned this—that nothing makes you women so angry and so scornful of a young and innocent lad as when he lets himself be checked by such—resistance!"

Ingunn stared at him, stiff with horror.

"Ay, had you been a pure young maid—never have I shamed a young maid, I am not like that. But you cannot ask me to believe you did not know full well how the dance would end that you led me the whole summer long?"

Ingunn continued to stare—slowly a blush crept over her grey face.

"I may tell you," said Teit coolly, "so much have I heard of you that I know of that man who served in your father's home—with whom you had a bastard when you were but fourteen—"

"He was no serving-man. And never have I had a child." Then she bowed low; with her arms clasping her knees and her head hidden in them she began to weep very softly.

Teit smiled doubtfully as he stood looking down at the weeping girl.

"I know not if 'tis he you wait for—to come back and marry you? Or if you have had others since— However that may be, he seems not to kill himself with haste, this friend of yours—I greatly fear, Ingunn, 'tis of no use you stay for him. For if you did that, there might easily come too many between you."

She sat as before, weeping silently and in bitter pain. Teit said, more gently: "Better take me, Ingunn, whom you have in your hand. I shall be—I shall be a *good* husband to you, if only you will put off this—flightiness of yours—and be steady and sane from this day. I—I am fond of you," he stammered awkwardly, stroking her bowed head lightly. "In spite of all—"

Ingunn shook his hand from her head.

"Weep not so, Ingunn. I have no thought of deceiving you!"

She raised her head and gazed fixedly before her. It would be idle, she guessed, to try to tell him the truth of what he had

heard. Such must indeed be the talk hereabouts, where none knew
Olav, and few had known her as other than a worthless woman,
the shame of her race, whom her kinsfolk had thrust aside in disgrace.

She had not strength to speak of it either.—But this new thing
that had befallen her with Teit—she thought she must tell him
how it had been brought about. So she broke silence: "I know
well that this is a punishment for my sin—I knew I sinned grievously when I would not forgive Kolbein, my father's brother—
I rejoiced when he was dead, and I thought of him with hatred
and lust of vengeance; I refused to go with the others to his funeral feast. He it was who was the chief cause that I was parted
from one to whom I was promised in childhood and would have
taken before all. Not one prayer would I say for Kolbein's soul,
though I guessed he might need all the prayers that— When they
said the *De profundis* at even, I went out of the room. And I
refused to go north with the others to his burial.

"God have mercy on me. I knew well that it is sinful to hate
an enemy after he has been called to judgment. Then you came—
and I was fain to think of other things—I was happy. And when
you would bear me company up in the weaving-loft—I had no
other thought but that you were a boy—and as it was with me
then, I had most mind to play and romp with you, for I would
think no more of the dead man; and when we took to throwing
the wool from the sacks at each other— But I never thought, nay,
I never thought, that if you were uncourtly and said lewd words
—I thought 'twas only that you were so young and wanton—"

Teit stood looking down at her with the same doubtful little
smile.

"Well—let that be so. I got you first against your will. But
afterwards—at night?"

Ingunn dropped her head, hopelessly. Of *that* she could say
nothing—she was scarce able to unravel it to herself.

She had lain awake hour after hour, crushed by dismay and
shame. And nevertheless it was as though she could not bring
herself to see that it was true—that now she was lost and branded
with shame. For already it seemed but as the memory of a dream
or an intoxication, her own wild merriment of the afternoon in
the wool-loft. And that Teit had caught her—but all the time his
image appeared to her as she had brought herself to see it after

Midsummer Night, when next day she had been angry with her-self for her foolish fear of him: for he was but a boy, a likable, clever, lively boy, who had brought her nothing but pleasure; a little wanton of speech, but then he was so young— And yet she knew, as she lay there, that now she had brought disaster upon herself even to death and perdition, and now she was an adulteress.

At last she had fallen asleep. And she was awakened by Teit taking her in his arms. She had not thought to bar the door—they never did so when they slept in the loft in summer. She no longer remembered clearly why she had not tried to be rid of him. Per-haps she had thought it would make her shame yet deeper if she now said she would have no more to do with him who had already possessed her—that she was loath to see him again and hated him. And when he himself came and she heard his bright young voice, she may have thought that after all she did not hate him so terribly —he was so simple-hearted and had no inkling of *what* he had brought upon her. For he knew nothing of her being bound to another, married in the sight of God.

Only next morning, when she looked at her misfortune in the clear light of day, was it borne in upon her that she must escape from this at once—must not let herself be dragged yet deeper. She felt that she herself had no power to do anything, of her own strength she could not break with him. But she had cried for help in her bitter woe— "Whatever may become of me, I shall not complain, if only I be saved from further sin—"

Teit stood looking at her. And as she still kept silence, he held out his hand to her. "Better not to quarrel, Ingunn. Let us try to agree and be friends."

"Yes. But I will not marry you. Teit—you must tell these friends of yours they are not to bring forward your suit—"

"That I will not do. And if your kinsmen say yes?"

"Still I must say no."

Teit paused for a moment. She saw his rage seething in the young man. "And what if I do as you wish—cease my wooing and come here no more? And if your kinsfolk should see for them-selves, in a little while, that you have strayed again into your old bad ways?"

"Still I would not marry you."

"You must not be too sure of finding me and catching me again,

if you should need me this winter. I *have* offered once to do
rightly by you, and you met me with scorn and cruel words."

"I shall not need you."

"Are you so sure of that?"

"Yes. Before I would send for you—I would cast myself into
the fiord."

"Ay, ay. That will be your doing and not mine—your sin and
not mine. Since you seem to think we have no more to say—?"

Ingunn nodded in silence. Teit paused a moment—then turned
on his heel, leaped across the burn, and ran after his pony.

She was standing in the same place as he came riding up the
path. He pulled up beside her.

"Ingunn—" he pleaded.

She looked him straight in the face—and, beside himself with
rage and agitation, he leaned forward and struck her with all his
force below the ear, making her reel. "A wicked wretch you are,
a cursed, fickle bitch!" His voice was broken by sobs. "And may
you have such reward as you deserve for the false game you
played with me!"

He struck his heels into the pony's sides, and the little jade
broke into a trot—for a few paces. But where the hill began, it fell
into its usual amble.

Ingunn stood watching the rider—she held her hand to her flaming cheek—but she was no longer angry with Teit for this. With
a strange and painful clearness she saw that Teit could but think
her what he had called her. And it added to her sorrow—even now
she could remember that she had liked him. And she pitied him,
for he was so young.

She would have to go home now, she thought. But she felt she
must break down at the thought of the house above—nowhere
could she turn without being reminded of this boy.

And yet she could not resist the rising thought at the back of
her mind—in a few months it would all be easier for her. When
she was no longer forced to think of—and a sudden pang of fear
came over her like a hot wave. Though there was little likelihood
of that— But would to God Teit had said nothing of it—she had
dreaded it enough already. Sick as she now was, with grief and
anxiety, she nevertheless knew that, when so much time had gone
by that she might be quite sure she was safe from *that*, then she

would not suffer so terribly. Then she would not feel, as now, that her *whole life* had been ruined by this disaster and this sin.

Old Mistress Aasa failed greatly during the autumn, and Ingunn tended her lovingly and untiringly. Lady Magnhild marvelled at the girl: for all these years she had seen her niece dragging herself about like a sleepwalker, doing only what she could not avoid, and that little as slowly as might be. Now it seemed that Ingunn had waked up; her aunt saw that she could work when she chose —she was by no means so incapable when she took herself in hand. Now and again the thought occurred to Lady Magnhild: perhaps the poor thing was afraid of what might become of her when the old lady was gone; her unwonted diligence was a prayer to them not to look on her too ungraciously when the grandmother no longer needed her care. Perhaps they had not been friendly enough to the poor, frail child.

Ingunn snatched at everything she could find to occupy her. When her hands were not full with the sick old woman, she applied herself to any work she could find—anything that might help her to keep her thoughts from the one thing to which they constantly flew back in spite of herself; she waited in breathless tension for her fear to be proved groundless.

All the thoughts with which she had played for years—of life with Olav at Hestviken, of Olav coming to take her away, of their children—it was like the touch of the angel's flaming sword merely to approach the memory of these dreams. She could scarce keep herself from wailing aloud.

She threw herself upon all such tasks as demanded thought—and told upon the body. She *would* not give in, if she felt sick this autumn—for she was not near so ailing as she had been the first days at Miklebö.

It had always been the way with her, that when she had been badly frightened, she felt giddy and had violent qualms afterwards. She had only to think of the day they drove over the rocks in the sledge, she and Olav. It was Yuletide, not long before they were grown up; they had taken it into their heads that they would go to mass in the parish church, and so they drove off in the dark winter morning, though none of the others at Frettastein would go to church that day—a strong south wind was blowing, with rain and mild weather. She remembered so clearly the long-drawn, dizzying fear that seemed to descend on her whole body and dissolve it as she felt the sledge swerve and slide backwards over the smooth ice-bound rocks—it came across the horse's quarters, as he struggled to keep his feet, striking sparks and splintering the ice, but was carried away and thrown down—Olav, who had jumped off to support the sledge, was flung headlong and fell on the frozen ground; and then she knew no more. But when she came to herself again, she was on her knees in the soft snowdrift, hanging over Olav's arm and retching till she thought her whole inside would be turned out, and Olav with his free hand was pressing lumps of snow and ice to the back of her head, which she had struck against the rock. This time too it was only fear that ailed her.

On the eighth day of Yule she sat alone with her grandmother —the others had gone to a feast. She had laid plenty of fuel on the hearth, for her feet were so cold. The flickering gleam of the fire lent a semblance of life to the sleeping face of the old woman in the bed—dead-white and wrinkled as it was. By the pale light of winter days Ingunn had often thought it already as peaceful as the face of a corpse.

"Grandmother, do not die!" she wailed below her breath. Her grandmother and she had been companions so long that they had drifted into a backwater of their own, while the life of other folk ran past outside. And she had come to love her grandmother in the end, unspeakably, she thought—it was as though she herself had found support, her only support, in the old woman, as she led her faltering steps, dressed her, and fed her. And now it would soon be all over—if only she could have laid herself down beside the aged woman. Sometimes she had dared to hope that this would be the end—she would be permitted to die here in her dim corner screened by her grandmother's protection—before anyone had guessed.

But now she would soon be dead. And then she would have to go out among the others. And she would be haunted by the terror that one day someone would see it in her.

But it was not certain, it was *not* certain even yet. It was only the fear of it that drove and forced the blood in her body: she had felt such violent shocks in her heart as almost to make her swoon. At times there was a sudden throbbing in the veins of her throat, and her pulses seemed to race through her head behind the ears. And that feeling she had had yestereven—and in the night—and today again, time after time, deep in her right side—like a sudden blow or thrust—haply it was but the blood hammering in a vein.

For even if there had been anything, 'twas not possible it had quickened, the way she had starved and laced herself tight.

The week went by, and more than once Lady Magnhild said to Ingunn that she must spare herself somewhat—the unwonted hard work must be too much for her in the end. Ingunn made but little reply and continued to tend her grandmother; but the active fit seemed to have left her again. She had slipped back into herself, as it were.

She felt as though the soul within her had sunk to the bottom of a thick darkness, in which it fought a blind struggle with the sinister foreign being that she housed. Day and night it lay tossing and would have room for itself and burst her aching body. At times she felt she could bear no more—she was in such pain all over that she could scarcely see—for not even at night did she dare to relax the bandages that caused her such intolerable torment. But she could not give up—she must get it to stop, to move no more.

There was one memory that constantly floated before her at this time; once, when she and her sister were children, Tora's cat had caught a bird which Olav had brought her that she might tame it. The cat had just kittened, and so she stole two of its young, ran down to the pond, and held them under water. She had expected them to die as soon as they went under. But it was incredible how long the little beasts kept on wriggling in her hands and struggling for their lives, while little air-bubbles came up all the time. At last she thought they were dead—but no, there was another jerk. Then she took them out, ran back with them, and laid them down by their mother. But by that time they were indeed lifeless.

She never thought of it as her child, this alien life which she felt growing in her and stirring ever stronger, in spite of all her efforts to strangle it. It was as though some deformed thing, wild and evil, had penetrated within her and sucked its fill of her blood and her marrow—a horror she must hide. What it would look like when once it came out into the light, and what would happen to herself if anyone found out she had borne such a thing—of this she dared not even think.

At last, six weeks after Yule, Aasa Magnusdatter died, and her children, Ivar and Magnhild, made a great funeral feast for her.

The last seven days and nights of her grandmother's life Ingunn had only slept in snatches, lying down in her clothes. And when the corpse was borne out, all she asked was to be allowed to rest. She crept into her bed; now she slept and now she lay staring before her, with no power to think of the future by which she was faced.

But when the feast came, she had to get up and busy herself among the guests. No one wondered at her looking like a ghost of herself in her dark-blue mourning gown, wrapped in her long, black veil. Her face was grey and yellow, her skin lay stretched and shiny over the bones, her eyes were wide and dark and tired —and the men and women, her kinsfolk, came up and said kind words of praise to her, almost all of them. Lady Magnhild had spoken of her faithfulness to the dead woman during all these years.

Both Master Torgard, the cantor, and the Sheriff of Reyne were among the funeral guests. And at once it flashed upon Ingunn— Teit! She had almost forgotten him. It was as though she could not make out the connection between him and her misfortune— even now, when she called him to mind, it was only as an acquaintance she had liked at one time, but then some ugly thing had befallen them, so that she scarce cared to think of him again.

But now the thought came to her: what had he said to his spokesmen when he withdrew his suit? If he had exposed her to them—ah, then she would indeed be lost. She must try to find out whether they knew aught. She felt like a worn-out, poor man's jade that had toiled in harness under a grievous load till she was almost broken-winded, and now was to bear yet more.

"You have not brought your clerk with you?" she asked Gunnar of Reyne, as indifferently as she could.

"Is it that Teit you mean? Nay, he has run from me. So now, you ask for him? They tell me he had errands hither to Berg early and late—is it true that 'twas you he was after?"

Ingunn tried to laugh. "Not that I know. He said—he said he

would send suitors to ask for me—and that you were to be one of them. I counselled him against it, but— Can it be true?"

The Sheriff's eyes twinkled. "Ay, he said something of the same to me. And he had the same counsel from me as from you!" Gunnar laughed till his stomach shook.

"What became of him, when he ran away from Reyne?" asked Ingunn, and she too laughed a little. "Do you know that, Gunnar?"

"We will ask the cantor—'twas to him he would go. Hey, Master Torgard, will you deign to come hither? Tell me, good sir—know you what became of him, that Icelander, my writer? Mistress Ingunn here asks after him—you must know he intended her such honour that he would sue for the hand of Ingunn Stein-finnsdatter."

"Nay, say you so?" said the priest. "Ay, he had many strange devices, my good Teit. So then, you are left to mourn his absence, my child?"

"I can do naught else. For he was such a marvellous cunning man, I have heard, that you, master, would send him to the Arch-bishop himself, since there was none other in this land who could make use of such skill. This must be true, I ween, for he said it himself."

"He-he, he-he. Ay, he could make up a tale. Half crazed he was, forsooth, though the boy could write better than most. Nay, he came in to see me awhile ago—but by my troth, I'll not have him in my household again—though he is a good clerk, but a madcap. So 'twill profit you nothing to weep for him, my little Ingunn.—Nay, but is it true—was the boy so bold that he dared speak of seeking a wife at Berg? Nay, nay, nay—" the priest shook his little birdlike old head.

So she guessed it could not be altogether true, what he had said to her that last day they spoke together. But now she had added this to her other anxieties—had she done a madly foolish thing in letting these men see that she thought enough of Teit to care to ask after him?

When the guests departed after the funeral, Tora stayed behind with her two eldest children and old Ivar Toresson of Galtestad. One evening when they were sitting together—they had brought out the treasures they had inherited from Lady Aasa and were looking at them—Tora said once more that her sister ought now to take up her abode with her.

Lady Magnhild said that Ingunn must do as she would: "If you would rather go to Frettastein, Ivar and I will not hinder you."

"Rather will I stay here at Berg," replied Ingunn in a low voice. "If you will still grant me lodging here, now that grandmother is gone?"

Tora renewed her demand: she herself had now five children and she had charged herself with the fostering of the motherless twins left by Haakon's sister, so she needed Ingunn's help.

Lady Magnhild saw a look of perfect misery in Ingunn's thin and wasted face, and she held out her hand to her. "Come hither to me, Ingunn! Shelter and food and clothing you shall have with me, as long as I live—or till Olav comes and takes you home; for I believe full surely that he will come one day, if God be willing and he is alive.—Think you," she said scornfully to Tora, "that Haakon will show his sister-in-law such honour at Frettastein as Steinfinn's daughter has the right to look for? Haply she is to dwell in her father's home and be nurse to his and Helga Gautsdatter's offspring! That Ivar and I will not consent to.—I had thought I would give you this"—she took up the great gold ring that she had inherited from her mother—"as a memorial of the faithful care with which you tended our mother all these years."

She took hold of Ingunn's hand and was about to put the ring on it. "But what have you done with your betrothal ring—have you taken it off? Poor thing, I believe you have worked so hard that your hands are quite swollen," she said.

Ingunn felt that Tora gave a little start. She dared not look at her sister—yet did so for an instant. Tora's face was unmoved, but there was an uneasy flicker in her eyes. Ingunn herself could not feel the floor under her feet—she clung fast to one thought: "If I fall into a swoon now, they will know all." But she seemed to be listening to another's words as she thanked her aunt for the costly gift, and when she was back in her usual place, she did not know how she had come there.

Late in the evening she stood by the courtyard gate, calling and whistling for one of the dogs. Then Tora came across to her.

There was no moon, and the black sky sparkled with stars. The two women drew their hooded cloaks tightly about them as they tramped in the loose snow and talked of the wolves, whose inroads had been very bold in the last few weeks—now and again Ingunn whistled and called in an anxious voice: "Tota—Tota—Tota!" It was so dark that they could not see each other's faces; Tora asked in a low and strangely dejected tone: "Ingunn—you are not sick, are you—?"

"I cannot say I am well," answered Ingunn, quite calmly and easily. "Thin and light as Aasa had grown at last, I can tell you it was a trying task to lift her and move her, day in, day out, for months. And there was little rest at night. But now it will soon be better with me—"

"You do not think it is anything else that ails you, sister?" asked Tora as before.

"Nay, I cannot think that."

"Last summer you were so red and white—and as slender as when we were both young," whispered Tora.

Ingunn managed to answer with a melancholy little laugh: "Some time I must begin to show, I wis, that I am on the way to thirty. Look at the great children you have, my Tora—do you remember that I am a year and a half older than you?"

In the darkness between the fences a black ball came rushing along—the dog jumped up at Ingunn, nearly sending her headlong into the snowdrifts, and licked her face. She caught it by the muzzle and forepaws, keeping it off as she laughed, and spoke to it fondly: "—And well was it the wolf did not get you tonight either, Tota, my Tota!"

The sisters wished each other good-night and separated.

But Ingunn lay sleepless in the dark, trying to bear this new anxiety—that Tora must have a suspicion. And the temptation came to her—what if she told Tora of her distress, begged her help? Or Aunt Magnhild—she thought of the lady's marked kindness that evening and felt tempted to be weak and give herself up. Dalla—it had also flashed across her mind, when she thought she could no longer bear this secret torment alone—perhaps if she turned to Dalla—

In breathless suspense she kept her eyes on her sister during the days Tora stayed on at Berg. But she could notice nothing—neither by look nor by word did Tora betray any sign that she guessed how it was with her elder sister. Then she went away, and Ingunn was left alone with her aunt and the old house-folk.

She counted the weeks—thirty were gone already; there were but ten left. She *must* hold out so long. Nine weeks—eight weeks—But as yet she had never clearly acknowledged to herself what the purpose was to which she clung, as she struggled on and suffered, as though stifled in a darkness full of formless terrors, with a dull pain over her whole body and a single thought in her head: that none must have any inkling of the misfortune that had befallen her.

The end that she saw before her—when she thought of it, she was filled with a horror that was like the stiffness of death; but it appeared to her that it was the end of the road, and she *must* reach it, though she would try to walk the last piece with closed eyes. Even when she sought a kind of easement by playing with the thought of crying for help, speaking to someone before it was too late—she never thought in earnest that she would do so. She must go on, to what she saw before her.

So far on in the spring the ground was almost always free of snow hereabouts. They would not find her footprints.—The great birch wood north of the manor stretched from the rocks where they smoked fish almost down to the lake. At its lower end it narrowed to a strip between crags—where folk hardly ever came, and where they could not be seen or heard from the house. The ice did not leave the bay so early. But on the southern shore and on the screes below the birch wood lay great heaps of stones that had been cleared off the fields in former times; there the people of Berg were used to throw down carcasses of horses and other beasts that died a natural death.

6

SHE had gone up into the bower where she had kept her things since Lady Aasa's time, one morning of early spring—it was a few days before Lady Day. She sat and shivered with fur boots on her feet and a big sheepskin cloak over her clothes; it was now colder indoors than out. Long, glistening drops kept falling from the roof past the opening, and the air quivered and steamed over the glimpse she saw of white roofs against the bright blue sky. She had taken the shutter from the little window to have more air—she could hardly get her breath, and she felt as though a heavy leaden hood lay upon her brain inside her skull; it pressed upon her so that the blood hammered in her neck behind the ears, and patches of red and black flickered before her eyes. She had taken refuge up here for fear anyone should speak to her—she had no strength to talk. But it was some small relief to be able to sit here in her prostration.

Ever afterwards she believed for certain that she had known what was coming when she heard the horsemen at the courtyard gate. She got up and looked out. That was Arnvid, the one who rode first through the gate; he had his black horse and the ring-bridle that he used when he went on a visit. The second horse she also knew to be his, a big-boned grey, which his groom rode. And the third horseman, he who was riding a high dappled roan, was Olav Audunsson—she knew that before he had come near enough for her to recognize him.

He looked up as he held in his horse, saw her at the window, and waved his hand in greeting. He was wearing a great black travelling-mantle, which lay in ample folds over the horse's quarters and covered his legs down to the feet in the stirrups. He had thrown back the hood, and on his head he wore a black, foreign hat with a high crown and a narrow brim—his fair hair fringing it all round and falling to his eyebrows in front. He had smiled at her when he threw up his hand.

Ever afterwards it seemed to her she had been awakened from a nightmare at the instant she saw him—Olav had come home. To her misfortune, it was true—he would crush her in one way or another—she faced that at once. But it was as though the blinding gloom fell away from her on every side, and the devils who had swarmed about her like the stirring of the darkness itself, so thickly that they jostled each other with elbows and knees, while they surrounded her and led her blindly with them—they fell away from her too. She seemed to know, even as she came down the stairs of the loft, that, now Olav was come, she could do naught else than tell him all and accept her doom from him.

Olav stood there with the house-carls who had come to take the strangers' horses—he turned toward her. With a pang of wounded pride she saw how handsome he was, and she had fallen away from him—those black clothes suited the bright fairness of the man so well. He gave her his hand. "Well met, Ingunn—" Then he had a sight of her wasted face. And, unheedful of good manners and of all the strangers who stood by, he threw his arms about her, drew her to him, and gave her a kiss full on the mouth. " 'Twas a long time you had to wait for me, Ingunn my dear. But now it is over, now I am come to take you home!"

He released her, and she and Arnvid greeted each other with a kiss on the cheek, as became kinsfolk.

She stood by while the young men cried: "All hail!" to Lady Magnhild. They told her laughing that Ivar was with them, but they had ridden from him up by the church—for neither the Galtestad sorrel nor his master was in good trim for speedy travelling.

"Nay, you know how angry he was with the haste you made in your young days," laughed Lady Magnhild. "But since you have put off that bad habit, Olav, I believe my brother has grown more and more fond of you!"

"Have I ever seen such a fair day?" thought Ingunn. The hard snow shone like silver in the spring sun, over the fields and out on the bay. After the mild weather earlier in the week, all the snow had vanished from the woods, and the bare ground shone with young grass, as though newly washed. Across the fields the aspen trees stood with pale green stems within the brown, leafless groves.

And she felt joy bubbling up in her heart—that the world was so full of sunshine and beauty and gladness. And she had put herself outside it, banished herself to her corner. For all that, it was a good thing that it was so good to live—for the others, for all who had not undone themselves. And when at that moment she felt a violent quickening of the child within her, her own heart seemed to stir and answer it—"No, no, I no longer wish you ill. . . ."

They sat at table, and Ingunn listened in silence to the men's talk. She learned that it was intended Arnvid and Ivar should go on the very next day, northward to Haftor Kolbeinsson, and place in his hands the third quarter of the blood-money for Einar. Olav held that it was more seemly he himself should not meet Haftor until he came to pay the rest of the sum, when at the same time he would receive Ingunn and her dowry at the hands of her kinsmen.

"You have no mind to go farther with us, I guess," chuckled Ivar Toresson. "I believe 'tis not your purpose to stir from Berg till you be driven out of the house!"

"Ay, so long as Lady Magnhild will grant me shelter, and fodder for my horse." He laughed with the others, at the same time giving Ingunn a rapid glance out of the corner of his eye. "Sooth to say, I have most liking to stay here, make an end of this matter between Haftor and me—and take Ingunn with me, so soon as I go southward to Hestviken."

"I doubt not that could be done," said Arnvid.

"Ay, I guess what you mean, and I thank you for it—but nevertheless I will not ask more help of you, Arnvid, since I can make shift without it. And I must do as I told you at Galtestad—go south and see how things look at Hestviken, before I bring my wife thither; and fetch the money I am to get in Oslo. And 'twill be far easier to collect the men who ought to be witnesses to our atonement if the feast be held at the time folk are on their way homeward from the Things—whether you wish that I shall receive Ingunn here or at Galtestad. Ivar is right in saying that, since this suit has been so long drawn out and tortuous, it should be brought to an end as openly as may be."

When folk went home from the Things—that was the middle of summer. The thought crossed Ingunn's mind like a whisper from the devils that had had her in their power the whole winter. But now she did not even feel tempted. It was impossible that she could go the rest of that road, now she had seen Olav again. All that she had fancied of her life at Hestviken with him and their children hovered before her mind. To that she could never return —if she tried to free herself of her secret in the gloom of night and hide it among the rocks, it would avail her nothing. Never more could she come to Olav.

Ivar only held up his hands in humorous amazement as he told the others that Olav had not yet set foot in Hestviken. Had anyone ever heard of such a man!

Olav laughingly excused himself—he turned red at the old man's teasing and it made him look very young. He looked younger, more like his former self, than when he was here last—though he now had some lines across his straight, round neck, and when he stretched, a red scar could be seen under his wristband. And his face was thinner and more weatherbeaten. For all that, he looked very young—and Ingunn guessed this was because he was so happy. Her heart sank sickeningly—would it be a *great* grief she was bringing upon him, when he heard that she had thrown herself away?

But he had been given grace, he had got his estate back, she understood that he was a man of some wealth. He had now sold Kaaretorp, the farm he had owned in Elvesyssel, where he had dwelt when at length he had been allowed to return to the country, last autumn. It would not be difficult for Olav to find a better match than she would have been—according to the agreement with her family he would have received no great portion with her, she understood.

Olav went out with her when she was crossing the yard to go to bed. "Do you sleep alone in Aasa's house? Ay, then 'twould scarce be fitting if I came in when you are in bed," he sighed, and gave a little laugh.

"Nay, we can scarce do that."

"But tomorrow night? Can you not get one of the maids to sleep in the house with you—so that we may speak privily in the evenings?"

He clasped her to him, with awkward haste, so hard that she uttered a groan, and kissed her before he let her go.

Ingunn lay awake, trying to think of the future. But it was like trying to clear a path for herself amid a fall of rocks too heavy for her to move. She had no power to think what would become of her now. Nevertheless, she had staggered as far as this in a blinding darkness that lived and moved with unseen terrors, and now she saw the day before her—even if it was as grey and hopeless and impassable as a rainy day in midwinter. Forward she must go: from what she had brought upon herself there was no escape, unless she sought refuge in hell.

She knew that she had lost her rights. She had lost them already in giving herself to Olav without the knowledge and consent of her lawful guardians—they had let her know that plainly enough. If her kinsfolk had afterwards been willing to grant her the right of inheritance, this was for Olav's sake—since they had changed their view of him and found out that it was more profitable to accept his offer of atonement and let him take her to wife in lawful fashion. What they would do when they heard that she had made it impossible for Olav to take her—of that she dared to think only vaguely. When it came to their ears that she was with child—and the father was a man whom it were bootless for her kinsmen to pursue. They would have to let Teit go—they could have no profit of him, and if they would seek him out and punish him, the shame would only be made worse—when it was heard that she had let herself be seduced by such a man.

No, she could not guess what they would do with her—and it. But tomorrow—or in two or three days at the latest—she would have to make trial of it. And, impossible as it was for her to imagine it—it was nevertheless as sure as death that when the birch was green, she would be sitting here with her bastard in her lap, and then she would have to accept all that her kinsfolk might visit upon her in their wrath at her bringing such shame on them all, and at being forced to support her and the child.

She had bowed so completely beneath her fate that her thoughts of yesterday seemed scarcely real, when she believed she could cast off her burden. Her only thought now was that she must drag this child with her all the rest of her life. Nor did she yet feel anything like kindness or affection for it; but it was there, and she must go through with it.

Only for a moment—at the thought that Tora might again claim her for Frettastein, and she saw herself with *her* child, two outcasts, living in Haakon's house among his rich children—only then did something wholly new awaken within her, the first tiny stirring of an instinct to protect her own offspring.

It was her brothers and sister who before all others had the duty of providing for their sustenance. That meant Haakon on Tora's behalf and her two young brothers, whom she had scarcely seen during these years while they were growing into men. Oh, but now she might perhaps dare to hope that Lady Magnhild would be charitable enough to let her remain at Berg, until she had given birth to the child.

Arnvid—she thought of him. If he would offer to receive them; he would be kind to them both. In spite of his being Olav's best friend—he was the friend of *all* who needed help. What if she told her story to Arnvid—to Arnvid and not to Olav? He could speak to Olav and to Lady Magnhild—and she would be spared what was as bad as walking into a living flame.

But she knew that she dared not do this. How she should find courage to speak to Olav she could not tell—but worst of all she feared to hide the truth from Olav. He it was who was her master, he it was whom she had failed, and all at once she felt that, when she had gone through this meeting with Olav, it would come about of itself that she must fall on her knees to God repenting her sin and all the sins she had committed in her whole life—*quia peccavi nimis cogitatione, locutione, opere, et omissione, mea culpa*—the words arose in her of themselves. For each time she had said them, kneeling by Brother Vegard's knee, they were now illumined and brought to life; as when the dark glass of the church window was suddenly illuminated by the sunshine—"because I have sinned most grievously, in thought, word, deed, and omission, *through mine own fault*."

She arose to her knees in the bed and said her evening prayers —it was long since she had dared. *Mea culpa*—she had been afraid of being saved from doing what she wished and accepting what she had brought upon herself. Now it dawned on her that, when she received God's forgiveness for the evil she had done to herself and to Olav, she would no longer desire to escape her punishment. The mere sight of Olav had been enough to make her see the nature of Love. She had done him the most grievous wrong. And when he suffered, she could not wish herself a better lot. And behind it she caught a glimpse, as in an image, of the origin of Love. In the cup which our Lord was compelled to receive that evening in the Garden of Gethsemane He had seen all the sin that had been committed and was to be committed on earth from the creation of mankind to the last judgment and all the distress and misery that men had caused to themselves and others thereby. And since God had suffered, because of the suffering her own fault would bring her, she too would desire to be punished and made to suffer every time she thought of it. She saw that this was a different suffering from any she had suffered hitherto; that had been like falling from rock to rock down a precipice, to end in a bottomless morass—this was like climbing upward, with a helping hand to hold, slowly and painfully; but even in the pain there was happiness, for it led to something. She understood now what the priests meant when they said there was healing in penance.

o   o   o

Olav and Ingunn were together in the courtyard at noon next day when Ivar and Arnvid were setting out. It was the same fine weather as the day before, thawing and dripping everywhere. The snow settled with a crisp little sound in the shrinking drifts, and the yard was full of tiny streams that washed smooth channels of rock in the winter's carpet of horse-dung and chippings of wood. Ivar was fuming because Arnvid wished to ride over the ice—it was certainly unsafe in many places off the Ringsaker shore; Ivar had once driven into a gap of open water many years before, and ever since he had been a great coward on the ice. But Arnvid laughed him to scorn—what, in broad daylight? Nay, kinsman! They would reach Haftor's before it was quite dark. Toiling uphill and down across country in this going—Arnvid swore he would have none of it— "If you can get your men to follow you, ride where you will, for me, but Eyvind and I will go our own way—"

But the three grooms were already far down the fields. The winter road from several farms higher up led through Berg and down to the bay; from there folk made their way south to the town, or north and west across the high ground on the other side and down to the ice of Mjösen.

Olav and Ingunn walked down with them—Arnvid and Ivar rode at a foot's pace. The snow was thawed away on the upper side of the track here on the sunny slope, and the water ran down. Arnvid warned Olav that he was being well splashed—Olav walked bareheaded, without a cloak, in a sky-blue kirtle reaching to the knees, light leather hose, and low shoes with long, pointed toes. His fine footgear was soaked and dark. "Ingunn is better clad to walk abroad—"

"I know not how she can bear it in this heat—"

She wore the same short, sleeveless sheepskin coat as the day before and tramped along in her fur boots—had done no more to deck herself than tying some red silk ribbons in her hair.

The air breathed warmly about them on the slope and there was a shimmer afar off wherever they looked.

" 'Twas over there we sat that time—do you remember?" whispered Olav to Ingunn. Today there were great bare patches of grass—even yesterday the whole had been silvery white, with only here and there a rock or a juniper bush showing. "We may look for a late sowing this year, since so much is thawed before Lady Day."

They stopped in the dingle and watched the riders. Arnvid turned once in the saddle and waved—Olav threw up his hand in answer. He broke off a branch of bramble and offered it to Ingunn, but when she shook her head, he plucked some of the berries himself, sucked them, and spat out the skins into the snow. "Ay, 'tis time to go back again."

"Nay. Stay a little. There is a matter I must tell you of."

"What is it?—You look so cheerless, Ingunn."

"Indeed, I am not cheerful," she managed to say.

Olav looked at her, at first in surprise—then his face too became serious and he looked half away again. "Is it that you think I stayed from you too long?" he asked in a low voice.

Too long. She would have said it, but could not.

"I thought of that," he said, gently as before. "I thought of you when I followed the Earl—I must tell you, I knew it was to share his outlawry. But he was my lord, Ingunn, the first lord to whom I had sworn fealty. 'Twas not easy for me to know what I ought to do. But I lost desire of food, Ingunn, when I thought of sitting down at Hestviken, eating bread and drinking ale, while he, who had helped me to get back all I possessed, was doomed to wander an outlaw in another land and had lost all he had at home.—But, you know, I did not believe it would be so many years— Think you that I failed you, when I followed the Earl?"

Ingunn shook her head: "In such matters you know well I cannot judge, Olav."

"I thought—" Olav drew a deep breath; "since I was such good friends with Ivar—and the fines for Kolbein were half cleared off —in good English coin—and you were affianced with my ring and gifts—I thought your lot would be a better one where you were. *Has* not your lot been a good one among your kindred, Ingunn?"

"Oh yes. 'Tis not of *that* I can complain—"

"Complain—?"

She heard the first faint catch of fear in his voice, summoned all her courage, and looked at him. He stood with the bramble in his hand, looking at her as though he did not understand, but dreaded what might be coming.

"Have you anything to complain of, then, Ingunn?"

"It was so ordered—that I—I had not strength to—I am no longer fit for you, Olav."

"No longer—fit for me—" his voice was utterly devoid of expression.

Again she had to rouse herself with all her force before she dared look at him. Then they stood staring each other in the eyes. She saw that Olav's face seemed to fade, congeal, and turn grey—he moved his lips once or twice, but it was long before he got the words out: "What do you mean by that—?"

Again they stood staring each other in the eyes. Till Ingunn could bear it no longer. She raised one arm and held it before her face. "Do not look at me like that," she begged, trembling. "I am with child."

After an eternity she felt she could hold out no longer; she let her arm drop and looked at Olav. His face seemed unknown to her—the lower jaw had dropped like that of a corpse, and he stared at her, still as a rock, and this went on and on.

"Olav!" she burst out at last, with a low moan— "speak to me!"

"What do you wish me to say?" he said tonelessly. "If another had told me this—of you—I had killed him!"

Ingunn gave a faint, shrill whine, like a dog that is kicked.

Olav shouted at her: "Hold your peace! You deserve no better —you vile bitch—than to die!" He thrust his shoulders forward as he spoke—again she whimpered like a beaten dog, stepped hastily away from him, and supported herself against the trunk of an aspen. The dazzling light from the snow-crust all around struck her with a sudden blow, unbearable; it made her close her eyes tightly, and she felt the pain shrivelling her body, as meat shrivels when it is thrown upon the fire.

Then she opened her eyes again, looked at Olav—no, she dared not look at him; she looked down at the brier with the red haws which he had thrown down on the snow. And she fell to wailing softly: "It were far better—it were far better—you did it—"

Olav's face contracted violently, became inhuman. His hands grasped the hilt and sheath of his dagger—then he tore it from him, belt and all, and flung it far away. It buried itself somewhere in the thawing drifts.

"Oh, would I were dead, would I were dead!" she moaned again and again.

She felt his wild, red, animal's eyes upon her—and, terrified as she was, her greatest wish was that he would murder her. She put her hands to her throat for an instant—whimpered softly—

The man stood staring at her—at the tense white arch of her throat, as she stood leaning against the tree. Once he had done it— the sword had been struck out of his hand, he was unarmed, and he had taken the other man by the waist and throat and broken him backward—had felt that never before had he put forth his strength to the uttermost.— And as she stood now he could see it— the shameless change that had come over her face, over her form —the mark of the other man.

With a loud groan, like the cry of an animal, he turned his head from the sight and fled up the path.

He heard her calling after him, calling his name. He knew not whether he had cried it aloud or only within himself— "No, no, I dare not come near you—"

She lay in a heap on the little spot of bare earth by the roots of the aspen, rocking herself and wailing. A good while must have gone by. Then Olav was there again. Now he stood bending over her, breathing down on her: "Who is father—to the child you bear?"

She looked up, shook her head. "Oh—'tis no— He was clerk to the Sheriff of Reyne. Teit was his name, an Icelander—"

" 'Twere a sin to say you were hard to please," said Olav with a sort of laugh. He took her roughly by the arm, gripped it till she wailed aloud. "And Magnhild—what says she to this? She laughed so merrily with the others yestereven—" he ground his teeth— "at me, I wis, silly gull that I was to be so glad and easy, never dreaming of such increase in my fortune. Oh—God's curse upon you all!"

"Magnhild knows nothing. I have kept it hid from every soul, until I told it to you but now."

"That was gracious of you indeed! I was to be the first to know! Now, I had always thought I could get my children my-self, but—"

"Olav!" she cried piteously. "Had you not come so soon"—her voice broke—"none would ever have known of it—"

Again they looked each other in the eyes for an instant. In-gunn's head dropped forward.

"Jesus Christ! You are not human, I trow!" whispered Olav in horror.

He straightened himself and stretched once or twice, and each time she had a glimpse of a red scar on his chest near the throat. He said, more to himself than her: "If they had brought me tidings that you were a leper—I believe I should still have longed for the day I could take you home.—'Wilt thou keep this woman in sickness as in health?' asks the priest at the church door.—But this —nay, this—! God forgive me, I cannot do it!"

He took her roughly by the shoulder. "Do you hear, Ingunn? —I cannot do it! Magnhild must—you must tell Magnhild I cannot. And since she has had no better care of you—this has befallen while you were in her charge, so she must herself— I cannot bear to see you again, before you are rid of it—

"Do you hear?" he repeated. "You must tell Magnhild yourself!"

Ingunn nodded.

Then he went up the road.

The ground was soaking wet where she sat, and she felt the cold stiffening and crippling her; it was an alleviation. She put her arm about the trunk of the aspen and leaned her cheek against it. Now it was time to search within herself for the consolation that was to come after she had told him. But she could not find it—only a bitter remorse, but not the contrition that brought hope. Her only wish was to be allowed to die at once—she had no strength to think of arising and going on to face all she must go through.

She called to mind all the words of comfort she had meant to say to Olav—that he should think no more of her; when he went out into the world, he must enjoy his happiness without thinking of her; she was not worth it. She saw now that it was true, and it was no consolation—that was the worst of all, that she was not worth his thoughts.

She did not know how long she had lain there when she heard the sound of sledges on the road. She struggled painfully to her feet—she was stiff with cold and her body ached all over when she moved—her feet were asleep and she could hardly stand or walk. But she made her way into the bushes and pretended she was eating haws as the two loaded sledges drove past. The workmen greeted her quietly and she answered them. They were folk from the farms above.

The sun had sunk a long way toward the west—the light on the snow was now orange, and the rising vapour began to be visible as a low-lying mist. She tramped hither and thither on the road for a while, not knowing where to go. Then she caught sight of some horsemen out on the ice—it looked as if they were coming this way—she took fright and turned toward the house.

She was about to steal into her own bower when Lady Magnhild came up to her from the other house. To Ingunn's scared senses her aunt appeared terrible, with her fleshy, florid face surrounded by its wimple, and her stomach thrust forward under the silver belt, with all the clatter of heavy keys, dagger, and scissors dangling at her side—like the time the mad bull came charging straight toward her. She put out her hand to the doorpost for support. But at that moment it seemed her powers of being frightened had been stretched too far.

"Holy Mary, where have you come from—have you been out loitering all day?—rolling in the road, one would think—you are smothered in wet and horse-dung up to your neck! What has come to you—and Olav, what is it with him?"

Ingunn did not answer.

"Do *you* know what took him to Hamar so suddenly? He came here and got out his horse, Hallbjörn could make nothing of him —he must go to Hamar, he said; but he left his bag behind, and he rode as though the devil sat behind him—'twas an ugly sight, the way he used his spurs, said Hallbjörn—"

Ingunn said nothing.

"What is this?" asked Lady Magnhild, flashing with wrath. "Do *you* know what is afoot with Olav?"

"He is gone," said Ingunn. "He would stay here no longer, when he had heard—when I had told him how it is with me—"

"—*is* with you?" Lady Magnhild stared at the girl—in her drenched clothes, her tousled hair out of its plaits and full of bark and refuse, her face a dirty grey and thin as a scraped bone—she was ugly, nothing else—and the way she held herself in the filthy wet sheepskin—

"Is with you!" she shrieked; she caught Ingunn by the upper arm and pushed her through the door, making her stumble over the threshold. Then she flung the girl across the room, so that she fell and lay in a heap by the draught-stone. Her aunt barred the door behind them.

"Nay—! Nay—! Nay—! 'Tis not I can guess what you have been doing!"

She took hold of Ingunn and pulled her up. "Take off your clothes—you are as wet as a drowned corpse. Ay, 'tis what I have always thought of you—half-witted you are; 'tis not possible you have your right senses!"

Ingunn lay in bed, half-numbed, and listened to her aunt's talk as she hung her wet things on the clothes-horse over the hearth. It was the first time in all these months she had lain down wholly undressed, and it was such a relief to be free of all these cruel bonds she had put upon herself—to get rest. It scarcely occurred to her that Lady Magnhild might justly have been far, far harsher with her—she had neither cursed nor struck her, nor dragged her by the hair—she did not even say much of what was in her mind.

Lady Magnhild took it in this way, that she demanded a full confession of how it had come about—then it was for her to see if some means could be found of keeping it hid.

She asked who was the father, but when Ingunn told her, Lady Magnhild sat for a long while perfectly speechless. This was so utterly beyond all she had ever believed possible that she could only think it must be so—the poor thing was something wanting. Ingunn had to give an account of all there had been between her and Teit—she gave short and broken answers to Lady Magnhild's rigorous questions. It was six months since she had seen him—no, he knew nothing of how it was with her—she expected the child in six weeks—

It was wiser to let the bird fly, thought Lady Magnhild. And there must surely be some means of keeping the girl hidden here in Aasa's house for the rest of her time; it could be said that she was sick—there were not many who asked after Ingunn; it was a lucky chance that she had lived so much in the shade all these years. Her aunt strictly forbade her to move beyond the door during the hours when the folk of the house were out of bed. Dalla would have to live with her for the present, and when her time came, they would send for Tora.

Ingunn lay still and let her weariness overcome her. It was almost good to be alive—her feet had grown warm between the bedclothes, and sleep poured over her like sweet tepid water. Half-dazed she heard Lady Magnhild discussing with herself how they might best smuggle out the child as soon as it was born.

When she awoke, she guessed it must be late in the evening; the fire on the hearth was almost burned out, but not yet raked over. Dalla sat on a stool beside it, nodding and spinning. Outside, a storm was rising—Ingunn heard the wind on the corners of the house, and just then something wooden clattered against the wall outside. She was still sunk in placid ease.

"Dalla," she said after a while. The old woman did not hear.

"Dalla," she repeated a little later. "Cannot you go out and see what it is that knocks so against the wall—see if you can move it—"

Dalla rose and came up to the bed. "So you are yet proud and grand enough to send folks on errands for you, lazy-bones! I am here to herd you, but not to run and do your bidding—shame on you, paltry jade!"

Lady Magnhild looked in on her niece for a moment once or twice each day; she gave Ingunn no more angry words—said very little to her at all. One day, however, she told Ingunn that she had found a foster-mother for the child—the wife of a cottar who lived in a clearing in the woods far to the north. It was settled that Lady Magnhild should send for her at once when Ingunn's birth-pangs came on; then they could get it out of the way as soon as it was born. Ingunn said nothing to this, and Lady Magnhild guessed it must be as she thought—the girl was only half-witted.

Then she was left alone with Dalla, day and night. She crouched, still as a mouse; if she did but move or breathe heavily, she feared Dalla would fall upon her with scorn and abuse, all the foulest and most cruel words she could think of.

Dalla and Grim had never been thralls in the way that folk in old time were as their masters' cattle. But in many places it had made very little difference between free-born and serf-born that the latter now had rights under the law. And least of all where it was a question of the descendants of the ancient noble families and their married servants who were the offspring of the old thrall stock of the house. It could never occur to such a master or mistress to part with such a couple, were they never so troublesome or incapable or sick or infirm; nor had it ever been the custom in these families to sell their thralls: an unusually good-looking or promising thrall child might be given away to a young relative or a godchild, and a thrall who gave far more trouble than service, or who was guilty of a misdeed, disappeared.—And even now the serf-born serving-folk hardly ever thought of anything but staying and earning their livelihood where they were born—in the inland districts. The honour of their master's house was their honour, its happiness and prosperity were theirs; they followed it in good and evil fortune, and the subject they threshed out again and again among themselves was the life of their masters in hall and chamber and bower, every scrap of it they could seize upon.

Aasa Magnusdatter had had Grim and Dalla with her since all three were children, and when she sent them to Steinfinn, it was as a gift from mother to son. Steinfinn's lot had been theirs, and since Aasa thought that his misfortunes were due to his marriage, they conceived a hatred for his wife, though they dared not show it. Although Ingunn by no means took after her mother, she had come in for a share of their ill will—without very much reason. But Olav and Tora had been their favourites among the children; these two were calm and considerate in their behaviour to the old bailiff and his sister—Ingunn was thoughtless and flighty, and they decried her yet more in order to exalt the others. And besides this, Dalla had been violently jealous all these years, that Ingunn and not she should have the care of Lady Aasa, and she saw the grandmother's fondness for the girl. And now that Ingunn had brought this unheard-of shame upon the Steinfinnssons and proved false to Olav, and had been handed over to Dalla, perfectly helpless and without the power of defending herself, the thrall woman took her revenge, according to her lights.

In the crudest and cruellest language she spoke at length of all the things of which Ingunn was only dimly aware—of Teit and of Olav—till the young woman was scalded with shame and wished the floor would open and hide her in the earth. Whether Ingunn sat or stood or walked, Dalla fell upon her with mockery for being so ugly. And then the old woman tried as well as she could to scare Ingunn out of her wits with talk of what awaited her when she should be laid on the floor; she predicted her the hardest of childbirths and said she could see it in her that she was to die.

Ingunn had always known that Dalla disliked her and counted her a fool, but she had never paid much attention to that. And it came as an altogether unlooked-for blow that the old thrall woman should apply herself to torturing her with such untiring malignity. Ingunn could guess no other reason for it but that she herself must be so disgraced and besmirched and abominable that those who had to be with her were minded to trample on her, as one tramples on a loathsome reptile.

So she gave up all thought of peace or preservation. That she might die was the best she dared hope. If only she might be free of this strange creature—for which she could still feel nothing but terror and hatred—she had no wish in the world but to be allowed to die.

Ten days passed in this way. Late in the evening they were sitting, each in her corner, Ingunn and Dalla, when someone came to the door. Dalla started up. "None comes in here!"

"Oh yes, I come in," said the man who stepped across the threshold; it was Arnvid.

Ingunn got up and went to meet him; she laid her arm about his neck and leaned forward to him—he was the only one she knew of on earth who would be good to her, even now. Then she felt him draw back a little and loosen the hold of her hands on his neck— and this sank into her, deeper than Dalla's abuse. Even Arnvid abhorred her—was she as befouled as that? The next moment Arnvid stroked her cheek, took her hand, and made her sit by him on the little settle by the fire.

"Go out with you, Dalla," he said to the old woman. "The Fiend himself must have put it into Magnhild's head to send that half-crazy witch to help you.—Or do you like to have her here perhaps?"

"Oh, no," she said weakly. And little by little Arnvid got from her something of Dalla's conduct—though it was not much that Ingunn could bring herself to mention. He took her hand and laid it on his knee. "Never fear—I trow you will be plagued with her no more!"

But there was so little that he could bring himself to say. He wished that she herself would tell him how Olav had taken this, and whether she knew what the man would do, or where he was now, or what was to become of herself; but it was impossible for him to speak of it first.

So Olav's name was never spoken between them, though Arnvid sat there a pretty long time. As he was going, he said: "'Tis an ill thing, Ingunn—I cannot help you. But you must try to send me word as soon as there comes a time when a man can be of use to you. I would fain have a word to say when they take counsel how you and the child shall be bestowed."

"There is no man can help me."

"Nay, that is true enough. You must put yourself in God's hands, Ingunn—then you know all will be well in the end."

"Ay, I know that. And you can say it. But 'tis not you that are in this case." She squeezed his hand in her distress. "I cannot sleep at night—and I have such dreadful thirst. And I dare not get up and drink for fear of Dalla—"

"Nay, nay," said Arnvid softly. "There is none of us that has known what it feels like to hang upon a cross. But that robber, he knew—and he hung there rightfully. And you know yourself what he did—"

Awhile after Arnvid had gone out, Lady Magnhild came and rebuked Dalla sharply. She bade her remember that Ingunn was Steinfinn's daughter, whether she had done wrong or not, and she was not to be troubled with unseemly prating from a serving-woman. And when Ingunn was in bed, Dalla came in with a great bowl full of whey and water and set it down on the footstool beside the bed with a smack, so that the drink splashed over. But in the course of the night, when Ingunn wanted to drink, she got a mouthful of refuse—it tasted like straw and sweepings from the floor.

Arnvid came in to see her next day, before he left, but they had not much to say to each other.

Ivar had come to Berg in Arnvid's company, but he did not go to see his niece. Ingunn did not know whether he was so angry with her that he would not look at her, or whether any had asked him to stay away so as to spare her.

Arnvid reached the convent of the preaching friars in the middle of the day and learned at once from the porter that Olav was there —he had come more than a week ago. He did not lie in the guest-house, but in a little house that the new Prior had had built in the kale-yard—he had bethought him that men and women ought not to be lodged together in the hostel, but that the women must stay outside the convent walls. But the women would not lie there, separated from their company and close to the graveyard. More-over the house was badly built, and draughty in winter, and instead of a hearth Sir Bjarne had had a stove built in the corner by the door, but it gave no heat, and the smoke from it would not draw out through the louver.

It was cold under the shadow of the church and chapter-house, and the thin coat of ice crunched with the jingling of his spurs as Arnvid walked through the garden. Here the snow had now thawed enough to leave the rows of peas and beans standing out as black banks with pale rotting stalks above. The women's house abutted on the churchyard fence; it was darkened by some big old trees even now, when they were bare.

The house had no anteroom; Arnvid walked straight in. Olav was sitting on his bed with his legs hanging over the side and his neck resting against the wall. Arnvid saw with a shock how changed his friend was. His ashen hair seemed faded, because his whole complexion was now the same, a greyish yellow, and it was so long since he had shaved that the lower part of his face seemed flooded—Olav was blighted and haggard all over. The fresh timber walls were still yellow, and there was some smoke in the room, but only a few embers glowed in the stove—and Arnvid felt that he had come into a place where all was wan and frozen.

Neither man noticed that they forgot their greetings.

"Have you come?" asked Olav.

"Yes—" said Arnvid stupidly. Then he remembered to say—as Olav knew it had been his intention the whole time—he had come to see Finn, his son, who was a pupil in the school. After that it occurred to him that he must tell Olav how they had fared with Haftor Kolbeinsson.

"How fared you, then?" asked Olav.

Oh, Haftor had been well pleased with the money—

"How long were you at Berg?" Olav gave a little frozen laugh. "I can see you have been there."

"I lay there last night."

"And how goes it there?"

"As you may well conceive," said Arnvid curtly.

Olav said no more. Arnvid sat down, and they were both silent. After a while a lay brother came in with bread and ale for the new-comer. Arnvid drank, but could not eat. The monk stayed for a few moments, chatting with Arnvid—Olav only sat and glared. And when the brother was gone, the silence fell between them again.

At last Arnvid pulled himself together. "What will you do about the atonement now, Olav? Will you give me and Ivar authority to act for you, when the matter is to be concluded? For you will have no mind to come north yourself and meet Haftor this summer?"

"I cannot see how I am to escape it," replied Olav. "She cannot journey alone over the half of Norway and home to me. There might be a danger that the next bantling was on the way before she reached her journey's end—" he smiled maliciously. "Oh nay, it were safer that I take her in hand myself; so soon as may be."

After a pause Arnvid asked, in a low and tremulous voice: "What do you mean by that?"

Olav laughed.

"Do you think of taking her to you after this?" asked Arnvid softly.

"You must know that, I suppose, you who are half-trained for a priest," said Olav bitterly. "That I cannot part from her."

"No," replied Arnvid quietly. "But I was not sure whether you saw that yourself. But, you know, none can force you take her into your house and live with her after this."

"I must have someone to live with, I trow, like the rest," said Olav in the same bitter tone. "I have lived among strangers from my seventh year. 'Tis not too soon to have a house and home of my own. But, you know, 'tis more than I had reckoned for, that she should bring into the household a brat ready-made—"

"Magnhild has provided already for the fostering of the child," said Arnvid softly. "It will be set out to nurse the same day it sees the light."

"Nay. I will not be shackled with any dealings in these parts. I will have nothing to do with anyone from here. Neither she nor I shall set our foot here in the north when once we have come away from it. In the devil's name, has my wife turned whore, I must be able to take her bastard into the bargain—" He ground his teeth.

"She is in such shame and distress now, Olav," pleaded Arnvid.

"Ay—we must smart, I wis, both one and the other, for the favours she allowed that vagabond Icelander of hers—"

"Never have I seen a child so wretched and cast down. Remember, Olav, when you had to leave her and fly the country—she was in an ill way even then, Ingunn. Weak she has always been, had little strength or wit to choose wisely for herself—"

"I know that well enough. It is not that I have ever thought her shrewd or firm of mind. But still this is a hard thing for a man to have to stomach.—Have they—" his voice suddenly failed him— "have they been *very* harsh with her? Know you that?"

"Nay, they have not. But it needs not much to break *her*. You know that yourself."

Olav made no reply. He leaned forward, with his hands hanging over his knees, and stared at the floor. After a while Arnvid said: "At Berg, I ween, there is none but thought you would put her away."

Olav sat as before. Arnvid dared not bring out what he had at heart. Then suddenly Olav himself spoke: "I said to her that I should come back—to Ingunn. Half a heathen she has been all her days, but I thought she had guessed so much—that we are bound together, while we are in life—"

Arnvid said: "When they wished to give her to Gudmund Jonsson, you know that would have been a right good match for her— but then she spoke as though she understood full well."

"Ha! But now, when she herself has broken her troth, she expects that I too shall go back on all I have spoken before God and men—?"

"She expects she is to die, I believe."

"Ay, that were the easiest way out, for both her and me."

Arnvid did not answer.

Then Olav asked: "I promised *you* once—that I would never fail your kinswoman. Do you remember?"

"Yes."

At last Arnvid broke the silence: "Ought they not to know it, Ivar and Magnhild—that you will take her in spite of all?"

He received no answer; and spoke again: "Will you consent that I tell them what you will do?"

"I can tell them myself what I will do," answered Olav shortly. "I forgot some of my things there too," he added, as though to soften it.

Arnvid said nothing. He thought that, in the mood Olav was in now, it was uncertain that they would have much comfort of him when he came to Berg. But he deemed he had no right to meddle with the affair further than he had done.

In the course of the afternoon, when Olav was ready for the road, he asked Arnvid: "When had you thought of going home again?"

Arnvid said he had not thought of that yet.

Olav did not look at the other, and he spoke as though he were ashamed and had difficulty in getting the words out: "I would rather we did not see each other again—before the atonement feast. When I come back from Berg, I would rather not—" he clenched his fists and ground his teeth sharply—"I cannot bear the sight of anyone who knows of this!"

Arnvid turned crimson in the face, but he swallowed the insult and answered coolly: "As you will.—Should you change your mind, you know the way to Miklebö."

Olav gave Arnvid his hand, but would not meet the other's eyes. "Ay—thanks for that—'tis not that I am ungrateful—"

"Nay, nay— You go south now, to Hestviken?" he asked nevertheless.

"No, I have thought to stay here—for a time. Haply I ought to find out if I am to prepare a home-coming feast or not—" he tried to laugh. "If she is not to live, there is no need—"

Ingunn sat crouching in the corner by the bed, and it was so dark both indoors and out that she could not distinguish who it was that came in, but she thought it was Dalla, who had finished in the byre. But the figure did not move, after closing the door behind it—and a terrible fear seized her, though she could not guess what it was that had come in; her heart flew up into her throat and throbbed like a sledge-hammer if anyone spoke to her. She struggled to quell her loud breathing and drew back into her corner, still as a mouse.

"Are you here, Ingunn?"

When she heard Olav's voice, it was as though her heart beat itself to pieces—it faltered and stopped, and through her whole body went a feeling that she was stifling to death.

"Ingunn—are you here?" he asked again. He advanced into the room—she could make out his form, square-shouldered and broad in his cloak against the feeble glow from the hearth. He had heard her groaning breath and felt about, trying to find where she sat in the dark.

And now terror gave back her speech: "Come not near me! Olav—come not near me!"

"I shall not touch you. Be not afraid—I will do you no harm."

She cringed away, speechless, fighting to overcome the terrible breathlessness that her fear had brought on her.

Olav's voice was heard, calm and level: "It came into my mind —'twere best after all that I myself speak with Ivar and Magnhild. Have you told them who is the father?"

"Yes," she whispered painfully.

Olav said, hesitating a little: "That was bad. I should have thought of it before—but I was so—surprised—I knew not what I said. But now I have bethought me, 'tis best I take upon myself the fatherhood. It will surely come out—such things are always noised abroad—and then we must say the child is mine. We must spread the report that I came secretly here to Berg last year at that time—"

"But it is not true," she whispered feebly.

"No. I know *that*." He said it so that it struck her like a whip. "And folk will surely doubt it—but that is all one, if they only see they must not speak their doubts too loudly. You must all say as I have said. I will not have it that you should keep such a child here in the Upplands; we should never feel safe that the story would not be ripped up again. You must take it south with you—

"Do you understand what I say?" he asked hastily, as she gave no sound beyond her heavy breathing in the darkness.

"No," came her answer all at once, clear and firm. It had happened to her before, very rarely—when tormented and frightened to the uttermost it was as though something broke within her mind, and then she was able to face anything, calm and composed. "You must not think of that, Olav. You must have no thought of taking me to you after this."

"Talk not so foolishly," replied Olav impatiently. "You ought to know as well as I that we two are bound to each other hand and foot."

"They told me—Kolbein and those—that there were many good and learned priests who judged your case otherwise than Lord Torfinn—"

"Ay, there is no case that all men are agreed on. But I hold to Bishop Torfinn's judgment. I gave him an ill reward for his kindness that time—but I laid this case in his hands and bowed to his judgment, when it fell out as I desired. And I must bow to it now likewise."

"Olav—do you remember that last night, when you came out to me at Ottastad?" Her voice was mournful, but calm and collected. "Do you remember saying you would kill me?—you said the one who broke troth with the other should die. You drew your knife and set it against my breast.—I have that knife—"

"Ay, keep it and welcome.—That night—oh, you must not speak of it—we swore so many oaths! I have since thought it was a greater sin, all we said then, than Einar's slaying. But I never thought it would be you who—"

"Olav," she said as before, "it is impossible. You could never have any joy of me if I came with you to Hestviken. I was sure of that as soon as I saw you. When you said you would come and fetch me in the summer—I saw that I had time enough to keep this concealed—"

"Ah—so you thought of that!" The words struck her like a blow, so that she threw herself upon the bed and clasped the bed-post as she broke into sobs, wailing in her abyss of shame and humiliation.

"Go from me, go from me," she whimpered. She remembered that Dalla might come in at any moment, bringing light into the room. At the thought that Olav might *see* her she was wild with despair and shame. "Go," she begged; "Olav, have pity on me and go!"

"Ay, now I will go. But you must know, 'twill be as I have said.—Nay, weep not so, Ingunn," he pleaded. "I wish you no harm—

"Much joy of each other we may not have," his bitterness got the better of him and he could not keep back the words. "God knows, in all these years—I often thought how I would make you a good husband—how I would do you all the good I might.—Now I dare give no such promise—it may well be difficult many a time to keep me from being hard on you. But, God helping me, our life will be no worse than we can both endure."

"Ay, would you had killed me that day," she wailed, as though she had scarce heard what he said.

"Be silent," he whispered, revolted. "You speak of killing—your own babe—and of my killing you—you are more beast than human, methinks; lose your wits when you see no escape. Men and women must bear resolutely what they have brought upon themselves—"

"Go!" she beseeched him; "go, go—"

"Ay, I will go now. But I shall come back—I shall come back when you have had this child of yours, Ingunn—then maybe you will find your wits again, so far that one may talk with you—"

She felt that he came a few steps nearer—and cringed as though she awaited ill treatment. Olav's hand felt for her shoulder in the dark; he bent over her and kissed her on the crown of her head, so hard that she felt his teeth.

"Be not so distressed," he whispered, standing over her. "I wish you no worse than— You must believe I do but seek a way out."

He took his hand from her and went out quickly.

Next morning Lady Magnhild came into her. Ingunn lay in bed gazing vacantly before her. Lady Magnhild's wrath was roused when she saw that the girl looked just as despairing today as ever.

"Have you not brought this misfortune on yourself?—and now you are to be rid of it far more lightly than you had a right to expect. We must all thank God and Mary Virgin on our knees that Olav is the man he is. But I say—God requite Kolbein as he deserves, for that he set himself against Olav's taking you long ago, and cozened that silly gull Ivar to be on his side! If they had only let Olav have you then, nine years ago!"

Ingunn lay motionless and said nothing.

Lady Magnhild went on talking: "Be it as it may, I'll not send for Hallveig at present. Since you are in such a wretched state, we may well doubt if it will live," she said consolingly. "And should it live, 'twill be time enough to speak of what will be best."

On the fourth day of Easter came Tora Steinfinnsdatter. Ingunn rose to meet her sister as she came in, but she had to take hold of the bedstead to keep on her feet, such was her dread of hearing what Tora would say.

But Tora took her in her arms and patted her. "My poor, poor Ingunn!"

And then she began to speak of Olav's generosity and of how black it would have looked if he had acted as most men in his position—sought to be rid of a wife who had never been given to him in lawful wedlock. "Sooth to say, I knew not Olav was so pious a man. He had much to do with the priests and the Church —I thought 'twas mainly for his own profit. I did not believe it was because he was so God-fearing and steadfast in the faith—

"And he will not claim that you part with your child," said Tora, beaming. "That must be such a comfort to you—are you not overjoyed that you need not send away your child?"

"Oh yes. But speak no more of that," begged Ingunn at last, for Tora never ceased her praises of this good luck in the midst of misfortune.

Tora said nothing of what she might have guessed or feared in the winter, nor did she censure her sister with many words, but tried rather to put a little heart into Ingunn: when relief came in a little while, she would find that the whole world would appear to her in brighter colours, and then there would come good days for her too; but she must not abandon herself as she did—she sat there in her corner all day long, never moved nor spoke a word unasked—only gazing before her in black despondency.

Dalla had taken Lady Magnhild's correction in such wise that never since had she opened her mouth to Ingunn. But she found ways enough, for all that, to torment the sick woman. Ingunn never dared lie down at night till she had felt under the bedclothes whether anything hard and sharp had been put there. And all at once she found a mass of vermin in her bed and in her dayclothes—they had been perfectly clean before. There were constantly cinders and chips and mouse-dirt in the food and drink that Dalla brought her. Every morning she tied Ingunn's shoes so tightly that they hurt her, and while Ingunn struggled painfully to loosen them, Dalla stood by with a sneering smile. Ingunn never said a word about this.

But Tora guessed at once a good deal of what had been going on—she took Dalla to task right heartily, and the old thrall woman cringed before her young mistress like a beaten dog. And when Tora saw that Ingunn could not overcome her terror if Dalla did but approach her, she drove the old woman out of Aasa's house for good. She helped her sister to be rid of the worst of the vermin, got her clean clothes and good food; and she checked her aunt when Lady Magnhild grumbled at Ingunn's ingratitude— saying that she herself had had a part in the disaster, and they had assuredly treated her more gently than she had a right to expect; she would put up with no more of this sullen crossness toward Ingunn. But Tora implored the lady—let them do all they could to make these last days easy for her; when she was on her feet again after her lying-in—it would be another matter. Then she would be strong enough to hear some grave words from them both.

7

SINCE Olav Audunsson had done penance for the slaying in the preaching friars' guest-house, he had formed fairly close ties with this monastic community; Brother Vegard, too, had been his confessor ever since he was a child, and he was a good friend of Arnvid Finnsson, who was one of the benefactors of the house. And before this last turn of events with Ingunn, Olav had had thoughts of joining the Dominicans as a brother *ab extra*. When the friars now saw that something weighed upon his mind, they left him in peace and avoided as far as possible lodging other guests in the women's house, where he lay. There was no little coming and going in the convent during Lent, for many folk from the country round were wont to make their Lenten confession here and celebrate Easter in the convent church.

Olav put off his confession again and again. He could not see how he was to make it in the right way—Ingunn could not have confessed yet, for Olav knew that Brother Vegard was still her confessor, and the monk had not been absent from the convent for six weeks. So Olav sat in the women's house and went nowhere—except to church.

But on Wednesday in Holy Week he thought he could not put it off any longer, and Brother Vegard promised to be in the church at a certain hour.

It felt cold and dark as he entered through the little side door from the cloister garth—it was the same spring weather out of doors. Brother Vegard already sat in his place in the choir, reading a book that he held on his knee, with the purple stole over his white frock. From an opening high up a sunbeam fell straight upon the pictures that were painted above the monks' choir stalls —lighting up the likeness of our Lord at the age of twelve among the Jewish doctors. "God, my Lord," prayed Olav in his heart, "give me discretion to say what I have to say and no more and no less." Then he knelt before the priest and said *Confiteor*.

With scrupulous care he rehearsed his sins against all the ten commandments, those he had broken and those he had kept, so far as he knew—he had had good time to think over his confession. At last he came to the hard part: "Then I confess that there is one to whom I bear the most bitter grudge, so that it seems to me most difficult to forgive this person. It is one whom I have loved with all my heart, and so soon as I heard what this friend had done to me, I felt I had been so deceived that thoughts of slaughter and wicked and cruel desires arose within me. God preserved me so that I curbed myself at that time. But so hard is it for me to bear with this person that I fear I can never forgive my friend—unless God give me special grace thereto. But I am afraid, father, that I must say no more of this matter."

"Is it because you are afraid you might otherwise disclose another's sin?" asked Brother Vegard.

"Yes, father," Olav drew a deep breath. "And it is for that reason that it seems so difficult to forgive. If I could tell the whole matter here in this place, I think it would be easier."

"Consider well, my Olav, whether it does not seem so to you because you think that, could you speak freely of the wrong your even Christian has done you, you own evil thoughts, your hatred and desire of blood, would then be justified according to what we sinful men call justice?"

"It is so, father."

The monk asked: "Do you hate this your enemy in such wise that you could wish him evil fortune every day upon earth and eternal perdition in the other world?"

"No."

"But you could wish that he might smart for what he has done to you, often and sorely?"

"Yes. For I can see naught else but that I myself must smart for it as long as I live. And I fear that, unless God work a miracle with me, I shall never more have peace in my soul, but wrath and ill will will arise in me time after time—for after this my affairs—my welfare and my repute—will grow worse, so long as I live upon earth."

"My son, you know that if you pray with your whole heart,

God will give you strength to forgive him that trespassed against you, for it has never yet been known that God was deaf to such a prayer. But you must pray without reservation—not as that man of whom Saint Augustine tells us: he prayed that God would give him grace to lead a chaste life, but not at once; it is in such wise men are wont to pray for grace to forgive their enemies. And you must not be downcast, even if God lets you pray long and persistently before He grants you this gift."

"Ay, father. But I fear I shall not always be able to curb myself while I wait for my prayers to be heard."

As the monk did not reply at once, Olav said hastily: "For it is so, father, that this thing which—which my friend—has done to me—has disordered my whole life. I dare not say more of it, but there are such difficulties— Could I say more, you would see that—this person—has set so heavy a load upon my neck—"

"I can guess that it is heavy, my son. But you must be steadfast and pray. And when on Good Friday you come forward to kiss the cross, look on it closely and reflect in your heart whether your sins did not weigh something in the load which our Lord bore, when He shouldered the sins of us all. Think you then that the load which your friend has laid upon you is so heavy that you are not able to bear it—a Christian man and His man?"

Olav bent so low that he touched the monk's knee with his forehead. "Nay. Nay, I think not that—" he whispered falteringly.

The night between Good Friday and Easter Eve Olav awoke drenched with sweat—he had been dreaming. As he lay in pitch-darkness trying to be rid of the horror this dream had left in his mind, their childhood came back to him in the very life: in his dream they had been boy and girl. But when he thought how all had promised then and how their future looked now, all that he believed himself to have secured through his constant prayers of the last few days seemed to fade away like smoke between his fingers. He drew the bedclothes over his head, and, lest he should burst into tears, he lay as a man lies on the rack, straining his whole will to a single end—the torturers shall not force one moan out of him.

That summer—that summer and that autumn, when she awaited his coming every night in her bower. Uneasy he had been; the guileless young heart in his breast had quivered with excitement and disquietude from the moment he awoke and saw that he was naked. But of *her* he had always felt easy. That she could fall out of his hands and into another man's—no, that he had never imagined. That last night, when he had come to her a homicide and an outlaw, when he had put the cold blade against her warm breast and bade her keep the knife for a token—it was not that he thought she might prove faithless. His thoughts were of himself, who was about to face an uncertain fate, young and untried and doubtful as he was.

When he crept close to her and hid his face in her wheat-coloured hair, it smelt like new-mown hay. And her flesh was so soft and limp, it always made him think of corn that had not fully ripened—was still milky. Never had he taken her in his arms without the thought: "I must not be hard-handed with her, she is so slight and weak; she needs my protection against every shock and scratch, for this flesh of hers cannot be such as heals quickly." And he had spared her all talk of that which weighed upon him, for he thought it would be a shame to shift any of his burden onto her feeble shoulders. Uneasy conscience, anxiety for the future—what should she understand of such things, with her childlike nature? The very insatiability with which she demanded his caresses, set herself to provoke them if he became absent for a moment or chanced to speak of any but their own concerns—this he took to be a kind of childishness. She had little more understanding than a child or an animal, poor thing—nay, he had often thought her like a gentle, timid beast—a tame doe or a young heifer, so fond of endearments and so easily scared.

Now he remembered that he had divined this at the same moment as he divined what it meant that she was a woman whom he would possess and enjoy—it had been clear to him that she was a weak and tender creature and that he must shield and defend her.

And now it appeared to him that this dream might have been sent him as a gift, though it had at first called up such grim torment in his mind. He had believed himself capable of wishing she might suffer abundantly for her weakness. Far from it.—He would do all in his power to help her to be let off lightly.

"My little doe—you have let yourself be chased straight into the pit—and now you lie there, battered and besmirched, a poor little beast. But I shall come and take you up and bear you away to a place where you will not be trampled upon and crushed."

—Now it was revealed to him that what had happened when he had taken her in his arms, plucked her flower, and breathed its sweetness and its scent, was only something that had chanced by the way. But what really mattered, when it came to the point, was that she had been placed in his arms in order that he might carry her through everything, take the burden from her and defend her. That was to be his happiness, the other was no more than passing joys.

Throughout the holy-days of Easter he was as one who had just risen from a grievous sickness—not that he had ever been sick in his life; but so he felt it. "My soul is now healed— Ingunn, you must know that I wish you naught but well."

He wondered whether he ought to tell his dream to Brother Vegard. But in these wellnigh twenty years during which the monk had been his confessor, he had never spoken a word to him in confidence outside the confessional. Brother Vegard Ragnvaldsson was a good man and a man of intelligence, but dry and chilly by nature—and then he had a sly and witty way of talking of folk, in which Olav delighted, so long as he was not himself the victim. Nor had he ever before felt any impulse to cross the fence that separated him and his confessor; rather had it seemed an advantage that the man outside the church was almost another person than the priest who heard his self-reproaches and guided him in spiritual things.

Before now he had thought of confiding this matter of Ingunn to the monk outside the confessional. But this would be like justifying himself and accusing her; so he would not. Doubtless Brother Vegard would soon be sent for to Berg; the poor soul must soon prepare herself to face the peril of death.

Then came the Wednesday after *Dominica in albis*.[1] As Olav was passing through the church door after the day's mass, someone touched his arm from behind.

"Hail, master. Is it you they call Olav Audunsson?"

Olav turned and saw a tall and slight, dark-complexioned young man behind him. "That should be my name—but what would you with me?"

[1] The first Sunday after Easter.

255

"I would fain speak with you, a word or two." Olav could hear by his speech that he was not from these parts.

Olav stepped aside to let the people come out of church and went a few paces along the covered way. Through the arches of the corridor he saw the morning sun just bursting over the blue-black ridges in the south-west, glancing on the dark open water between the island and Stangeland and lighting up the brown slopes, now bare of snow.

"What would you, then?—I cannot call to mind that I have seen you before."

"Nay, we can scarcely have met before. But you will surely know me by name—Teit Hallsson I am called; I am from Varmaa-dal in Sida, in Iceland."

Olav was struck speechless—Teit. The boy was shabbily dressed, but he had a handsome, dark, and slender face under his worn fur cap, clear tawny eyes, and an arched jaw with a mass of shining white teeth.

"So now maybe you guess why I have sought you out."

"Nay, I cannot say that I guess that."

"If you knew of a place where we could talk privily," said Teit, "it might be better."

Olav made no reply, but turned and went in front under the covered way round the north side of the church. Teit followed. Olav was aware as he walked along that no one could see them. The roof of the corridor came down so far that people outside could not distinguish who was moving in the shadow behind the narrow arches.

Where the corridor followed the curve of the apse, there was a way into a corner of the graveyard. Olav led the other by this path and leaped the fence into the kale-garden. This was his usual way to and from church; it was shorter for him.

When they reached the women's house, Olav barred the door behind them. Teit seated himself on the bench unbidden, but Olav remained standing and waited for him to speak.

"Ay, you can guess 'tis of her, Ingunn Steinfinnsdatter, I would speak with you," said Teit with an uneasy little smile. "We were friends last summer, but now I have neither seen nor heard aught of her since early autumn. But now the talk is that she is with child and near her time—and so it must be mine. Now, I know that she was yours before she was mine, and therefore I thought I would speak with you of what we should do—"

"You are not craven-hearted, methinks," said Olav.

"No man can be possessed of *every* vice, and I am free of this one—" the boy smiled lightly.

Olav still held his peace, waiting. Instinctively he gave a rapid glance at his bed: his arms hung in their place.

"So long ago as the autumn," Teit began again, "I let her know that if it could be so ordered, I was willing to marry her—"

"*Marry* her!" He laughed, two short blasts through the nose, with mouth hard set.

"Ay, ay," said Teit calmly. "Meseems 'twas no such unequal match either—Ingunn is no nurseling, and her name has been in folk's mouths once before. None had heard from you for ten years, and it seemed little likely that you would ever come back. Ay, *she* talked as if she believed it, and so she sent me packing; and I was angry, as well I might be, at such fickleness and said I would go my way, if she would have it so, but then it would be bootless to send for me later. She has not done so either—not a word have I heard from her, that she is in distress—and I know not if I would have gone to her now—I parted from her in no friendly fashion—

"But when I heard that you had come back and had been at Berg—and that you would have no more of her and went your ways when you saw how things were—then I took pity on her after all. And now they say she lies shut up in one of the outhouses and is given nothing to live on but dirty water and ashes in her porridge, and they have beaten her and kicked her and dragged her by the hair, till it is a marvel she is still alive—"

Olav had listened to him with frowning brows. He was about to answer gruffly that these were lies; but he checked himself. It was impossible for *him* to discuss this matter with Teit. And then he reflected how it would add to all their difficulties if these rumours got abroad.—And to how many people had this young coxcomb boasted of his paternity?

Teit asked: "Is it not so that you are a good friend of this rich Arnvid of Miklebö in Elfardal, her kinsman?"

"Why so?" asked Olav sharply.

"They all say he is helpful and good—the friend of every man who needs help. So I thought haply it were better if I betook me to him first, not to the Steinfinnssons or the old man at Galtestad. What think you of that? And if you would give me a token to your friend, or let one write a letter to him and set your seal on it—"

Olav sank straight down upon the bench. "Now methinks—! Is that your suit to me—I am to back your wooing?"

"Yes," said Teit calmly. "Does it seem so strange to you?"

"It seems strange to me indeed." He burst into a short, harsh laugh. "Never did I hear the like!"

"But 'tis seen every day," said Teit, "that a man of your condition marries off his leman when he wants her no longer."

"Have a care of your mouth, Teit," said Olav threateningly. "Beware what words you use of her!"

As though absently, Teit took the little sword that hung at his belt and laid it across his knees, with one hand on the sheath and the other on the hilt. He looked at Olav with a little smile. "Nay, I had forgot—'tis here in this room you use to strike down your enemies?"

"Nay, 'twas in the other guest-house—and as for striking down, we came to blows—" he checked himself, annoyed at having been drawn into saying so much to the man.

"Be that as it may," said Teit with the same little smile, "since it seems now that I have more part in her than you—"

"There you are mistaken, Teit. Never can you have part in her —Ingunn belongs to *us*, and whatever she may have done, we will never give her away outside our own rank."

"Nevertheless it is mine, the child she bears—"

"Know you not, with your learning, Icelander, that an unmarried woman's child follows the mother and has her rights, even if it be a freewoman who had been seduced by her thrall?"

"I am no thrall," said the Icelander hotly. "Both my father and my mother came of the best stock in Iceland, though they were poor folk. And you need not fear that I shall not be able to support her, if you do but give her a fair dowry—" and he enlarged on his future prospects—he would become a man of substance if only he came to a place where he had opportunity to exercise all his art and knowledge—and he could train Ingunn to help him.

Olav called to mind the bookbinder who had been here in his youth—a master craftsman whom the Bishop of Oslo had sent up to Lord Torfinn, that he might finish the books that had been written in the course of the year. Olav had accompanied Asbjörn All-fat to the room where they work—the wife was there helping, boring holes in the parchment, many sheets at a time, and between whiles she pushed with her elbow the great kneading-trough which she had hung by her side; within it lay her child, shrieking and grimacing and dropping the morsel it had been given to suck —till Asbjörn bade her give herself a little rest and comfort the child. He felt sorry for her, said Asbjörn. When their work was done, the Bishop sent her a winter kirtle besides the man's wages, calling her an able woman. Olav had seen them the day they departed: the master rode a right good horse, but his wife was mounted on a little stumpy, big-bellied jade, with the infant in her arms and all their baggage stowed about her.

Ingunn thrust into such a life—holy Mother of God, no! That was not even to be thought of. Ingunn outside the rank in which she had been born and brought up; it was so crazy a thought—he simply could not understand how it had come about that a fellow who stood so utterly outside had fallen in with her.

He sat watching Teit with a cold, searching glance as the other was speaking. Amid all the rest he saw that the boy was likable in a way. Unafraid, accustomed to make his own way in the world, Olav could guess; it would need no small thing to wear him down or quell his cheerful spirit—he was so quick to smile, and it became him well. He must have grown a tough hide in his roaming life among strangers, knaves, and loose women; but— He himself had now roamed about the world for nine years; he himself had had a hand in doings that he did not care to think of when he came home to settle. But that anyone from *that* world should have stepped between him and Ingunn, should have touched her—

Touched her, so that she lay there at Berg awaiting the hour when she must go on her knees upon the floor and give herself over to the pains and humiliation of childbirth—Ingunn's child. No one, she had said, when he asked her who the man was. He remembered that he himself had said: "No one" when she wished to know who had helped him to escape to the Earl, when he ran away from Hövdinggaard. And in those years when he had followed the Earl he had met so many, both men and women, who, he knew, would be "No one" to him when once he was settled at home in Hestviken—he had known many lads like this Teit, had caroused with them in comradeship and liked them. But then he was a *man*, nothing else. When any from that world outside crossed the bond that held a man to his wife—then the life of both was stained for all time. A woman's honour—that was the honour of all the men who had the duty and right of watching over her.

"Now, what say you?" asked Teit, rather impatiently.

Olav woke up—he had not heard a word of what Teit had just been saying.

"I say, you must put this—folly—out of your mind. But see that you get you out of the Upplands as quickly as you can—take the road for Nidaros today rather than tomorrow. Know you not she has grown-up brothers?—the day they hear of their sister's misfortune, you are a dead man."

"Oh, that is not so sure. If I say it myself, I am none of the worst at using arms. And I hold, Olav—since she was once *yours*—that you might well do something to help her to marry and retrieve her honour."

"So you think I would count her case bettered if she married *you*?" said Olav hotly. "Hold your peace, I say—I will hear no more of this fool's talk."

Teit said: "Ay, then I must go to Miklebö alone. I will try it—will speak with this Arnvid. *I* hold that her case will be better as my wedded wife than if she is to be left with these rich kinsfolk of hers till they have tortured both her and our child to death—"

"But I once said that myself," thought Olav, wearied out— "torture her and the child to death.—But then we were not to have a child—"

"For I have seen myself the plight she was in with the folk of Berg, ere ever this came about. And I cannot be sure that *she* will not count it a gain if she gets a man who can take her far away from this part of the country and from all of you. 'Tis true, when first she had let me have my will with her, she turned clean round, raved at me like a troll. But maybe she was affrighted—haply 'twas not so senseless as I thought at first. And until this time we had always been friends and agreed well together, and she never made it a secret that she liked me as well as I liked her—"

Liked him—so there it was. Until this moment Olav had felt no jealousy, in such a way that he could fix it on this Teit—it was *she* and her disaster that had troubled him to the depths of his being. The cause—had been "No one" to him too. But so it was, she had liked this rascal and been good friends with him the whole summer. Ay ay, in Satan's name, the boy was comely, brisk, and full of life. She had liked him so well that she let him have his will —afterwards she had taken fright.—But she had given herself to this swarthy, curly-haired Icelander, in the kindness of her heart.

"So you will not give me any token or message to Miklebö that may serve me in good stead?" asked Teit.

" 'Tis strange you do not bid me go with you and plead your cause," said Olav scornfully.

"Oh nay—I thought that were too much to ask," replied the other innocently. "But I had it in my mind, if perchance you were bound thither in any case, that we might travel in company."

Olav burst into a laugh—a short bark. Teit rose, took his leave, and went out.

As soon as he was gone, Olav started up as though from sleep. He went to the door, and saw as he did so that he had picked up his little axe—a working-axe that had lain on the bench beside his hand among knives and gouges and the like. Olav was engaged in making some footstools for use in the church—the Prior had said they wanted some, and Olav had offered to make them.

He went into the convent yard and through the gate. The lay brother who acted as porter was standing there idly. Olav went up to him.

"Know you aught of that fellow yonder?" he asked. Teit was striding up the hill toward the cathedral; no others were in sight just then.

"Is it not that Icelander," said the porter, "who was clerk to Torgard the cantor last year? Ay, 'tis surely he."

"Know you aught of the fellow?" asked Olav again.

Brother Andreas was known for the strictness of his life, but his chastity was of the kind that has been likened to a lamp without oil: he had not much charity toward other poor sinners. He then and there bestowed upon Olav all those chapters of Teit Hallsson's saga which were known to Bishop's Hamar.

Olav raised his eyes to the churchyard wall, behind which the young man had just disappeared.

No greater harm could possibly befall than that the man came off scot-free.

.   .   .

Next day the sky was again blue and the air quivered with warmth and moisture about the bare and brown tree-tops. As Olav entered the courtyard of the convent late in the afternoon, the cook, fat Brother Helge, stood watching the pigs, which were fighting over the fish offal he had just thrown out.

"What has come to you?" he asked. "You were not at mass today, Olav."

Olav replied that he had not slept till near morning, and so he had overslept himself. "But I wonder if you could get me the loan of a pair of skis about the house, Brother Helge." Arnvid had asked him to come north to Miklebö after Easter; he thought of going today.

But would he not rather ride, suggested the lay brother. Olav said that with this going he would get on faster by following the ski-tracks through the forest.

He had just shaved himself when Brother Helge came to the door of the women's house with his arms full of all the convent's skis and a wallet of provisions over his shoulder. Olav had cut himself over the cheek-bone and was bleeding freely—the blood had run down his cheek and stained his shirt; his hand was covered with it. Brother Helge could not stop the bleeding either, and he wondered that such a little scratch could bleed so much. At last he ran off and came back with a cupful of oatmeal, which he clapped against the wound.

The sweet smell of the meal and the coolness of it against his skin sent a sharp thrill of desire and longing through the man—for a woman's caresses, tender and sweet, without sin or pain. It was of that he had been robbed.

The monk saw that a veil came over Olav's eyes; he said anxiously: "Methinks, Olav, you should give up this journey of yours —inquire first, in any case, if there be no other man in town who goes that way. 'Twas not natural that a paltry cut should bleed so freely—look at your hands, they are all bloody."

Olav only laughed. He went outside, washed himself in the puddles under the drip of the roof, and chose a pair of skis.

He was standing in the room, fully dressed, telling the lay brother about his horse and the things he was leaving behind—when there was a sharp ring of steel somewhere. Both men turned instinctively toward the bed. Kinfetch hung on the wall above it, and it seemed to them both that it shifted slightly on its peg.

" 'Twas your axe that sang," said the monk in a hushed voice. "Olav—do not go!"

Olav laughed. "That was the second warning, think you?— Maybe I shall bow to the third, Helge."

Hardly had he uttered the words when a bird flew in at the door, fluttered hither and thither about the room, and flapped against the wall—it was incredible how much noise the little wings made.

The cook's round red face whitened as he looked at the other— Olav's pale lips seemed livid.—But then he shook his head and laughed. He caught the bird in his cap, carried it out of the door, and let it go.

"These tomtits are ever perching on the log walls, scratching and pecking at flies at this time of year; the noise they make every morning— You are easily served with portents, brother, if you reckon it one when the tomtits fly indoors!"

He took up the little working-axe and hung it to his belt.

"Shall you not take Kinfetch?" asked Brother Helge.

"Nay, she would be unhandy to drag on this journey." He bade the lay brother put away the battle-axe together with his sword, took a ski-staff that was tipped with a little spear-point, and then with a farewell to Brother Helge he set out.

It was full moon as Olav mounted the slopes under Furuberg. The sunshine had paled, the sky had become dull and chilly—grey and thick in the north. It looked as though there might be snow. Olav halted with the skis on his shoulder and looked back.

In the fading sunshine the lowlands looked bare and dark and withered—patches of snow were few and small. In the town the dark roofs of turf or shingles and the bare branches of the trees clustered about the bright stone walls of Christ Church, with its heavy, lead-roofed tower standing out against the pale and ruffled waters of the lake. Olav cursed within himself at the feeling of depression that came upon him—well, it would be bad luck if snow came just when he had to find his way through the woods. He had passed that way only once before, and that was in Arnvid's company, so that they dashed along and took short cuts over the roughest ground—on skis Arnvid could outrun any man he knew.

It chanced that he knew which of these little huts on the out-skirts of the forest the Icelander had taken for himself; a foul murder had been done there in Bishop Torfinn's time: a father and his two children, a son and a daughter under age, had killed and robbed a prosperous old beggar. Since then folk had not cared to live there. But this Teit was altogether penniless.

Olav pretended to himself that he had no plan—it must fall out as fate would have it. Teit might have set out for the north the day before, or he might have thought better of it, given up that idea. But if that were so, Olav saw at once he would have to keep him to it again; he could not have this man going at large in these parts. He would have to get him to Nidaros, or to Iceland—any-where out of the way.

He pushed the door; it was not bolted. The cover was over the smoke-vent, so it was very dark; the little room was cold and dismal, with a raw smell of earth and mouldiness and dirt. But Teit sprang out of bed fully clad and looked as fresh as ever—a fleeting smile came over his face as he saw who his visitor was.

"You will have to sit on the bench—I cannot set out a seat for you, for there is not a stool in the place, as you see."

Olav seated himself on the fixed bench. So far as he could see, there was not a loose piece of furniture in the hut—only some fire-wood lying about the floor. Teit threw some on the hearth, blew it into a flame, and opened the vent.

"And I cannot offer you a cup of welcome—for a very good reason. But you gave me none yesterday either, so—"

"Did you expect it?" Olav laughed grimly.

The other laughed too. And again Olav felt that there was a sort of charm about the lad—barefaced perhaps, but spirited, un-daunted by poverty and desolation.

"I have changed my mind, Teit," said Olav. "I am on my way to Miklebö now. And if you think it may serve your turn to speak with Arnvid Finnsson—you are welcome to join me."

"Ah—but, sooth to say, I have not my horse with me now. But maybe you can get me the loan of one?" He laughed as if he had made a good joke.

"I go through the forest, on skis," said Olav curtly.

"Ah. Such conveyance I can well find. I have seen a pair out in the shed—" he darted out and came back with them. The ski was split for a good part of its length and the hide of the *aander* was almost worn away.[2]

Teit fastened on his belt and sword and threw his cloak about him. "Ay, now I am ready when you will!"

"Food you must take, I ween?"

"Nay, such heavy gear I thought to spare myself—for a good reason."

Olav felt very ill at ease. Was he to share his food with a man whom perhaps he would afterwards—break peace with? And something prompted him to offer the lad the whole; Teit must have gone very short of food lately.—But in any case that would have to wait till they came up into the hills.

"Think it well over, though, Icelander," he said, almost threateningly. "Might it not be foolhardy for you to join company with me through the forest, think you?" He felt he was giving his conscience a little more than its due in saying this—it might sound like a sort of challenge. What would happen was uncertain, but in any event—

But Teit only smiled coldly and slapped his sword. "Methinks I am better armed than you—I believe I will venture it, Olav. And for that matter—a great man like you does not cast his hawk at every fly."

As they were going out, Olav looked back at the hearth; the fire was now burning briskly.

"But—will you not put it out?"

"Nay, I care not. 'Twill be no great harm anyhow if this hut be burned up."

As soon as they stepped outside, Olav noticed that the mist in the air had now grown so dense that he could look at the sun—there was a grey veil before it.

The surface was good when they reached the high ground. Olav kept to the northern slopes of the ridge that lies between Ridabu and Fauskar. As far as he remembered, he ought to go due

[2] In some districts of Norway a pair of skis consisted of one *ski* (left foot) of naked wood and one *aander* (right foot), which was a shorter ski, covered on the under side with hide, preferably sealskin, with the hair on. This made the *aander* run very smoothly downhill and prevented balling on wet snow; uphill the hide acted as a brake against backsliding.

265

north and then slightly to the north-east; then in the course of the afternoon he would come into a tract that contained not a few sæters belonging to farms in the Glaama Dale, and they would be sure of finding shelter for the night. The evenings were already long.

The snow lay six or eight feet deep on these slopes, and after the thaw of the last weeks' mild weather and the sudden frost, it gave excellent going. But ever and anon Olav had to wait for Teit, who lay floundering, sunk in masses of snow. He was just as likely to fall at the top of a slope as at the bottom.

"I think we shall have to change skis," said Olav after a while. The hide of Teit's *aander* was so ragged that Olav simply ripped it off.

The change did not help Teit much; it was marvellous how many tumbles the boy got. He lost his ski and went through the frozen crust up to his waist, laughing at his own clumsiness as he scrambled out.

"You are not much used to running on skis, Teit?" asked Olav; he had been far down a bush-grown scree after the other's ski.

"Not much." Teit's face was red as fire from his struggles and he had scratched both face and hands on the frozen snow, but he laughed heartily. "At home in Iceland I never set foot on a ski. And here in Norway I have not tried the art more than two or three times before today."

" 'Twill be hard work for you to cover the long road to Miklebö, then," said Olav.

"Oh, I shall come through well enough—have no fear of that."

"God knows if he even sees how it plagues me to run back and forth in my own tracks like a dog to pull up him and his skis," thought Olav. Aloud he suggested that they might rest awhile and take a bite of food. Teit was quite willing, and Olav broke off branches and laid them on the snow.

He looked the other way while the lad was eating. "Ay, he suffers no want who is victualled by convent folk!"

The sky was now grey all over. From where they sat, high on the shaded slope, they saw nothing but forest, ridge behind ridge, blue-black beneath the heavy sky; in the valley that lay just below them the forest looked black as coal around a little white patch— a lake or a marsh.

But round about the birds began to pipe and chirp in tones of spring—a little uncertain and hesitating in the face of the weather that was coming. Now and again a sough went through the forest, advancing from ridge to ridge. The land to the northward was wrapped in a snow-squall, which hid the dark-grey cliff and the wooded slope below it—it was coming this way.

"Nay, Teit—we must go on."

Olav helped the Icelander to bind his skis securely. And then this sword—for a man who fell at every turn. He could not help saying it—sword and skis do not go together.

" 'Tis the only weapon I have." He drew it and handed it to Olav, with some pride. It was a good weapon—a plain hilt and a fine blade. "That is my whole patrimony—all my father left me. And I will never part with it!"

"Is your father dead?"

"Ay—three years ago. 'Twas then it came into my head to try my luck in Norway. Well—I made for Fljotshverv first, to Mother. She ran off from Father and me when I was seven winters old and I had not seen her for ten years—she had found one she wished to marry, and then her conscience smote her for having been a priest's paramour so long. But she would fainer see my heel than my toe—ay, there had been lean years in our part of the country, and the children swarmed on their farm; I could never find out how many were mother's and which belonged to the other women—"

"Nay, Teit—" Olav leaned forward on his skis and set out again.

Tacking this way and that, he plunged down; the ground was broken here—he had to crouch under the trees. The sun had beaten down on the snow and left the ski-track standing out like a ridge. But yon fellow must get on as best he could.

Down by the tarn he stopped, waiting and listening. A gust of wind swept the ridge, there was a creaking and grating and soughing through the forest. Ah, at last, there came the sound of skis on the frozen slope.

Teit accomplished the last lap in fine style and came down to the tarn. He was white all over from his falls, but he grinned with all his gleaming teeth and his grazed and ruddy cheeks.

"Soon I shall be as good a ski-runner as a Norseman!" He showed what he had done with his awkward cloak—by degrees it had become so ragged that he had thought it as well to thrust his arms through two of the holes and fasten his belt outside. Thus he was rid of *that* hindrance.

"Are you very tired?" asked Olav.

"Oh no." He put his hand to the back of his neck and rocked his head a little: just there in the bend of the neck he was stiff and sore—it felt as if the devil himself had caught him there.

Olav himself felt a slight stiffness in the same place—it was the first time he had been on skis this year. So he could imagine what the other felt. And all at once there came into his mind—his rowing to Hamar with Ingunn on the lake; he was only a boy at the time, and he had toiled and pulled at the oars, but his neck ached worse and worse and he clenched his teeth, spurted, and would not give in and show that he was tired; he felt perfectly hopeless— "Shall we never get there?"

He looked at Teit—and clenched his teeth. He must stifle this feeling that tried to get the better of him. He would think of her —how *she* was suffering now; of the hatred and loathing that had filled him when he heard of her ruin; of all the hopes that had been destroyed. "And we shall live in the shadow of this sorrow and shame all our days." But here was this malapert youth, who was the cause of their misfortunes—and had no idea of it all. They went on side by side across the flat, and Teit chattered incessantly, puffing and blowing and groaning—asked Olav questions about the animal tracks they saw—old trails that glistened on the frozen crust, fresh ones of elk that had gone through—boasted of his newly acquired skill as a ski-runner. He confided in him, almost as a boy confides to his father.—And more than anything else Olav felt a kind of pity for this fatuous simplicity. No! This was so utterly preposterous—

The first hard grains of snow began to drizzle down as they entered the forest on the other side of the tarn. And the daylight was already on the wane. They had not gone far up the slope when they found themselves in a flurry of snow. Olav pushed on, stopped and waited for the other, who was hanging back—pushed on again. Now he was restlessly longing to make an end of this journey, to come under a roof—and at the same time he shrank from thinking of what then. From the height where they had rested, he had seen that beyond the ridge they were now on was a higher one, and at the top of it were some white patches on which there seemed to be houses. They might be crofters' homes, they might meet folk tonight—or they might be sæters, which was more likely. It must fall out as it was fated.

Higher up there was a strong breeze against them. For a time the snow had fallen thickly in great soft flakes, but now the wind lashed their faces with hard, dry grains; the whistling sound of the snow seemed to fill the whole forest with a sharp note that penetrated the droning and howling of the wind in the fir-tops. And the weather was felt the more since the dusk was now growing rapidly denser.

The ski-tracks had vanished long ago, a good deal of fresh snow had fallen already, and where it had been blown into drifts, their skis sank in deep.

Again he had to stop and wait for Teit. The Icelander drew up beside him, groaning as if his chest would burst; breathless, but as cheerful as ever, he said: "Bide awhile, friend—let me go ahead and break the trail."

Olav felt his will sink impotently—before this feeling that arose within him, which he must grapple with and trample underfoot ere he could do aught to this boy. He flung himself forward and ran on with all his strength. Now and again he had to halt and listen whether the other was after him, but he never waited till Teit had quite overtaken him.

It was almost dark when they reached the clearing. It looked like a little cluster of sæters. Through the snow and the darkness he had a glimpse of scattered black objects—some might be large rocks, but some were huts.

Olav threw down the wallet as soon as they were inside the dark hole, took out his tinder-pouch, and set about striking fire. He knelt over the hearth, breathing upon the little flames that struggled to catch the half-damp twigs—heard Teit's cries of satisfaction as he looked about him in the little cabin. There was hay on the pallet, a skin coverlet, and some sacks for pillows—and the boy strode into the black hole beyond, a sort of shed of stones and turf. There were bannocks, Teit announced, and a tub of whey and water; he came into the opening with a baler in his hand and offered Olav some of the half-frozen drink.

"To be sure, Teit, we are in a Christian land; folk do not go from their sæters without leaving behind the wherewithal to keep body and soul together, should any need it when faring through the forest."

Teit stretched himself on the pallet while they took their meal, lying with his knees drawn up and his head low on account of the smoke; they could not make a draught, for the little room was so narrow that the flames might catch the bedstead or the pile of fuel on the floor. Olav sat on the bench opposite, in spite of the smoke, which tore at his chest and made his eyes smart. The man sat with his arms crossed, staring under drooping eyelids into the fire and listening to the boy's chatter, silent as a stone. 'Twas all folly; neither the weather nor the road was anything to talk about —had he not been burdened with this companion, who was like a new-born calf on skis, he would have run hither in half the time. But the fool talked as though they had been comrades in the mightiest adventures and dangers.

"Are you tired?" asked Teit, suddenly aware that the other had not replied a word to his flood of talk. He made room on the pallet—"Or maybe you will lie inside?"

Never, thought Olav. Share a couch with this guest for a night —no. There was reason in all things.

"Nay, I am not tired."

He tried to collect his thoughts. For they seemed to be slipping away from him all the time—Ingunn and he were *married;* he must keep that clearly before him; and therefore Teit *must* be put out of the way; he had ruined her from pure frivolity, but this non-sense the boy talked about repairing her misfortune—the young goat could do nothing there; he must do it himself, the little that could be done. Hide the shame. Believe—let folk believe what they pleased, so long as they saw where he stood and where her kinsmen must stand with him—he acknowledged the child for his and intended to defend his word against any who dared to utter doubts aloud.

"When did you hear these rumours?" he asked abruptly. "That she is—in trouble? This must have got abroad quite lately?"

Teit said ay, 'twas not so long since he had heard it. Some people he knew in the town had a daughter who was married to one of the crofters under Berg. And both they and their daughter had seen her walking hither and thither on the slopes below the manor in the evenings—but now of course it was light till late at night.—Teit dwelt upon their gossip.

Olav sat listening with lowered brows. The blood began to surge in his ears. But this was better. Let the boy keep on; now he would soon get over this unmanly—kindliness, which had been in a fair way to corrupt him.

"And what of you?" asked Olav; his mouth was twisted into a sort of smile. "Could you forbear to let them know that this was your doing?"

"I dare say I said some such thing."

"Have you spoken of it to others?"

If it could be made to seem like crofters' tattle and naught else, that would be bearable. Carry one's head high among one's equals, look them straight and hard in the face, and pretend to have no inkling of what was murmured behind one's back—malicious gossip that the maids had carried to their mistresses—

Teit said, with some embarrassment: "I had been so furious with her that it made me glad when first I heard she was so heavy on her feet.—The devil knows she was light and quick enough last summer—like a cat that strokes herself against one's leg and slips away when one tries to take her up. Then at last, when I had got her in my clutches—"

Olav hardly heard what the other was saying—the blood hummed and hammered so in his head. But this was enough, it had given him back the will to revenge—and a dear vengeance it must be, for it would be long ere he forgot this that he had just heard.

"—But the next night she had changed her mind again, barred her door against me. And when I came to her and spoke of marrying, she drove me from her as though I had been a dog—"

"Then I almost think you must put this marriage out of your head, Teit."

Warned by the ring of the man's voice, Teit looked up—Olav had risen to his feet and held the little woodcutter's axe in his hand. Quick as lightning the boy seized his sword and drew it, as he leaped to his feet. Olav was seized with a wild joy on seeing that Teit now grasped it all—the boy's face seemed to blacken with rage; he saw he had been fooled and he met the other's wordless challenge with an eager cry of youthful valour.

He did not wait for Olav to attack, but dashed in at once. Olav stood still—three times he warded off the boy's strokes with the head of his axe. The lad was deft and agile, Olav saw; but not strong in the arm. When Teit cut at him the fourth time, Olav swerved unexpectdly to the right, so that the sword caught him on the left arm, but the young fellow lost his head for an instant. Olav's axe struck him on the shoulder, and the sword fell out of his hand. He bent down to pick it up with his left, and then Olav planted the axe in the skull of him; the boy fell on his face.

Olav waited till the last spasms had left the body, and a little longer. Then he turned him over on his back. A little blood had run down through the hair, making a streak across the forehead. Olav took the corpse by the arm-pits and dragged it out into the dairy-shed.

He went to the door of the sæter—night and wind-driven snow, the roar and soughing of the wind in the forests. He would have to wait here till daylight.—Olav lay down on the pallet.

So many a man had fallen by his hand, of greater worth than this one.

Olav threw more wood on the fire. He must shake off this unwholesome—remorse, or whatever it was. Teit had brought it on himself. Bishop Torfinn himself had said a ravisher who was slain by the maid's kinsmen must be reckoned almost as a self-slayer; he had begged his own death. Teit—had begged his own death. It were absurd that he should feel it as anything worse than—than felling a man in battle. Teit had fallen weapon in hand—there lay his sword on the floor.

Never could he settle Ingunn securely so long as this wretched jackanapes could run hither and thither blabbing of his misdeed, the nature of which he had not the sense to see.

Olav was so cold that his teeth chattered, though one side of him was being baked as he lay. But his elkskin coat stuck to his back, wet and stiff and icy cold, and his footgear was wet through. And he felt the wound he had got on his left arm—he had forgotten it, but now it ached and smarted.

He heaped fresh fuel on the hearth. If the hut burned, let it burn.

Nay, but he must preserve his life for Ingunn's sake. Long enough she had had to wait for her husband—he must not be missing when she needed him most.

"Nay, my good Teit, 'tis *you* must give way, for *I* will not." He struggled to hiss out the words; the other was pressing on his chest with all his weight, and Olav could not get a hold, his strength seemed to be taken from him. Teit showed his whole white row of teeth, smiling as frankly as ever, though the back of his head was split open. "Cannot you see it, you wretched half-wit?—the woman is mine, so you must give way—take yourself off—"

He was awakened by his own hoarse cry as the nightmare left him. It was almost entirely dark in the room, with only a little glow from the embers. Wind and snow came in through the walls —and the elkskin qerkin was like an icy coat of mail.

Olav got up and went into the dairy, fumbling in the dark. The dead man lay there stiff and still, cold as ice. He had only been dreaming—he must have slept for several hours. He fed the fire again, nor could he endure to sit and stare at it—so he had to take to the pallet again. He got the sacks of hay under his back and the skin coverlet over him as well as he could.

Now and again sleep wrapped him as in a mist, and each time it veiled his thoughts he was awakened by the same dull throbbing pain within him—the smarting of his wound was only an echo of some deeper hurt. Then he was wide awake and lay thinking round in the same ring.

That fellow had got his deserts. He had had to kill so many a better man in battle, and never taken it to heart. There might be sense in pitying Ingunn, but not this one—no. If there were none to mourn the lad, either here or in his own land, that were well; then no innocent would suffer because the guilty had found his punishment. These years, first with his uncle and then with the Earl, ought to have been enough to harden him. This was uncalled for—he had got his deserts. And so on, round in a ring.

He started up—no, it was only a dream that Teit stood there in the doorway with the baler, offering him a drink. He lay safe enough where he should lie. "Oh nay, Teit, I am not afraid of you. And if I am afraid, you never had the wit to know what it is I am afraid of. My poor little Ingunn, you must not be afraid of me."—He was wide awake again.

Then there was this new burden that he had to face—what should he do? Give notice of the slaying at the first house he passed, when he came down from the wilds? And take upon himself this new case of manslaughter before he was wholly quit of the old one, with weregild and fines?—And feel the common talk barking in his tracks—what quarrel could such a man as he have

had with that vagabond Icelander?—ay, to be sure, 'twas Ingunn
Steinfinnsdatter— No, not that either.

But then—how was he to be rid of the corpse?

So many a better man had he seen fall from the ship's side and
be lost in the sea. So many a good thane's son of Denmark must
have been left to the wolf and the eagle after the Earl's attack. But
that was the Earl's doing, not his; it had never been his fault if a
dead man was left without Christian burial. And since he was so
soft that the mere slaying of such a one as this Teit, his wife's
paramour, weighed upon him, he would be ill fitted to go through
with the other thing, which *was* sin. *That* would be a sin that he
could not throw off.

But if he declared Teit's slaying at his hands, then they could
not even *pretend* that Ingunn's honour was saved.

At last he must have fallen asleep and slept long and dream-
lessly. The sun shone in through the cracks between the logs when
he opened his eyes. The hearth was black. He heard nothing of
the wind—not a sound but the black cock's note from far and
near, and now and again a belated chirping.

He stood up, stretched and rubbed himself. His arm was stiff
and rather sore—not much. He went to the door and looked out.
The world was white and the sun was high in a blue and cloudless sky. The mist had sunk and lay like a white sea, made golden
by the sun, with points of rock and wooded ridge jutting out, and
they were golden with fresh snow on which the sun was shining.
The white carpet of the hillside sparkled red and blue; hare and
bird had already printed their tracks in the fresh snow, and the
call of the black cock resounded everywhere in the woods.

In this infinitely white world of wild, snow-covered forest he
stood, the only human being in the wastes, and knew not where
to hide that other little carcass, the dead man. Break through the
carpet of snow and bury him—no. It must be done in such a way
that beasts could not come at it—that he would not have. Let it
lie and be found when folk moved up to the sæter—that was impossible; then it might come out who the dead man was—and
after that all the rest.

The two pairs of skis stood in the drift beside the wall, snowed
under. Olav took the good pair, which he had borrowed from the
convent, cleared them of snow, and laid them down. He clenched
his teeth firmly; his face grew stiff and blank.

He went in and smoothed out the couch. Then he fetched the corpse and laid it there—tried to straighten it out. There was clotted blood and brains in the hair, but not much on the frozen grey face. He gaped hideously, Teit. Olav could not get the mouth and eyes closed. So he covered the dead man's face with the worn and blood-stained fur cap.

Underneath the ashes he found some sparks, and when he laid on bark and twigs and a mass of wood, the fire soon burned up. There was a load of hay in the dairy; Olav brought it in and threw it down between the hearth and the bed. His foot stumbled against Teit's sword—he picked it up and laid it on the boy's breast. Then he scraped up an armful of bark and twigs and threw it on the heap of hay.

Now the fire was burning briskly on the hearth. Olav took a long stick and raked the brands into the hay—with a flicker and a hiss as they caught the bark the flames shot up. Olav sprang out, carrying the skis under his arm, and waded up the slope through the fresh snow.

Up at the top, where the wind had bared the old crust, he halted, knelt, and bound the skis fast to his feet. Then he took the staff in his hand. But he stood there till he saw the grey smoke curling out of every crack in the walls. He repeated the burial prayers in a low voice—almost overcome by terror: was this blasphemy? But it seemed he had no choice—a dead man lay within; he *must* do it.

He had left his axe in the hut, he remembered, and the wallet, but it was empty. Now both the whey-vat and the store of bread would be burned; it was a small matter among all the rest, but— Never had he disdained God's gifts; the smallest piece of bread that he dropped on the floor he would take up and kiss before he ate it. This was almost the only thing he remembered of what his great-grandfather had taught him.

To hell with it. In the wars he had seen whole storehouses of food and franklins' homes given over to the flames. And better men than this one had been caught in the fire, both living and dead. Why should he count this as so much worse—?

In old days they burned their fallen chieftains thus. "I have given you a funeral pyre fit for a sea-king, my Teit—with your sword clasped in your hands, food and drink beside you."

The smoke kept creeping out—now it enshrouded the whole

sæter. The fire shone through it—the first flames found their way out under the eaves. Olav set out swiftly, with no trail to follow.

When the sæter-folk came up in the summer, they would find the bones among the ashes—he tried to console himself. He would be laid in Christian ground in the end.

He swept down to a watercourse, while his ears sang and the snow spurted from his skis; flew across the bottom of the slope, halted on the other side, and looked back. The fine, long hump of the ridge he had left stood out golden in the sunshine against the blue sky. In one place a little cloud of dark smoke was spreading.

An hour later he crossed the top of a fence, buried in the snow, into white meadows. There were houses here; the snowdrifts made them level with their surroundings in many places but smoke was rising from a louver. There were tracks between dwelling and byre, and fresh refuse on the midden.

Olav looked out over the landscape as he brought himself to a standstill. The country was white, tinged with yellow, and blue in all the shadows. Far to the northward he had a view of a broad valley in which were great farms.

Say that he had quarrelled with his companion last night and it ended in their seizing their weapons. And then brands from the fire had been flung into the straw.

He pulled himself together and set out again over the fields.

Late in the afternoon he came to Miklebö. Arnvid was out—had started for the woods two days before with both his sons to look for capercailye. But his house-folk gave their master's best friend a good reception.

Olav was out in the courtyard next day at sunset when Arnvid and his sons came home. Magnus was leading the horse—both it and the men wore snowshoes—and it was packed with knapsacks and the like and a fine bag of game. Arnvid and Steinar were loaded with skies and bows and great empty quivers.

Arnvid greeted his guest with quiet heartiness, the sons received him frankly and becomingly. They were half-grown now, two fine, fair-haired, promising youths.

"As you see, I changed my mind—"

"That was well." Arnvid smiled a moment.

"But—have you fared through the forest with no weapons but that little spear?" asked Arnvid as they sat talking while the food was being brought in.

Olav said no, he had had an axe with him too, but he lost it yestereve; he was cutting some branches to make a bed—ay, he had found a shealing and slept in it. Graadals booth?—it might be that. Nay, in the snow and the darkness he had not been able to find his axe again. For that matter, he had given himself a scratch on the upper arm as it flew out of his hands.

Arnvid wished to see the wound before they went to rest. It was a clean, straight slash—looked as if it would heal quickly. But how Olav could contrive to wound himself just there, Arnvid could not make out—well, these old axes with a long pointed barb at each end might play one many tricks—and surely they were unhandy for lopping branches.

8

INGUNN had the child on the third day after Hallvard's Mass.[3] When Tora lifted the new-born babe from the floor, the mother clasped her head in her arms and shrieked, as though afraid to see or hear.

When Ingunn was put to bed, Tora brought her the child, ready wrapped.

"You must *look* at your son, sister," Tora implored. "He is so pretty—he has long, black hair—"

But Ingunn shrieked and drew the coverlet over her face.

Tora had sent for the priest the evening before, when the case looked ill; and as she thought there was little life in the boy, she asked him to baptize him before he left. They asked the mother what name he was to have, but she only groaned and hid under the bedclothes. Neither Magnhild nor Tora cared to recall any of the men of their kindred in this child, and so they asked the priest to give him a name. He replied that today the Church commemorated Saint Eirik, king and martyr, and therefore he would call Ingunn's child after him.

[3] May 15.

Tora Steinfinnsdatter was both angry and sorrowful as she sat with this ill-omened little one, her own nephew, on her lap, and the mother would take no notice of him.

On the third day after the birth Ingunn was very ill. Tora guessed she was suffering from the milk, which was now bursting her breasts. She was unable to move, or to bear any one's touching her, and she could not swallow a scrap of food, but complained of intolerable thirst. Tora said it would be much worse if she drank—the milk would then rise to her head: "Not a drop dare I give you, unless you will let me give you Eirik—" But still Ingunn would not take her child.

In the evening, when Tora was preparing the boy for the night, she chanced to upset the basin of water, and she had no more warm water in the room. For a moment she was uncertain what to do. Then she wrapped a cloth about the naked child and bore him to the bed. Ingunn lay in a feverish doze, and before she could prevent her, Tora had laid Eirik on his mother's arm and gone out.

She made no haste in the cook-house—but all at once she was struck with fear and ran back. In the doorway she heard Ingunn's loud and piercing sobs. Tora rushed forward and pulled back the coverlet. "In God's name—you have not done anything to him!"

Ingunn did not answer. Eirik lay there, with his knees drawn up to his stomach, and his hands to his nose; small and thin and brownish red; the warmth of his mother seemed to do him good. His wide, dark eyes looked as though he were thinking.

Tora drew a breath of relief. She took the basin that Dalla brought her, lifted the boy, and finished washing him. Then she wrapped him in swaddling-clothes and carried him back to the bed.

"Shall I lay him beside you?" she asked, as indifferently as she could.

With a long-drawn plaint Ingunn raised her arms, and Tora laid the child in them. Her hands trembled a little, but she made an effort to talk in a calm and level voice as she propped her sister up, laid Eirik to her breast, and strove to get him to suck.

After this Ingunn obediently took the boy when Tora brought him and laid him to her breast. But she remained as sorrowful as before and seemed to have lost heart entirely.

She was still in bed when Arnvid came riding one evening to Berg. Lady Magnhild had sent word to Miklebö as soon as Ingunn was delivered.

Arnvid came into the room, greeting Lady Magnhild and Tora as calmly and courteously as though nothing unusual were afoot. But when he came up to the bed and met Ingunn's look of mortal dread, his own face became stiff and strange. A burning flush spread over her face and throat as she fumbled shyly with her thin fingers at her breast—drew her shift together and turned the child's face, which was instantly convulsed in a scream, toward the man.

"Ay, is he not what women call pretty?" said Arnvid with a smile touching the child's cheek with one finger. " 'Twas a shame you made such haste to have him christened. You should have been my godson, kinsman."

He seated himself on the step beside her bed and slipped his hand under the bedcover so that he touched the child's head and the mother's arm. It was uncanny, the way she trembled—and then came what he was waiting for, Lady Magnhild asked after Olav.

"I was to give you all greetings from him. He parted from me at Hamar, would hasten home now; he thought he could be back here about the Selje-men's Mass; [4] by that time Ingunn should be strong enough to go south with him." He pressed her arm tightly to make her keep calm.

He replied to Magnhild's and Tora's questions, told what he knew of Olav's plans. All three made as though all was well—though each one knew that they all thought the same: how would life shape itself for these two? Here lay the bride with another man's child at her breast, and the bridegroom knew it, as he rode south to make his house ready to receive its mistress.

But at last Arnvid said he would fain speak a few words with Ingunn alone. The two ladies stood up; Tora took the child from its mother to carry it to the cradle.

"And this one?" she asked. "It is Olav's wish that he shall go southward with his mother?"

"Ay, so far as I understood, that was his wish."

Then he was left alone with her. Ingunn lay with closed eyes. Arnvid stroked her under the roots of the hair, wiped away the

[4] July 8.

perspiration. "Olav bade me stay here till he himself can come and fetch you."

"Why so?" she asked in fear.

"Oh, you know—" he hesitated. "Folk are a little more wary of what they say when there is a danger their talk may reach a man—"

Beads of perspiration came out on Ingunn's forehead. She whispered almost inaudibly: "Arnvid—is there no way out—for Olav —so that he may be free—?"

"Nay.—Nor has he given any sign," Arnvid added, "that he wished it."

"If we besought—the Archbishop—on our knees—promised to do penance—?"

"His Bishop could give him leave to live apart from you—if Olav would ask it of him. That he will fetch you home and live with you—this he does of his own free will. But no man can sunder the bond there is between you, so that Olav could freely take another wife—not even the Pope in Romaborg, as I believe."

"Not even if I went into a nunnery?" she asked, trembling.

"So far as I know, you must have Olav's consent to that. And he would not be free to marry again. But to be a pious nun I trow you are the least fitted of women, my poor Ingunn.

"Then you must remember what Olav himself said to me. It was he who once staked all upon the judgment of Holy Church in the question whether you two were husband and wife or not. He himself called for Bishop Torfinn's decree, whether your living together were binding wedlock according to God's law and not fornication—and Lord Torfinn said yes to that. Strict as this Bishop was wont to be toward ravishers and all who violated the honour of women, he claimed on Olav's behalf that this man should be suffered to do penance and make atonement with Einar's kinsmen.—Do you understand—Olav *cannot* depart from his own word, nor will he either, he says.

"Nay, here I talk on, forgetting that you are still weak. Be easy now, Ingunn—remember what manner of man Olav is. Stubborn and headstrong; when he wills a thing he must have it. But you must have heard the saying, trusty as a troll—"

But it could not be seen in Ingunn that she had plucked up heart. The other women were mightily consoled when they knew for certain that Olav Audunsson would make no ado, but would take to himself the wife he had once claimed in so boastful and headstrong a fashion—and bear with her ill conduct in the meantime. Ingunn's kinsmen, Ivar, her brothers, and Haakon, when they heard of the whole matter, said that Olav had injured them all so deeply, by first taking the bride to himself, then summoning her guardians before the Bishop's court, and finally by killing Einar when he called him to account—that it was no more than justice if he held his peace, cloaked Ingunn's shame, and did what he could to put a good end to a bad business. Moreover, Hestviken was far away. And even if folk in the south got to know that his wife had had a child by another man before Olav Audunsson married her, he would not be worse wed than many another good and worthy man. No man in his native district need know more than that, unless they themselves were foolish enough to let it come out that she had already been bound to Olav before she had the child, in such a way that some priests in any case would say the boy was begotten in adultery.

This was pointed out to Ingunn by Ivar and Magnhild. She listened to them, palefaced, and dark about the eyes; Arnvid saw that she was greatly disturbed by what they said.

"What say you to this, Arnvid?" she asked one day when Ivar and Haakon had been sitting with her, discussing their view of the case. She now left her bed in the daytime.

"I say," replied Arnvid quietly, "God knows 'tis an ill thing it should be so—but you must see yourself, there is some truth in it—"

"You say that—you who call yourself Olav's friend!" she burst out angrily.

"That I am—and I thought I had shown it more than once," replied Arnvid. "And I will not deny that I have my part of the blame for the bad turn all this has taken. I counselled Olav unwisely, perhaps—I was too young and lacking in wisdom—and I should not have stayed in the guest-house that evening, when Einar picked a quarrel with us. But I shall do my friend no good, nor will you either, if we hide our heads under our wings and refuse to see that the Steinfinnssons too have *some* right on their side!"

But Ingunn burst into tears. "Not even you wish Olav better than this! None of you count his honour of any worth, none but I—"

"Nay," said Arnvid —"and now he must lie in the bed you have made for him."

Ingunn's weeping stopped suddenly—she raised her head and looked at the man.

"Ah well, Ingunn—I should not have said it. But I have been stretched upon the rack of this case of yours so long now—" he said wearily.

"But what you said was true."

The child lay in the bed screaming; Ingunn went and took it up. Arnvid noticed again what he had seen before—though she handled the little one tenderly and seemed to be fond of him, she always seemed to touch her child rather reluctantly, and she was very clumsy when she had to tend the boy herself. Eirik indeed always screamed and was restless and fretful in his mother's arms; she could only quiet him with the breast for a very little while. Tora said this was because Ingunn was depressed and uneasy, so that she had little milk for him; Eirik was always hungry.

This time too he had soon finished sucking, and then he lay grimacing as he pulled at the empty breast. Ingunn gave a little sigh; then she fastened her clothes, stood up, and began to walk up and down the room, carrying the child. Arnvid sat looking at them.

"Will you accept it, Ingunn," he asked, "if I offer to foster the child? I will bring up your son in my house and be to him as I have been to my own sons."

Ingunn did not reply at once; then she said: "You would be a faithful kinsman to the boy, I know that. You had the right to expect that I should thank you for the friendship you have shown me all these years, better than I do.—But should I die, you must—you must take care of Eirik—then 'twill be easier for me in my last hour."

"You must not speak of such things *now*," said Arnvid, trying to smile. "You who are just up and out of danger."

When Eirik was six weeks old, the woman came with whom Lady Magnhild had bargained early in the spring—that she should receive and foster a child that would be born in secret at Berg. Now the rumours about Ingunn had got abroad nevertheless. So many different things were said as to who might be the father—but most people thought it was that Icelander who had been so often at Berg last summer—now he was gone, doubtless run away for fear of the woman's rich kinsmen. Now the foster-mother, Hallveig was her name, came one evening to Berg to ask what had become of the child—she had heard no more of the matter.

Before Lady Magnhild had thought of what she should say, Ingunn came forward and said she was the mother of the child, and Hallveig should take it with her when she went home the next day. Hallveig looked at Eirik and said he was a fine child; while waiting for her food, she took him up and laid him to her breast.

The mother stood over them and looked on while Eirik took a full draught—it must have been the first time in his young life that he had drunk his fill. Then Ingunn took the child and carried it away to her bed; but the woman was shown into another house, where she was to sleep. It was intended that she should ride home betimes next morning, before folk were about upon the farms.

The sisters were left alone in Aasa's house, and Tora lighted the holy candle, which they still burned every night. Ingunn sat on the edge of the bed with her back turned to the child; Eirik lay against the wall, cooing cheerfully.

"Ingunn—do not this thing," said Tora seriously. "Do not send your child away like this. It is a *sin* to do such a deed, unless you are forced to it."

Ingunn said nothing.

"He is smiling—" said Tora with emotion, beaming at the boy. "Look at your son, Ingunn—he can smile now—he is so sweet, so sweet—"

"Ay, I have seen," said Ingunn. "Many times he has smiled of late."

"I cannot understand that you *will*—that you *can* do this."

"Cannot you see that I will not bring this child of mine under Olav's roof—ask him to foster this brat that a vagabond clerk has left behind—"

"Shame on you for speaking thus of your own child!" exclaimed Tora, revolted.

"I am ashamed."

"Ingunn—be sure you will regret it as long as you live if you do this thing, sell your child into the hands of strangers—"

"I have now brought myself into such a plight that I can never cease to regret."

Tora answered hotly: "You speak truly, and on that score there is none on earth can help you. With Olav you have played right falsely, there is none of us but thinks that—and your shame falls heavier on him than on the rest of us. But if you will be false to your child too—the guiltless young being that you have housed forty long weeks under your own heart—I tell you, sister, I cannot believe that even Mary, Mother of God, will pray for mercy on the mother who betrays her own son—"

"Beware, sister," said Tora once more. "You have wronged us all, and Olav worst. There is only left this boy, him you have not yet failed!"

No more was said between the sisters. They went to bed. Ingunn took the boy with her. She lay with her lips pressed against the silky, moist skin of the child's forehead and heard her sister's words ring and ring again within her. Even as Eirik's little head lay now against her throat, lay Jesus Christ against His mother's bosom in the image in church. What did He think of the mothers who flung a little boy from them? "And He called a little child unto Him and set him in the midst of them—" On the wall of the church in Hamar there was a painting where He hung nailed to the cross between two thieves, but beside Him stood His mother: fainting with sorrow and weariness she watched by her Son in His last agony, as she watched over His first sleep in the world of men. Nay, she saw it now—she dared not pray to Mary's Son for forgiveness of her sins unless she stopped here. She dared not pray Christ's mother to intercede for her with her Son if she held fast to her purpose and betrayed her boy.

"Ingunn," whispered Tora, weeping. "I spoke not so harshly to you because I wished you ill. But it will be worse than all the rest if you forsake your child."

Ingunn's voice was as hoarse as her sister's as she answered: "I know it. I have seen that you are fond of Eirik. You must try—when I am gone, you must—you must look after Eirik as well as you can."

"I will—as much as I dare—for Haakon," said Tora.

None of the three slept much that night, and just as they had fallen into a doze toward morning, Lady Magnhild came and woke them. The woman was ready to start.

Tora watched her sister as she wrapped the child—"I do not

believe she will dare to do it," was her hope. Then Lady Magnhild began again with her talk that Olav had transgressed so deeply against them all that it could not be called sheer injustice if he had to suffer Ingunn to take her child south with her. They need not have it at Hestviken; Olav could very well have it fostered outside.

Then Ingunn seemed hard and resolved as she carried the child out and gave it to Hallveig and watched her and the little boy who accompanied her ride away with it.

At breakfast-time it appeared that Ingunn had left the house. Arnvid and Tora ran out to search for her—she was walking hither and thither in the field behind the barn, and, beg as they might, they could not get her to go in with them. Tora and Magnhild were quite bewildered—it was dangerous for a married woman to go out in this way, before she had been churched—and what were they to say of a mother in Ingunn's case? Arnvid thought they must send for Brother Vegard, for Ingunn ought to obtain absolution and make her peace with God and the Church before Olav came back, so that they might go together to mass, when he had received her with her kinsmen's consent. He himself promised to stay with Ingunn and keep watch over her until he could get her to come in.

Once they came right up to the birch grove north of the manor. Arnvid followed close on the woman's heels—not a word could he find to comfort her. He was as tired as a drudge and hungry; the afternoon was far spent, but when he begged her to use her wits and come in with him, he did not get so much as a word in answer; he might just as well have spoken to a stone.

Then she went up to a birch tree, laid her arm against its trunk, and ground her forehead on the bark, uttering groans like those of an animal. Arnvid prayed aloud for God to help him. He guessed she must be half mad.

At last they reached a little knoll, where they sat side by side in silence. All at once she tore open her dress and squeezed her breast so that the milk spouted in a thin jet onto the warm rock, where it dried into little shiny spots.

Arnvid jumped up, caught her round the waist, and set her on her feet, shook her this way and that. "Now you must behave yourself, Ingunn—"

As soon as he took his hand from her, she let herself fall at full

length; he raised her again. "Now you must come in with me—or
else I'll take and *beat* you!"

Then her tears came—she hung in the man's arms and wept im-
passively. Arnvid kept her head buried against his shoulder and
rocked her this way and that. She sobbed till she could sob no
more. Then she wept silently, with streaming tears, and now
Arnvid could fasten her clothing over the bosom; after that she
allowed herself to be half led, half dragged home, till he could
hand her over to the women.

Late in the evening Arnvid sat out in the courtyard talking to
Grim and Dalla—when Ingunn came out of her door. As soon as
she saw the old people, she halted in fear. Arnvid rose and went
up to her. Dalla went in, but Grim stood where he was, and as
Ingunn came past him by Arnvid's side, he raised his hairy old
face and spat at her, so that the spittle trickled down on his bushy
beard. When Arnvid took hold of him and pushed him away, he
made some nasty gestures and muttered all the coarsest names the
thralls of old had for loose women as he turned after his sister and
left the yard.

Arnvid took Ingunn by the arm and drew her indoors. "You
cannot look for aught else," he said, half in anger and half consol-
ing her, "than to suffer such things while you are here. It will be
easier for you when you come away, where folk know not so
much of you. But go in now—you have tempted fate more than
enough in running out today, and now the sun is going down."

"Stay a little while," begged Ingunn. "My head is burning so—
it is so good and cool here."

It was rather dark for the time of year; clouds were spreading
over the whole sky, and in the north the sunset turned them to
gold. A rosy light came over the valleys, and the bay reflected the
glory of the clouds.

Ingunn whispered: "Speak to me, Arnvid.—Can you not tell me
something of Olav?"

Arnvid shrugged, as though impatiently.

"I would but hear you speak his name," she said plaintively.

"Methinks you must have heard it often enough these last
weeks," replied Arnvid with annoyance. "*I* am sick of all this long
ago—"

"I meant it not so," she begged quietly. "Not of how useful a man he might be to us and such things. Arnvid—can you not speak to me of Olav—you who love him? For you are his friend—?"

But Arnvid would not say a word. It occurred to him that now he had allowed himself to be tormented year in, year out by these two; he had done so many things that were like cutting into his own flesh and turning the knife in the wound. He would do no more.—"Come in now—"

Tora met them and thought that she and her sister might well sleep in Magnhild's house tonight. It was so cheerless in the other house, now the child was gone.

When they were about to go to rest, Ingunn asked her sister to sleep with Lady Magnhild in the chamber: "I am afraid I shall get but little sleep tonight, and sleeplessness is catching, you know."

There were two bedsteads in the room. Arnvid slept in one, and Ingunn lay down in the other.

For a long time she lay waiting for Arnvid to fall asleep. The hours passed; she felt that he was still awake, but they did not speak.

Now and again she tried to say a Paternoster or an Ave, but her thoughts roved hither and thither and she could seldom repeat a prayer to the end. She said them for Olav and for Eirik; she herself must be beyond prayers, since she had determined to cast herself into perdition with her full knowledge and will. But since she *had* to do it, perhaps she would not be given the very hardest punishment in hell—even there she thought it must be an alleviation to know that when she cut the bond between them and plunged into the depth, she left Olav a free man.

She could not feel that she was even afraid. She seemed worn out at last—hardened. She did not even desire to see Olav again or her child. Tomorrow Brother Vegard would come, they had told her; but she would not see him. She would not look *upward*, and she would not look *forward*, and she recognized the justice of her perdition, since she refused to receive anything that was necessary to her soul's salvation. Repentance, prayer, work, and the further pilgrimage of life, seeing and speaking to those with whom she must dwell, if she should try to live on—the thought of all this was repulsive to her. Even the thought of God was repulsive to her now. To look *downward*, to be alone and surrounded by darkness —that was her choice. And she saw her own soul, bare and dark as a rock scorched by the fire, and she herself had set fire to and burned up all that was in her of living fuel. It was all over with her.

Nevertheless she said another Paternoster for Olav—"Make it so that he may forget me." And an Ave Maria for Eirik—"Now he has a mother in me no longer."

At last Arnvid began to snore. Ingunn waited awhile, till she thought he was sound asleep. Then she crept up and into her clothes and stole out.

It was the darkest hour. Behind the manor a wing of cloud rested upon the ridge and seemed to cast its shadow over the country. The woods surrounding the farm were steeped in gloom —a thin grey vapour floated over the corn and gathered about the clumps of trees, effacing their outlines. But higher up, the sky was clear and white and was palely reflected in the bay; on the heights beyond the lake there was already a gleam of the coming dawn above the woods.

At the gate of the paddock Ingunn stopped and set the stakes in after her. There was not a sound in the summer night but the grating of the corncrake. Dew dripped from the alders on the path by the burn and there was a bitter scent of leaves and grass in the darkness of the thicket.

The grove went right down to the manor hard. And now Ingunn saw that the lake had risen greatly while she had been lying in. The water came over the turf and covered the shore end of the pier.

She stopped, uncertain—in an instant terror quickened within her and shattered her hardened resolve. Nay, for this she had no heart—wade through the water out to the pier. She wailed helplessly in her fear. Then she lifted up her dress and put one foot into the water.

Her heart seemed to thrust itself into her throat as she felt the chill water running into her shoe; she gasped and swallowed. But then she ran on, wading through her own fear, tottering unsteadily over the sharp stones of the beach. The water splashed and gurgled about her with a deafening noise as she went forward. Her foot reached the pier.

It was flooded for a good way out; the plank bent between the piles, it gave under her feet, and the water came far up her legs. Farther out the planks were just above the surface, but sank under as soon as she stepped on them. Each time she held her breath in fear of losing her foothold and falling into the lake. At last she reached the extreme end of the pier; it was clear of the surface.

There was nothing left of her callousness now—she was beside herself with fright. But her trembling hands busied themselves blindly with what she had thought out beforehand. She took off the long woven girdle that was wound thrice about her waist, drew her knife, and cut it in two. With one piece she bound her clothes together around her legs below the knees—that she might appear seemly if she should drift ashore. The other piece she tied crosswise over her bosom and slipped her hands underneath—she had thought that it might be over sooner if she did not struggle as she sank. Then she drew a last, long breath and threw herself in.

Arnvid half woke, lay in a doze, and was on the point of dropping off to sleep again when, with a dull thump of the heart, he started up, wide awake—and knew that what had half awakened him was that he had heard someone go out.

He was on the floor in an instant and over by her bed, fumbling in the dark. The couch was still warm, but empty. As though still distrusting his own senses he searched on, along the logs of the wall, the head of the bed, the foot—

Then he thrust his naked feet into his shoes, slipped his kirtle over his head, groaning the while—he did not even know how long it was since she had gone out. He set out at a run straight through the corn and came down into the meadow that led to the lake—there was someone on the pier, he made out. He ran across the meadow and heard his own footfalls thudding on the dry turf. On reaching the water's edge he ran on, wading until he could strike out and swim.

Ingunn awoke in her old bed in Aasa's house. At first she was aware of nothing but that her head ached as though it would burst and the skin of her whole body was as sore as if she had been scalded.

The sunshine poured in; the louver was open and she had a glimpse of the clear sky. The smoke, which showed blue under the ridge of the roof, turned brown in the bright air outside—it was caught at once by the breeze and whirled among the grass on the roof.

Then she remembered—and fell almost into a faint. The feeling of relief, of being saved, was so overpowering—

Arnvid came up at once from somewhere in the room. He supported her with one arm and put a wooden cup to her lips. There was tepid water-gruel in it, with a flavour of herbs and honey.

Ingunn drank every drop, keeping her eyes on him over the rim of the cup. He took it from her and put it on the floor, then seated himself on the step beside the bed with his hands hanging between his knees and his head bowed. It was as though both were overcome by a sore sense of shame.

At last Ingunn asked in a hushed voice: "I cannot think—how was it I was saved?"

"I came at the last moment," said Arnvid shortly.

"I cannot tell," she began again. "I am so stiff in all my limbs—"

"Today is the third day. You have lain in a swoon—'twas the milk went to your head, I wis—and you had grown so cold in the water, we had to pour hot ale and wine into you. You have been awake before this, but haply you do not remember—"

The bad taste in her mouth seemed worse than before and she asked for water. Arnvid went out for it.

As she drank, he stood and watched her. He had so much at heart that he knew not what to take first. So he said it without more ado: "Olav is here—he came yesterday in the afternoon—"

Ingunn gave way, sick and dazed. She felt herself sinking down and down—but deep within her there was a little spark that was alive and tried to catch and break into flames—joy, hope, the will to live, meaningless as it was.

"He was in here for a while last night. And he bade us tell him as soon as you were awake. Shall I go and fetch him now?—the others are in the hall—'tis breakfast-time—"

After a moment Ingunn asked, trembling: "Said Olav aught—have you told him—of this last?"

Arnvid's face contracted suddenly—he set his teeth in his lower lip. Then it burst out of him: "Had you no thought—have you no thought, Ingunn, of where you would be dwelling today if you had carried out your purpose?"

"Ay," she whispered. She turned her face to the wall and asked in a low voice: "Did Olav say *that*? What said he, Arnvid?"

"He has said naught of that."

After a while Arnvid asked: "Shall I bring Olav in now?"

"Oh nay, nay—wait a little. I will not lie here—I will sit up—"

"Then I must send in one of the women—you have scarce the strength to dress yourself?" asked Arnvid doubtfully.

"Not Tora or Magnhild," Ingunn begged.

Then she sat on the bench by the end wall and waited. She had put on her black cloak, without really knowing why she did so; and she held it tightly about her and drew the hood over her head. She was white and cold in the face with fear. When the door opened—she had a glimpse of the man stooping as he came in—she shut her eyes again and her head sank on her breast. She planted her feet hard against the floor and held on to the edge of the bench with both hands to master her trembling.

He stopped when he had passed the hearth. Ingunn dared not raise her eyes; she saw only the man's legs. He wore no shoes, but tight-fitting buff leather hose, split and laced over the instep—she fixed her eyes upon this lacing, as though it would save her from her crowding thoughts. Such a fashion of men's hose she had never seen before, but it was cunning—they could thus be made to fit the ankle like a mould.

"Good day, Ingunn."

His voice went through her like a thrust, she sank yet farther forward. Olav came on, now he was standing just before her. She saw the hem of his coat; it was light blue, came down to the knees, and had many folds—her eyes stole upward as high as to his belt. It was mounted with the same silver roses and the buckle with Saint Olav's image; he had a dagger with an elk-horn sheath and silver mountings.

Then she saw that he was standing with outstretched hand. She laid her thin, clammy hand in it, and his closed about it—his hand was rough and dry and warm. Quickly she drews hers back.

"Will you not look up, Ingunn?"

She felt that she ought to rise up and greet him.

"Nay, sit still," he said quickly.

Then she looked up; their eyes met, and they continued gazing into each other's face.

Olav felt all his blood being sucked back to his heart—his face was frozen and stiff. He had to set his teeth; his eyelids drooped half over his eyes and he could not raise them again. Never had he known that a man could be struck so powerless.

The boundless pain and distress in her poor eyes—it was that which drew his soul naked up into the light. Away went all that he had thought and determined—he knew right well that they were great and important things that now dropped from his mind, but he had not the power to hold them fast. He was left with the last, the inmost cruel certainty—that she was flesh of his flesh and life of his life, and this could never be otherwise, were she never so shamefully maltreated and broken. The roots of their lives had been intertwined as long as he could remember—and when he saw that death had had hold of her with both hands, he felt as though he himself had barely escaped from being torn to pieces. And a longing came over him, so intense that it shook him through and through—to take her in his arms and crush her to him, to hide himself with her.

"Perhaps you will grant me leave to sit down too?"—he felt so strangely weak in the knees. Then he seated himself on the bench, at a little distance from her.

Ingunn's trembling increased. His face had been hard as stone—grey around the bloodless lips, and his strangely bright blue-green eyes had stared sightlessly under the drooping lids. "O God, God, have mercy upon me—!" As yet, she thought, she had not fully guessed the extent of the misfortune she had caused—but now she was to know it; she read that in Olav's face of stone. Now, when she could bear no more, came the worst.

Olav glanced at her under his half-closed lids. "You need not be afraid of me, Ingunn." He spoke calmly and evenly, but there was a slight hoarseness in his voice, as though his throat was not quite clear. "You must not think any more of what I said when I was here last—that I might prove a hard man to you. When I said it, I was still—wild—about this. But now I have bethought myself, and you must not be afraid. You shall live at ease in Hestviken, so far as depends on me."

Ingunn said, in a low, despairing voice: "Olav, you cannot—We cannot dwell together in Hestviken after this? How will you live there with me, remembering every day—"

"If I must, I can," he said shortly. "There is no help for it, In-gunn. And never shall you be reminded of it by me. That you may depend upon—safely."

Ingunn said: "But you are not one who forgets easily, Olav.

Oh—! Do you think you could do aught else but remember, every night when you lay down by my side, that another—"

"Ay—" he broke in. "Then you must remember," he went on, calmly as before, "Hestviken is a long way off—farther than you think. You will see, Ingunn, that it may be easier for us than we believe, when we live so far away from the places where all this has befallen us.—You will never see any sign in me that I remember it," he added hotly.

Ingunn said: "Olav, I am crushed and broken.—And if it be true that there is no way at all of setting you free, now that I have disgraced myself— But I do not see that it can be so, since they said once that they could part us, though we had been betrothed since we were children and we had slept in each other's arms—"

"I have never asked if I could wriggle out of my marriage. In all these years I have counted myself bound and been content that it was so, and I am still content. Such was my father's will. I am not one who forgets easily, you say—no, but I cannot forget this either, that we were betrothed to each other by our fathers when we were so young—and as we grew up together we slept in one bed and ate of one dish, and most of what we owned was in common. And when we were grown up, it was with us as you said.— There may be many things for which I must answer before God's judgment-seat," he said in a very low tone; "so I may well forgive you!"

"That is handsome of you, Olav, and it is good to know it. But now I will ask you to wait a year and meanwhile to let this matter rest. I am weary and sick, maybe I shall not live so long. Then you will be glad that you can take a wife to whom no blemish clings—that no woman without honour has ever been mistress of your house, or brought shame on your bed and board."

"Be quiet," whispered Olav huskily. "Speak not of that. When they told me what you had tried to do—" he stopped, overcome.

"I shall scarce have the strength to go to such a deed another time," she said; a quiver, a sort of smile, passed over her face. "I shall be a pious woman now, Olav, and repent my sins for such time as God wills I shall live. But I believe it will not be long—I believe I bear death within me already."

"You believe that because you are not yet over your sickness," said Olav sharply.

"Tainted I am," she wailed—"faded. I have lost all my fairness, so say they all. Little skill have I had all my days, and now I have lost heart and strength—what profit or joy can you have of such a wife as I? You have sat here and never looked at me once," she whispered shyly. "I am not much to look at, I know that. And 'tis no wonder you are unwilling to come near me. Think of it, Olav—you would soon feel it unbearable if you had such a wretched wife by your side day and night, always—"

Olav's features grew yet stiffer; he shook his head.

"I marked it already when you came in," she whispered almost inaudibly, "and you did not greet me with a kiss—"

At last Olav turned his head slightly and looked at her with a melancholy smile. "I kissed you last night—more than once—but I trow you did not feel it."

He passed both hands over his face, then bent forward, with both elbows on his thighs, and rested his chin in his hands.

"I dreamed a dream last spring—'twas Good Friday night to boot—I have thought of it often since. I remembered it so clearly when I awoke, and afterwards I have not been able to forget it. Now I will tell you what manner of dream this was.

"I dreamed I was on a hill in the forest, where all the trees were cut down, so that there was no shade—ay, the ground was hot there, and you lay in the full blaze of the sun, on the heather—there was heather and cranberries all around the stumps. You lay still—I know not whether I thought you slept—

" 'Tis strange—in all these years I have roamed about the world I often wished you would show yourself to me in dreams. You know that there are means one can use if one would dream of one's dearest friend—many a time I tried them, though you know I have never had a very firm belief in such devices. But I used them many times while I was still in Denmark, and also since. But I never saw you—

"But I dreamed this dream on Good Friday night, and I saw you as clearly as you are sitting there. You still seemed a child; we were both children, methought, as when we were together at Frettastein. Your hair had come unplaited, and you had on your old red gown of wadmal, but it had rucked up and I saw your legs bare to the knee—you were barefooted—

"Then a viper darted out of the heather—"

Olav drew a few heavy breaths; then he went on: "I was so

affrighted that I could not move. And this seemed strange, for I am bold to say that if only I can *see* the danger, I am not easily frightened—but in this dream I felt a terror beyond bearing—when I think of it, it seems I have never known what terror was, before or since. The snake moved through the heather, and I guessed it would strike you.

"But it did not move all the time after the manner of vipers; sometimes it thrust its way along as caterpillars do, and then it was no serpent, but a fat, hairy caterpillar—but then it was a viper again, coiling in the grass. It seemed to me I had a knife in my hand, and I thought I would strike the snake over the neck with a stick and kill it—'twould be easily done. But I dared not, for it turned into a caterpillar again.—Do you remember how I was a boy—how unspeakably I loathed the sight of worms and cater-pillars, and maggots worst of all? I strove to hide it, but I know that you saw it."

Again he passed his hands over his face and breathed deeply.

"Ay, I stood there as though stunned. And then the snake lay about your foot, and now it was a viper, and it coiled about your calf, but you slept on as soundly as before. And then the snake raised its head and darted hither and thither in the air and flickered with its tongue. Now I know not what I shall say—there was a horror in it, yet I was drawn to look upon it; nay, it was as though I waited with delight for it to strike.—I saw that now I could easily take it by the neck, but I dared not. And—and—I saw that it was seeking out the place, on your instep, where it could set its teeth in deep.—But I felt—pleasure—in looking on at this. And then it struck—"

He stopped abruptly, with closed eyes, and bit his lip.

"Then I awoke." Olav strove to speak calmly, but his voice was thick. "And I lay and was angry with myself, as you know one often is when one has behaved in a dream as one would never do awake. For, you know, then I should have killed the snake. And I ween I would never have stood idly and watched my worst enemy asleep if a viper crept upon him, nor would I have thought it any delight to see it strike.— But there were not many things in the world, I wis, that I would not have done for you, when we were children.

"And I have thought and thought upon this dream—"

Again he broke off abruptly—sprang up and staggered a few

steps away from her. Then he turned to the wall and threw himself against it, with his arms raised in a cross and his head buried between them.

Ingunn rose and stood as though thunderstruck. Something was happening that she had never dreamed possible. Olav was weeping —it was as though she had never thought he could.

The man sobbed aloud—strange rough and raw noises were torn from his chest. He made a great effort and forced himself to silence; but his back quivered, his whole frame was shaken. Then his tears broke out again—at first in little gasping spasms, then another storm of harrowing sobs. He stood with one knee on the bench, his forehead against the wall, and wept as if he could never cease.

Ingunn stole up, beside herself with terror, and stood behind him. At last she touched his shoulder.—Then he turned round to her, threw his arms about her, and crushed her to him. They sank into each other's arms as though both seeking support, and their lips, open and distorted with weeping, met in a kiss.

KRISTIN LAVRANSDATTER
Sigrid Undset's masterful trilogy

"No other novelist has bodied forth the medieval world with such
richness and fullness."   —*New York Herald Tribune*

The acknowledged masterpiece of the Nobel Prize–winning Norwegian novelist Sigrid Undset, *Kristin Lavransdatter* has never been
out of print in this country since its first publication in 1927. Its
narrative of a woman's life in fourteenth-century Norway has kept
its hold on generations of readers, and the heroine, Kristin—beautiful, strong-willed, and passionate—stands with the world's great
literary figures of our time.

THE BRIDAL WREATH

The first volume of this masterwork describes young Kristin's
stormy romance with Erlend Nikulaussön, a young man perhaps
overly fond of women, of whom her father strongly disapproves.

FICTION/0-394-75299-6

THE MISTRESS OF HUSABY

Volume II tells of Kristin's troubled and eventful married life on
the great estate of Husaby, to which her husband has taken her.

FICTION/0-394-75293-7

THE CROSS

The final volume shows Kristin still indomitable, reconstructing
her world after the devastation of the Black Death and the loss of
almost everything that she has loved.

FICTION/0-394-75291-0

Available at your local bookstore, or call toll-free to order:
1-800-793-2665 (credit cards only).

Printed in the United States
by Baker & Taylor Publisher Services